Love in the Time of License

By

Darnell Clevenger

1

She dated her lineage from Eve, not the Eve of the ripe red apple but rather the temptress of the golden autumn leaves, although pre-apple time is an important part of the history, an integral part since it, along with the apple itself, is not only the symbolic means to a desired end but also the storied crescendo that gives cymbalic as well as dramatic climax to the first bite.

Eve was not an innocent, by any means, not a cutesy post-puberty darling all decked out in her gingham pinafore, lecherously seduced by some licentious eighteen-year-old-villain sprouting the first faint wisps of a moustache, or by a dirty rich old man with no hair on his chest and night-dribbles on his chin, no matter what the feminists tell you. She was born fully aware of her true value in the marketplace. Possibly because she was created from a rib which had already been corrupted by means of becoming mortal flesh, possibly because of the Darwinian composition evolution had given her, possibly because this story is being written by a male—in any case she not only realized from the first instant of conscious thought that a bird in the hand might be considerably better than two in the bush, but that two women in a man's bedroom are not necessarily more desirable than one in the bush, so to speak, if the, uh, charms of the one in the bush are well sculpted, have not been thoroughly explored in any recent sense by the bird hunter, and/or are minimally hidden for maximum attraction.

When she awoke out of nothingness she was lying on her back, staring up at a pair of brown eyes that somehow set her juices to flowing. She stretched slowly, sensually, instinctively covering her nipples with one arm, her pubis with the other hand, all the while staring into those startled eyes, watching them as they seemed to glaze over with unconscious desire.

"This creature," she told herself amusedly as her eyes wandered down the solid length of the male being, "wants to enjoy the use of my body, but he hasn't the slightest idea that he does or how to go about it." Suddenly another thought came to her and she found herself giggling uncontrollably at the mystery of life. "But neither do I at this moment in non-time, yet—not consciously anyhow."

And so she stood, posing naturally, exposing herself hopefully to the boorish lout who, after curiously inspecting her body from head to toe and then that little piece of himself which, apparently of its own accord, had become tumescent, turned away to watch the fish frolic in a nearby brook, playing with his tumescent part all the while, just as he always had whenever the urge arose.

"I'll show that bastard," thought Eve, chagrined at being so thoroughly discounted.

And so she searched for the Great Serpent. She seemed to have an innate sense of his existence, not to mention his location, as if he were nothing more than an extension of her psyche, or as if she had committed the same act over and over throughout eternity until even being dipped in the River of Forgetfulness could not completely erase its dim, shadowy outline from the depths of her unconscious self. Without hesitation she headed directly for the apple orchard and there, coiled at ease under the Golden Delicious Tree this time, she found her mark.

"Hello, Eve," Great Serpent hissed with a sly smile. He, of course, was fully aware that their encounter was but one enactment among a multitude in the archetypal pattern of their existence. He also believed that whether the encounters were dreamed or real was irrelevant to those involved in them. "I'm honored and not a little turned on by your visit. I do assume it's me you're searching for."

"Who else could it be, Tragic One?" Eve started to simper but immediately, intuitively realized that the Great Serpent was immune to flirtation, although not to feminine charms in general, or masculine ones as far as that goes. She wondered if he was actually sexless or if he combined both sexes in his one self and thus had no need of exterior objects of gratification.

Whichever the case, she felt only irritation. She didn't like a world in which any rational creature that seemed to have the appropriate masculine tools might be immune to her feminine charms. On the other hand, after a moment's consideration, somewhere deep in her interior depths she realized that he was definitely not asexual and that she had enjoyed his charms more than a few times throughout eternity.

"Is this a social visit, Eve, or are you here on our...," he leered at her," hmmm, ongoing business venture?"

After a penetrating glance at Great Serpent's eyes, Eve chose the direct approach. This slippery snake, she reasoned, could not be tricked by a mere mortal. He could read her mind as easily as if she were explaining all of her thoughts in clear, concise sentences. Moreover, he seemed to have some innate sense of what the future held in store for the two of them."

"This Garden is a boring place, Serpent."

"That's Great Serpent to you," Satan hissed, smiling internally with the good humor of an actor performing a favorite role, one he has completed times innumerable with innumerable variations. "I need to retain my image for the posterity of humankind. Moreover, our relationship in the Garden, as usual, will be too short for familiarity of discourse. Only the repetition will re-occur eternally, not the duration. But repetition in and of itself at the divine level does not warrant such informality. That is reserved for the mortal, for the finite, as I might say—for those beings which are uniquely the same yet never the same from beginning to end."

"Oh, Great Serpent," our little Eve bowed her head in exaggerated sarcasm, "I think this place is boring."

"You know," Old Nick advised in a sympathetic aside, "the next time you should look around before you begin acting out The Great Tragedy, become familiar with the plants and animals, enjoy a few sunrises and sunsets, take a swim in the lake, sunbathe, picnic, hike in the woods, get to know your partner, explore his body in complete safety while there are no negative consequences, no mosquitoes or poison ivy, no yucky and painful pregnancies, and no taboos at all. Enjoy innocence while it lasts. Overlook the boredom for a while; it will eventually dissolve into action anyway, and not necessarily action of your liking.

Moreover, once you go into exile you'll sleep through the sunrise, be too tired to enjoy sunsets, swim in polluted pools, bask under a cancerous sun, fight beasts and insects in the woods, and never, ever know your partner except in the physical sense," he leered, drooling slightly over his final words.

"That oaf you call my partner is nothing more than a boy in a man's skin."

"You and you only can help him become a man, even here in paradise, and much more pleasantly than out in the world of sorrow, laughter, pain, and death, and without the heartbreaking consequences of childbirth. How many times throughout eternity have I tried to convince you of that? And how many times have you ignored my advice?"

"I don't want a relationship in an emotional vacuum, Great Serpent. I don't want a relationship with a creature who would as soon watch the fish in the brook as ogle my body. I don't want to play games with a child who might bounce from my bed at any moment to go play with the animals in the woods. I want devotion from my partner. I want full control over my relationships."

"You know what all that entails, not to mention that it's next to impossible?"

"I have an inkling, but my intuition tells me that this is another point in the story where you're supposed to advise me," Eve smiled innocently.

Great Serpent shook his head in utter pity for Adam and sympathy for Eve. "This creature," he told himself, as he always did at this point in the infinitely repetitive story, "would make a fitting partner for me in my kingdom, except that she does not want the absolute control of master to slave that I have, no matter what she thinks. She wants to control through temptation and conflict, not realizing how temporary temptation must be in a mortal world. Besides," he chuckled without humor, "she would always try to control me, the master, and she just might be even more devious than I am if given the potential to improvement that eternity grants when there is no symbolic Styx in between moments of awareness. I might become another Zeus, sneaking around to conceal my affairs from my consort if I took her as my mate."

"You have a choice," he spoke, unable to keep the slight tinge of envy out of his voice. "You can retain your innocence and remain in the Garden, or you can forfeit that childish innocence and thus be condemned to the world I spoke of a few moments ago, the world of opposites. Here in the Garden everything is pleasure and contentment. Out there in the desert pain and sorrow counterbalance the good things. For all positives there will be negatives. For all love there will be hate. For all peace there will be war. For...but of course you know my spiel by heart, unconsciously if not consciously, so I see no need to repeat it verbatim. Suffice it to say that if I could I would probably make the same choice that you will. Existence is of little real worth without the fear of non-existence to enhance its simple pleasures. Your image of a vacuum was very apropos. My eternal existence is so very, terribly ethereal. That is the tragedy of eternal existence. We gods soon enough become incapable of emotional attachments, or of any truly deep feeling whatsoever."

"What if I choose to remain in the Garden?"

The Great Serpent smirked at the speculative glint in Eve's eyes. He had seen it before, how many times!

"You have been created a creature of free will. It is your choice." He laughed, not a pleasant sound, at what he considered one of his brother's greatest obfuscations. "But you are predestined to fall from grace and wander lost in the wilderness until the Final Judgment. So you will choose to do those things which will exile you from the Garden. That is how you have been created, to plague your fellow creatures as they will plague you."

"You call that free will?"

"I didn't create this tragedy. Nor did I define it. God created it. You humans define it ad nauseam, sometimes with great insight, most of the time, though without much subtlety but with excessive dogmatic fervor, at first, then with decreasing ardor as time passes. It's the same with all of your toys and inventions. You suffer and sacrifice and maim and cheat and kill to get something you want. But you soon ignore it, or experience it thoughtlessly, without feeling, as do most creatures with the familiar, as do children with their toys."

"You're avoiding the question, Great Serpent. I was referring to your comments on free will. First you tell me that I'm free to follow where my spirit might lead me, that I can choose to remain in the Garden if I so desire. Then, in the very next breath you tell me I'm doomed to, what did you call it, 'fall from grace,' and wander in the wilderness of suffering and pain and, ultimately, death."

"You, My Dear, are simply too simple to understand such an extremely complex idea," the Serpent imitated Eve's former sarcasm. "You have been created with the mental ability to choose whither thou willeth, within the parameters of your mortal flesh and the limitations of the good earth, of course." Old Nick grinned hugely, as if at some cosmic joke he alone shared with God. "But my Angelic Brother already knows what choices you will make. He determined it so in the creation of your flesh and the limited capacity of your human brain."

"So, what you're saying in all honesty is that I will choose to leave the Garden because I really have no other choice."

"I didn't think you would understand me."

"Oh, I do understand you all right. Your tongue is as forked as it always has been, I expect. And your mind is as…shall we say 'subtle' in spite of the obvious paradox? I almost said fallacy, but I suddenly remembered my place in our little, eternal tragicomedy. What I don't understand, however, is why you think I'm so simpleminded as to not see through your intellectual nonsense."

The Great Serpent shrugged what would have been his shoulders if he had been so constructed as to have shoulders. He grinned, showing his ivory fangs. He wriggled and squirmed with pleasure.

"I like it so much when you and I have these intelligent dialogues before you have to go trick Adam into eating the apple," he whispered affably, a dry, gourd-like rattle of a sound.

"I detest talking to Adam. He's such a bore in this early period of his development, although you already seem well aware of that."

"Yes, and, except in isolated instances, he really doesn't improve much through repetition or age, nor does his progeny, except for isolated examples, if my intuition is giving me the straight scoop. I suppose that's a major part of the reason I now eternally repeat my errand to you. After a few trillion attempts at seducing my supposed mate in this early stage of our existence, or at the least of having an intelligent if not meaningful conversation, I've given up." Eve shuddered, "My fear is that, if I keep foreshortening the story of our creation and few moments in the Garden, you'll become the hero of the piece rather than the villain, and I'll thus wind up your mate rather than Adam's. After all, I am the only possible heroine," she added, glancing slyly at the Great Serpent, "although there are two possibilities for the male role. Or am I mistaken?"

"Would that be so bad?" the Great Serpent preened, ignoring her question, not because of its lack of potential validity, but precisely the opposite. "You would become queen of the Underworld, be wealthy beyond your wildest dreams, have eternal life, own infinite slaves, do anything your heart desires. What more could you wish for?"

"I have eternal life now through repetition. Once I leave the Garden I'll have pleasure, suffering, death, and forgetfulness, which will make life bearable, even enjoyable at times. What more could I wish for?" Eve didn't try to hide the note of sarcastic mimicry in her voice.

"Me," the Great Serpent again preened as he slowly turned into a facsimile of a handsome young stud as bare as Adam but considerably more interesting to Eve in that his anatomy portrayed a mental willingness and physical readiness far beyond Adam's garden variety of knowledge or experience, or inclination.

"Oh, my goodness," Eve exclaimed, unable to control her palpitating heart, not to mention the warm sap flowing pleasurably through her loins.

Adonis stood before her. His golden locks shimmered in the sunlight filtering downward through the leaves of the apple tree. His deep blue eyes promised roiling depths of superhuman passion, dangerous and explosive pleasures prolonged until the body would tremble uncontrollably, pleasures pleading for release yet at the same time begging mutely for the rippling ecstasy to go on and on forever.

"Shall we?"

And they did the dance of love (love?) until they were both sated.

Great Serpent returned to his customary form.

"I always look forward to that little tryst as the human tragedy begins to unfold in each of its cycles," he murmured pleasantly.

"Why not visit me during my part of the coming tragicomedy?" Eve stretched luxuriously. "You could come to me while Adam is working in the fields or hunting in the woods, or off to the wars. If we were careful no one would be the wiser, and so Adam would never know."

"I do visit you, my love. I visit you and your daughters in many guises, depending on your sexual preferences during any given moment of a cycle. I do it by proxy," he leered at her and pretended to twist the end of a mustache not there. "My Brother won't allow a more personal approach. He doesn't want any of us gods, ummm, or should I say angels—he doesn't want us interfering directly in the affairs of you mortals. He believes personal, direct interference might corrupt the living tragedy by adding a humanly discernible deus ex machina which could possibly destroy the tragic balance between hope and despair, a balance necessary in order to maintain sanity on the one hand and evolutionary advance on the other."

"If I chose to remain in the Garden," Eve speculated, "I wouldn't have to suffer all the negative extremes. You and I could make love whenever we had the urge. And I could maybe teach Adam to enjoy the game also. I would have two sex partners."

The Great Serpent chuckled coldly, "Much of that was my line earlier. But eternity in paradise is not all it's cracked up to be. It's easy to become bored when existence is all smooth contentment and physical satisfaction. And boredom is a terrible thing. It led me to rebellion. It leads me to cruelty in my kingdom. It leads me to, as you so quaintly put it, 'make love to you' during our short time together in the Garden, in spite of the fact that you are already promised to Adam, or maybe because of that fact. It leads me to continuously war against my Brother, in the limited, often petty ways He allows. Besides," he chuckled again, "like I told you, you'll choose to leave the Garden. You do every time. It's predestined."

"Yes," Eve snorted, "but it's also really my choice. Isn't that what you said?"

"I suppose it's time for you to visit Adam now," Great Serpent spoke with little enthusiasm, ignoring her comment, "to prepare him in all ways for The Great Temptation."

And so Eve and the Great Serpent went forth to visit Adam in his natural castle. They found him sitting by a brook, watching several fawns frolicking in the distance while a grizzly nearby fished for its <u>pre</u>-Darwinian supper. (Or should it really be some kind of berry that grizzly was eating, something not so suggestive of the struggle for survival?)

"Death exists here in the Garden?" Eve commented sarcastically as the bear flipped a large salmon onto the bank, pounced, and began tearing it from its mortal skin.

"We all have to eat," Nick again shrugged what might have been masculine shoulders in different circumstances. "Besides, fish are lower creatures. They don't really feel death."

"Is there an infinite supply of them?"

"Possibly. I don't know."

"Is there an infinite supply of humans?"

"I don't know," the Great Serpent frowned. "Why?"

"I just wondered," Eve smirked. "If there is, then none of us would ever get to repeat ourselves. Would we? The totality would never reach the end of existence so the individual could never begin again. No ending, no beginning. Yet you and I both know that we act out this little farce over and over and over. We know that, but," her voice became thoughtful and her eyes stared into infinity, "what we don't know is no more than a dream—a dream from out of the grave maybe."

"Hummmm, how does one reach the end of eternity? So what are you trying to say?"

"Nothing really," Eve laughed. "I was just trying to establish in my own mind that we humans are distinct creatures in each repetition of the cycle, that the world of animals and plants really does exist for us, that although we might destroy it in one cycle, it will not really die but will be born again in another cycle. I don't understand how that could be true if there is an infinite supply of all living and non-living creatures."

"And you really wanted to establish that you are godlike in that you have meaning in God's eye," Nick smirked. "Isn't that what you really mean? You saw the grizzly kill the fish. You could kill the grizzly if you had the right weapon. But can something kill you?"

"Yes."

"Not in the Garden. But outside, yes."

"And so that's what separates us from the gods?"

"Yes."

"Out there, in the world to which we are doomed, we die only to be reborn again. And again."

"Yes."

"And the gods never die."

"Yes."

"Thus we live many lives, all previous ones forgotten, while you go on and on and on with never a change in the electrical impulse of consciousness. No interruptus to jump-start another existence which, arguably because the mind sees it as entirely new and different, really is a different existence."

"Yes."

"I think it's time for me to begin preparing the stage so that I can successfully tempt Adam with the apple."

"Yes."

2

And you know the rest of the story. It took Eve several days to wean Adam from his most irritating childish ways, but she enjoyed the contest, if it can be called such. Not as much as the outcome, she has always claimed, but I have my doubts about her sincerity in this specific situation and its repetitions.

In any case she sought out Adam, who was lying on his side by a murmuring brook, in the shade of an ageless oak, a blade of grass hanging from his lips, his eyes lazily following the meanderings of several spotted trout. Being our original ancestor, symbolically at least, Adam left us with many of our masculine characteristics, not the least of which is that of couch potato, lawn potato in Adam's case, a characteristic Eve has tried to change drastically down through the ages, with mixed results for her temperament and Adam's peace of mind.

Eve stretched out on the opposite bank, facing her prey, pulled a long blade of grass and dangled it between lips slightly swollen and scarlet from a quick, surreptitious massage moments before, and forced her eyes to follow the swimming fish, feigning ignorance of Adam's proximity.

Often over the next hour she fought a smirk which struggled to curl her lips and crinkle her heavenly blues. She continuously fought the urge to smile at her prey, but only occasionally did she let an oblique glance slip over one part of his body or another.

Adam remained ignorant of the creature's intent. He had heard God's explanation of what his relationship would be with it, but God might just have some ulterior motive for pushing the association, a motive unfathomable to mere humans. Adam knew about fornication from watching the animals. They seemed to enjoy each other during certain periods of the year. He wondered if his relationship with this new creature would be the same, a few moments of pleasure followed by a long period of foraging for a pregnant mate and then child protection duties for an indeterminate time, only to have the process repeat itself annually until he became too bored to perform any of the expected duties and so would turn himself out to pasture, so to speak. Presently he had his freedom. He could do what he wanted whenever he wanted. Should he trade that for an occasional moment of intense physical pleasure?

But, he reminded himself, his Father had said this new creature would become a companion and helpmate, someone for him to talk to and someone to lend him a hand when he had things to do. What things, he wondered. He didn't know of anything he needed help with. As for companionship, he could play with any of the animals he wanted to when he felt lonely.

Adam glanced at the creature on the far bank of the stream. Again he felt the pleasurable stirring in his loins, which irritated him. He frowned. He glared at the creature, suddenly angry that it had invaded his territory, angry even if it was a gift from his Father, blithely ignorant that some of his antagonism stemmed from an unwarranted, preordained jealousy, daring the oddly shaped creature to so much as mumble a greeting in his direction. But as it seemed to be completely unaware of his presence, he became irritated at being ignored. The irritation turned to anger. Several times he almost shouted for the thing to go someplace else; this specific section of the stream and its banks were his. After a while, however, he began to feel a sense of guilt, as if he rather than the creature were the interloper, which made him so furious that he finally did shout:

"Go away, you wretched creature! Can't you see I'm counting the fish in this section of the stream? I'm busy. Go bother someone else."

The creature didn't respond, as if it had not heard or understood his words.

"Go away or I'll stone you."

The creature remained motionless.

Adam rolled over until he found a pebble. He threw it and hit the creature on the leg. A satisfied smile twisted his lips and sparkled in eyes the blunt color of hickory bark.

A moment later the smile of satisfaction turned to dismay. A pout swelling its tempting lips even more, the creature glanced his way momentarily, looked deeply into his eyes, accusingly, then turned back to the fish.

Worse, God shouted from on high:

"Adam, remember what I told you the other day. I made this new creature for you, as a friend and companion. Her name is Eve. You are a male. She is a female and helpmate. Male and female, like the animals of the forest and the birds and bees of the air, remember? You've been studying them. You should know by now how much fun they have with each other. Or are you as retarded as you were in the last cycle?" the Lord growled the final sentence to himself before again addressing Adam, "Now play nicely and no fighting." God chuckled and again spoke too softly for Adam to hear, "You'll have plenty of time for that later." Adam cringed more at his father's tone than at the words. The blade of grass dropped from his lips. His eyes watered. He forced his gaze to return to the trout, but after God's pep talk he couldn't keep from furtively glancing at the creature, often.

"A female," he thought, over and over, trying his damnedest to focus on his memory of the games the animals played with each other.

It was impossible, however. His mind, as yet no more disciplined than the mind of most animals in their childhood, refused to concentrate for long. His eyes wandered with his mind, from the trout in the stream to a herd of does and fawns frolicking in the meadow nearby, to flickering shadows just beyond the edge of the woods, shadows he felt were leopard cubs cavorting with their mother.

He rose lazily and wandered off to watch the fun, having again totally forgotten Eve, whose eyes flashed blue fire at the desertion.

"I'll get even for that," she growled, angrily slapping the surface of the water.

The splashing result of her slap turned her frustration to laughter, then to sadness. The fish turned at the sound of the slap and stared curiously at her.

Her laughter dying in her throat, Eve murmured softly, a note of melancholy entering her voice, "After Adam catches a few of your friends and I broil them over an open fire, a slap like that will send you skittering for the shadows."

Adding an expressive damn to her comment, she set off after Adam, more than ever determined to tempt him, if for nothing more than to teach him a lesson in diplomacy. As she started through the stream, however, she caught a glimpse of her reflection in the water. She hesitated at the sight of the brown-skinned, blond image: the innocent blue eyes, wide, round, expressive; the strong face with pouting lips and large nose; the slightly flared hips molding into a firm, flat belly; shoulders barely wider than hips, but covered with skin softer than goose down; the pert, not-quite full breasts of a girl recently having passed through puberty; pubis as blond as the hair on top; long, shapely legs.

"Well," she murmured, pleased, "God has done himself proud this time. And me," she giggled a moment later. But her giggle quickly turned to thought.

"Is that all there is to it?" she asked herself. "Or is there something I've forgotten from the other times?"

She studied the fawns and does. A huge buck strolled out of the woods toward the gamboling animals. On the far side of the stream a black bear rolled itself into a ball and then stood on two legs and stretched as high as it could. Moments later a female with two cubs joined the bear and the four animals ambled off through the trees.

An idea tugged at Eve's consciousness. She walked back to the stream and studied her reflection once more.

"They have hair all over them, even on their faces," she informed herself. "I don't. I'm completely naked except for the hair on my head, this little tuft down here and in my armpits, and a little down on my legs. Adam can see everything, every single blemish. There's no mystery. Nothing left for the imagination. No sense of something new, of an adventure to come. No reason he should want to explore me. Except for the coarsest purpose, of course," she giggled, "which isn't all that bad." A moment later she added thoughtfully, "If that's all he wants, and he gets it, he'll turn back to his flora and fauna gazing, satisfied and bored with me. I've got to figure out a way to make him think he missed something, a way to make him imagine that there's always something new and interesting hidden in my being, make him think he never quite gets it all. Otherwise he'll never be mine entirely. He'll always be wandering off for one reason or another because by nature he's a fiddle-footed, fickle, self-centered lout."

So saying, Eve marched purposefully into the woods. In less than two hours she returned, a new Eve. In her hair she had entwined a yellow rose surrounded by violets. Every hair on her head had been stained with the juice of the black raspberry, her lips with the juice of the strawberry, her cheeks with powder made of finely ground limestone. Her breasts peeped through golden leaves held in place by a thin red vine tied seductively below her shoulder blades. A mini-skirt of similar leaves had been fashioned low on her hips, to some extent covering her to barely below the cute little cheeks of her butt. Her outfit accentuated the sensual roundness of her breasts, the soft curve of her hips, and the unending flesh of her legs.

She smiled at her image in the stream before setting off in pursuit of Adam. She found him in the deep, dark woods studying a cloud of harmless mosquitoes. (For your edification, the mosquito had not yet learned to bite. That would come after the fall.) He glanced at her, quickly glanced away as if caught in a shameful act, shyly glanced at her again, and forced himself to gaze into her eyes. "Do I know you?" he mumbled curiously.

Eve smiled slyly. With a little improvement on God's natural design, she had put Adam in his proper place. "I don't think so, yet," she simpered.

"I'm sure I've seen you somewhere," Adam muttered insistently, trying to ignore the leafy splendor of the creature's fur and concentrate on answering his own question.

The creature's face, he decided, was bizarre; he had never seen anything exactly like it before. Its eyes, rimmed with a black substance bleeding a reddish liquid onto white pupils, were somewhat similar to those of a grumpy black bear he had once come across in the deep forest. But they weren't the same at all. The bear was grumpy because he had not slept for several days and nights. His eyes were red for the same reason, or so he claimed. This creature before him didn't look grumpy. It was actually showing its teeth in what it must mean as a smile. It surely wasn't tired either. It was prancing around moving its hips and other things as if limbering up for a race.

Adam wondered about the creature's mouth, asking himself if it had fallen and bruised its face.

The white stuff on its cheeks was attractive, he thought, as was the leafy fur.

Adam wondered if he were being challenged to a race in some kind of sign language. Excitement tingled through his groin. He too began flexing his body.

Before he could react the creature had moved its body close to his and was matching his motion move for move. He found this enchanting. From time to time their bodies touched at the hips or chest. At each touch excitement flooded his groin with pleasure.

"I'm a woman," the sensually undulating creature whispered softly in his ear once when their bodies seemed to adhere longer than usual.

"Ah-hah!" Adam exploded. "Father told me about you. He said I should play with you. Be nice to you."

"Yes," Eve murmured, breathing softly against the other ear. "You should, because then I'll be nice to you."

"But you don't look like the woman he told me to be nice to," Adam complained petulantly. "I like for things to look like they should."

"No you don't."

"I don't?"

"No."

Eve's answer startled Adam into silence. For a long time he gave in to the sensual enjoyment of their bodies moving rhythmically as one—a soft touch, a moment of warm fusion, separation, again a soft touch.

"Why don't I?" he asked, trying unsuccessfully to recapture his former peevish unconcern.

"Because you're a man. So you have a man's mind and a man's

imagination. You need something to feed them both. Otherwise they'll never grow beyond the boundaries of this place."

Something clicked in Adam's thought process.

"I'm a man?"

"Yes."

"You're a woman?" "Yes."

"Men are males?"

"Yes."

"Women are females?"

"Yes."

"Father said we should enjoy each other like the animals do."

"Well, not in those precise words, but you've got the general idea all right."

Eve snuggled closer to her prey as she spoke. She could feel Adam's growing desire to accept her advances. She took his huge paw in her dainty little hand and led him deeper into the woods, for some reason embarrassed not by the romantic foreplay and their mutual acquiescence, but by the coming act itself.

I wonder if it was actually then or nine months later that Adam really understood that he had tasted the fruit of the forbidden tree.

3

I met Eve during my second week at Echo Creek University, known as Echo Creek College until faced with a period of declining enrollments and near bankruptcy, at which time, under the astute leadership of a new president with advanced degrees in physical and mental education, the Board of Trustees changed the moniker, built a bigger gym and football complex, gave the rest of the campus a general facelift, and lowered academic requirements, both entry and exit, while at the same time making public records which showed that those requirements had been raised to more stringent levels of expectation. Enrollment increased immediately, as did retention and graduation rates and, as a result, even more importantly, finances. The trustees were pleased. The administration was pleased. The faculty was pleased since their salaries were also raised. The state Board of Education was highly pleased. And so were staff, townspeople, and most students, actual and potential.

Echo Creek University, or ECU, as it is presently known, and pronounced Eck U, as a not-very-subtle take-off on Echo, was established within decades of the founding of Echo Creek itself, as an institution of higher learning for the local elite. Only one portrait of the founder exists today. It hangs in the boardroom, centered on the wall behind "The Throne," an ornate chair traditionally occupied by the president during the semi-annual board meetings. Offers of several million dollars have been made for the picture by collectors of Echo Creek trivia, but the Board continues to reject each offer. Why, I don't know, unless they're holding out for more money. The portrait can't be of much value otherwise, and it clashes terribly with the ultra-modern décor of the room, including an elongated oval table and matching chairs which could have been designed by El Greco if he were into fusing Danish modern and imitation King Arthur.

Anyhow, ECU's founder was one Terry Sloth, a sleepy-eyed, long-nosed creature whose fortune came from industrious parents. Terry's father owned an international lumber company as well as several furniture factories of multinational renown. His mother was a famous model and writer of romances. They died in a forest fire when Terry had barely reached his sixteenth birthday. After their death, much of their wealth disappeared into the coffers of the church, creditors, and other financial pirates. More slipped into the pockets of those who, under the guidance of Terry's self-appointed guardians, sold the remaining holdings. However, enough remained that Terry, his children, and his children's children for half a dozen generations could have lived like kings without stooping to labor of any kind, mental or physical.

In spite of his wealth, Terry was a poor student, an odd paradox never understood or accepted by any of his friends and peers among the wealthiest classes. He failed kindergarten, barely slipped through first grade because of a kind-hearted teacher and, well, with parental diligence, a lot of brown-nosing, clean living in public, and a little graft here and there, made it through elementary and high school one week to the day before his twenty-fourth birthday, in plenty of time to assume his rightful role of leadership in society, which primarily consisted of hereditary membership on three boards of financial institutions; one high school board, inasmuch as it was illegal to serve on a school board other than the one in whose jurisdiction one lived, except for private high schools and that would come later in his life; six church boards; the board of the local hospital, of which he would become president for life when he reached thirty years of age, since his parents had financed eighty percent of the construction of the institution and had insisted on including the provision for his life-time tenure in the charter; a half dozen or more boards of institutions of higher learning; and the state board of the Masonic Lodge.

However, at twenty-four Terry was not yet ready for entry into adult life. He wanted his entitlement to four years of higher education. Nay, he craved four years of college as the normal adolescent boy craves the movie actress, saucy and sensual, who struts her stuff on the screen before him, or, maybe more aptly defined, as the stallion craves the mare in heat in the adjoining stall. There was nothing subtle about Terry's desires. Anything he desired gave him an erection. That, in essence, was how he became aware of his desires.

In his innocence, Terry applied to the state university, basing his application on his academic record. Needless to say, he was rejected. No one in the university registrar's office made the connection between him and his dead parents. His mother had used an alias for her professional work. His father had always used his middle name and the initial of his first name on public and business records, while Terry reversed that process on the line which asked for his father's name and occupation.

He tried the same process on 321 other applications to institutions of higher learning around the state and nation. The result differed only in the length of time it took for the rejection to reach him.

However, lucky for Terry, a group of local high school teachers had banded together to form a preparatory link between Echo Creek High and the state university. They had formulated a series of course offerings; published them in catalog format complete with course number, title, and brief description; and submitted the result to the State Board of Education for approval, which they promptly received eleven years, seven months, and three days later. Lucky for Terry, the merry band of teachers did not have means or faculty to offer more than a fraction of the needed courses in any given year (one of them had already died), but by changing academic-specialty hats semester by semester, they were able to offer the first two years of college over a period of four years, free to all comers since faculty remuneration amassed rapidly, in the form of state and federal aid and charitable contributions, inasmuch as the group had no administrative structure in the first years of their existence with which to share their income and inasmuch as, for reasons of prestige, the high school furnished them classrooms for close to nothing. And so Terry slipped through his first two years of college without leaving Echo Creek High School or meeting any impossible obstacles along the way, although all of the gang actually shuddered every time he entered one of their classes.

From this ideal makeshift institution Terry transferred to the state university. His grade-point average had been sufficient for transfer, albeit too mediocre to predict future success. He failed his first semester at the state university, and his second, and third, at which time, discouraged, his determination shattered, he anonymously (to all except the university's president and a select few professors of academic power and renown) donated several million to the college of business, in which he was attempting to major, by the way, with an equal sum to the college of liberal arts and sciences. Afterwards his academic ability and his grades improved. He eventually graduated but was discouraged from pursuing a graduate degree in spite of his avid desire to do so. He turned to the pursuit of money, a poor substitute, he often told himself, for the advanced pursuit of ideas, but an alternative goal, nevertheless, something to give his life meaning.

In his later years, when the money chase had lost its zest and he felt his mortality creeping closer day by day, he began searching for the pearly gates of immortality. He contacted the president who had taken control of Echo Creek High's preparatory link to the state university system. Unknown to him, the original founders of the link had all gone on to join the celestial educational institution. But they had eventually created and left behind a well-padded and not at all underpaid administrative structure which had become so entrenched in the link that many in Echo Creek and surroundings found it almost if not completely impossible to think of the two as anything other than a single entity. Faculty and staff were hired by the administration/ link to perform tasks in the same way that any employees of any institution, public or private, performed tasks for wages. The link itself, of course, or the administration (no one is certain because the two are still inseparable to historians) upgraded the title of the institution from College Link to Echo Creek Community College.

Terry became known in Echo Creek history as the man who further upgraded the status of ECCC to ECC, from two-year college to full, four-year college and, later, just before his death, as president and most influential member of the board of trustees, to four-year and graduate university, and thus eventually to ECU. He gave oodles of money for the upgrades and, in that way, purchased a degree of immortality as well as an honorary doctorate in humane letters, the first time, and an honorary doctorate in educational administration for the second major contribution. Immediately afterwards he authorized one of the graduate faculty, a historian and would-be scholar, to write his memoirs. The thin tome was published two days before Terry's death. He died happy, his greatest dreams realized.

4

Back to my first meeting with Eve: I had made a date to eat lunch in the Student Union with a couple of the guys I had met the week before at Orientation; we were all in the same small study group. They were new students also but not from Echo Creek.

When I arrived at the Union, they were sitting with a bunch of other students, all crowded around one of the larger tables, all with food and drinks on the table in front of them. The Student Union was an inexpensive food court, subsidized by the federal government in one way or another, I suppose. At noon when classes were in session and during the evening, it was a noisy, unruly, open rectangle made of glass, steel, cement blocks and tile with square metal tables and an excessive number of chairs inviting occupants to each table.

"Hey, Donjon," one of my new acquaintances greeted me, raising his hand with a feigned cool indolence. Named Bartholomew Kane by not-very-sensitive parents, he was a proposed business major and star centerfielder. He came from a nearby small town; he reached Echo Creek U. by means of small-college baseball skills and substandard academic background and potential, or so he claimed.

At Orientation they asked a lot of hokey questions, trying to make us new students feel at ease and, I suppose, trying to get a feel for the new student body and how they would fit in. In our group each one of us had to answer the question "Why did you come to Echo Creek University?" Bart said he came to play baseball. When pinned down to why Echo Creek and not some other college, he grinned and said he wasn't the bookworm type and so his grades weren't good enough to go to a better school. That got a laugh from well over half of the students, a glare from our orientation leader and the other students. The truth, I have no doubts, was that he wound up at ECU because of substandard skills in baseball, although the same was probably true of academics as well.

The comment, which I took as sarcasm because of the look on Bart's face as he spoke, appealed to me so I made a point of talking to him during breaks.

Dan Borrell, another new student at the table and also from Bart's hometown, had been in our orientation group as well. He was a basketball player, tall and lanky. He had laughed openly at our orientation leader's irritation and volunteered that, like Bart, he had come to Echo Creek U. to play ball, basketball not baseball, but ball nevertheless.

"If it wasn't for the chance to play basketball I'd go work in a factory or something," he shrugged, "or I'd go someplace where I could get the major I want. You know, like learn how to manage a store of something."

Anyhow, Bart's greeting served as introduction to the unknown students at the table. Another casual nod from Dan served as the model for other greetings.

There was only one vacant chair, beside the girl who turned

out to be Eve. I plopped into it and immediately slumped into my normal sitting style, something similar to that of a Raggedy Andy doll.

Eve was talking to a girl on the far side of her. The guy to my left was involved in a heated discussion with the girl next to him. As far as I could make out, because of the general noise that made hearing most of what they said next to impossible, and because of their face-to-face, low-even-though-intense conversational style, I decided they were discussing their mutual class schedules. After a few minutes of listening and understanding a fraction, albeit a small fraction, of what they were saying, and of watching their facial expressions and body language, I came to the conclusion that they were sweethearts from high school, one of the smaller county high schools. After a few more minutes of listening and watching I concluded that the guy had promised to take some class at ten in the morning, a composition class, I think. The girl had signed up for the class at ten but the guy hadn't. It seems he had heard something negative about the teacher assigned to that section of the course, like maybe he was too demanding, and so had signed up for a different section, with another teacher, but he had failed to tell his girlfriend. She came across irate. He was apologetic. She was threatening to dump him if he didn't start communicating better. He was promising greater reliability in the future. I guess he might have been horny, I don't know.

Across the round table Dan and Bart were schmoozing a couple of girls they had cornered between them. I couldn't hear a word they were saying, but the girls exuded a lot of smiles, giggles, and more-than-friendly body wriggles, so I figured my two new friends were doing okay.

To their left slouched two guys and a girl who seemed to do more gawking around the room than talking to each other. And, again, like I said, the girl who I later learned was Eve was talking to the girl on the other side of her. Since the table contained an equal number of male and female students, I figured the girl next to Eve must belong to the gawking guy beside her, even though he was involved with the girl on the other side of him and the guy beyond her.

Which left Eve as my intended—or so I figured.

So I studied Eve. If she was meant for some kind of a blind luncheon date, I wondered if she had come to the feast as innocently as I had or if she had been forewarned that a single guy would appear at her side, made not from a feminist rib but from the fusion of an egg and sperm, invited not by God but by a couple of guys he hadn't known for very long.

So, ignored by every one of my table mates after the brief flurry of noncommittal nods, I gawked and continued inventorying Eve out of the corner of my vision. She was choice flesh above the table, dishwater blond hair to her shoulders; sparkling blue eyes shaded by downy brows and lashes, suggesting an innocence belied by a saucy nose a little wide for her face; lips naturally curled as if from laughing or sneering too much at the world around her; and breasts worthy of Helen but not large enough to be made of silicone. All encased in a blouse neither form-fitting nor big enough for four of her, the only two styles prevalent at both our table and the others around the room.

I scooted my chair closer, unconsciously, I like to think.

"Are you crowded?"

Eve turned toward me as she spoke. Sweat broke out on my brow, and other, more private parts. I wondered what variety of red my face had become. I glanced at the couple to my left. They were oblivious to anything except each other. Nobody else at the table seemed to be aware of me or of the question. The girl with whom Eve had been talking had turned to the boy beside her, hurriedly, as if relieved to be free of Eve's attention. The two were already deeply engrossed in conversation.

"No," I blurted, "just trying to get cozy so we can talk and I can hear what you're saying."

Eve rolled her eyes, but she did smile ever so slightly.

"Just what I need in my life, another Don Juan."

"Better a Don Juan than a Milty Milktoast," I laughed through my embarrassment.

She looked at me with what I like to think of as more interest than curiosity.

"You don't really have the look of a Don Juan type," she smirked.

"I'm not," I shrugged, my nerves having returned to their former lethargy. "I don't have the right looks and girls make me nervous."

"I don't know whether to consider that as honesty or a line of bull."

As she talked Eve looked me straight in the eyes as if she were trying to penetrate beyond the surface to the core of my being, to see if the words came from a sincere source.

"Some of each," I tried for what I thought sounded like a truthful answer.

"Or the 'Look how humble I am' line."

"You don't like me or you don't like men in general?"

Eve laughed out loud at my question, "You really mean, 'Look at me. I'm a hunk. Any woman worthy of her sex would be attracted to me. So if you're not you must not like men.' Isn't that what you mean?"

"No, that's not what I meant," I fought a losing battle with sudden irritation. "What's the matter with you anyhow? I was just making stupid conversation and you tell me I'm a liar and don't really mean what I said. Why didn't you just tell me I was being stupid? That would have been more correct." I laughed, although without any humor in it. Actually it felt more like a series of burps.

She smiled and rolled her eyes.

"You shouldn't call somebody stupid when you don't know them."

I found myself returning her satirical grin in spite of my anger.

"But you can call them dishonest?"

"I never thought of a man's line of manure as being particularly dishonest, not in any personal sense. I've always figured that it's a relative characteristic of the sex, like size and strength and aggressiveness." She laughed suddenly, a delightful trill of momentary happiness. "You men never change, no matter how old you get. You're always trying to impress us females, always trying to show us how strong or intelligent or kind or whatever you think you are, anything that gives you an advantage in the sex game." She shrugged, serious. "I figured yours was the humility line."

"You have a bad impression of men," I commented, not knowing what else to say.

"Maybe," the smile had disappeared from her eyes and lips. But a moment later those same blue eyes sparkled again, "But some of my very best friends are men. Uh, boys, I mean, mostly."

"That sounds like a racial allusion."

"More like borrowing from racial allusions in order to make a satirical comment on gender relations, which are treated a lot like racial relations these days, which is kind of idiotic." Eve shrugged, the bare hint of a smile on her lips. "I guess I'm as prejudiced as anyone else in this ridiculous world we live in, against men, against other races, against other cultures, against other social classes, against anything different. You name it, I've doubtlessly got it. And anyone who says they haven't is lying, to themselves if to no one else."

"Wow! Cynical!" I blurted.

She shrugged, her piercing blue eyes studying my face again, "We all generalize, and over-generalize, and generalize without sufficient facts, or too often without any facts at all, I think. But anyway," she shrugged again, "I know I'm being pedantic, but how could we think at all without generalizing? In chaos? We're too limited mentally for that. Actually," her teeth nipped at her upper lip and her eyes concentrated on the infinite space over my left shoulder, "we organize the chaos around us according to pre-conceived notions and relationships, notions and relationships that are formed by the specifics and similarities existing in that very chaos. The more intelligent among us are probably more open to new relationships, new ideas, and new facts. The less intelligent probably force everything new to fit old, familiar patterns or condemn whatever they can't. The more intelligent are probably more open to modifying their notions to fit new relationships and ideas. And facts, of course. But, to put the whole thing in a really simplistic nutshell, reality exists in the eyes of the beholder, or at least has a heck of a lot more influence there than in its own essence."

"I don't think it's as easy as all that," I shook my head, becoming interested in her comments, startled into the pedantic myself by a woman interested in talking about something other than people or things. "I figure there're lots of intelligent people who reject the Big Bang theory out of hand, simply because it doesn't easily conform to the words in the bible. Others accept it as established theory and try to reconcile it with their Christian beliefs, or with whatever religion they believe in, maybe claiming that's the way God started the universe, not by separating earth and water, but by creating the birth of time and space out of a concentrated ball of matter, which he might or might not have made in the first place."

"You think the Big Bang is questionable?" she asked, although, from the look on her face, I think she really wanted to point out that I had either missed or changed the substance of her comments.

"I'm not the only one," I felt my stubborn nature rising to the fore, while at the same time I wondered at my arrogant presumption. I was talking as if I knew what I was talking about.

"It's a hypothesis, you know, although they teach it as fact. But it's really no more than speculation, mathematical and scientific speculation."

"Which surely makes it more believable than religious speculation simply because the people who postulate it are educated, highly intelligent scientists."

Her lips tilted in a slight sneer as she spoke.

"Yeah, well," I reacted, "the medieval scholastics were the most highly educated people of their time also, but it didn't make them right or more thoughtful and more open to new ideas and facts."

"We've gotten a little off the track here," Eve smirked, but I thought I noticed a flicker of interest somewhere deep in her eyes. "We were talking about intelligent people, not educated people."

"Before that we were talking about prejudice as a result of overgeneralization. Besides, it's generally the most intelligent people who get an education. Yeah, I know, not always," I quickly inserted as her eyes sparked and she started to speak.

She giggled and said, "A pedantic Don Juan, that's what you are. You seduce women through their minds."

It was my turn to roll my eyes.

"You're new on campus this semester," thankfully she turned our conversation to a personal level, away from the freshman one-upmanship we had begun.

"Yeah," I answered. "You too?"

"No, I started at midyear. This is my second semester coming up." Noting my quizzical expression, she added, "I'm from

Midport. I didn't graduate until this spring, but I finished all my requirements and everything else in the fall semester so they let me enroll in college before officially graduating. The college and Midport have an agreement about that."

"A brain," I commented.

"A woman with a brain—how unusual," she smiled conspiratorially.

"A beautiful, um, girl with a brain—I don't find that any more unusual than a handsome boy with a brain, like me," I grinned.

"Nice catch," she laughed, a husky sound in the shrill tide around us. "But do you really think I'm just a girl?"

Accepting the challenge, I looked her over from top to bottom, slowly, caressingly, eventually returning my eyes to hers. She was no longer smiling. Her eyes were studying my face as if to find part of her answer there. When my eyes touched hers, her gaze held mine.

"I don't know when a girl becomes a woman or a boy becomes a man," I admitted, half serious, half sardonic. "The law claims to know, but it can't be trusted very much. Besides, to state the obvious, a boy has a man's body long before he becomes a man in all ways. No doubt it's the same for a girl and woman, although I've never been one," I smiled in order to emphasize that I was joking. "So, how far are you along the process?" I tried for a sardonic grin in imitation of her earlier one.

Ignoring the question and the tinge of sarcasm in my comments, she asked, "Are we talking about sex here?"

"Not really," I shrugged, feeling a little put out by the simplistic bias of the question, "although that's part of it. Not the sexual act so much as the physical ability to do the act and suffer any consequences, not necessarily the willingness to do it although that's part of the whole process, I suppose. But, man, your reaction was so simple, so common, like you've got sex on the brain. You sound like all the other girls I've talked to on campus. There's a lot more to being an adult than…."

"I know," she interrupted impatiently, "but I'm not used to talking about much of anything but sex with boys. That's all they seem to be interested in, besides sports."

"You didn't answer my question," I ignored the bias in her remark.

"How would I know?" she laughed again, the melodic sound echoing in my cavernous depths. "I think I'm a woman, but you ask a lot of older people I know and many will tell you that I'm a conceited, snot-nosed kid."

"Hey," her words covered my face with a spontaneous grin, "maybe we've got a lot in common after all."

"So it's all relative," she added, ignoring my comment.

"No doubt it is, although that doesn't tell us anything of value," I agreed, shifting gears into serious overdrive.

Momentarily I wondered if what we were having was a rare introductory college conversation, one that occurred seldom and then only between two serious students, not the majority, one in which everything but the kitchen sink is thrown out to impress the other student. I wondered if talking to Eve was some kind of special experience, or if we were just two more college freshmen trotting out all our repertoire to make an impression.

"So what's your name?" I asked when she remained silent and seemed on the verge of turning back to the girl on the other side of her. I didn't want to lose her yet.

"Eve," she rolled her eyes, "and don't make any snide comments about purity or the Garden of Eden or Adam or any other biblical stuff. I've had enough of them to last a lifetime. And no, I don't want to go out for ribs this evening. That one really makes me see red." She glared at me as if I had broken some kind of sacred vow.

After a few minutes into our conversation, I had decided to ask her if she lived on campus or off and what her phone number was. But as our conversation progressed I kind of lost my nerve.

We turned to personal matters. Her link to Bart and Dan was Midport and sports. She too had been an athlete at Midport High, four years of both softball and basketball, but she did not expect to play sports at Echo Creek U. She was a full-time student and worked part-time to support herself. And she planned on double-majoring in accounting and finance, as well as completing an MBA before she left college and took a job. So she didn't have time for sports.

"I don't really like the idea of spending five years in college, but with the MBA I should be able to get a really good paying job," she explained.

Our half-hearted conversation came to an abrupt halt when she suddenly glanced at her watch, exclaimed that she barely had time to rush to her dorm room before class, grabbed her books, and made for the door. No phone numbers were exchanged, no promises to meet again some other day. She shot from her seat and disappeared in the swarm of students jamming the main exit. For some reason I felt no major sense of loss, only a feeling of something unfinished.

The others at the table glanced up as she scrambled to her feet but immediately returned to their conversations. No one seemed to notice me still sitting there. I sat quietly for a moment, glancing around, ignored. Then, as if finally realizing that my main purpose for being in the Union was lunch, my stomach growled. I made my way to the cafeteria line and returned with a hamburger, fries, and soft drink. The others had all left by then.

5

I didn't connect with Eve again until well into the next semester. I saw her around campus occasionally, walking in the distance, in the library studying, sitting with friends in the Union, or waiting to enter a classroom. We nodded when our eyes happened to meet, but neither made any attempt to strike up a conversation.

Yet something must have hooked my unconscious self and dragged it along in her wake, because one cold but kind of balmy Saturday afternoon when I found myself off work for the day and unable to study, I set out for what I told myself was a walk without defined destination. Yet I headed straight to the house in east Echo Creek where, according to Bart and Dan, Eve boarded with an elderly couple. My nerves pounded louder and louder the closer I approached the house; my lungs shrank with every step as if I were running cross country. I almost walked on by but at the last moment forced myself to turn onto the sidewalk leading to the house.

Eve was sitting on the porch, cuddled in one corner of a swing with her arms wrapped around her chest and her legs drawn up under her, snow boots sticking out from under a light winter coat, a sock cap hiding most of her blond curls, her lips and cheeks pinched red by what must have been a long time outside in the cool air.

Wordlessly she motioned to the empty space beside her. Nervously I plopped down.

"For a while I thought you were just walking by," she smiled, her eyes glinting mischievously.

"I almost did."

My voice shivered. I shivered.

"Are you cold?"

"Yeah," I lied.

"I'm glad you didn't walk on past," she spoke softly.

"I am too," I tried to laugh but my voice still shook ever so slightly.

"Because I've been bored to death since I quit studying an hour ago and I was hoping somebody, anybody, would drop in," she giggled at her little joke.

At her laughter my nerves quit playing bongos in my lungs. My ego whispered that she had been thinking about me but she didn't plan on admitting it.

"Let's go for a walk," I offered through an inane grin.

Without a word, still giggling uncontrollably, she bounced up from the swing and down the steps onto the sidewalk. I followed in a more dignified manner, although I felt like giggling idiotically right along with her, and dancing for joy as well.

We walked silently for some time, Eve a foot or so in the lead, in the direction I had been walking before stopping. We soon reached the edge of Echo Creek, passing dirty mounds of snow scattered along the sidewalk. The street became a two-lane road. We continued into the countryside, between fields of snow, under a pale sky recently washed and rinsed, our path lighted by an anemic sun that floated in and out of frozen white clouds.

Eve slowed down until we were walking side by side. "What made you come out to see me after so much time?" she asked. "I mean, it's been over two months since we met and you haven't tried to see me or even talk. All you've done is nod or wave when we pass by each other on campus, and even that not all the time. And you never talk to me when we're both in the Union at the same time." Giggling, she imitated my swagger for several minutes, comically, occasionally waving or nodding abruptly as if to someone passing by.

"You're always with other students," I offered lamely, although I readily admitted to myself that my desire had been intimidated by my fear of rejection.

"I'm glad I was alone today then," the sardonic glint had returned to her eyes, "or you might have walked right past, pretending you didn't see me or that you were too preoccupied to do any more than wave and hurry on your way."

She again imitated me walking and waving, watching me from the corner of her eyes.

"When it comes to girls," I tried to laugh but failed, "I'm about the biggest coward you'll ever meet."

"Good," she declared and took my hand with hers. "I never did like the Casanova type. I don't want some man who's gonna move on as soon as he gets what he wants."

"Sex without commitment?" her comment startled the words out of me.

She shrugged and grinned before turning serious, "That's

right. I don't have anything against sex if it's with a guy I think I'd marry. But I don't sleep around with just any guy that smiles at me," again that quick grin that made me want to giggle with her, "or that takes me to a movie or out to eat or something. I like guys and I like to go out on dates and things. But what I really, truly want, sometime, is a permanent relationship, one accepted by society and the church, with children. I don't plan on living in sin or as a social outcast or without real commitment from both of us. I don't plan on being a single parent. And I don't plan on growing old alone. Do you?"

For the first time I began to question my need to see her again. She must have read the shock on my face because her laughter trilled again and she squeezed my hand.

"I don't plan on getting married now, silly! And not with you. When I find the right man, I'll settle down. But he'll have to have money or be on his way to making it, lots of it. I don't plan on growing old poor. Do you?"

"Well, I don't know," I mumbled, too startled to think clearly. "I never thought about it." I hesitated before bumbling on, "I guess, yeah, I'm like everybody else. I'd like to be rich. But, uh, there are other things more important than money."

"Like what?" she asked skeptically.

"Well, like love and friends and…."

"Sure, I agree, those things are important," she smiled earnestly. "But they've got nothing to do with money. I'll have friends whether I'm rich or poor. And love too."

"Yeah," I agreed without thinking and therefore oozed some more pedantic nonsense. "Friends won't leave you just because you become rich. But love? What if you fall in love with somebody poor, or somebody who's not really interested in making lots of money?"

"I won't," she stared at me, her upper lip curled at the corner.

"What if you do?" I insisted.

"I won't," she reiterated, irritation in her tone. "Love isn't something that just happens."

"Sure it does," I disagreed.

"No, it doesn't. You might be attracted to some guy. You know, the way he smiles or looks at you might get you, or the way he walks, or his shoulders, or something. But that's not love. That's just physical attraction. You might see a guy and say, 'Man, I'd go to bed with him in a minute.' But that's not love, that's passion. Love is something that grows with time together."

"Well, it's gotta start somewhere," I declared, irritated because I suddenly realized that, down deep inside, I really believed in love at first sight.

"Yeah, but passion doesn't turn into love unless you nurture it. Just because you sleep with a guy a few times doesn't mean you've gotta marry him and live happily ever after. You can up and leave him before he starts growing on you. There are other fish in the brook."

I didn't know what to say to her comments so I didn't say anything. We walked in silence for a long time. Eventually we reached a crossroad and turned left, over gravel lined with trees and occasional snow drifts. If the semi-balmy weather held, I thought, all the car-polluted snow would be gone in a couple of days. If the air warmed a little more and that brought a heavy rain, the world would be clean again for a while.

"You don't believe in romantic love," I blurted, my ego disturbed by her words. "You don't believe a boy and girl can see each other for the first time and know right away they can't do without the other one.

She squeezed my hand and laughed, "Do you?"

I thought about her question before I answered. I had always thought of myself as something of a pessimist, yet I believed in romantic love. The images of the widow and Allie Lizardus slipped unbidden into my thoughts. Allie and I, we had had our childish fling, better said, our hot, bumbling experiments, that one summer. The very next school year Papa Lizardus had sent her to a private school in the East. I had only spoken to her once since then, when we accidentally bumped into each other on the street downtown, a couple of months after my graduation from Echo Creek High and hers from the prep school she had attended. Our conversation was stilted, forced, and quickly terminated by her evident embarrassment. For a long time after our sensual, bumbling games, she had disturbed my sleep at night, my reveries by day, with her chubby body, but then the widow entered and exited my life, leaving behind a memory almost as real as the widow herself to caress me in my dreams. But the sharpness of that too had faded with time, to be replaced by or merged with others which floated through my existence without becoming more than a yearning, vague at times, more intense at other times, but never more than a night-time desire unrequited.

I had always thought I loved the widow, not Allie, who had been no more than an object of curiosity and childish lust, a pleasant toy I found one nice day and played with for a while and lost and occasionally recalled, at times, even feeling a sense of emptiness at the loss sometimes. The widow, however—I had been certain that I loved her. Yet I had let her slip not only from my life but also from my daily thoughts and dreams, not completely by any means, not to the extent that I had let Allie slip into the nethermost regions of my unconscious self, but definitely from being the central figure of my reveries to being a cameo character.

"Yeah, I do believe in love at first sight," I answered her question stubbornly, pushing the doubts aside. "You can't help falling in love. You just do. And you can't help how you act when you're in love."

"My God," she trilled with laughter. "That's rubbish. It makes great love stories about characters like Romeo and Juliet or Julien Sorel and Madame de Renal or, one of my favorites, the story of Jake Barnes and Lady Brett Ashley." She glanced at me, to see how I was taking her cynicism, I think. "I love romantic stories, especially tragic ones," she continued after a moment. "I get all teary-eyed when I read them, or see them in a movie or on the stage. But I can't picture myself doing what Juliet did—killing myself on the body of my dead lover because of an overwhelming sense of love and loss, or being unable to commit myself to any other man because I can't have the one I want, or sacrificing my good name and social standing, my future happiness on this earth, for some man I happen to want at a specific time. Can you imagine doing that for a woman?" she asked after a moment.

I thought about her question in uncomfortable silence as we continued walking, now hand in hand.

Finally I blurted out my thoughts, uncertainly, "I don't know. I want to say yes. But I don't know. I mean, maybe I don't have the guts to kill myself even if I was madly in love and the girl I loved wouldn't have me or died for some reason. Even if I thought I couldn't live without some girl, I don't know if I could kill myself over her."

"You're no fun," Eve giggled. "You don't have to be so honest. You could pretend like you're a true romantic rather than a fair-weather one."

"I thought you didn't like romantics."

"I didn't say that," Eve shook her head as if in disgust. "I said people can control who they fall in love with. Love is something you earn, not something that jumps out and grabs you from nowhere. It's like a feeling you develop with time and shared experiences, like an old married couple or two sisters. You don't just see somebody and fall head over heels in love. That only happens in fiction and movies, and stuff like that. In real life, love comes out of doing things together. You know, like sitting beside each other in school for years on end or taking a walk in the cold and talking about dumb things," she laughed suddenly and squeezed my hand.

"You think we're falling in love?" I asked with a nervous grin.

"You haven't been listening to me very well," Eve threw her hands in the air and rolled her eyes in mock consternation. "I said you don't fall in love like suddenly and accidentally. How many times do I have to say it? You slide into love. Or you stroll into love. Or you roll into love—if you let yourself or if you're not on your guard. It takes time and togetherness. It doesn't happen in just an afternoon." She again squeezed my hand, laughing playfully. "Maybe after a few dozen of these walks we might."

"Well crap, what about a mother and her baby?" I felt my stubborn, argumentative self raise its hackles.

"We were talking about romantic love."

"Love between parents and children, between friends, between a boy and a girl—the only difference is sexual desire."

"No, it isn't, and not all parents love their children."

"Yeah, I know," I agreed, thinking of the parents of some of my friends, "and they show their love in lots of different ways."

"You can say that again," she spoke thoughtfully. "But we were talking about love, not how you express it, and love between a boy and a girl, not the love of parents for their baby. That's different. The baby is part of them. They probably feel an emotional attraction for a new baby like I might feel a physical attraction for a new guy I meet." She paused and glanced at me from the corner of her eyes. "The mother probably feels it more because she's lived with the baby inside her for a long time. But it's still just a general attraction, not yet focused on a specific baby with all its individual characteristics and not yet developed into a need to be with the object of love. That begins to happen when she first sees the little thing and starts feeding and taking care of it. Her attraction becomes love as time passes and as she nurtures the baby and her own feelings for it."

"Wow, that's cynical!" I couldn't help exclaiming. "You don't believe that complete strangers can fall in love the first time they meet?"

"You asked that before and, no, not in love," her upper lip

curled in a sneer. "I've already told you. They can be attracted to each other, or just one of them might feel the attraction," she giggled, "like in unrequited attraction."

I grinned tentatively at her little joke.

"But love? That's a lot more complicated than two warm, living masses being pulled toward each other by the laws of human gravity. Like I said, first there's the tug inside you by one thing or another, by a level of sophistication in dress or speech or movement, by a glance or a smile, or maybe by sexual vibes. It's no more than one more appeal to something inside you, an appeal that swings you toward the orbit of this new person. You might not even be aware of it. It's like a tiny spark dropped into grass. If the grass is dry enough and the wind is right, the spark might grow into a raging fire. If not, if you're careful you can still nurture it and it might at least grow into something you can warm your hands with on a cold winter night, something with enough heat so you won't be too cold and lonely as the years pass. But at the same time you can always put the fire out if it has something about it that you don't like."

"That's scary," I mumbled almost to myself.

"Scary?" she seemed surprised at my reaction.

"So much for the wild, irresistible hurricane force of true romance," I couldn't help shrugging my shoulders and shaking my head to show my consternation even though I was being a little sarcastic.

"You mean true passion, Donjon."

"No, I don't," I disagreed. "I mean what I said, true romance. I mean the way a guy feels for a girl when he can't stand being away from her, when she's all he can think of, her smile, her chatter, the way she looks at him, the way she walks away from him, the way...."

"Yeah," Eve rolled her eyes, "and after he's crawled in bed with her a few times, he finds it not so difficult to stay away from her. The more they make out the less attractive he finds her physically. You know that old saying, familiarity breeds contempt. I wouldn't go all that distance with man/woman togetherness, but I do think being together for years breeds a sense of the commonplace and the monotony inherent in it."

"What about marriage?"

I realized that my voice had become strident with anger, as if I were reacting to an attack on my person or on something I held sacred.

"What about it?"

"People fall in love and then get married. They don't get married and then fall in love."

"Maybe," Eve stared as if I were some kind of naïve child, "and maybe people think they're in love when they get married. And maybe a lot of them grew up as childhood sweethearts and so had a long engagement, even though not formally. But I bet most of them are 'in love' with marriage more than with their bride or groom; otherwise, they'd just be lovers until they got bored with each other and started looking for greener pastures. They think they're in love with a person but they're really in love with the mystery of the wedded state, with some romantic or spiritual ideal they have of two lovers growing old together, or they crave the social status marriage gives them. Or they want to get their wife or husband before the market dries up and only the culls are left, so they marry the best they can find at the time. Or they want children and social acceptance both, and marriage is the best place to get them. Or, like me, they don't want to grow old without the companionship of children and grandchildren and a beloved mate tied to them legally and socially and spiritually, as well as by the bonds of time. There are lots of reasons people get married, I believe," she ended her lecture, "and among the young, one of the major reasons is, uh, romantic passion, or passionate romance, or, better said, a little romance and a lot of passion. They call that love, but it's the aura of the first experiments with sex."

"You don't call it love?"

"Not really, I don't think, although I guess I could," she acquiesced begrudgingly, "but it's a flame that way too often burns out quickly and leaves only embers, which can turn cold without new fuel."

"Fuel?"

She shrugged, "Yeah, fuel, like kids and other things in common, especially friends and relatives and a past and, yeah, friendship and intimacy.

At the next crossroads we turned to retrace our steps. As if by spoken accord, we avoided the subject of love and related topics for the rest of the walk. When we reached the house where she was boarding, Eve excused herself, saying she had to study and then get ready for a date that evening. We exchanged phone numbers. I promised to call and then trudged home, my emotions on a roller coaster, up one minute, down the next, up from memories of our time together, down because Eve had a date with some unknown male for the evening, up from the memory of her hand in mine, down because, except for giving me her telephone number, she had avoided any and all discussion of our potential future together, and way down in the dumps because of her cynical attitude toward love and romance.

6

Monday pounced as usual and so I again settled into my routine—classes, study, classes, study, part-time work at a local service station and garage, more study, more classes.

But Eve controlled my thoughts, first the reveries that helped make some really boring lectures sufferable, and later my dreams, day and night, in which she replaced all other stars, temporary and long-standing, as the semester progressed. When I could I pumped Bart and Dan for information about her—her family, her past, her character, her interests, whatever they were willing to share, truth or fiction. At first they seemed reticent to tell me anything at all about Eve. I eventually learned that each of them, at one time, had had the hots for her, that probably they still did but without any hope of their desire coming to fruition. Bart's reticence, I think, came from jealousy. But Dan's feelings seemed to have moved on to other females, partially at least. When they did open up I found they either knew most of Eve's personal and family history or they were really inventive. But then, small towns are pregnant with rumors motivated by a mixture of familiarity and imagination, truth and fiction, and Bart and Dan both loved the rumor vine.

Eve, I learned, was an only child in a certain sense, in divine as well as human law, since her mother apparently never gave birth to another. On the other hand, she was the only child legally recognized by her father, John Gardener, although not his only child by any means, if Bart and Dan and the rumor mill were correct. According to my two friends John chased the girls more than most of us poor males had the energy and time for. Some say, I have learned since then, that as far as progeny goes John would have been considerably better off liking the boys. His continuous philandering from his pre-puberty days well into his dotage would not, if that were the case, have populated the earth with so much fruit, palatable and unpalatable, sweet and sour.

However, I am only concerned with two early proofs of his predilection: Ron and Reno Tynsdale. A long time before he married Eve's mother, John had these two illegitimate sons by a girl named Leda Jones, who in turn was Eve's mother's first cousin.

Leda lived in Ur, an imitation Bavarian town northeast of Midport. She was an airy girl, not much more than a child at her first coupling with Eve's father, who was known at that time of his life as The Gardener, not simply because of his proclivity for sowing his seed in any available soil, fertile or infertile, lush or arid, virginal or exhausted, but more importantly because of the vitality he brought to his calling.

On the other hand, one of the two nicknames most commonly applied to Leda was Airhead. The other was Sexpot, although the latter's common usage was pretty well limited to the male population between the ages of ten and ninety.

Leda and John met at the Annual Halloween Festival of Ur, a public street carnival invariably taking place on the last Saturday of October. Barricades were set up at each end of Main Street and half a block from Main Street on each of the three side streets inside the barricades. No one not wearing a costume was admitted to the festival, which was one of the most popular in the county, if not the entire state.

John had just celebrated his sixteenth birthday when he first attended. However, he looked much older than his years, with or without a mask, so he had no problem ordering booze which, in turn, made it easier for him to score with older women. It was like a form of identification, relationship, or thought. Establish an a priori assumption and logic easily does the rest. John was drinking. Only people over twenty-one are allowed to drink legally. Ergo, John was legally over twenty-one. Not really uncommon logic, I believe, and rampant among John's conquests.

The problem was, or should I really say that John's advantage was, that he existed, morally, long before the cultural preoccupation (obsession might be a better word, actually)-before our cultural obsession with making all male creatures adult and child conform to female standards of conduct, emotion, thought, and legal standing, or, as a majority of our male citizens might insist, long before women decided they have the right to all the freedoms, physical as well as social, that men have traditionally considered their own. Thus he was free of certain standards of conduct which limit a man's freedom of action to that defined by a woman's freedom of the same.

Be that as it may, however, John attended the Annual Halloween Festival of Ur shortly after his sixteenth birthday. He attended alone as was his habit. He drove the family car, as was not his habit since he had taken his driver's test and passed with excellence on his birthday. In fact, it was his first time driving the car without an adult beside him.

And in second fact, during the evening (and into the wee hours of the night) he dented all four fenders and the door on the passenger side, the four fenders while parking at the festival, in lover's lane, and at Leda's house, the door while turning a corner on the way out of Ur—some other incompetent had parked too close to the corner of the street onto which John wished to turn. After each of the four accidents John thought fleetingly of notifying the other car's owner. That would be the honorable thing to do. But it would have been such a drag finding the owner if he/she was at the festival. On the other hand, if he/she resided in one of the houses by which each car was parked, and some more than half-drunk kid walked up to his/her door, knocked, got him/her out of bed, and told him/her that his/her car had been dinged and dented—well, John was no Ezra Pound but he did have a fertile enough imagination to conjure up some of the worst possibilities. And if he knocked on a door behind which the owner(s) did not live? After several seconds of positive consideration, in each case, he opted for the safer choice of flight. He made the right choice, most of you would probably agree, since the police never came looking for him, and so his parents' titanic wrath was the only punishment he received, a punishment which soon spent itself in fatherly expletives and such commonly inane motherly questions as "How could you?"

The next evening John returned to the crime scene, and the next, until one night the last of the revelers staggered home, their final drunken shouts echoing in the debris left for the wind and the street cleaners. Later John confirmed another date for late the following evening, one he didn't plan on keeping, said goodnight with a feigned passionate kiss, and drove off into the darkness, leaving his summer sweetheart with a womb no longer fallow.

Within a week he was happily plowing another field, one that had been plowed and re-plowed, but a soft, earthy, sun-drenched field worthy of all his heated skills and effort, nevertheless. He never again returned to Leda and never answered her calls, even after he learned through the teen grapevine that she was pregnant.

So Leda, alone with her burden, found a creature more amenable to both holy and civil matrimony. She easily seduced a man named Tom Tynsdale, a farmer by trade, and convinced him that she was pregnant with his spermatozoa.

Tom had failed math almost every year of the twelve he attended school. Ergo, he believed her since the logic of math and the illogic of conception, at least in terms of the process, are as integrally related as are all opposing forces in the dialectical imperative. They married, set up house, worked, had children, two sons, as was to be expected given Leda's innate integrity, and lived contentedly for the rest of their mortal lives—mostly so, anyhow, although there is some evidence that Tom strayed from the marital bed a few times during his middle years and that Leda lost her way even more often.

And so we finally get to the core of the matter. Tom and Leda Tynsdale gave legal birth to two strapping boy twins named Ronald and Reno, the very same two that were a number of months earlier naturally conceived by Leda and John the Gardener. Tom never in his life doubted that he was the sire of the twins. Not so the twins although, by the time of their birth, Leda had convinced herself that Tom was their biological father, a belief she never recanted, even on her death bed. Therefore, John's participation in the matter was and still is irrelevant, for all practical purposes, (i.e., social, psychological and biological) except for historians and gossip mongers such as myself, and of course a few genetic traits.

The story of Ron and Reno is one of conflict. They clashed even before the moment of conception. While John grunted in the throes of orgasmic delight, a sharp pain paralyzed him for what seemed like minutes but in actuality lasted only a split second or two. It was almost as if the flow of his sperm had divided itself into two warring factions, each trying to destroy the other and thus enter solo into Leda's body. The two sides seemed to be fighting with saw blades. John felt as if someone were reaming his sperm canal with a roto-rooter. The pain was excruciating. He screamed. Leda hugged him tighter, kissed him more passionately, absolutely certain she had pleasured him far beyond what mortals can physically stand and that he must therefore love her dearly.

Soon, however, the pain of battle was transferred to her non-virginal waterway. She mimicked John's screams, wondering even in her hurt if she was having an orgasm. She had almost decided to give up sex forever when the pain turned into a rushing sense of movement headed directly for her womb, as if John's sperm could not wait to enter the deepest, darkest, most sacrosanct part of her being. The thought actually did give her an orgasm. She forgot her pain of moments before.

The mortal conflict between Ron and Reno had begun. Sperm Ron won the battle by means of a sneaky kick to Sperm.

Reno's flagellum. Sperm Reno, on the other hand, won the race because of the head start given him by the kick. But Sperm Ron was so close behind him at the wire that he did not have time to block the passage. Both lived to fight another day.

And fight they did.

After a round of sex, Leda enjoyed nothing more than a lethargic snooze wrapped in the arms of her present lover, in this case John. So, when the uncontrollable jolts and shudders of orgasmic pleasure had subsided, leaving her languidly cuddly, she scurried to the bathroom to wash her crotch, planning, once cleaned and blow-dried, to slink back to the warm bed and John, who had begun to snore even before she slipped out from under the sheet.

She didn't quite complete the round trip, however, before the next fight began. Gamete Ron, furious that he had lost the race, attacked Gamete Reno just as the latter plunged toward Leda's anxiously awaiting ovum. Gamete Reno defended himself with a tremendous series of primitive karate kicks and punches, but to no avail. Gamete Ron hung on for dear life. Squealing, biting, scratching, cursing in simple gamete talk—the combatants tumbled headfirst into their temporary refuge only to find that they had been bested in the race by almost a dozen other interloper gametes. Suddenly, in unison, as if by mutual agreement and carefully prepared battle plans, the two enemies turned on those who had dared sneak in ahead of them. The liquid ambient became a red froth. Five would-be fetuses died instantly, ripped apart by tooth and claw. Three bled to death, flagella torn from their wee little bodies. The others retreated hastily, frightened beyond realization that death lay in flight as well as in battle.

Leda had just stepped from the bathroom when the final spermatozoic struggle began with Gamete Ron's vicious attack on his adversary, for the ovarian prize of budding fetusdom and, ultimately, life itself. The spasm of pain was so intense that she sank to the ground screaming. John didn't hear, either because he was sound asleep or, more probably, because he was snoring too loudly.

Leda passed out momentarily, but the extreme severity of the pain radiating from deep in her uterus jerked her back to consciousness immediately. She screamed again, and again, and again, unable to move. The ripping and tearing increased in a crescendo of sharpened knives. Leda shrieked wildly. John mumbled slurpily. Leda writhed on the floor until the terrible pain diminished. Then she crawled on hands and knees to the bed but was unable to pull herself up into it, so she poked John awake. He grumbled but did help her by pulling weakly on her arms. Then he quickly dropped off to sleep again. She cuddled beside him and, her uterus still sore, waited for him to awaken, wanting more than anything to punch him in the groin. That, she thought as she finally dozed, would wake him sufficiently to understand that she was hurting, and maybe even enough to commiserate with her suffering. The last images that drifted through her mind as she gradually slipped over the edge were those of the venereal diseases she had read about.

What she didn't know was that the excruciating pains in her womb had heralded a tie in the struggle between Gametes.

Ron and Reno. Bloody, torn from stem to stern, flagella mashed and chipped, leaking life-sustaining fluids, each reached the egg and dived in, exulting that he had won. Leda's warm, hurting body began healing both of her developing children, while each of those dropped off to sleep also, unaware that the other had survived the most crucial but one of all races before birth and that their conflict was doomed to continue in the months and years to come.

When Leda's time eventually arrived Reno entered the birth canal first and without hindrance because Ron hadn't the slightest idea he was sharing his Edenic womb with any other creature, let alone the very one that had tried to destroy him nine months earlier. As far as he was concerned he was lying face to face with a mirror image of himself. Reno was just as oblivious to his surroundings. Actually both twins had become complacent in their insulated, sound-proofed food sacs, each believing himself the chosen of some esoteric, multi-named, but benevolent divinity whose primary purpose for existence was to cater to the needs and the desires of his favorite creation, who, of course, was precisely the one doing the thinking at any given moment.

So anyhow, Reno stuck his head in the canal first and started to crawl through leisurely, as if what he was doing was the most natural thing in the world and had nothing at all to do with the claustrophobia that would haunt the remainder of his living years, as if, in fact, he was on a spelunking vacation in some pristine cave. However, he had no sooner wriggled head, arms and shoulders into the narrow space than Ron decided it was time for him to explore what might be at the other end of the tunnel that had begun tempting him several days previously, the day he had first noticed its soft, elastic spasms. After his first notice of it, it had become even more alluring because it seemed to suggest fresh air as opposed to the fetid atmosphere of his liquid surroundings of the moment.

With a smile of anticipation he dogpaddled toward the opening and…stopped, alarmed. He had run into what seemed like somebody else's rear end, face first. It wasn't his own, he decided at contact, although he did actually feel around to make sure nature hadn't inverted his body parts as a joke.

Stunned, he slipped backward and tried to study the soft protuberance. As he did so, he noticed the two appendages that seemed to be running or swimming in place. They were familiar. He felt below his own butt and, as he figured, found two of the same type of attachments.

"So," he asked himself rationally although he couldn't actually formulate any worldly language yet, "are there two of me?"

He reached forward to pinch the waving add-ons, to find out if it hurt.

Nothing happened, nothing to him that is. He felt no pain at all. As for the attachments to the alien butt, however, they kicked frantically and seemed to scoot further into the butt in front of them. Or was it, he wondered, that the butt scooted further into the tempting tunnel-like apparatus, dragging the attachments with it?

Suddenly the violent anger returned, after nine months of

quiescence. Alone, as he thought, in his own silent world, he had felt nothing but peace and goodwill to all. Now that an alien creature had appeared in what he considered his own personal slice of Mother Earth, a kaleidoscope of emotions surged through him, ranging from curiosity to rejection, love to murderous hatred. The latter emotion remained a long-term guest after the others had become vague memories. He had lived at peace too long, with himself and with his ambient. The call to violence came as a welcome relief.

He charged the appendages that had invaded his kingdom and guarded against his entry into the tunnel-like structure and wherever it might lead. Viciously he charged, toothless gums and no-nail fingers set to rip and tear.

At that very moment the ends of the appendages slipped into the tunnel and disappeared. Ron hesitated, startled. He glanced around suspiciously. Nothing. Insight smacked him in the stomach. He gasped. He realized that the image which for months he had accepted as nothing more than his own reflection had been, in actuality, a living creature other than himself. He cursed vilely. His temper exploded; he smashed at his liquid ambient and at the walls which contained it.

Poor Leda! She had just given a relatively easy birth to a healthy baby when, suddenly, painful irregular spasms began pummeling her insides like sledge hammers pounding spikes.

She howled and howled again and again.

His mind cleared by his tantrum, Ron abruptly directed his anger toward a specific target, Reno. Wild with hate, he charged into the birth canal. At the moment he burst forth into fresh air, though, something strange happened to him. He lost his ability to move through the new medium in which he found himself. He roared his disapproval. He threw his arms and legs in all directions, kicking and swatting at everything that moved within his view. When the doctor bent over him, cooing softly, he bloodied the man's nose. When the doctor, irritated, swatted him a little harder than normal on his butt, he tried to kick the man's eyes out, missing and hitting him in the chin instead. When the doctor plopped him down at his mother's side, he grabbed her nipple and squeezed, accidentally, of course, since he had no control over his appendages, let alone his body. In his anger and frustration he simply struck out blindly at everything within range. It would be months before his mind could again coordinate his body with the murderous strength and cunning it had previous to his birth.

When, however, his mother pushed her nipple at his mouth, he gurgled, his temper settled, he slurped, and then he slept. His life settled into a routine: eating, sleeping, eating, howling, eating, sleeping…well, you get the picture.

Ron was an easy kid to raise, as long as the people around him gave in to his desires even before he had them. Within hours of his birth, whenever he woke and began yowling, Leda stuck a nipple in his face until he began to suckle. He couldn't seem to shriek and dine at the same time. She also learned quickly that Ron would not share with his twin and suckle one nipple while Reno suckled the other. If Reno was nursing when Ron began howling, she had better pull Reno off the tit and put Ron on, immediately. Otherwise Ron's furious howls turned to screeches so frightening and continuous that many times the neighbors reported her to the police for child abuse. First come, Ron served, and equality of individual rights all be damned, she soon decided. Let Ron have the nipple whenever he so wished. Reno could wait.

After the fifth time the city police appeared and hauled her off to jail, leaving two yowling kids in the care of a father whose feeding skills were negative at that point in his children's development, Leda wised up. When Ron yelled for milk, she gave him milk, even if that meant putting up with Reno's whimpers for a while. She soon realized that the older twin would quit whimpering and find something to play with until she decided to feed him, like his finger or toes or penis, anything protruding, it seemed.

She did the same after the children were weaned and Ron still refused to share his feeding time with his twin or wait his turn. She simply took the food source from Reno and gave it to Ron. She could be assured that as soon as Ron was satisfied he would drift off. She could also be assured that Reno would not bring the police to her door.

Eventually the twins began to ambulate on their own. Immediately the violence of the ante-birth rivalry began anew. One day when Leda left the two alone on the floor of their room, Ron picked up a toy clock and bashed his brother on the head with it. Reno squalled. Leda came running. Reno jabbered in explanation, pointing to the clock with one hand and holding his head with the other.

Ron ignored the uproar and continued to play with the clock, pushing it along the floor while making what he thought of as motor noises but what Leda mistook for rhythmic humming. She soothed Reno until he stopped his blubbering, then picked up Ron and crooned a lullaby, trying to get the toddler to imitate her. But he preferred the sounds he was already making.

And so peace among the Tynsdales depended almost completely on Ron the younger. One day, however, Ron escalated the rivalry. He enticed his brother into the barn with him and then up the ladder into the haymow. For an hour the two played on top of the bales of straw until, in the distance, they heard Leda calling them.

"No talk Mommy," Ron said, smirking and pulling his brother's hair until the boy whimpered.

"Mommy," the older toddler shouted when Ron let loose. Still shouting, he crawled toward the huge door through which the bales of straw were lifted into the mow.

"No talk!" Ron growled.

His brother refused to obey.

"Mommy call," he declared and tumbled off one bale onto another on his way down the stacks of straw toward the open door. "Mommy," he shouted. He struggled to his feet and again shouted and tumbled once more.

"Dumb shithead," Ron snarled, wobbling toward his brother.

He fell. He caught his foot on the twine binding as he flopped from one bale to another. In his effort to recover his balance, he jumped for a bale two rows away and one layer lower. The twine around the bale had broken. As Ron felt his feet sink into the loose straw, he tried to leap again, his arms waving frantically, still trying to catch his balance. He didn't. One foot caught on the single twine holding the bale of loose straw together. He felt himself falling. With a frightened shriek, he kicked his feet and twisted his body. His foot caught, then slipped from the twine, sending his legs flipping over his head. Body cartwheeling, arms swinging frantically, he smacked into the wall by the door. For a while he was too dazed to move. Then his brother's voice worked its way through the thick fog surrounding his brain. Ron sat up slowly, carefully. Reno stood beside him, less than a foot from the open door.

"Ronnie hurt?" he asked.

"Dumb shithead," Ron growled.

"Ronnie falled," the boy giggled.

"Reno fall," Ron snarled.

He pushed his brother through the window.

Ron heard a startled squeal, a split second of silence, and then a dull thud as the body landed on a pile of manure twenty feet below.

In his halting, broken English, Ron told everyone that he and his twin brother had been playing peacefully on the wooden floor of the haymow, in the center, far from the window, when Leda called. When he heard her voice, Reno had turned and toddled across the floor toward the window, had tripped on a bale of straw, and had tumbled right out the window. Ron couldn't stop his twin because he had been sitting on the floor with his legs crossed, making toys of straw. His brother had been standing beside him, admiring the toys. Ron heard his mother's voice but turned his head in the direction of the ladder well, away from the hay door. When he turned back, at the sound of stumbling feet, it was already too late. He glanced up just as Reno tripped and flapped out the door.

Ron invariably ended his story with the words "Like chicken" and a hysterical giggle. Everybody thought the hysteria signaled grief over what had happened.

Reno denied Ron's version of the story and offered his own, but no one listened because his linguistic skills were cruder than those of his brother and because Ron was considerably noisier, not to mention more aggressive and funnier.

Reno, by the way, had suffered no more than a broken collarbone, a dislocated shoulder, and an inch or so of manure plastered all over his right side and most of the rest of him. So those inclined to believe his version of the fall were easily convinced by Ron's adherents that Reno was lying or, at the least, was trying to make a mountain out of a termite hole.

7

Ron was popular from birth, although God knows why. From the very beginning he was one of those people who scare those who know him and yet are loved in return, as some love an abusive spouse, a brutal dictator or, more to the point, a threatening god. Whereas Reno was quiet and introverted and thus generally ignored, Ron simply smiled, a crooked smile that most considered cute, plus a little threatening, and all opposition folded. That same cute smile became a manly one as he grew to adulthood.

After The Accident, as Leda and Tom were disposed to call Reno's fall, peace reigned in the Tynsdale household for several months. The twins were not involved in another life-threatening incident. As he grew through childhood and puberty, Reno diligently avoided being alone with Ron, although it was impossible and he suffered for that, often barely avoiding life-threatening resolutions to some incident caused by his brother. He became even more withdrawn, more the loner and serious student. He had few friends and the ones he did have were also solitary, introverted, and studious creatures. Slowly he became an avid reader. He taught himself to play the guitar. The few sports he did become involved in on a continuing basis increased his solitary habits—long-distance running, swimming, bicycling.

After passing through puberty he quit attending church. All four Tynsdales were, or had been, regular church-goers, Leda because she believed absolutely in an afterlife that one entered through the portals of God's institution on this earth. She had no doubt whatsoever that belief in God and His Son as defined by her church, good works, and The Golden Rule all together formed the only key that opened the gates to the Eternal Kingdom, and that the dogma of her personal church was by far the most important ingredient of the three. She did her best to follow the church's teachings as she understood them. Her greatest fear was that she might have misinterpreted some minor church precept during her many years of faithful devotion. Mostly, however, she felt deeply sorry for other people, for those many who consistently misinterpreted church dogma and for the multitudes of other misguided fools the world over who attended false churches. There were so many of them, the misguided people as well as the false churches. She sometimes wondered how the devil would find room in hell for all of them. She never wondered the same about God for He could do anything, even forgive her minor transgressions.

Tom, on the other hand, attended church more as a means to keep Leda happy than as a means of attaining heaven in the afterlife. Not that the man didn't believe in an afterlife. He was human. He was a creature of his culture. He was not a free thinker, not even much of a thinker, by any stretch of the imagination, the only really independent and rebellious "thoughts" in his life having been about sex, booze, and flight to some tropical paradise where he could get away from it all—it all meaning not only his family and social obligations but also what he had become, and work, by all means work.

At first, Ron attended church because he had no choice. Later, as he assumed some of the responsibility not only for himself but also for his relationships, he chose to attend. He early understood that becoming a member of a church, a church accepted by the culture in which one lived, had many advantages, financial as well as social. Luckily his parents had chosen the church attended by most of the community leaders so he did not have to switch institutions. By the time he passed beyond puberty he was teaching Sunday school to his peers and was in charge of the children's wing. The pastor was planning Ron's future as a leader of the church and, ultimately, as a holy man in his own right. The president of the town's only bank had added his protection and begun to instruct Ron in matters of money and banking, at times giving him odd jobs around the bank, envisioning the day when the youngster would enter the bank as teller and work his way up to the vice presidency and, at the president's retirement, to the presidency itself.

Ron was quite content with the way his life was developing. He had no desire to become a preacher. The prestige of the job attracted him, but the thought of living in gentile poverty the rest of his life turned him off. He wanted prestige all right, but he wanted money even more. From what he could understand of the adult world, being a bank official offered both, especially if he became an elder of the church, as the present president had.

Ron envisioned himself in his mature years as a wealthy family man, wise from his studies and travels, a respected image of success, and, almost as satisfactory as being financially sound, a leader in both church and society.

So he planned his future even before he passed his mid-teens, although there is no evidence to prove that his plans were at all conscious. He got himself a girlfriend named Doris. She was a cute little bit of fluff from one of Midport's leading families, not necessarily bright but an excellent student by sheer effort and demure personality; accommodating; blond since blond was the in thing; smaller than Ron, which made him feel stronger and more in charge; and popular with the students and teachers who counted. Moreover, shortly after entry into the second grade she began taking professional lessons in song, dance, gymnastics and tennis. When Ron took up with her in the seventh grade, she seemed well on her way to becoming a cheerleader and drum majorette en route to a position of social, in other words popular, leadership.

Of course Ron had considerable help in the formation of his lifetime plans, from Leda if not from Tom except by acquiescence, Tom being a couch potato by avocation and thus not helpful in much of anything having to do with family and household.

Leda, on the other hand, from the beginning, organized children's parties for Ron's acceptable classmates, not to mention brunches for mothers and soirees for all potential patrons, mothers and fathers. She it was who groomed Ron. She it was who recommended her son for leadership in the children's wing of the church. She it was who suggested to the church minister that her son would make an excellent Sunday school teacher. And not least of all, she it was who implied that Ron desired nothing more in life than to become a minister of the faith, an implication she believed since it was her desire.

Reno became lost in the daily domestic flow. When not at school or somewhere running, biking or swimming, he could be found in his room reading or picking at the guitar his parents, in their own words, had been "suckered" into giving him for the first Christmas after his tenth birthday. Generally the only recognition he received were orders to tone down what both parents and Ron called "that damned noise."

Unlike his brother's, Reno's fantasies inclined toward the heroic. One day he dreamed of becoming a fireman and saving children, old women and pets from burning buildings. The next he might dream of becoming a soldier whose primary duty was to invade foreign countries in order to return kidnapped beauties to their proper home or of becoming a policeman with the skills of Batman and Spiderman combined. A few times, in a moment of mother/son intimacy, he confided his dreams to Leda, who was not one to mince words or encourage mental sloth in her children. She pooh-poohed what she considered Reno's childish naiveté and suggested that a more logical route to success might be college, which could lead to positions with greater rewards.

Reno tried to accept her advice, but his mind invariably returned to the fantasy world of fiction and to the mind-numbing exercises of fingers on chords or legs and arms moving his body through water or air. He had few friends, none very close. When he entered junior high school, he was asked to join the swim team, a junior branch of the high school varsity squad, but, uninterested, he refused. He occasionally joined a group of neighborhood kids on a bicycle outing or on a swim day at the public pool, but rejected overtures to further what he considered excessive shared activities.

Two weeks after they reached their twelfth birthday the twins found themselves at home with no adult supervision. Their school had been cancelled for a teacher conference, a fairly common occurrence in their school system. Tom was working the farm somewhere; Leda was on one of her all-day shopping excursions with friends.

Reno had been practicing on the guitar since the day he received it. So far he had refused to take lessons. For some reason which he himself was unable to explain, he insisted that if he learned on his own he would become a better player. So every evening for an hour after the evening meal he plunked away at the chords, laboriously picking out song after song until, on the day in question, he had a repertoire of twenty seven songs that he had learned to play by ear, although in his version of each song only the chorus was actually recognizable.

In spite of their at times irritated shouts for him to quit making such nerve-shattering noise, both parents had become semi-proud of Reno's accomplishment. But Ron detested guitar music, especially guitar music played by his twin. More than one dispute had broken out between the two brothers over Reno's insistent twanging, a considerable number of which had resulted in physical confrontation. Ron had sworn a private vow to destroy the guitar whenever he could do so with little chance of being caught or, if caught, punished.

"You're such an ass," he had exploded often enough when he

and Reno were alone. "Do you think anyone really enjoys listening to that discordant crap?"

"Hey," Reno growled, "I play it for my own enjoyment."

"That's bullshit and you know it," Ron snarled. "You do it to torment me."

So, came the day in question. As I said previously, there were no classes because all the teachers were off on another conference, a type of outing they refused during the summer months or on vacation days, since that would interfere with their earned free time. Tom left at his normal time. Weeks previously, Leda and friends had designated the day for a shopping excursion in spite of, maybe because of, it being a day with no school. Tom and Leda had discussed the potential danger of leaving the twins home alone together and decided that the boys had become responsible enough to refrain from fighting and to take care of themselves, for a few hours at least.

They could have been right, you know. All might have gone well. But Leda had not been gone for more than fifteen minutes when Doris showed up with her budding breasts and blue eyes pleading to be cuddled and mauled, if not loved and respected.

Reno reclined on his bed fingering and occasionally twanging his instrument when Doris knocked. He had closed the door so his plucking would not irritate Ron any more than usual. Thus he didn't hear the door open and close, nor did he hear the ensuing giggles that moved erratically from the living room to Ron's bedroom.

It was some time before he realized that a third person occupied the house with him and his brother. The awareness at first came through a series of shrill but muffled giggles from across the hall. He immediately recognized the vocal chords from which the cries erupted.

"Sexy Doris, the Brain-dead," he grumbled aloud, intentionally striking another discordant note in the series he was practicing.

He tried to continue with his music, tried to force his concentration to the guitar, away from the incessant giggles of physical delight and the occasional amused laughter of his brother, but to no avail.

The couple seemed to be wrestling, play wrestling. The alternating giggles and guffaws, on one hand, and wild bouncing which shook the entire house, on the other, were interrupted by long moments of silence occasionally followed by the headboard bumping into the wall or the thud of someone falling off the bed, in turn succeeded by another round of giggles, guffaws and trampoline-like bouncing.

Reno's nerves frayed. His imagination taunted him. His playing became even more discordant than usual. He pictured the two in Ron's bedroom, Doris with her blouse unbuttoned to the navel, her bra unsnapped to allow Ron access to her BBs, her skirt hiked almost to her crotch, her face flushed and her hair disheveled, yearning for Ron's hand at her groin but too scared of the consequences to allow him complete access. Once more Reno tried to concentrate on the song he was playing. Once more his mind strayed to the noises sifting through his closed door.

He fought the tumescence in his groin, forced himself to count by threes to one hundred, then by fours, but he gave up at thirty-two. His mind couldn't overcome the vision painted by his imagination. He put the guitar away and grabbed a novel. The words made no sense. He tossed the book on the night-stand and buried his head under the covers, blocking out the sounds from across the hallway. But his imagination boiled, his tumescence became painful. He had never caressed a girl, never kissed one, never held one's hand. He had never traded notes with a girl or shared secrets. He had never had a girlfriend at all, not even for the brief period of a single recess, playing on the monkey bars together or swinging side by side. All his under-standing about girls came from television and movies, from the children's and teenage novels he had read, and from watching girls with other boys. He discounted the example of his teachers and his mother and her friends. They weren't really girls, if they ever had been.

He cursed and rolled off the bed, deciding on a bike ride to cool off.

He had barely finished pulling on and tying his sneakers when the giggling from across the hallway turned to a shriek of pain and fear. He bounded from the bed but froze with his hand on the doorknob.

A thunderous silence followed the scream.

Reno listened. A barely audible mumble seeped through the gaps around the door. He continued listening, hopeful that the scream had been in play or the result of an accident, and that the two across the hall would resume their friendly game. He didn't want to remind Ron of his presence, let alone interrupt him.

Reno flopped back onto his bed, grabbed the novel, and again tried to read. For a while he made some headway, plowing through the words even as they faded in and out of his brain without making much sense.

Then the noises began again, the muffled giggling, the bumping, the scraping, and, worse, the interspersed silences. Muttering curses to himself, he once more dropped the book and headed for the door, determined to escape his emotions in a grueling bike ride.

He made it into the hallway.

Doris shrieked, a wild cry drenched with pain and fear. Reno charged. His shoulder slammed into Ron's door before his hand twisted the knob. He rebounded to the center of the hallway. Blind anger spurted into his brain. With a feral cry he raised his foot and kicked, hitting the knob, twisting his ankle, and staggering into the room like a drunken kangaroo.

Doris lay sprawled on her back in the middle of the bed. Her long hair spread angelically around startled, frightened eyes. Her unbuttoned soft, white blouse had been wrenched down over her virginal shoulders, effectively trapping her arms at her sides. Her bra had been ripped open. It covered her navel rather than the two small, elastic, tempting mounds that protruded from her chest, their nipples red and raw. Her jeans lay in a dry puddle on the floor beside the bed. Her panties clung to her hips in disarray. Her slender, passionate, terrified legs kicked at the air above Ron's hips.

Ugly curses issued from her sweetly swollen lips.

Face satyric with desire, jeans beside hers on the floor, underpants around his ankles while his bare bottom pumped the air, holding his prey down with his body, one arm scrabbling at her breasts, the other at both thrusting groins in continuously failed attempts to push her panties aside and at the same time penetrate her innocent flesh, Ron swiveled his head when Reno crashed through the door.

At first he didn't seem to recognize his brother. His face remained charged with desire. His body continued its frantic movements.

Slowly, however, the disturbance registered, as it did a second earlier for Doris, who squealed and struggled and tried to reach the blanket pushed off the foot of the bed and at the same time attempted to cover her breasts with the other arm.

Neither arm could move from her side, however, which sent her into fits of alternating fury and shame.

"Get out!" Ron shouted suddenly, his mind ripped from the cloud of passion. "I'll kill you, you bastard! Get the hell out!"

Reno almost obeyed. He was accustomed to flight when his twin's anger erupted. But Doris began sobbing.

"Help me," she cried. "He's hurting me."

The girl's plea called to the heroic compassion in Reno's heart. His valor swelled and throbbed. Ron changed before his eyes, grew hair on his legs and horns on his forehead. Doris's soft hand beckoned Reno's manhood, calling to the epic hero in his mind and the romantic hero in his loins.

He charged. Awkwardly Ron tried to scoot backward, attempting in one hasty motion to push to his knees, divest his ankles of his underpants, and slip off the foot of the bed onto his feet.

He didn't make it. He was sliding off the bed, his ankles still bound, when Reno's shoulder drove into his side. The two boys slammed into the door of the closet, knocking it off its roller at one end, ripping the track off the wall at the other, and tilting the entire door outward before it ripped from the track. Its fall broke the lamp on the nightstand, gouged a hole in the top of the stand, and slashed sheet and mattress. It bounced off Doris's head and back as she scrambled to avoid its unwitting attack.

For the first time since their birth, Reno found himself in the winning position during a battle—on top. He squirmed until his knees rested on Ron's biceps, his butt on his twin's chest. Ron thrashed and bucked, screeching curses and threats. But Reno clung to his position like a monkey clinging to the back of a hysterical zebra. He was driven to it. He couldn't straighten up because a corner of the folding door had fallen on his back. The point gouged his spine every time he straightened in the slightest or Ron bucked too high. The same thing happened every time he drew his fist back to put an end to Ron's pestilential babbling.

Doris came to his aid. As the door bounced off her back, frightened out of her wits by Reno's savage attack and uncertain as to what was molesting her from behind, she kicked out blindly. Her dainty little foot connected with the end panel of the door, folding it neatly into the next one. Like an accordion, the panels folded into each other along the foot of the bed and over Reno's back until the entire apparatus dropped flat on the floor, neatly folded and at peace with the world.

The door no longer threatened to gouge a hole in Reno's spine each time he moved. However, it no longer protected his rear either.

He hit Ron on the nose, glorying in the cry of pain and outrage that followed his blow. He raised his fist to smite the evil despoiler of virgins again, the grandeur of his heroism swelling huge and warm in his chest.

The blow never landed.

Instead a warm and soft but sharp-boned body pounced on his back, kicking, clawing, and screeching for him to quit hurting Ron. The attack stunned him, knocking him onto his side and paralyzing his mind for a split second, the time needed for Ron to scramble out of his clutches.

"What the hell did you do that for?" Reno tried his best to ask Doris. "Here I am trying to save you from this brute and you attack me. I'm the hero of the story. You're the damsel in distress. You should welcome me with open arms."

But nothing functioned, not his voice, not his arms or legs, nor the mind that controlled them.

Worse, Doris continued the attack. Neither the ferocity of her swooping pounce from the bed nor the resultant collision with Reno's body slowed her down. She began kicking him in the chest and face even before he came to a flopping stop beside her.

Frantically he rolled out of her reach, only to meet Ron's fists and feet from the other side. Doris chased him across the floor raking his back with her fingernails. Reno tried to fight her off. His elbow connected with her chin, eliciting a shriek of pain and anger, and a renewed frenzy to her attack. He swung a fist at Ron's face and felt something soft give. The next moment Doris again pounced on his back. One arm crushed his throat. The other raked fingernails down his face, furiously trying to blind him. Ron hit him in the face with the broken lamp from the nightstand, then in the stomach, then in the face again. Reno felt something crack in his nose. Warm blood spurted over his face, flooding into his mouth as he tried to breathe. He choked and coughed violently. The base of the lamp smashed into his forehead, bounced off an ear, and thudded once more against his broken nose. He screamed at the pain, but he didn't hear the scream. He had passed out.

The pummeling continued unabated until Doris noticed that her erstwhile savior had stopped moving. Frightened that he might have died, she clambered to her feet and frantically began dressing.

"What're you doing?" Ron quit pounding on his brother to glare at her.

"I think Reno's dead. I think we killed him," she whispered hoarsely, completing the hooks on her bra. "I can't be here when they find him."

"You can't be here when who finds him?" Ron asked curiously, searching for a pulse on Reno's wrist as he spoke.

"The police!"

Doris's voice trembled with her fright.

"You're talking crazy. Nobody's going to tell the police or anybody else anything about this." Ron's voice became conspiratorial. A sardonic smile split his swollen lips. "If he's dead, we'll dispose of the body and tell everybody he left and we never saw him again."

"How are you going to explain all that?" Doris pointed.

The metal track from which the closet door had hung clung

to the wall by one end. Several of the plastic hangers had broken, their pieces and the clothing they were in charge of cluttered with shoes and dirty clothes on the bottom of the closet. The door itself had wound up folded on the floor, lying diagonal to the closet and bed. The nightstand lay on its side, one leg missing, its upper side having received two deep gouges. Bits of the lamp were scattered around the fallen stand. The base was still clasped in Ron's hand, ready to again become a weapon.

Reno lay on his back, unable to move the tiniest fiber of his body. His shirt had been almost completely destroyed in the battle; it hung in tatters from his neck. Blood dribbled from his nose and small pools of it welled to the surface of cuts and scratches on face, chest, and arms. His eyes were half open. He felt dead but somewhere in the chambers of his mind bits and pieces of the conversation echoed.

Ron shrugged, unworried, "I'll tell Mom that Reno tore up my room before he ran off."

"But what about the police?" Doris wailed.

"You'll back up my story," Ron stared at the frightened girl as the seconds ticked by. She began to fidget. She licked her lips continuously but erratically. Her eyes darted around the room. She could not meet Ron's stare. "Won't you?"

Reno wondered vaguely if the words were a threat.

"Yes," Doris answered hurriedly, "but I've got to go."

"What the holy hell do you mean, you've got to go?" Ron growled. "You can't go till we get rid of the body."

"I can't do that," Doris's words erupted from her throat as a breathless squawk. She moved toward the door, her hands stretched out in supplication. "I can't do it. They'll catch us. Don't ask me to, please."

"Shit!" Ron growled. "I bet you'll rat me out."

Doris continued toward the door, her eyes frightened and pleading, her body shaking violently, uncontrollably.

"You killed him too," Ron stepped toward her, poised like a cougar on a ledge, its prey trapped below it. "If I go to jail, you do."

"I didn't mean to," Doris wailed.

"Neither did I," Ron spoke thoughtfully, moving closer to his prey. "But what the hell," he grimaced evilly. "I can't say I'm sorry we did it."

"You did it," Doris moaned. "I only tried to protect you."

"Come on, Doris," Ron scoffed. "You were kicking and hitting him like you wanted to tear him to pieces."

"No, you were the one that hit him with the lamp. I just slapped him." Doris again edged toward the door, Ron following her step by step. "Yeah, well, you kicked him too, and choked him, and scratched him."

"I didn't do it. You did."

"Who the holy hell are you trying to convince?" Ron scoffed brutally, "me or you?"

"I didn't mean to," Doris's denial swelled into a wail of despair.

"Me neither," Ron smirked at her fear. "But I hope he rots in eternity."

"Why?" Ron's words momentarily erased her fear. "He's your brother."

"Yeah, he is, every minute of every hour of every day."

Startled by the hateful intensity in the boy's words, Doris blurted, "What did he do to you?"

Ron glared at her. She winced, thinking he was going to hit her. "He's my twin," he turned his glare on his brother.

"What's so bad about that? I wish I had a twin sister. We could share lots of things."

"Jesus Christ but you're dumb. Most people get to be individuals. No one judges them by other people." Ron shrugged, admitting a slight fallacy in his argument. "Oh, if a guy messes up, people compare him to his folks or maybe his sister or his brother. You know, they'll say he's a chip off the old block or just like that good-for-nothing brother of his, if they're bad too. If not, if they're okay but he's not, they'll probably feel sorry for his family and say he's just a bad seed. But the guy, he won't accept that at all. He'll think he's an individual because he doesn't have a twin brother. Understand?" Ron glared at Doris and shook his head angrily at the blank stare slowly turning once again into fear and despair. "Me, I've got a mirror image I have to live with every damned day of the year. He'll probably follow me through eternity too."

"That's silly. You're not like Reno."

"Yeah, I am. We're two sides of the same coin." With a quick, humorless grin at his conceit, Ron added, "He's tails. I'm heads."

Doris giggled nervously, happy that Ron's temper seemed to have subsided.

"But that's not the real point," Ron continued. "And it's not the real point that people are always mixing us up. I get so damned mad when somebody tells me I really look like Reno or that something I do or say is exactly what my brother might do or say in the same situation. It's even irritating when they say my brother wouldn't do that, just because of the comparison; people are always comparing us and I hate it."

"But that shows you're not alike."

"Don't be an ass. The problem is we're too much alike and I don't like it. It makes me miserable. But that's still not the real point. Reno ruined my chance to be me and only me."

"But you are you," Doris exclaimed, perplexed at Ron's reasoning.

Ron sneered and shook his head. He wondered why he had ever hooked up with such a dunce. Then he glanced at her body and his question was answered.

"What I can't figure," he changed the subject, "is why you attacked him. He jumped me to save you, you know." He gazed at her, grinning cruelly.

"I know," Doris refused to meet his eyes.

"Why did you take my part then?"

"I don't know. He was hurting you," she whispered.

"I was trying to force you to do what I wanted. You were struggling and crying for me to stop. That's why he attacked, a white knight to the rescue of the fair maiden," Ron's voice turned mocking. "So why did you help me. I was the one hurting you. Reno was the one trying to save you. Do you like for me to hurt you?" The cruel grin swelled like an erection.

"No, I...," the sound hesitated submissively, as if impeded by engorged lips. "I just..., I love you, Ronnie. He kept hitting you and I...it made me mad. I don't know what happened." Doris began to cry softly.

The sound, and the anguish deforming her face, irritated Ron. A curse rose to his lips but erupted stillborn into the air.

Reno moaned.

Startled, his attackers swung in his direction.

"It looks like the bastard isn't dead after all," Ron glared at Doris.

"Thank God," Doris prayed fervently.

"Thank God, shit! We didn't hit him hard enough in the right place. So maybe I should hit him again."

Ron picked up the broken lamp and stepped toward his brother.

"No!"

Ron grinned wickedly, "Why not? I'd get rid of two birds with one lamp, so to speak: my shadow and this black desire in me to find out what it's like to kill someone."

"Why do you want to kill someone?" Doris whined.

"You've never wondered what it would be like to kill somebody, to maybe bludgeon them to death or cut their throat and watch them die?"

"No," Doris again edged toward the doorway, horror twisting her face into an ugly mask.

Ron glanced at Reno, who was trying to sit up.

"You have no intellectual curiosity, Doris. In fact, I don't think you're curious about anything not common and normal. I know you're curious about my body," he grinned lasciviously. "But I wouldn't call that abnormal or uncommon. Besides you're scared to go all the way. A hand job, that's all I ever get." He laughed. "I like it. I like it. But I'll get the rest of it sooner or later, one way or the other."

"That's what you were trying to do when your brother at-tacked us," Doris sniffed. "You were hurting me."

"Hey, only in the judicial system can you lead a guy on and then draw a line in the sand and say no more, that's as far as we go. Not in real life unless the guy's a miserable wimp, controlled by his fear of the police and courts."

"I have to draw a line somewhere. You won't."

Ron shook his head in disbelief, "Why should I?"

"You don't care about anyone but yourself. If you want to do it, then I'd better do it or else."

"Or else what?" Ron scoffed.

"Or else you'll make me do it.

"I suppose I've forced you to do everything we've done," Ron sneered.

Doris's eyes misted over. A tear trickled down the edge of her nose. Her lips quivered.

"Yes, at first," she mumbled, choking on muffled sobs.

"Come on, Doris," Ron jeered. "You've been all over me since the first time we were alone together. I was only returning the compliment."

"That's a lie."

Ron grinned and looked at his brother, who was still trying to sit up.

"What we're going to do," he glared at Doris, "is tell Mom that we were talking in our room and Reno was in his room with the door wide open, strumming his guitar—just strumming it as loud as he could, not actually playing anything. I thought he was doing it just to irritate us so I told him to quit. Mom will believe that because she knows how much I hate that damned guitar and she thinks Reno strums it sometimes just to annoy me."

"Does he?"

"Who knows and who cares? Mom thinks so because I tell her so." He smirked. "We'll tell her that's why Reno got mad and attacked us."

"She won't believe us," Doris said skeptically.

"She'll believe it if I tell her it's the truth, especially if we both swear it."

"I don't know," Doris muttered dubiously. "Reno will tell her what really happened, won't he?"

"Yeah, he'll say you were screaming so he thought I was hurting you, maybe trying to rape you. Mom will have her doubts about that because she thinks Reno lies all the time about me and what I do and don't do because he's jealous of me."

"You really think that will work."

"All you've got to do is say we were talking and laughing when Reno attacked us. Maybe we had gotten a little noisy with our laughing—we can say that. But we have to insist that we hadn't done a thing to Reno except for my telling him to shut his door or not play his guitar so loud."

"What if she doesn't believe us?"

"She always believes me. And she likes you because your dad is a bigwig in town. So if we both say the same thing, she won't have any doubts."

"What about your dad?"

"He's irrelevant."

So, the upshot of the clash was that Reno lost his guitar for a month, lost his allowance until he had paid for the damages to Ron's room, and temporarily lost some of his social privileges, all of which he didn't much care about. He couldn't have played the guitar during that first month anyway since two of the fingers on his right hand had been broken in the scuffle. He spent the first two days after the incident in the hospital, the doctor being worried that he might have some brain damage from the blows to his skull. The broken fingers and the scratches on his face and back and the bruises covering most of his torso and head had healed in a month, sufficiently for him to recommence playing the guitar. But it took more time for his fingers to return to their former flexibility and for his emotions to once again yearn for the instrument. His hatred for his twin deepened considerably during the incident and its aftermath.

Ron and Doris continued boyfriend/girlfriend until Doris became pregnant and, at Ron's insistence, had an abortion. After that their relationship deteriorated until, having found a new girlfriend and bored by the sameness of what he was getting, Ron told Doris to get lost. She languished for days. Her parents became deeply worried about her health, so much so that they consulted the family psychiatrist. He suggested rest, love, and six treatments at several hundred dollars each. However, miraculously, Doris recovered before the day scheduled for the first treatment. The varsity quarterback, having learned that Doris and Ron were no longer an item, asked her out for a movie, a hamburger, and a little after-hours petting party in his new Mustang.

At the formal insistence of the family psychiatrist, nevertheless, she did take the complete round of treatments in his office, but they seemed somewhat anti-climactic after the date in the Mustang with one of the school's real hunks. They did serve an important purpose, though. At the psychiatrist's suggestion, and with his help, Doris began taking birth-control pills regularly. The result was that she and her new boyfriend enjoyed themselves thoroughly, experiencing the pleasures of the flesh without any of the consequences brought about by natural cause-to-effect possibilities—uh, mostly, but they were lucky in that sense because the hunk was not monogamous by any elasticized stretch of the imagination. They remained together for almost a year, not the school record by any means but one that a lot of married couples should try to emulate.

8

And so, Ron and Reno were Eve's half-brothers on her biological father's side (which she supposedly never knew), second cousins on her mother's side, although they were old enough to be her uncles because of the time lag between their birth and hers, a time lag caused mainly by her father's slowly declining interest in sex. By the decade of his thirties he still became horny every few weeks in spite of his growing aversion to the game, however, a bio/psychological condition that normally disappeared just long enough for him to pop. A few seconds later he would roll off, exhausted and satiated for another few days. It was during one of these intermittent moments—Eve's mother had been noted over the years to refer to them as momentary irritants, kind of like a mosquito bite except that with a mosquito you generally know you have been bitten—it was during one of these moments of arousal that Eve was conceived, an event you could call miraculous because of the odds against it happening with no more than a thrust or two of Eve's father's pocket-size poignard.

In any case, on the very day of Eve's conception the twins celebrated their fifteenth year of existence in this funny world of ours.

Nine months later, being in most ways quasi-normal males,

they could have cared less that a squalling bundle of flesh had fought its way out of its mother's womb, or that this bundle of flesh and blood was related to them. During most of the day in question Reno was strumming his guitar, riding his bicycle, or reading a meaningless novel. Ron was working at the bank part time, chairing a meeting of Youth for Putting God Back in the Church, getting some innocent into trouble, and/or playing bedroom games with his latest squeeze.

The first the twins paid much attention to the bundle of flesh, blood and bones was at the annual family reunion during Eve's thirteenth year al aire libre. She had begun her monthly bloodletting the previous summer. In my imagination her chest had swollen enticingly, her twin buds pointing slightly above the horizon. Her hips had rounded temptingly, virginal yet but enclosing all the promise of Homer's Sirens. And her smile! Ah, her smile. Her eyes! Her lips! Her…Helen couldn't have been anything but a pale reflection.

According to Eve, as well as other sources, the twins raved about her beauty, Reno in the quasi-songs he wrote, Ron in meanderings of his mind since he never shared his most private thoughts with anyone, although the movements of his eyes when Eve was around told the story. The two of them indulged Eve as any doting uncles might indulge their favorite niece, and maybe a little more.

When Eve passed through puberty without ritual but with a significant amount of ogling from the male portion of the local species, the twins had long settled into their adult existence. Far from the expectations of parents and friends, after several false starts Reno had become a policeman. He had grown up a romantic, a worshipper at the shrine of love and heroism. Yet, paradoxically, or was that logically, he believed in the absolute necessity of authority. The universe after the fall from grace, he avidly believed, consisted of the struggle between good and evil which, in human terms, manifested itself as a psychological conflict in each and every individual, a conflict that ended only at death. When an individual chose good over its cruel enemy, he increased harmony in the universe and, logically, decreased discord. The moment that evil was destroyed, he was convinced—the moment that good triumphed in the struggle and evil disappeared forever from the universe, in that moment the heavens would open and the human spirit would fuse with the divine will. Humanity past and present would cease to exist as the unique and separate entities we consider ourselves, entities which in reality are processes yearning toward fusion with the divine spirit, and would merge eternally into an all-encompassing wholeness. Or should I say wholesomeness?

Reno also believed that the good among us are responsible for the bad. We know what is best in the long run not only for ourselves but also for the others. We have all been divinely selected to guide the others on the righteous path, with force if necessary.

And so he chose to become a policeman. His goal was to help as many fellow humans as he could desert the pathless wilderness of evil for the asphalt and concrete highways of good, gasoline fumes be damned, whether they wanted to or not. He knew what was best for them. He had seen the light.

He took pleasure in wearing a uniform respected by at least some of the population. He enjoyed his small share in making the roadways safer from speeders and reckless drivers. He enjoyed arbitrating disputes, violent or not, between family and friends, and others. He relished confronting criminals and hauling them off to jail. He loved the sense of authority and value his job gave him. In short, he had found both his vocation and his avocation. He was a happy camper in this temporary existence of ours, much more so, I expect, than many of his fellow beings.

And he fell in love with Eve when he first noticed her as a post-pubescent teenager. She became the little sister he had never had, a soft, fuzzy little creature that brought warmth and affection into an otherwise somewhat sterile life. He took her to the movies, stuffing her with popcorn and candy, squired her to town functions when she wanted to go but had no one else she would accept as escort, guarded the home front when her parents wanted a night out on the town, spent lots of evenings strolling with her through the neighborhood, and generally became her protector and brother.

"He was just like the older brother I always wanted," Eve once confessed, tears in her eyes. "I could tell him anything and he wouldn't get uptight and yell at me or say I couldn't do this or had to do that. He'd tell me what he thought, then ask me what I thought, and we'd talk until I realized what the real problem was and what I had to do. I loved him, but I never treated him very well after I met Ron."

Ron also fell head over heels in love with little Eve, although his emotional if not physical attraction seemed to stem from jealousy of his brother, and did not manifest itself in action until several months after Reno had been squiring her around town.

Unlike his bachelor brother, Ron had married, not young but married nevertheless. His wife was an American beauty—a cheerleader in high school, a sorority president in college, and in married life Midport's social leader. She had never won a beauty contest, mainly because she had never entered one. She had never entered one because she refused to become involved in anything that might lead to being typed nothing more than a hunk of flesh, albeit a desirable hunk. Moreover, even though she refused to admit it to any living soul other than herself, she had neither the physical beauty nor the necessary talent to compete above the local level. The men around Midport, however, from puberty to the walker, if their eyes were any indication at all, considered her a decent, and universal, work of natural female art.

When Ron began dating her, Mary was an elementary school teacher and secretary to the local Republican Party. After their marriage she added other duties: member of the DAR and almost perpetual president of the female branch of the Masonic Lodge, not to mention actual or honorary member of the board of most charitable and capital fund drives that were grown annually, or periodically, in Midport's social gardens. As well, she had most of her statistically allotted two and a half children, having given the additionally allotted half child to a sister who preferred raising children to laboring in the community garden.

Ron had moved into a permanent supervisory slot in the Bank of Midport immediately out of college. Within five years of becoming a full-time employee, he had been named the youngest vice president the bank had ever had, a deserved honor acclaimed by most of the town's leading citizens and trumpeted throughout the region by the *Midport News*. Three years later, not quite to the day, he drove his personally designed golf ball off the third tee at the country club and smack into the bank president's temple, the president having been standing several yards ahead and to the right because of Ron's noted penchant for hooking off the tee.

Ron was properly upset. Mary was properly upset. The wife of the president was properly upset. All three mourned suitably. After an appropriate amount of time had lapsed, Ron became president of the bank. Mary became Mrs. President. The ex-president's wife became Mrs. Chairman of the Board, the helpmate of Midport's richest man. The ex-president moved on to better things if the public eulogies about him in this life were any indication of salvation in the next, and if the eye of the needle is not really a deterrent to entry into paradise.

And so Ron became one of Midport's leading actors. He dreamed of becoming a star on the national and, of course, the international stage. On those days when his interpersonal skills seemed at low ebb, he envisioned himself as Chairman of the Federal Reserve or of the World Bank. On more enjoyable days, he pictured himself in the White House, commander-in-chief of a great military, arbiter of peace or destruction. No wimp would he be as a leader, he swore in his daydreams. Other nations would knuckle under or face Armageddon. The inability of his nation to bring peace and prosperity to the world, at any cost, frustrated him, as did his own failure to fully manipulate the disparate elements of his own bank board—even of his own family, if truth be known.

And so Eve tripped into the adult world and first Reno then Ron became enamored of her charms. Eve, of course, became enamored of being enamored of. She loved all the little gifts and the envy of her friends, and the attention, especially the attention. Mainly, though, after she passed through puberty, she loved being what she often called "slobbered over" by two men she considered handsome, sophisticated, successful, and safe. Her relationship with Reno, however, changed after Ron began paying court to her whims, as she herself has confessed often enough.

"You don't know what it was like being sought after by two older guys," Eve once confided when we were talking about Ron and Reno and her relationship with both of them. "It was like..., well," her blue eyes took on a glazed, dreamy cast, "like I was really something. Reno treated me like a little sister, but I could tell I turned him on," she grinned contentedly. "Not at first, not when I was a little girl, but later, after I really developed," her hands falsified herself as a buxomly woman. "He was always such a gentleman, though. Sometimes it made me so mad, the way he controlled himself. I'd flirt with him something awful, to get him to make a pass at me, even if it was withdrawn the next moment." She hesitated, her impish grin breaking through a fleeting cloud of melancholy, "But he never did. I was such a little bitch. I wanted more than anything to break through his reserve just to prove I could do it. But now, I'm glad I didn't."

"Hey, a good man is harder than hell to find," I quoted, or

rather misquoted, pedantically. "If you ever do find one, cherish him."

"I will," she laughed, squeezing my arm, "if I ever come across one again."

"Point taken," I rolled onto my side and ran my hand over the smooth, warm skin of her belly. "I reckon Ron is more akin to the man you love."

"The man I love?" she giggled, clasping my hand in hers and moving it to her right breast. "Man? Love? You mean the boy I love to make love to, don't you?"

"Okay, okay," I grumbled, irritated that she had never told me she loved me. "What about Ron?"

It was Ron of whom I was mainly jealous of course. The tendency toward rape and philandering must exist in the majority of the males of the species. Else we would never have been much shakes at war and hunting and running the gene machine. Fuse that characteristic with our covetous and possessive tendencies, and it's a real miracle that women have domesticated us to the extent they have. On the other hand...but what the heck, I'll let some woman or the experts wonder about the loyalty of women down through the ages from the tree to the two-car garage. I have trouble enough understanding my own sex. Or should that be gender?

Whatever—back to Ron and his character. Whereas Reno had showered Eve with attention from the time she emerged from puberty, Ron became overtly interested only after she began strutting around town with Reno. One day during her fifteenth summer she received an invitation to a birthday party for Ron's daughter, Tandy. She didn't like Tandy, considered her a spoiled brat, cruel and self-centered. Besides, the girl was a mere child of six. But an invitation to the home of the president of Midport's only bank was simply too exciting to refuse. So she called Reno and cancelled their movie date for the night in question.

"Reno was upset," Eve confessed one day when we were sitting in the dorm room of one of her girlfriends, who had gone home for the weekend. "But he didn't say much, only that he'd miss my company at the movie, and he told me to have a good time at the party."

"Did you?" I asked, more to keep the conversation going than because I was interested.

"Not really," she shrugged, lifting her legs from where they rested on my knees and dropping them onto my lap.

I was sitting at one end of a broken-down couch, in Levi's, a tee shirt, and sneakers. She wore shorts and a loose blouse. Her sandals had been tossed on the floor near the bed. Lying on her back, eyes closed, head on the arm rest, bare legs stretched out so her calves were resting on my lap, she sent my blood skyrocketing up the heat scale every time I glanced at her.

"Ron knew about my monthly evenings at the movies with Reno, I suppose. We had been going to the movies together for a long time, it seemed to me." She paused to swipe at her eyes. "Ron was nice to me at the party. Tandy sure as hell wasn't. Nor was Ron's wife," Eve giggled. "What a dunce she was…still is. Afterwards I never heard from any of them until just before my next movie date. Ron called and asked me to go with him and Tandy to a movie, on the evening that I was supposed to go with

Reno. And what did I do? Well," she smirked, "nice levelheaded twit that I was, I accepted and called Reno to cancel our date.

"That's when he told me I should avoid getting caught alone with Ron. I asked him why, but he wouldn't give me a reason. I got upset, although I think I was really more upset with myself than with him. I told him he was jealous. He laughed but I could tell he was hurt by what I said. I don't know why, but that made me even madder, so I told him he didn't need to see me for a few months. What a little bitch I was," she smiled ruefully. "I treated him like a lover rather than the guy who had begun to play the role of my brother. My only excuse is that I was really impressed that Ron had taken an interest in me, and I was ready to throw Reno over for a chance at a friendship with a man like his brother. Yeah," she laughed mirthlessly at my sarcastic grin, "my female ego was flattered and swelling with conceit. Reno was really worried about me though, in spite of all the names I called him. He called my parents to warn them about Ron, but my mom got upset with him too. I think she would have sold me to Ron for an entry into high society," she giggled as if picturing what might have happened to her if her mother had sold her into white slavery.

"I think I'd like your cousin Reno," I commented, not knowing what else to say.

Her eyes became moist as she continued.

"My mom was really pissed. She told Reno how she had heard rumors that he had always been jealous of Ron and had maligned him often while the two of them were growing up. She said that Ron was one of the most respected citizens of Midport and that she actually trusted him more than she did Reno, who was, after all, just a cop."

"I don't think I'll like your mom."

"She's okay," Eve shrugged indifferently. "Besides," she showed me her impish grin before lifting her leg and digging her heel into my gut, "what makes you think you'll ever meet her?"

"I thought you shared all your treasures with your mom," I returned her grin, trying for an indolent look.

"I do," she laughed out loud, her voice husky, soft, like it became when she was aroused, but with a slight hint of sarcasm hidden somewhere. "That's why the question."

I grabbed her foot as she lifted it to kick me again. In a few seconds we were wrestling. She raised her other foot for a kick, playfully giggling. I pushed it aside and, with a rolling dive, landed on top of her soft heat, between her thighs. She fought to get her hands and feet under me for leverage against my weight. I rolled and flopped to stay precisely where I was. Suddenly, as I rolled to the outside of the couch, she twisted and rolled with me. We crash-landed on the floor, me on the bottom, on my back, she on top, squealing happily. My lower back lit on her shoes. Her knees lit on my solar plexus. Each and every atom of air in my lungs exploded outward—a bacterial nightmare of what atomic warfare must be like. I flopped and gasped, a grunting microbe with its oxygen supply cut off. Eve attacked. Before my oxygen returned—before I could breathe again, I felt my groin readying itself for the promised heights of pleasure. So much for survival always being the primary human drive, I thought, as I struggled to catch my breath and return her wild kisses at the same time.

Before long, somehow, I found myself on top, Eve's legs wrapped around my hips, pulling me into a soft warmth promising unimaginable pleasure. I don't know when or how we undressed, but I remember that soft, white, naked body melting into mine as my hands roamed its curves and my own burning flesh surged with excruciating bliss into hers, soon afterwards exploding into brilliant fireworks straight out of Eden.

We visited our personal paradise often that day, our second and longest immersion in the raptures of the flesh. During the long, sensual hours, as I explored her hidden delights by the sun's rays shining through the single window in the dorm room, I would have followed Eve into the arms of Satan himself. As evening approached reason returned, but I was still in love and had become an even firmer believer in the law of ownership by means of possession. Eve was mine. I was hers.

<h1 style="text-align:center">9</h1>

Sometime after I first walked out to Eve's place, I found myself in Bart and Dan's dorm room. Dan and I had just shared our last class of the day. Afterwards he had invited me to his room for a beer. My next shift at work didn't begin until the next day and I didn't have much homework for the weekend, so I accepted. Bart was already there.

Their room was dorm-room symmetrical, and symmetrically messy, although there's always the possibility that my first impression was slightly off. In the few times we hung out together I considered Dan as the neater and cleaner of the two, in person anyway. In their room twin beds rested head first against the back wall, a couple of feet from the side walls. End tables took up a small square of the space between the beds and the side walls, in the far corners. Bookshelves, stretching up to just below the ceiling, served as headboards for the long, narrow beds. The room's two windows, small, their bottoms shoulder high to a man as tall as Dan, bathed the room in twilight. Beneath the windows, backs to them, idled two desks with swivel chairs, and a dorm-size fridge in between. At the foot of each bed a tall chest of drawers stood at sloppy attention. And against the front wall, from the side walls almost out to the doorway, which opened in the middle of the room, the college had constructed closets, almost as an afterthought, it seemed. The tracks for the sets of hanging closet doors drooped in places as if something heavier than the doors had been hanging on them at times. Both closet doors stood open at each end.

The room looked like it had just served as playpen for a couple of mischievous puppies during their dog-pound recess. On the end tables rumpled clothing almost hid the alarm clocks. Baseballs, two ball gloves, a metal bat, several batting gloves, a pile of baseball caps, shoes with the spikes almost ripped from the bottoms, and a few books filled some of the space on one bookshelf. The other was a little neater. It contained mostly books, papers and pencils in no order that I could ascertain. Only one old basketball and a pair of sneakers that could have been Dan's back when he was in junior high adorned its shelves, most of which were bare. On the desks papers were piled high, mingling with a few articles of clothing and several books. Discarded clothes, pop and beer cans, a few ripped candy wrappers, and other unidentifiable items occupied both chairs and desks. I saw no place on either for working or sitting space. Packed atop the tall, muscular chests were trophies alongside personal mementoes, possibly reminders of childhood experiences. Scattered around the floor and under the beds lay dirty, rumpled clothing, food wrappers and containers, empty condom wrappers advertising past conquests, and wadded papers all suggestive of class assignments, or maybe tests over and done with.

A beer relaxed on his stomach, balanced by two hands as if one alone might let the can tilt if not aided and abetted by the other, Bart lay on his bed, watching the little that could be seen of a tiny television screen plopped on top of Dan's chest of drawers, its flickering screen facing the other bed and thus causing Bart to watch it from a 45-degree angle. Bart was wearing a holey pair of sneakers and soiled sweat pants that might have fit him twenty some pounds and several inches in the past. Intense concentration was frozen on his face, which registered no change of expression when we entered. I can't recall the name of the soap he was watching.

"Look what the garbage truck dropped in front of me on my way out of class." Dan laughed as he jerked his thumb in my direction, threw his backpack on his bed, and turned back toward the door, adding, "Be back in a sec. I've gotta see a dog about a pony show."

Bart waved his hand toward Dan's bed and said, "Have a seat!"

His eyes never left the screen. He never said another word but did take a swig of his beer. I sat down and watched the screen, uncertain of the meaning behind the mostly unintelligible words the two actors were screeching at each other. About all I could make out was that one was male and one female, that both seemed angry about something, that both were better looking than most of the people I came in contact with on a daily basis, and that both were dressed to the hilt and standing in some kind of mansion. I think the title of the soap made some kind of reference to our daily lives, but what it could be relative to mine I couldn't tell.

Dan returned a few minutes later.

"Turn that damned thing off," he complained as he opened the fridge and extracted two cold beers. "I can't stand stupid shows like that one and you know it."

"It's no worse than the silly crap you watch," Bart shrugged, trying to empty his beer as he talked but finding it impossible to talk and drink at the same time. After he finished his sentence he chugged the rest of the beer and tossed the can toward his desk. It lit where aimed, but slid off and landed on the fridge before toppling off and bouncing under Dan's desk. Without another word, the remote in his hand, Bart rose, stepped slowly to the fridge, and opened another beer before punching the button to turn the tv off.

The program had ended just before he stood up.

"Okay?" he asked Dan, the makings of a sneer marring the grin on his face.

Dan shook his head and frowned but said nothing.

"So, now that the noise box is off, how about a game of poker?" Bart grabbed a deck of cards off his desk and plopped back onto his cot as he spoke, but this time in a sitting position.

"For matchsticks or toothpicks maybe," I grunted. "I'm broke except for seventeen cents. Tomorrow is payday."

"So's Bart," Dan laughed, "except for his bag of pennies."

Bart set his beer can on the floor and began shuffling the deck.

"We cut the deck and draw one card for seventeen cents. High card wins."

"No way," I laughed. "If I lost I'd be flat broke. I'd probably have a nervous breakdown worrying about needing some of that seventeen cents and not having it."

Dan shook his head, smiling. Bart frowned and made one last try at getting me into a card game. Dan had warned me earlier, though, that his roommate considered himself a card shark and would attempt to get me in a game.

"He's got a game on most every night," he complained, "lots of nights till three or four in the morning."

"Do you play?"

"I played a couple times early this semester, on Saturday evening when I didn't have to get up in the morning. But I'm no good at the game; I lost everything early. I can't afford to lose money, so I quit and haven't played since."

"Does Bart win?

"I don't know. He says he does. But he never has any money, or at least he says he doesn't, so I don't know whether to believe him or not."

"What did you think of Eve?" Bart asked after we had settled in, to drink and talk, not to play poker.

I shrugged, wondering what to say. It was none of his business, I figured, but then he and Dan had set me up with the girl.

"She's got one sexy body," I tried for a leer to go along with the one reference that I hoped might avoid any explanation of what my future with Eve might be.

For a moment I thought Dan was going to hit me. He clinched his fists, frowned, and took a menacing step toward me, then stopped, staged a bawdy laugh and declaimed, "You can say that again. And again. And again and again and...." As he finished emoting I wondered if he had been serious with the body threat.

"Cut the crap, Dan," Bart interrupted with a growl, jumping to his feet as if ready to attack. "You know damn well I don't like dirty talk about Eve."

"Okay, Bart," Dan held his hands up, palms forward in a conciliating gesture. "I know how you feel about her. But hell, man, she's female and that makes her fair game for us Casanova types. Right, Donjon? He took a step in my direction before turning to face Bart, grinning lasciviously all the time, as if trying to irritate Bart in spite of his words. "You can't expect any red-blooded male not to slobber all over himself whenever she smiles at him. Just recall, if you can, Bart, old buddy, those legs, those slender hips, that full set of knockers, and those eyes, and those lips just waiting to be kissed, and...."

"Oh, go to hell, Dan," Bart snarled, his face twisting into what must have been meant for a smile but looked more like a grimace of pain. "She isn't like what all you guys think. She's a nice girl. She'll make some guy a good wife someday."

"You wouldn't want to be 'some guy,' would you?" Dan teased his roommate. "And I've heard you say worse things."

"If she'd have me, I might," Bart ignored the teasing tone and the second sentence. "But you damn well know she won't have anything to do with me anymore."

"You called her a tease one time," Dan reminded his roommate. "You had a pretty convincing argument."

"Yeah, I was a frigging liar too." Bart had plopped down on his twin bed again as if standing up was too much for his legs. "And mad as hell at her for ditching me. Me, Bart Kane!" he raised his voice sarcastically. "I thought I was really something back then. One of the greatest shortstops to ever play at Midport High. A guy who could have any girl he wanted. I'm damned if I could figure out why she rejected me. Why? Hell, how could any girl possibly do such a thing? So I decided she really only wanted to play the field, that she was a whore at heart, a woman who wanted to sleep with any man she could get her hands on."

"Hey, man, there's gotta be something wrong with any female that can resist your charms," Dan spoke softly, grinning from ear to ear.

"You've finally got that figured out. After how many years? You're too slow to be in college, Dan. You should be out digging ditches."

"And you should be following in Einstein's shoes. I know. Someday I'll know my place. But not today. Today I dream about getting Eve in the sack."

"Just stay the hell out of my way in your dreams, and in mine too," Bart's smile as he spoke seemed a mixture of anger, sarcasm, humor, and regret.

"So you don't think Eve can be made?" I moved the conversation back to me and Eve.

Bart stared at me.

"Come on, man," Dan laughed, "at the right time with the right guy and a good line—any woman can be had. It's that simple. All you have to do is prepare the time with the line and convince her you're Mr. Right, Mr. Right at that moment anyway. If you succeed, you're in her pants. If not," he grinned with an exaggerated lascivious leer, "no doubt the game was fun."

"Yeah," Bart joined in, "sometimes the chase is a hell of a lot more fun than the prize, specially if you're so damned drunk you lose track of the difference between beauty and the beast."

"Hooo, hooo," Dan hooted. "You should know. That witch

you brought home last night looked like she'd been in a train wreck."

"I was a little out of my mind," Bart leered. "This morning, when I woke up and saw what I'd been playing with last night… man, I was sick. I couldn't get her out of here fast enough."

"Maybe I shouldn't have gone next door to sleep," Dan aped Bart's leer. "We could've gotten her out the door before going to sleep."

"I doubt it," Bart grinned ruefully. "I was so drunk I thought I was in bed with a soap star. No way would I let her leave. No way. Hell, if there'd been a church handy, I'd be a married man today. I was in love, in love with the most beautiful girl on campus."

"All kidding aside, do you want to know the truth about us and Eve?" Dan changed the subject, speaking to me, a hurt, rapt expression on his face as if his brain was possessed by sad but beautiful memories whose brilliant rays were reflected outward with such force that they radiated from his eyes and the very pores of his skin. "Eve was the best-looking girl at Midport High. There was a time, in our sophomore year, when I thought we'd be mates for life. She was one hot tamale and I was stuck in the sauce, stuck permanently, I thought. What the hell, though," loss echoed emptily in his tone, "she didn't feel the same way. She was just in it for the fun, she said when she dumped me because I was getting too serious. 'Too serious,' those were her words, not mine. I was in love. I didn't know from serious or anything else. I was ready to commit."

"At what age," I asked doubtfully, wondering if he was pulling my leg for fun, again; I'd learned soon after meeting him that he was a convincing actor, "sixteen?"

"Yeah, about that," he grimaced, "fifteen when we started seeing each other, sixteen when we broke it off. But those were the best months of my life. They were like a dream, one of those wet dreams when the angels sing and you're with this fantastically sexy girl and she begins...."

"What's she really like?" I interrupted his rant, curious about what he thought and not a little turned off by his words.

"She knew how to make me happy," the lascivious grin returned as he talked. "I don't know where she learned how, but I guess I really didn't care at the time. Only afterwards, when I was bitter because she ditched me and because, I figured, she had been at it with other guys—that's when the whole idea of how she had become so good at the game began to upset me."

"Jealousy," Bart began to sing, laughing.

"Don't give me that crap, Bart," Dan groused in semi-good humor. "You've cried in your beer more than once about how the two of you had something heavy going last year before she dumped you and how you'd take her back any day of the week. And yeah," he continued sheepishly, "I damned well would also take her back any day of the week and twice after church on Sunday, just like you. But we both know she never goes back with any guy she dates and dumps."

The conversation continued with Eve at its center but with little real meat to the plot until my mind began to wander. I became a little suspicious of the roommates and the tales they were spreading in my presence. Were they serious? Or were they playing a game? Why would they set me up with Eve if they both still had the hots for her? And why would they set me up with her and then tell me how they still ached for her? Strange, I thought, all this yearning and self-pity being aired in my presence. It sounded a lot like the melodrama of the soaps they watched.

A few weeks later, Dan and I were sitting in an off-campus bar having a beer. It was one of those bars that don't question a patron's age as long as he doesn't cause trouble or get too drunk to walk out the door under his own steam and in a semi-straight line. And as long as there are no police in attendance.

The problem was that Dan was getting a little soused. We were only on our third or fourth beer, but he had been slightly blotto when we met at his dorm to walk to the bar. In any case he was already slurring his words when he broached the subject of Eve.

"That girl over there" he nodded toward three girls, college girls no doubt, sitting near the back wall, in the corner farthest from the bar against the west wall, "the one with the long blond hair, she reminds me of Eve. She got up and walked to the john a while ago. And boy is she stacked."

I glanced at the girl he was referring to. She was facing away from me, talking to two companions, a blond with short curly hair and a brunette with straight, shoulder-length hair. Both girls looked like they spent a lot of time out in the sun or on a tanning bed. I couldn't see much of the girl Dan was referring to, only her long, slightly wavy blond hair, a few inches of her green blouse showing on her shoulders, and one elbow that draped outward a few inches from the side of her chair.

"So, go for her," I laughed.

"I would," he got this hangdog expression in his eyes and around his mouth as he spoke, as if somebody he loved had offered him a bone to assuage a deep hunger and then yanked it away just as he was getting ready to taste it. "But, you know, I've never gotten over Eve, not totally."

"You know," I groused, "when it comes to Eve, I'm never sure how much to believe you. One time you say you aren't interested in her at all anymore. Then the next time we talk you moon around about how she dumped you, or how you'd take her back in a moment, or what a great lay she was. What's wrong with you anyway? If you still have the hots for her, why'd you set me up with her?"

He laughed, but there was no humor in the sound, "Who knows for sure? It was one of those spur-of-the-moment things. You know, me and Bart had just met you. We liked you. It seemed like in every orientation meeting, if we weren't sitting beside you, we were sitting beside this same bunch of freshmen guys and girls. Toward the end of orientation week we all started talking about not losing track of each other, so we decided to meet once a week for lunch. Then Bart and me, we ran into Eve, so we invited her. But she made it uneven on the girls' side, so we invited you. We both liked you and we also wanted to get back on Eve's radar. So what the hell! We didn't figure you'd get anywhere with her. You're not her type, not really, and she's not yours. We figured maybe you'd date her for a while, until she got bored and broke it off. By that time maybe one of us would have a chance again." Once more that humorless laugh. "Hell, I hoped to be shacking up with her soon, just like old times."

My irritation skyrocketed, but with an effort I tamped it down. I knew I was angry not only because Dan was talking about Eve as if she was nothing but a piece of tail, but even more so because he seemed to be belittling me.

"What do you mean not her type? What's her type anyway? And what the hell type am I?"

Dan grinned. He realized that he had gotten my goat and seemed tickled by it.

"Let's see. What the holy hell type are you?" His laugh oozed with drunken humor. "I haven't known you very long. But I've got you pictured as kind of an odd mixture of nerd and wannabe adventurer. You're not into organized sports, but I've heard you're a pretty good athlete, not varsity material but still you can hold your own in pickup games. That's what the kids that know you from high school say. You're not the tough guy type and you don't run with them, so I figure you're not a wannabe bully. The kids who've known you since high school say you've always got your nose in a book or you're out playing ball of some kind, or swimming, or having a drink with the guys," he paused and grinned again, "except when you're working or getting in trouble. They say you work a lot but you're not really ambitious. You're kind of a loner."

My reaction was irritation once more, although he was partially right about my life style, or maybe the irritation rose up because he was totally right. I didn't have a great deal of ambition, not financially anyway, not at the time, not enough to major in business or any other money-oriented program. I wasn't even sure why I was in college. I didn't study any more than I had to in order to get by. I didn't have the slightest idea what I wanted to major in, although I often told people I did. I was lost and stuck in the middle of the road that led where everyone seemed to think young people should go, through college to a good job, whatever that was. Me, I'd rather be enjoying my life, but I wasn't always sure how to do that to maximum advantage. I was easily bored. So I was always looking for something to keep me busy. But it had to be something I enjoyed doing, whether work or play.

"Would you quit bullshitting me and come clean about you and Eve, damn it," I shook my head to express my irritation and disgust. "You and Bart are the same. One moment you brag about screwing Eve, as if she was nothing more to you than some female to sleep with. The next you cry in your milk about how much you still love her, how she dumped you, and how you'd take her back in a heartbeat. What I'd like to know is why you want her back if she was nothing but a good lay. There are plenty of those around for the picking. And why did she dump you anyway if she liked you enough to screw you?"

I thought for a minute that he was going to throw his beer at me, or take a swing. Anger turned his face into a shriveled mass. His eyebrows furrowed. His teeth gritted. His fists clenched. He remained frozen that way for a long time. Then he suddenly relaxed and grinned ruefully.

"Ah," he released his breath as if he had been holding it since my comment. "You're right. I owe you the truth. We did set you up expecting it not to work out between you and Eve. We were both hoping she'd turn to one of us when the two of you bombed. But, hell, we both know she won't. Yeah, she might spend a night with one of us, or a few hours in our room, given the right circumstances. But there's no way she'll ever date either of us again, not except maybe on some special occasion, which you know as well as I do will take a miracle to happen, because she'll never be short of men standing in line for a chance to date her, no matter how much the odds are against that chance. She's got too much on the ball to ever be short of men drooling over her. She's beautiful. She's sexy as all hell. She's fun to be with. She knows how to make a guy fall all over himself to please her. She makes a guy feel like he's something special. She's smart as a whip. She's...."

"Why'd you break up with her then? Or did she ditch you."

For a long time I thought he wasn't going to answer me. He glared at me, took a long slug of beer, then glared some more.

"Okay," he finally broke the silence. "Nobody I know of dated Eve for very long. Nobody. All through high school and even down in junior high some guy would chase after her. Eventually she'd say he was her boyfriend. But not for long, then some other guy was after her. Later, in high school, when she started in on the dating game seriously, it was the same thing. She'd go out with a guy for a while. Then, boom, he was out and she was alone and soon another guy was dating her. Nobody seemed to know why. If they did, they weren't telling. In our sophomore year, though, the word got out. Guys started saying it was her," he chuckled sarcastically, "cousin that was keeping her from any guy for very long. He made her dump them after a few dates. If they wouldn't take no for an answer, he did things that made them think he'd kill them if they didn't leave Eve alone, like start nasty rumors about them, or almost hit them in his car, or have some older tough guy threaten them. He really hit one guy a year ago that was chasing Eve."

When I snorted in disbelief, he shrugged and continued.

"Believe it or not. The guy he hit was a good friend of mine. Eve really turned him on, like, I mean, he couldn't think of anything else. He even quit running around with any of his friends to be with her more. He didn't talk to me for weeks. Then she ditched him. He was a mess. He kept after her, cornering her after school, at the movie theater, any place she went alone. Calling her. Going to her house, even though she wouldn't answer the door and her mom would tell him to leave and never come back. Then one night he was out late, drunk, heading toward her house, crossing a dark street, when a car came out of nowhere and hit him. Banged him up pretty bad. Broke his leg. The police never figured out whose car it was, or said they didn't anyway. But some of the guys Eve had dated knew, or they said they did. I didn't believe them until my breakup with Eve."

Dan quit talking in order to finish his beer and get another.

After a few slurps of the fresh one he started talking again. "I was dating Eve when the bastard threatened me. I ignored him but then I got to talking around. It was then I started totally believing what some of the guys were saying. A couple of days later, when Eve told me she wasn't going to see me anymore, I decided not to push it."

He shrugged his shoulders in what I took for embarrassment.

"But, you know, dating her was the greatest two and a half months of my life. It started at a football game, on a Friday night, believe it or not. Hell, I knew who Eve was. Midport doesn't have that many students. Every guy in school knew who Eve was. But I hadn't really talked to her much, you know, maybe just to say hello and ask how she was doing. That kind of thing. I was backward with women then." He frowned apologetically, more to himself than to me, I think. "So, anyhow, I was sitting in the booster section at the ball game, something I never did much. I always figured all that yelling and stomping was silly, except for using it as a screen to watch the cheerleaders," he leered and raised his bottle to let the barmaid know he wanted another one.

When she looked at me I shook my head no. A few silent moments later Dan had his beer, ordering another as she set the bottle in front of him. He watched the girl leave before tilting the bottle. After a long chug he started talking again. I realized he was drunk as a skunk; otherwise, he wouldn't have been talking honestly about his relationship with Eve, I don't think. "We met at a football game," he repeated, "in the booster section. I was with some friends. We saw this bunch of girls sitting at the top of the section, all in a row, like bottles of beer on the wall." He chuckled at his own funny.

I ignored it.

"A couple of the guys knew some of the girls. So up we went, right behind them. Six little tomcats in a row sitting behind six little pussy cats in a row. I was sitting behind Eve. She ignored me at first. But with a little help from my friends and one of the girls, by halftime I was sitting beside her. By the end of the game, I had a date for later that night. After that," he shrugged and chugged the rest of his beer, then grabbed the last one the girl had set in front of him, "it was just a matter of time and patience, and a good line here and there. We were in bed, in her house, in less than a week. Her parents were out of town for the weekend. Man, was that a weekend I'll never forget. It's like a dream that keeps coming back over and over. I hope it never fades." Dan grinned, a grin that was a cross between dreamy smile and wanton leer. "After that, what is there to say? I couldn't get enough of her. She must have felt the same way about me, either that or she's one hell of an actress. I guess you can say I grew up in that time, became a man."

"So you let her cousin scare you out? Why? Didn't Bart say he's just a banker?"

"Yeah, he's a banker. But he can be pretty damn scary. Date her long enough and you'll find out."

I asked him what he meant, but he just stared at me for some time and then off into space. In hopes he might get back into a talkative mood, I ordered two more beers, one for me and one for him. He finished the beer and ordered another without saying a word. His eyes seemed to alternate between blank and dreamy. I decided to wait him out, hoping he would talk some more.

Finally, the words coming out in a deep slur, he said, "She's a good woman, Eve, but she doesn't know what she wants, not really. She thinks she does. But, hell, that damn cousin of hers has got her mind so full of money and ambition and big houses and…," he stopped, drooping over his beer as if he had lost the thread of what he wanted to say. "She won't stay with a guy that ain't got the same ambitions she's got, if he don't already have money. I mean, nobody can be that warm and cuddly and then kiss a guy off the next minute. I used to go over to her house after school, when her parents weren't home. We'd cuddle. We'd talk about the future. You know, going to college, getting married, both of us working so we'd have plenty of money and a nice home, having kids, raising them so they'd be ambitious too. We'd make out, and cuddle, and talk more about what life together was gonna be like. She wanted us to have two kids, a boy and a girl. We'd get them into everything: piano lessons and sports and dance and band. Social clubs and things. We'd have four bedrooms, a bathroom for each bedroom, a family room, a den, a formal dining room, basement, a three-car garage and a big yard with lots of trees and flowers. Jesus, I worried about how all that stuff would get clean, but she didn't want to hear that kind of thing. She'd get mad when I said I didn't want to spend my life mowing a yard and trimming flowers. But she never said I wouldn't have to. She just refused to talk about it. If I insisted, she'd shush me with a kiss or something and again start talking about all the things we'd have."

"The nesting instinct," I commented pompously.

"What?" Dan glared at me like I'd suddenly sprouted horns or hair all over my body.

"Women are like that. They start screwing around with a guy, the first thing you know they begin thinking about having children and building a palace for the kids to grow up in. Feathering the nest." What a pompous ass I am, I thought as I finished talking. But the thought did nothing to my ego except make it laugh at itself and then continue spouting the very same pretentious crap that had made it giggle in the first place.

"You're full of shit. You don't know a thing about modern women. Some of the ones I've gotten in the sack were only interested in having a good time. But not old Eve baby. She wanted promises that I'd work my butt off to get her the kind of life she wanted, a life with lots of luxury and comforts."

Angry sarcasm slurred the last few words of the final sentence.

"I can't understand her. She's such a nice girl, a really nice person. But she's so damn…."

His voice trailed into silence, as if he couldn't find the right word to finish his thought.

"Materialistic?" I ventured.

"Yeah. Greedy, maybe."

"But you'd go out with her again in a minute," I laughed, "If she'd have you."

"Yeah," he admitted, "if that damned so-called cousin of hers would let me."

With that final comment Dan clammed up, changing the subject and refusing to talk any more about Eve or her cousin. Every time I inserted either name into our conversation, he simply stared at me and changed the subject again. Eventually I realized that he was too drunk to talk at all. I helped maneuver him to his dorm room, half carry being the key words here.

Bart had a similar story. To hear his tale, I didn't have to wait while he got drunk. All I had to do was lose a few dollars at poker.

I stopped by their room a couple of weeks after Dan bared his soul. It was Saturday evening. Dan knew several upper classmen who shared a house together off campus. They were throwing an open-house bash. Price of entry—your own booze and a little extra. When I got to Dan's dorm room, Bart was alone, drinking a beer and watching tv. I knocked. He yelled. I entered. I had to laugh. He was in the same position he had been in the other time I visited the room: lying on his cot, watching Dan's tv at an angle, a beer balanced on his stomach and held in place with two hands.

"Where's Dan?"

I didn't ask the question until I'd studied the soap opera for a few minutes.

"He had to go home."

I waited but he didn't explain why.

"He was supposed to meet me here. We were going to some party he knew about."

"Yeah, I was thinking about going too."

"Why'd he go home?"

Shrug. Chug. Burp. Finally a few words, "He didn't say why, just said he had to."

"You going to the party?"

"Nope. Don't know where. Don't know the guys. I was going with Dan."

Shit."

"Yeah."

Keeping his eyes on the tv, Bart motioned toward the fridge.

"Stick around. Have a beer. My soap'll be over soon." I grabbed a beer and sat on Dan's bed, waiting, trying to keep my eyes from gravitating to the boob tube. An impossibility. For some reason I can't sit near a television when it's running and ignore it. My eyes and ears seem to have a mind of their own in such circumstances. So I watched the end of Bart's program with him, relieved when it was over. But not for long because as soon as Bart switched off the boob tube he grabbed another beer and a deck of cards. He eyed me as he shuffled, a shit-eating grin on his face.

"You got any money this time or you gonna chicken out again?"

Two-man poker isn't my idea of an exciting time, but I figured that, if we got started, some other guys in the dorm might show up and buy in. I was wrong. We played for a couple of hours while I lost the money I had planned to party with that weekend and eat on until Friday, when my next paycheck was due. That didn't put my mood into chuckle overdrive, by any means. Bart, on the other hand, became more and more pleased with himself as he won more and more of my money and drank more and more of his own beer. Before long he was bragging about his past conquests, the conquest which had left the most impact on him apparently being the one with Eve, since he dispensed with most of his other ex-girlfriends in a few sentences but he began talking about Eve by the third game and was still talking about her as I left.

"Don't get me wrong, man," he called from his cot, where he was counting his earnings, as I opened the door. "Eve's a good woman. She'd make any man a great wife."

I no longer recall exactly how the conversation unfolded. It was too disjointed and I was too bored, and tired. But let's pretend that it went a little like the following, like I always pretend I know what I'm talking about:

"Like most of the guys I knew, I'd been hot after Eve since down in junior high, and even earlier. She was something—a good athlete, played in the band and was really something to watch on the dance floor, oozed sex, liked men. Or boys, I guess you'd have to say. I mean, she wasn't like so many girls that just want a boyfriend for sex and social standing," he grinned lewdly at his image. "She really liked being around the guys: dating, playing sports, dancing, going to the movies, talking, whatever. She didn't seem to feel complete without a male or two or three in tow." He sniggered and shook his head. "It caused a lot of friction, a lot. Guys were always fighting over her. But the thing is, she didn't like that. If she saw guys fight over her or heard about it, those guys were on her shit list from then on. No matter what. No matter how long. I don't ever recall her taking up again with a guy she ditched because he got in a fight over her." He paused for a long moment before adding, "I don't really remember her ever going back with any guy she ditched, no matter the reason."

"What the hell does she want? I mean, you and Dan, both of you, think she's something. But both of you say she goes through men like I go through water. Or you go through beer and soaps," I laughed as I spoke, not knowing how Bart would take the jibe.

He simply grinned and upped the bet I had just made, "Beer, soaps and poker chips—that's me. What more does a man need?"

"Maybe a woman."

"Now you're talking. Either call my bet or the pot's mine."

I threw in my hand, not for the first time.

"I don't know why she uses and discards so many guys," he said after raking in the pot, throwing out another ante, and beginning to shuffle the cards. "Me and Dan have talked about that a couple of times since we've been roommates. Dan thinks she hasn't found the guy she's looking for but me, I think she likes me too much." He laughed good-humoredly at his own joke before continuing, "I don't think she can be satisfied by only one guy. She needs lots of them. I don't know if it's her ego or if it's a physical thing. You know, too much female testosterone in her genes. But she can't seem to stay very long with one guy. Slam bang and she moves on to another," this time he cackled at his joke. I wondered if the guy was getting drunk or if he was just high on winning my money.

"What about that cousin of hers, Ron something or other? Dan said he's the one that won't let any guy date her very long."

"Maybe," Bart shrugged and started dealing the cards. "He might be part of the reason. I guess. But I think Eve's the real problem. I don't think she can put up with one guy for a very long time without wanting to check some other guy out. You know, kind of like the guy always wanting to see what's on the other side of the mountain. For Eve, it's what's that guy way over there like? What's he got that this guy don't?"

"So she's easy?"

"No, I didn't say that," for the first time Bart seemed irritated at me. "If you wanta know about her sex life, ask her."

After that, we played a few more desultory games but he refused to say any more about Eve, ignoring my questions.

Finally he said he'd had enough poker for one night. I finished my beer and headed for the door as he flipped on Dan's tv and settled in to watch some cop show, throwing those parting words at me as I walked across the garbage-strewn floor.

10

After the day I walked by Eve's house and somehow found the nerve to climb her steps, I didn't see her again for some time, not in the Union, not in the library, nor walking on campus. Bart said she was dating an upperclassman. Dan agreed, but insisted that she only saw him occasionally, that she wasn't out and about much because she worked, had an extremely heavy academic load, and was spending her spare time studying, at home or in the library.

It was evident that both had talked to Eve since I had. It was just as evident that neither intended to help me connect with her. They both rejected my pleas for her phone number or even her class schedule; I could have called her or accidentally found myself outside one of her classrooms when the class let out. For some reason I'll never be able to explain, except as cowardice, I would rather talk to her on the telephone or bump into her on campus than climb the porch steps again and knock on the door of the house where she was living. The thought of possible rejection on her doorstep turned my guts to jelly. Even worse was some elderly woman answering my knock and announcing that Eve did not want to see me, then or any other time.

So I began to wander by both Union and library occasionally and, finally, one blustery February evening I ran across her sitting in the undergraduate reading room with a large stack of books on the floor around her and one open on her lap.

She didn't glance up as I slowly approached and stopped near her, although her eyes flickered in my direction at one point, I thought. Maybe. She continued reading in any case, brow knitted, full lips pursed, fingers hesitantly starting to turn the page.

I waited for several minutes, the fragile shell of my ego beginning to crack along its fault line. Luckily my anger intervened.

"Hey, are you ignoring me on purpose?" I blurted.

My words brought Eve's eyes bouncing up, seemingly startled. Her mouth opened but no sound came out.

"I've been trying to find you ever since that afternoon we walked together."

Even to my own ears what I said sounded a little silly.

Her eyes sparkled, her mouth curled irritably, her body tensed, then, as if she finally recognized me for who I was and the recognition eased the building irritation in her, she smiled.

"Did you forget where I live?" her smile didn't quite erase the sarcasm in her words.

"No, I...," I stammered, trying to come up with an astute answer.

"Let's go over to the Union for coffee," she interrupted laughingly, "before you go into cardiac arrest."

Her words embarrassed me even further. I could think of no retort. My mind stumbled back over my behavior since our last meeting. She was right, of course. I should have gone directly to her house. But I had lacked the necessary nerve or self-confidence or conceit or whatever it is that makes a man believe he's not only absolutely worthy of his lady love but also totally irresistible to her. What can I say? She was correct in her assessment of me as being no Don Juan, not by a long stretch of the imagination.

Eve talked most of the way to the Union, giving me the opportunity to put a few Band Aids on my damaged ego. She did not have time for a social life. She had taken a part-time job at a popular restaurant downtown, one that catered to the business crowd at the lunch hour. She waited tables five days every week, two hours every day, and she worked some evenings. When you added that to being enrolled in the maximum number of semester hours she could take, she spent most of her free hours studying.

"It's hectic," she chattered away, apparently having forgotten my reticent behavior over the past few weeks. "My tables are filling up when I arrive and they're still full when I leave for class, but my customers have their dessert and coffee before I do leave and my boss takes care of anything else they might need, like another cup of coffee. He also collects my tips and keeps them for me. And the busboy clears the tables so I don't have to wait around to do that and wind up late for class. They're really pretty good to me. Maybe you could get a job there too," she wound up, her enthusiasm mounting as she talked.

"I have a job," I mumbled, still humbled by the truth in her earlier comments.

"Oh, yeah, sure, I remember now what you told me," she continued chattering. "You work in a service station that's a garage too. I don't suppose you plan on making that a career."

"Jesus, Eve," I huffed, "you don't have to go to college to change the oil in a car, no more than you do to serve a meal." "I didn't mean exactly that, silly," she trilled as we barged through the doors of the Union. I bee-lined for one of the few empty tables, several yards in advance of her, so if she spoke again I didn't hear what she said.

I reserved the table by putting her books on it. As I did so, she completed her thought, "I wondered if you plan on owning a service station or garage, or maybe working your way up in a car agency? If you studied business in college you'd have a big advantage over anyone who didn't."

"Yeah, I guess," I answered noncommittally as we weaved through the randomly placed tables and chairs toward the cafeteria line. "But I don't plan on being a service station or garage owner." "What then?"

She turned to the cashier to order a cup of coffee. I got a Coke. She insisted on paying, which put another small dent in my male ego, but it helped my billfold, which was kind of flat those days, so I only blustered a little.

"I don't know," I answered honestly after we had taken seats facing each other across the small table.

"You and lots of other kids," she shook her head as if in disgust. "You need a plan. Everybody needs a plan. It's kind of like a scientific experiment. You've worked at odd jobs, you say. You've studied a lot of subjects in school, like math and science, literature, history, and other things. You know people who work at different jobs, like parents of your friends, your parents and relatives, or other people you know for some reason. You like them or you don't like them. You like the way they live or you don't. You know that some of them take really fun vacations and have nice houses and cars, and maybe a cabin on a lake somewhere. Others are really intelligent or nice, some of them stupid or not so nice. You get to know your teachers and something about their families and lives. So you begin to formulate a general hypothesis about what you'd like to do with your life. You tell yourself you'd like to be a teacher, or a banker, or a whatever. Maybe you change what you'd like to become more than once before you graduate from high school. Maybe you don't. You go to college thinking you know what you want to be. Maybe you change your goal in college. You decide you don't want to be a biologist. You want to be a stock broker instead. But the really important thing is, you start college with a general plan. You don't just show up and hope you'll stumble onto a major that turns you on."

"Why not?" I said indifferently. "I don't know what I want to do the rest of my life. How could I when I'm barely eighteen. Why should I make decisions about what I'll enjoy doing when I hit forty or fifty. Why not just go with the flow. I like to read so I'll major in literature." I grinned, not really wanting to get involved in a serious discussion about college. "On the other hand I like math also and that's more masculine, don't you think? Or I could take up one of the sciences. Or history. I'd look good in a tweed coat, puffing on a pipe, giving lectures on the Civil War or France under Napoleon."

"Don't be facetious," Eve glared at me. "Besides, who wants to be a teacher? They don't make much money."

"Money?" my scorn must have shown in the way I pronounced

the two syllables, I guess. At that period in my life I had decided that making money smacked way too much of materialism.

"Don't give me that silly crap about money being unimportant as long as you like what you're doing. Only kids who don't have to worry about clothes, tuition, room, and board spout that crap, and they don't really believe what they say. They just think they do."

"How do you know what other kids believe or don't, Eve? You're no mind reader."

"What makes you think I'm not?" Eve giggled.

"Come on," I laughed. "Next thing you'll tell me you're a witch too."

"No," she studied me over her cup as she took a sip, "I don't believe in that crazy stuff. The supernatural, turning humans into mice, making sacrifices to the devil or some other creep—that's for the stupid and strange. I had a girlfriend once who believed in that kind of stuff. She always wanted to hold séances or go out to the town cemetery on a night with a full moon, and other silly things. I went to the cemetery with her once. She took a dead cat along that she'd found on the highway. She buried it on the grave of an old man that had just died. She didn't like him for some reason and she said the cat's soul would chase his for all eternity. She didn't say why she didn't like him or what made her think the cat's soul would chase his forever. And I didn't ask. By the time she got that stinky cat in the ground, mumbling and chanting all the time, I'd had enough of her, I'll tell you. So that night was the end of our friendship. I don't much like to waste my time with fools."

"What happened to her?" I asked, my curiosity piqued by the story.

Eve shrugged, "She kept coming around the house for a long time. I refused to talk to her. She'd call. I'd refuse to talk to her. I got so I wouldn't answer the phone when I thought she was on the other end. She'd try to corner me at school or fall in beside me when I was going from one class to another, trying to start up a conversation. The first few times I told her to stay away, but she was persistent, so I just ignored her, walking away if I could. She finally gave up."

"Is she here at ECU?"

"No, she got pregnant during our senior year. She and the guy got married right after graduation. Why?" Eve asked, grinning sarcastically. "Did you want to look her up?"

"No," I laughed again, trying to sound as sophisticated as I felt. "I agree with you about the supernatural crap, although there've been times when I was alone at night, in the country or on a really dark and deserted street, that I've got a funny chill in my spine. Or I hear or see something out of the corner of my eye that doesn't seem quite real, and my heart quits beating and I can't breathe and icicles grow up my spine, and then suddenly I'm panting like mad and my heart is pounding away and all I want to do is run as fast as I can anywhere, but away from where I am. But I don't." I grinned at Eve. "You know why?"

Eve returned my grin, conspiratorially, "You don't want to think of yourself as a coward and you don't want to admit that the supernatural might really exist, especially to yourself."

"Yeah," I admitted. "Once I let one of the phantoms get to me, I might be running scared forever."

"I feel the same way."

"Keep them chained in the depths of the Id and never let them free."

"Uh-huh."

"Do you really think there are no such things as werewolves and ghosts and things?"

"Of course," Eve grimaced with disgust and moved her empty cup, pushing the rings of water this way and that. "Let's talk about something else, like plans. I really think education wastes a lot of human resources."

My bewilderment must have shown on my face because she laughed.

"Plans, plans, plans—we were talking about plans before you changed the conversation to phantoms."

"I changed the conversation?"

She giggled at the exasperation in my tone. I liked her giggle. Except for the pitch it could have been a chuckle. I liked her laugh. I liked her smile. I liked her voice and the agility of her mind. Most of all, though, being who and what I am, I liked her body, all the soft curves in the right places, perky breasts just right for a story about Goldilocks, hips with a tingling swing that my eyes couldn't leave alone, arms and legs sculpted by an active life—the perfect female creature put together by some classical Greek artist who enjoyed soft, subtle, lovely, youthful feminine curves.

I was hooked. And she knew it, knew it and delighted in it, as she delighted in all masculine adoration, I began to learn as time passed and our relationship flourished. But then I can't deny that I've always liked female attention.

"I didn't change the conversation. You did."

"Whoever changed it isn't important," she put a stop to the disagreement. "We were talking about all these kids coming to college without knowing what they want to major in. A lot of them don't even want to be here. They come because their parents insist on it. Others come because their friends do, still others because they don't know what else to do or because it's the in thing. And worst of all are the ones like Bart and Dan, the ones that come to college so they can play ball or participate in some other extracurricular activity, like partying." She grimaced, then shrugged, "About the only thing you can say for them is that they help improve faculty and administrative salaries and erode educational quality, so those who just want to graduate without a great deal of work can do so a little easier."

"I don't see any of that as a problem," I tried to shake off the pessimistic mood her words were pushing me toward, "as long as they can hack the academic stuff. That's what bothers me, all the kids in my classes whose IQ seems to be at the junior high level or lower—Huxley's brave new working class in college, reading Shakespeare so they'll have an easier time finding the up and down buttons."

Eve gave me a friendly shove, "Quit being such a snob or get out of the lifeboat. Everybody knows college is just like high school. If you stay around and take the right professors and classes, and study or cheat when you have to, you'll get through, unless your IQ is down in the moronic range. No professor wants to flunk many students. If they did, there'd be fewer teaching jobs and fewer jobs for administrators as well as staff, and lower salaries. We wouldn't have such nice facilities. All the sports programs would suffer, so a lot of fans would be turned off and quit donating money to the colleges."

I laughed, "Jesus, Eve, I've only known two other people as cynical as you are."

"Are you talking about those two friends of yours that died attacking the high school?"

"How did you know about Cass and Adam?" I blurted, mortified although I should have known that she would be aware of my relationship with them. Not many of my fellow students during my final years in high school, or my other acquaintances, including my family, to tell the truth, had let me forget about Cass and Adam. Somehow I still felt guilty, not only about what my two friends had done but also about my not being with them when they did it, as if I had helped plan a reprehensible crime but had been too cowardly to carry out my part in it and so had betrayed my best friends, sending them to their death while I hid under the bed.

"What did you expect?" she watched me curiously. "The majority of the students here are from Echo Creek and the small towns scattered around this part of the state. The ones not from Echo Creek read the news and watch TV or listen to gossip. What your friends did was big news, national news. Your name was linked to theirs over and over." She studied me, gloatingly. "You're an infamous celebrity and I have the inside track. All of my friends will be green with envy, although most of them wouldn't want to be seen with you. It might hurt their date value among more acceptable males, ones with higher social standing and, from what you keep saying, more immediate financial potential."

"It won't hurt your date value to be seen with me?" I bristled.

Mocking laughter flickered deep in her eyes before expanding into a brilliant smile. When she smiled like that her whole person sparkled like whitecaps dancing merrily over a sunny sea. Me, I found it impossible to keep my bristles from folding, softened by the joie de vivre she exuded.

"It was really stupid of me to take your comment personally," I admitted glumly.

"Uh-huh," she agreed, "but logical, I guess, since I really have been avoiding you, even though deep inside me I truly did want you to catch me." An imp twinkled in her smile. "You know, like in the old movies when men and women really seemed to like each other: Tarzan chases Jane. Jane runs, making sure Tarzan can keep up, until she finds a place good for the catching. Then she stumbles or pretends to turn at bay. Tarzan catches her. She's happy. He's happy. Cupid is happy. Fade out so the ideal is not sullied by reality."

I had to smile in spite of my attempts at self-control. Eve was so unpredictable. One moment I absolutely knew what she was going to say. The next she threw me a curve ball. At times she seemed one of the straightest of the straights. Other times I didn't have the slightest idea where to file her in my scheme of society's fits and misfits, although I was certain, somehow, that she belonged more in the former than in the latter category, but that for some reason she occasionally enjoyed slipping into the latter as some people of the blue-collar class enjoy dressing up on a weekend and hobnobbing with their cousins in the white-collar class, or as some of the rich enjoy slumming occasionally. "Let's be serious," she continued. "According to the press, your friends were born trouble, 'Satan's Boys,' as one reporter liked to call them. They were like serial killers, he once said, starting out with simple crimes like peeking in windows or vandalizing public property, and slowly advancing to the serious stuff like torturing animals and killing people. You weren't given a glowing report either. He said you were the 'craven coward' right in there with the planning and everything, but calling in sick the day of the shootout."

"Nobody ever proved that," I groused, ashamed.

"No, you're right, but other newspapers said, in some cases, or suggested, in others, the exact same thing."

And every one of them is part of the Lizardus chain, or copied their news from one of them, I thought, squirming in spite of my attempts to maintain my cool, not quite sure whether to say nothing or to reveal some of the suppressed frustration. My dad's words of caution on that fateful day echoed from somewhere deep down inside me. I studied Eve, wondering just how much I could trust her. I wanted to. I had never confessed my role in the plans for the shootout to any person except my father. Finally I opted for a hypothetical confession.

"Let's say I was lucky that day, when Cass and Adam died. Let's say they stopped by for me and I was ready." A huge, black cloud began to swell inside me, turning the world a dull melancholy, as memory's sorrow swept over me like a dust storm. I felt like an insect sucked inside a sweeper bag. My voice sounded to me as dull as my feelings. "Let's say it was like this: My dad's shotgun was tied around my neck and I had his rain slicker on to hide the weapon, like we had planned. I heard Cass honk; he was driving his sister's car. I started out the door just as Dad came in it, coming home even though he was supposed to be at work, because he'd forgotten something. He looked at me and he looked around as Cass pulled away from the curb, probably frightened by Dad showing up when he did. When Dad looked back at me, he knew something was terribly wrong. He knew and I knew he knew and so I just watched Cass and Adam disappear down the street." I paused to clear my throat before continuing, as if in a plea for absolution, "Adam kept looking back at me, something miserable or lost, or maybe even something hopeful, in his eyes. I'm sure there was something there, like he was sending me a message," once again I tried futilely to clear the dusty obstruction in my throat. "You know, maybe he was trying to signal something he really wanted me to know about before he died. But I couldn't…uh, I couldn't see what it was. He was too far away."

Eve stared at me, an odd droop to her lips, which I took for commiseration but which could as easily have been scorn. My mind whirled crazily, chased by memories of that day and of the weeks that followed as I became the central figure in everybody's morbid curiosity about Cass and Adam and their suicidal attack on Echo Creek High School. The problem was, I could never give a clear, easy answer to why my friends did what they did. I denied that I had had anything to do with their plans, as my father ordered, although I don't think many people actually believed me. I had been in on the planning, of course. Whether from the beginning or not, I don't know, nor do I know if I sat in on all the later planning. But even to this day I don't for the life of me understand why I went along as I did or why Cass and Adam followed through, unless it was that they simply got caught in a trap of their own making and couldn't back out without taking a devastating blow to their pride, both to their self-esteem and to their esteem for each other. As for outside reasons, social reasons, I've always thought the major causes weren't a few little or big things, but rather the "sea change" taking place in our culture during our youth, a rapid but profound and ever continuous clash between the old and the new, in both our personal and our public lives, which Adam and Cass couldn't cope with.

Maybe that's why I followed along in their wake, because of the sea changes and the resultant motion sickness I felt as I was tossed back and forth between my family's beliefs and ideals and all those other ones I absorbed at school. Or maybe I followed along simply because I didn't want to chance losing their friendship. That is, I followed along until luck stepped in and saved me. And I was faced with the question of why, because I was a suspect in a conspiracy to commit murder and because I was the closest friend of the two culprits and, mainly, because I myself needed an answer. But it's a question I couldn't answer then and one I still can't answer, not satisfactorily, not to the press or police, inasmuch as they expected a simple answer which would put me in jail, and definitely not to myself.

On the other hand, it might all have been just a game at first. Cass enjoyed games of intrigue and so did Adam, but Cass actually seemed to thrive on the planning and preparation even more than on the games themselves. He could have expected to stop at any point in the attack but somehow got so carried away with the process that he couldn't put on the brakes, not until it was too late anyhow. Who really knows, though? It could be that Cass really believed some of his own far-out ideas, like that this life is just one more in an infinite series, kind of like one of Jorge Luis Borges's labyrinths or a complex computer game. Whatever he wanted, he would not have found it difficult to convince Adam to go along.

Yet all his antagonism toward the governing elite and major institutions of Echo Creek couldn't be discarded if a person honestly wanted a peek at the forces triggering what he did. It could have been as simple, or as complex, as that. He saw corruption and incompetence and he wanted to do his share to destroy them, even if doing so meant his own destruction. That would have been true especially if he didn't consider the end of this life as permanent, but rather as a passageway to another and another and another existence.

I tried to explain all the above to Eve. She said she understood. To this day I don't know if she really did.

"The closest I've ever come to an answer that, well, that others might accept and that doesn't make Cass and Adam out as senseless murderers," I reflected, "is to blame the continuous changes brought about by technology and science, in cultural and social values, in our beliefs and in what is and what isn't acceptable.

When the moral soil you walk on every day keeps shifting under your feet and what's taboo today may be all right tomorrow, or vice versa, and the next day it's not okay again, or it's acceptable over here but not over there, or it's acceptable with one group of friends but not the other, or at school with the teachers but not at home with your parents, or the reverse—when our moral values become so nebulous, so diverse, so flexible that you can ignore them or apply them as you wish, you lose perspective. You lose it because so many of the changes you have to make from one group to the next are not superficial but rather fundamental changes, and because there's so much disagreement about what is right and what is wrong that your moral compass goes absolutely haywire. You could probably handle the continuous shifting of moral quicksand under your feet, the continuous emotional instability, if there was a generally high standard of social and spiritual conduct among our country's leaders, local and national, in the church and in the government, and in our schools and universities." I grimaced at Eve's doubtful look, and finished with a lame grin, "But there isn't, not as far as I'm concerned.

The majority are terrible role models with respect to honesty and integrity, or true understanding of the working class and the poor, and the kids, especially the kids."

"Now who's the cynic?" Eve asked me, the imp again in her smile, but only partially because under that soft light in her eyes flickered a hint of understanding and sympathy.

I wondered if she thought this was all an intellectual game we were playing, in a pale imitation of the academic process in which we were immersed—I playing the lecturing teacher, she playing one of my star pupils, listening with open mouth and from time to time asking a probing question or inserting a meaningful comment meant more to impress than to learn.

"Yeah, I know, that's probably too farfetched as an explanation. It sounds more like a speech prepared for an antiestablishment political rally."

"Yes," Eve's hand touched mine, which lay on the table in front of me, before withdrawing. "It's probably a lot simpler than that. I read once that Cass's lack of real parents and a lack of true moral fiber in Adam's parents were the real causes of what they did."

"Add it all in the mix and figure it out with chaos theory, maybe we could come up with a really valuable explanation, but what person who knows how to do that would care enough to actually do it," I laughed at my own conceit. "But I'd say they were well adjusted, just rebellious kids who did a lot of things simply because they weren't supposed to and could get by with them. Cass would get a kick out of reporters blaming the loss of his parents for his escapades, and more especially for his personality, or character disorders, or whatever you want to call it. Ha, even suggesting he had a personality disorder would have tickled him. Adam? His mom was a bitch but he had a great relationship with his dad. Both Adam and Cass would have laughed for weeks if they had read all the psychological babble that tried to make them out as mentally or psychologically maladjusted. They considered themselves freethinkers; all others they considered mental robots."

"I wish I had known them," Eve almost whispered the words. "But, still, they had to have something wrong or different, about them. There are millions of kids in the school system that don't like it, even hate it, but they don't shoot it up. Lots of them would like to probably, but they don't, and not all of them just because they're cowards or unthinking robots who do what they're supposed to do simply because that's what everybody expects."

"We're right damn exactly where I wind up in conversations like this always. Lots of people break the law, but a hell of a lot more don't for one reason or another. Why, when so many laws are hypocritical and favor the rich?"

"You can't blame society, or the laws, not to mention that it won't do any good if you're looking for someone or something you can punish for its guilt. It's a little hard to penalize an entire culture, don't you think?"

What I took as her sarcasm irritated me.

"I wasn't blaming society," I grumbled. "Nor was I trying to find someone to punish. I was trying to explain what might have set Cass off. But, you know, maybe more than the actual speed of change caused by technology, it's that we know about it." I fumbled for words, afraid I was entering an area I hadn't given a great deal of thought to, not enough to have organized a clear, logical explanation of, anyhow. "I mean," I grinned inanely as the satirical words of one of my professors popped into my mind, words he used to poke fun at student comments on a recent exam we had taken, "back during the pre-historical period of the Industrial Revolution, there were the telegraph, telephone and radio. They made the world smaller, a lot smaller than sailing ships and stagecoaches. They moved new ideas around more quickly and into more isolated parts of the world.

But they didn't penetrate every corner of the earth. You had to have wires to use them. Lots of places in the world didn't have those wires, so we didn't know much about those people, unless they had a major plague or war. Even then we received only one general picture, not much disagreement about what was going on. Then a lot of our kids started going off to war in exotic places and returning with new morals and new ideas. Then jet travel and television were invented. Change became more rapid but most of it remained superficial and what was essential didn't have a disruptive impact within a single generation, but rather again speeded up the normal flux of change from generation to generation. And, of course, foreign ideas began to penetrate into more and more isolated areas. The world shrank further, faster. But you still needed wires or visitors from other parts of the globe in order to exchange ideas. Change was still measurable, new ideas and their impact still traceable along the wires. But," I shrugged, feeling mentally lost, "along came the computer and wireless communications, and I now feel like a mental sponge that's being irradiated continuously by new ideas and values. I feel like the earth might if it were alive. I'm continuously being bombarded by atoms of new ideas and values from every part of me, atoms that aren't always recognizable as related in any way, shape or form to my world view, personal, social or spiritual, as uprooted and chaotic as it has become."

My words slipped off into temporary stasis, along with my mind. Eve stared at me with pursed lips. I turned to forming watery designs on the table with my glass.

"I think I kind of understand where you're coming from," she commented after a long silence. "We're a generation caught in some kind of atomic vortex formed by the clash of ideas and values and emotions from all over the world. No other generation has had so much information at its fingertips as we do, especially so much contradictory, unedited, often worthless information flying at us from all directions. Many of us adapt to the continuous attacks by withdrawing into the familiar and rejecting anything unfamiliar. Others seem to thrive in the vortex, making their way through the labyrinth of words as if that's their natural medium. But," with a thoughtful frown she returned the subject to where it had been, "I still think there had to be something wrong with your two friends or they couldn't have shot all those people. To me, that's self-evident."

Those words with reference to Cass and Adam were so familiar that I didn't react. The problem was, when they were still alive I had considered them normal, as normal as anybody else. Since their death almost anybody who mentioned them referred to their abnormality as a commonplace, so much so that doubts had begun to penetrate the cracks of my armor, but I still couldn't accept that they were not just normal kids whose reaction to our absurd, corrupt and essentially avaricious world and its base in the eternal flux, albeit no longer the flux of foot travel, but rather that of rockets and the Ethernet, had driven them to extremes of absurdity in thought and action—in truth though, no more so than that of the world at large, although my reaction was probably skewed by the feeling that if they were abnormal, then so was I. And to that my ego found it difficult to acquiesce, although I actually prided myself in what I considered my individuality. Go figure!

"I guess," I answered Eve's conclusion. "But what was wrong with them could have been no more than a minute vacuum where a thread of reason should have been."

Eve stared at me as if I had suddenly sprouted two heads, "You're not making sense."

"If they had left a political manifesto—you know, if they had given a political reason, or even a cultural one, or a religious or economic or racial one—or any kind of absurd but acceptable reason, I guess, they would have been called terrorists or heroes. But no one could come up with a suitable rationale for their attack, not even suicide since they left no note, so they had to be nutcases. They lost it and struck out blindly, like a wounded beast. That seems to be the general consensus, anyhow. But I don't agree. They didn't strike out blindly. They planned their attack carefully and logically. They struck the easiest, most defenseless target, the one that represented the greatest degree of corruption and inefficiency in their world, the greatest amount of waste and, for society at large as well as for them, the greatest emotional investment. I guess, if you really need a term for them, you could call them anarchists, but that's a really empty word."

My own reasoning befuddled me and it had begun to vibrate in my voice. "The thing is," I began again, hesitantly, "for most of us moral values are too often for dressing up in on Sundays, like a suit and tie. The rest of the week we put our old clothes back on because we don't want our Sunday-go-to-meeting clothes to get dirty. On Sundays we go to church, fold our hands in prayer, sing hymns, and parade a moral piety we reserve for special occasions, like Sundays and religious holidays, and with family and such. The rest of the time we sure don't turn the other cheek if someone slaps us on one. More than likely we try to do it to them before they can do it to us. But we still try to keep up the Sunday façade."

"Earlier I thought you sounded like some kind of fanatic idealist," Eve put in when I stopped talking, my hands busy forming watery circles with my glass, my mind trying to slip out of the nervous fog that had settled around it. "Now you're sounding childish and bitter."

I shrugged, hoping that the movement didn't seem flippant.

"I guess I'm kind of on a downer. It's nothing new. I get depressed whenever I remember Cass and Adam, maybe because I can't really explain why they did what they did and I need an explanation that satisfies me, not one that other people think is correct, but I never come up with one that does the job." I met her eyes for a fleeting second. The concern radiating from them made me feel a little better about myself. I wondered if I didn't enjoy wallowing in self-pity.

"Let's talk about something else then."

"Like what?"

"Like me!" she laughed, standing up and posing with her high breasts thrust forward, her hands on her hips, and her deep blue eyes beckoning with an inviting softness that mocked itself, before again taking her seat.

My juices flowed like molten lava. My body perked up. My mood changed immediately. I even found myself grinning like a boy on the verge of tasting a special treat. Yet I was well aware that her pose had not been serious.

"Ha," I chuckled spontaneously, glad to have the subject changed, my nerves already beginning to stabilize, "is this going to be an evening of true confessions? Do I pass the crying towel to you now?"

She smiled, wistfully maybe, and regaled me for the next quarter hour with the same details of her young life that she had talked about on our first walk together. She enjoyed school, but primarily as a means to a good job and decent life. She really enjoyed the competition for grades, the companionship with others her own age, the structure and sense of purpose, and even the extracurricular activities. She admitted that she enjoyed the process of learning and the knowledge that resulted from that process, but she couldn't claim to love learning for the pure joy of knowing new things or expanding her mind. Rather, what turned her on was learning new things that could be applied to the real world and, most importantly, to her own life and experiences. No true scholar she, but rather an apprentice of the world. "Bart Kane graduated with you. He said you got the best grades in your class."

"Bart's a gossip," she laughed. "He's told me a lot about you too."

"You talk to Bart much?" A twinge of jealousy turned me blue for a moment. Bart's story about his relationship with Eve and what he still felt for her flooded through my mind like a tsunami, trailing Dan's story behind it.

"Not a lot, really," she spoke as if she had caught me with my eyes on an interesting part of her anatomy. "We have a history class together, U. S. History. It's in Lizardus Hall, in the big lecture hall, on the first floor. You know." She paused until I nodded. "We've sat together once or twice. And I see him three or four times a week in the Union or on campus. I can't very well avoid him. The campus is pretty small and he's an old friend."

I shrugged, noncommittally, I hoped, wondering about the use of the word 'friend.'

"I see other friends from my high school sometimes, also," her smirk returned. "Why?"

"No reason," I lied. "I was just making conversation and couldn't think of anything else to ask.

"You could have asked me for some specifics about my high school years."

"You told me a lot of things the time we went for a walk, when I came out to your house and found you sitting outside on the porch. You were the editor of your school newspaper during your junior and senior years. You were class president all four years. You played the clarinet in the band in junior high and high school both. You played guard on the women's basketball team and also played softball. And, what I like most, you were the vale-dictorian of your senior class. Did I miss anything?"

"I was on the debate team for four years and captain for three," she smiled.

"I'm sitting with a celebrity," I grinned inanely, happy that she was smiling again, but at the same time bothered by all those kids throughout history who had not been active in much of anything, as children or as adults.

"If I had to choose one characteristic that defined me the most, it would be my competitiveness. I like to win. Sometimes the competition itself turns me on but, whether it does or not, winning does. You'll find out if you hang around me for very long. I hate to lose."

11

During the next week our relationship became more substantial. We met three times, as much at Eve's insistence as at mine. Our first real date took place at an off-campus hamburger joint. We had finished our meals and were dawdling over Eve's coffee and the remainder of my Pepsi, comfortable in each other's company, I like to think, though the flow of the conversation often seemed like the sputter of an old Model T Ford being cranked in sub-zero weather.

"I don't see anything wrong with being a little materialistic," Eve reacted to some comment of mine about idealism or altruism or some such thing. "I want a husband with a good salary and I want a career of my own. I want a nice home. You know, I don't want my children to have to share their bedrooms and I don't want to live on poverty hill. I want a den where my husband and I can get away from the children whenever we feel the need, where we can keep our household papers and accounts and where we can do whatever homework we need to do for our jobs. I want a room for the family to get together to play games and watch television, or just talk about our children's school and friends, and their ideas and what they want to do when they grow up and, you know, about world problems and religion and all that. I want my own car. I want a two-car garage so I don't have to park out in the snow and rain. I want enough money so we can travel on vacations and stay in nice hotels. When the children are grown and out on their own, I want enough money for two vacations a year, one inside the country and one to other exciting places like Europe and South America and Australia."

We were sitting in a rectangular room with booths lined around the outer walls. An unswept aisle of dingy tile separated us from the long counter and its line of round metal stools covered with cracked red plastic. Clusters of ketchup bottles and salt and pepper shakers hovered in front of every other stool as well as on the table of each booth, dried bits of their contents stuck to them and to the table around them. Well-used menus stood on edge framing each cluster, splotches of food staining their dingy plastic covers.

The lower section of the outer wall seemed to be made of concrete blocks covered by a thick coat of once-white paint. From table top to ceiling, running the length of the room, a single window looked out on the parking lot and the busy street beyond. The window hadn't been cleaned for a couple of decades, at least.

We were sitting in a booth at the rear of the room. The shabby red plastic covering on the benches was stained and cracked. Scratches marred what had long ago been a bright red Formica table top.

You know, I have a tendency for my mind to doze off, go blank, when people are saying things that don't much interest me. It's not a good habit to have, but it's one I've never been able to break no matter how much I try to concentrate. When this happens, I think some people can see the fadeout in my eyes. Anyhow, I must have gone blank and Eve must have noticed my glazed stare because she suddenly glared at me, slowly, dramatically lifted her cup for a sip of coffee, and carefully replaced the cup on the saucer, in the exact same position it had been in before. She swallowed slowly, obviously, all the time staring into my eyes, not romantically by any stretch of the imagination.

I became self-conscious. So I tried a big gulp of Pepsi. Too big! My throat became flooded as my mind hurriedly tried to force the entire gulp down the narrow passageway into my stomach. I choked, almost spitting the whole gob onto the table. A dribble of Pepsi got through the blockade. My eyes watered. My throat ached. I forced myself to swallow the rest in spite of the hurt. Slowly the blood faded from my face. My eyes dried out a little. The ache disappeared. And my throat and lungs quit gulping on their own. I coughed and sputtered but that too finally stopped.

"What?" I asked when my voice box finally began functioning again.

Eve shook her head disgustedly. "I was talking about some of my dreams for the future. You know, for the good life. I want my share of the American dream and I was telling you about some of it," she kicked me lightly under the table, "in case you're interested."

"I am," I made an effort to rise to the occasion, but I couldn't get enthused about marriage, having two and a half kids, going to work every day in order to bring home enough loot for all the trimmings, and growing old together. Talking about sex and other things we could do together in the here and now might have kept my enthusiastic interest.

Our second date took place in the library, an intimate study session—you know, one of those sessions in which you study each other more than you do the written word, but a session that makes you feel good about your study habits nevertheless.

By the end of the week I was beginning to have difficulty sleeping because my mind spent the dark hours stimulating itself with erotic visions of myself and Eve in a variety of fictional love scenes and my body spent those same hours in rising sensual reaction to the pieces of fiction my mind couldn't seem to let go of. By the weekend I was too wasted, in all ways physical and emotional, to compete tenaciously at tiddlywinks, let alone tennis, which might be one reason why Eve decided to keep me around. We met that Saturday at the ECU tennis courts and she trounced me 6-0, 6-3, 6-4, 6-1. I stomped off the court in disgust after the fourth set. She chortled all the way to the Union, where I had to buy, and then all the way to her room where the reward for the loser was worth the trouncing.

"Where did the Carsons go?" I asked curiously when Eve invited me in.

I knew that she was not supposed to have guests under any circumstances when the elder Carsons were not at home.

When she had moved in she had been given a list of "Thou shalt 'nots,'" a list she had shown me in our recent study session and over which we had both laughed and commiserated. "Thou shalt not" number one was no guests unless expressly approved by Mr. and Mrs. Carson. Number two stated in plain English that under no circumstances was Eve to have guests when the Carsons were absent, no matter whether the guest or guests had been previously approved or not.

"They left for Chicago last weekend," Eve smiled in complicity. "They won't be back till next Sunday."

My adrenaline kicked in with that news. Or was that testosterone? Whatever, a tidal surge moved in my groin.

"Why didn't you tell me this last week? I didn't work Tuesday and Thursday. I could've come over," my attempt to keep the complaint out of my voice failed.

For a moment she simply stared at me silently, as if she was trying to decide what to say.

"The final for my summer class in finance was last Thursday. You do remember I took a summer class in finance, don't you?" She smiled to soften the sarcasm. "I spent most of the week studying, except for the time I spent at work and with you. And no, I didn't study alone all the time. Bart came over to study with me on Tuesday and a group of us met in the Union on Wednesday for a study session.

"Bart came over here? I saw him yesterday and he didn't say anything about it."

Jealousy clobbered me in the gut and sent my tongue flapping out of control, although I well knew that she had made no commitment to me or me to her.

"The bastard," I grumbled on. "He didn't say anything about it."

She shrugged, the motion of her shoulders pulling her blouse tight against the nipples of her breasts, and slid forward until those same nipples and breasts were pressed against my chest.

Her arms encircled my back. Her eyes turned soft and inviting. My mind shifted into another channel, one where violent gusts of wind created vacuums in their wake, making it difficult to breathe.

"He knows we're seeing each other," she spoke with her forehead against my chin and her hair stifling my breath. "Maybe he was worried about how you'd react."

"Or maybe he simply didn't want me to know he'd spent a day with you alone, here."

I once again reminded myself that we weren't engaged or anything serious like that, so she had a right to see another guy if she wanted to, even if for more than a study session, but I don't think any part of me except my reason agreed with the conclusion.

Eve's soft warmth clinging to me from chest to thighs quickly smothered my resentment, turning it into a swollen, uncontrollable desire aware of nothing but itself. Our lips fused. My tongue slipped between her lips, excitedly exploring the moist depths beyond. Her tongue seemed to intercept mine timidly, as if afraid to allow my pulsating member deeper ingress, yet at the same time yearning for the very penetration another part of her was halfheartedly pretending to deny me. Then slowly, hesitantly, sparring aggressively one moment, retreating shyly the next, her tongue submitted to the size of my passion, retreating to the bottom of her mouth, where it stretched out luxuriously, expectantly, while mine continued probing the inner depths.

Our bodies struggled desperately to become one as we stumbled and wobbled up the stairway and into her room, none too soon tumbling onto her bed, still mostly clothed in spite of our frenzied attempts to remedy the situation. Her body fired mine with molten desire. Her writhing became so wild that I felt myself slipping into the blinding chasm of uncontrollable pleasure. Frantic, I withdrew far enough to cool my building passion and pull her bra down over her breasts. For some reason I couldn't get the damned thing unsnapped. My fingers seemed swollen and stiff. I backed off far enough to rip my clothes off. When I turned back to her, she too had stripped and was lying on her back, waiting, her eyes smoldering as she watched my antics, a smile of what I hoped was anticipation on her lips.

When I left several hours later, at Eve's insistence, I was a man reborn. Her assertion that I couldn't spend the night, in spite of my pleas, made no big dent in the swollen armor of my ego. I was so high on requited passion that I didn't feel my shoes touch the sidewalk once on the way home.

That night, when I slept, I dreamed of an angel all silky skin and soft curves, her sensual young body beside mine in bed, beckoning, her eyes smiling shyly, her body burning to the feathery touch of my fingers, her hot flesh shivering in nervous anticipation as I hovered over her, my passion swollen and bouncing its desire.

The next afternoon Eve was waiting for me when my last class ended.

"Hi," was all she said as she clasped my arm and grinned that knowing smile of hers.

I must have spouted something inane because she giggled and said, "I love you too, silly, but we can't go back to my place now. The Carsons came home in the middle of the night. Can you believe it? A week before they were supposed to? They weren't enjoying themselves, they said. But I'll bet the money they were spending scared them to death; they're both such scrooges, especially Mr. Carson."

The Carsons had apparently spent all the money they planned to spend on vacations for some time, because they stayed home the rest of the summer, not even taking a weekend to visit relatives that they surely had somewhere, appearances to the contrary. So my sex life, after such a fantastic surge, once again retreated into its private world of dreams and yearnings, only occasionally, surreptitiously, reappearing when the Carsons had gone shopping for a few hours, when I could cajole my dad out of his car for an evening, or, as summer meandered into fall, when Eve and I were lucky enough to find a grassy, secluded spot on our sometimes afternoon or evenings walks.

12

Late one Saturday evening in September, at the end of a pleasant Indian summer day, Eve and I wandered out Echo Creek, on an old road we had not walked together before. I had worked most of the morning and afternoon and had studied the early part of the evening away. Eve studied in the morning and worked in the late afternoon and into the early evening, after which we met for coffee in the Student Union and then decided to take a walk together.

Eve became strangely quiet after we left the Union. A few times I tried to start a conversation but soon gave up and decided to enjoy the simple pleasure of walking quietly beside her, her warm hand in mine.

A full moon had appeared pale white on the horizon, a horizon at the lower edge of a sky still blue from the light of a sun no longer visible, as we came to a wooded area I had explored more than once as a child but hadn't entered for several years. The trees hovered dark and inviting on the east side of the road, most of the underbrush and saplings having been cleared out, and kept out, by the farmer who owned the woods. It was rumored that he planned on dividing the woods into parcels and selling the parcels as building lots, some day.

But he hadn't yet.

On the far side of the woods, near the eastern edge, hid a small clearing in the form of a lazy L. Or so it had in my memory. I guided Eve toward that clearing, in spite of her protests.

"It's late," she complained. "Mrs. Carson will be really upset if I come traipsing in after she's in bed."

"Tell her you had to study for a test or something, or you had to stay late at work."

"You want me to lie," she accused me.

"It's not a real lie. It won't hurt her and it'll help us," I excused myself, irritated that she was making such a big deal out of something so logical and insignificant.

"I've got to be in by midnight," she finally acquiesced. "The Carsons go to bed at midnight on Saturday."

Those words set my heart to pumping. We had over three hours to do what had been foremost on my mind most of the day and had become an absolute fixation during the past hour, as we sat and talked over our coffee and tea: Eve half clothed, Eve with only her panties on, Eve in the nude, the two of us in one compromising position after another, both of us naked but definitely no longer in the Garden of Innocence, the…well, you get the picture. My mind had been tormented all day with sensual pictures conjured up by my body in extreme heat. I don't know how I found the time to concentrate on my work.

But then I guess I should be honest and admit that I didn't, not all the time. Hmmm. Admittedly not most of the time.

So, I slowly maneuvered Eve to the clearing, or so I imagined at the time, although when I think back on those fabulous days of our budding love affair, I wonder if I wasn't myself maneuvered into thinking I was the one doing the maneuvering. But it really doesn't matter, does it? After all, imagination is the father of belief and belief is the Siamese twin of truth, the two being inseparable if not identical in our minds in spite of our insistence to the contrary. They're kind of like the conundrum of the chicken and the egg.

Grass and weeds covered the ground like a shag carpet, especially near the tree line on the southern edge of the clearing. We lay down on our jackets, snuggled together against the chill of the evening. It didn't take long for us to turn the temperature up, however, as our bodies frantically strained to become one.

"Let me," Eve's voice rasped, husky and breathless.

She caught my hands, pulling them away from her youthful breasts and forcing them to remain motionless at my sides. Swiftly she jumped to her feet, her breathing harsh in the silence of evening. I couldn't see the features of her face, her expression or what gleamed in her eyes. Sunlight had disappeared and twilight was rapidly fading into the dark of night. The moon had not yet risen high enough to smile over the treetops, although a few stars twinkled overhead, pale and distant. But I watched her body appear bit by bit as she hastily discarded pieces of clothing until she stood above me, naked, her breasts and hips as pale as the few stars above, the rest of her still stained from the previous summer's sun, or possibly a tanning booth..

Soon she was kneeling beside me, her soft, warm hands stripping me article by article until I lay naked and at her mercy, my erection throbbing in those same hands. Her hands moved. Her hot, moist lips enclosed the head. The pleasure mounted until I felt the explosion building higher and higher, unstoppable, and then…I exploded, the earth faded, became a dream of reality as I floated somewhere in the dark sky among the millions of tiny, twinkling stars that had somehow appeared out of nowhere. And the moon! Yes, the moon also had felt my pleasure and sparkled bright and full, orange, grinning happily, just above the treetops.

"You liked that?" Eve's voice finally penetrated the fog of pleasure that pervaded my being.

Within minutes I returned her gift. My hands explored her soft curves from knees to breasts. My tongue worked its own magic as her lips had worked theirs. Her sighs turned to frenzied groans. Her body kicked and twisted uncontrollably as she climaxed. Eventually the spasms slowed and then stopped completely. Her body relaxed. Her eyes closed. I rolled over onto my back, my arms at my sides, my eyes gazing almost unseeingly at the multitude of tiny stars on their black satin background. Her warm moist hand found mine and our fingers entwined. We lay in blissful silence for how long I don't know, until, without a word, we joined together for another long, long journey to bliss, together this time.

"We need to go. Mrs. Carson is a bitch when anybody breaks her rules."

I think I had been asleep when Eve spoke. Her words seemed to come from a great distance. I shivered., for the first time aware of the cold seeping up from my bare legs, creeping under the jacket with which I had covered my torso.

By the light of moon and stars we hurriedly gathered our clothes and dressed. We retraced our steps to her place in silence, her hand in mine at times, my arm around her shoulders at other times, our hips lightly touching from time to time.

"Do you love me?" Eve suddenly asked when we had traversed a little over half the distance to her place.

I must have hesitated too long because she swatted me on the arm and said, "You don't really have to answer if you don't want to." She laughed as she spoke, although the sound came out more of a growl. "But if you don't answer, I'll put your name in red ink on my black list."

"Of course I do," I tried to sound enthusiastic but the words tripped over each other in my hurry to get them out, causing me to stutter and turning my voice into a pompous imitation of itself.

"Well, say it then," annoyance floated in the depths of her words. "Say you love me."

"I love you," I again tried for enthusiasm and sincerity of course. But irritation was probably predominant.

"You're supposed to be the romantic one and me the pessimist," she squeezed my hand playfully as she spoke.

"I thought I got to be the disillusioned romantic. That's not the same as a full-fledged romantic dreamer."

"Don't be silly. You're too young to be disillusioned."

"Come on, Eve," I complained. "We've gone over this before. It's not how old you are that counts. It's how much experience you've packed into the years you've lived."

"Whoo, whoo," she laughed, imitating an owl. "Listen to the man-about-town! Isn't he a cosmopolitan gentleman!"

"I didn't mean that, Eve," I defended myself seriously, although

I knew Eve was teasing me. "It's us, all of us. It's our culture. I mean, it's this modern world we live in. Nothing is taboo. Kids experiment with sex and booze and drugs and anything else they want to by the time they hit puberty. If they don't actually do those things, they see them done on tv or they read about them in newspapers or novels. Or they hear their friends talking about them. They...." "Where did all that silly crap come from?" Eve laughed. "You sometimes come up with the dumbest things. And are you saying you'd rather live back in the Middle Ages?"

"No, that's not what I'm saying." I tried for a sensual laugh. "I like what we did. Yum, yum!" I grabbed her and we wrestled playfully for a few seconds, until she elbowed me in the ribs and we continued walking. "It's that you, we, I mean, we humans can't have everything. We always have to give up something."

"Poor, Donjon," Eve interrupted laughing. "He can't have me and Mary and June all at the same time. He has to make a choice."

"Ha, ha, ha," I grouched, not seriously. "But that's the essence of the problem. It's a dialectical world all right. It doesn't take a genius to figure that out. But one extreme generally excludes the other, although everything seems to merge at those same extremes in the physical world. You can't have night and day at the same time, or winter and summer, just partially this and partially that like twilight or fall. With the emotions, though, the problem is even more exclusive. Having one means giving up the other, like hating someone means you sure as hell don't love them, and hate and love don't merge at the edges. They're mutually exclusive not only at any given moment, but also in terms of development. It's the same thing with innocence and experience. Once you get experience, even a smidgeon, all those hot dreams of innocence are gone, permanently. By the time most of us get into high school, all of those beautiful visions of our innocent years are gone, long gone. We've found out that girls are made of skin and bones and flesh and smells just like boys are. They like to do the same things boys do. No more fantasies and beautiful, irrational dreams about making love as if in paradise. Making love is just having sex."

"You don't think sex is great?"

"Yeah, I do," I laughed, trying for a Bogart voice.

"I remember thinking a lot about having sex before I did it the first time. The dreams were so fantastic. I always thought they were realistic, until I did it. Then I thought the fantasies were a lot better," she giggled shrilly and squeezed my hand. "But now I think the real thing is better."

"How do you know?" I insisted. "Can you remember, really remember, what your dreams about sex were like?"

"I had a wonderful time. It was a really nice evening." Eve said, ignoring my question as we turned up the sidewalk leading to the Carsons' porch. Suddenly she giggled, "But don't think I'm going to make an honest man out of you just because you couldn't resist destroying your innocence with my real body."

With a quick kiss on the cheek and a light squeeze of my hand, she skipped up the steps onto the porch, opened the door, and disappeared, leaving me standing alone on the dark sidewalk, halfway between porch and street. I froze for a moment, staring at the door through which she had fled, my mind a lonely blank. The house was dark, although an occasional pale flicker of light suggested that someone was watching television. The street behind me was deserted, but I had no other choice. I turned and ambled into the deeper darkness, hurrying from streetlight to streetlight as if the shadowy world in between held creatures, or maybe just ideas, real or imaginary, which I couldn't face without losing too much of my sense of self. As I scurried along the street I couldn't help wonder if I might have been wrong, that the real and imaginary did meet at the edges in some way, like night and day, and summer and winter, forging ideas and beings that were not quite either/or, like maybe us humans, for instance, with all our dreams of eternal pleasure in a perfect world.

13

A couple of weeks later Eve and I were again lying in our private spot in the wooded clearing. The night air stirred from time to time, slightly, a feathery caress moving over my exposed skin, warm, soft, almost indistinguishable from Eve's fingers caressing my body. We had made love, deep, passionate, exhausting devotion on the altar of each other's flesh. I lay on my back, my eyes half closed, lethargic, enjoying the velvet warmth of Eve's body nestled at my side and the pleasant aftermath of sexual satisfaction that seemed to linger on forever. It was on evenings like this one that I gave fond thanks to the widow for her marvelous, loving lessons. Without her I would still have been a naïve bumbler in the art of sex, even worse than I probably was, although my ego still can't control my wavering between feelings of inadequacy, on the one hand, and conceit on the other.

Multitudes of stars twinkled in the black dome above. I saw them. Somewhere down in the unconscious depths of my being they filled my soul with beauty and the vastness of the universe. But, languid in depletion of my sensual energy and in my sated hunger, I didn't completely register their existence, or even that of the velvet dome they decorated. My conscious self felt little more than a vague sense of my lassitude and the pleasant feel of Eve's naked body against mine. "Did you ever wonder if there really are planets with intelligent creatures on them up there somewhere?"

Eve's whisper seemed to rise from far away, as if the words were spoken in town, maybe on campus, and had to make their way through the night air and the trees of the woods in order to reach my ears. At first I couldn't react. I tried but my mind continued paralyzed from the lingering pleasure and deep contentment of our earlier activities.

Eve punched me in the ribs, tenderly, playfully.

"I'm talking to you, Donjon. Don't go to sleep on me."

"I know…I'm not," I forced myself to mumble, trying but failing to sound rational. "Yes."

She giggled and again punched me, tenderly.

"Yes what? Yes you wonder if there are planets up there or yes you haven't gone to sleep on me?" I forced myself to wake up and talk.

"They're beautiful, some twinkling while others remain so terribly motionless and noncommittal, and lonely. I like to imagine the stars as tiny diamonds, uncut, some sparkling when you look at them, others cold, unfeeling, ice crystals without a sun to help them express themselves, just awaiting their turn to preen and show their true selves, the vast swarm of them eternally unmoving. And those wispy clouds in the east, floating toward us, they suggest a living force moving them, like the tides are moved in the sea and the seasons are moved by the sun and the planets and…everything expressing the delightful, sometimes content, sometimes angry, often cruel, always unsettled nature of whatever it is that created it all. I…."

"I didn't realize that you had such deep feelings," Eve snuggled closer, then chuckled. "With some work you could maybe turn those statements into poetry."

"You don't feel the beauty all around us," I asked, trying to keep the disappointment out of my voice. Her tone seemed to hide a note of sarcasm, "and the loneliness, the awful desolate emptiness that pervades everything?"

"Of course I do," she caressed my ear with her lips as she spoke. "I wasn't being sarcastic if that's what you think. I was really thinking how your words made the night sky even more beautiful than it was. When you mentioned the clouds I saw them for the first time, but I also saw the dark shadows of the trees around us, shadows without tiny sparkles of light to offer hope. There aren't any lightning bugs out tonight to soften the despair I can feel in the darkest shadows. Some nights, when I'm walking on campus or sitting out on the Carsons' front porch… when I'm alone and it's cloudy and I can't see any stars, those nights I feel so lonely I want to run to the closest lamp or human sound, just to make sure there are other people awake and conscious, alive like me.

"Some nights when I'm lying in bed with the curtains open, and I can see stars, I don't feel the loneliness. It's as if my mind—not my brain, but something inside me that seems to reach out and touch an eternally comforting essence—it's as if there is something touching me with its being, trying to comfort me, telling me, not in words but in feelings, in a vague, yearning sensation, that a god who really cares about me does exist, and that I was somehow created within that divinity's essential nature and will someday return home to it, to fuse my being with its being, forever. Before that moment, and afterwards, however, I too often get this terribly empty mood. It's like there's no meaning anywhere. Not here on earth. Not out there in that vacant black hole we call space. And I get cold all over, deep inside too, all of me floating cold and empty in the cold, empty universe. There's no end. There's no place where the fireplace is warm and waiting for me, where love and an eternal, continuous feeling of being at home, of happiness and deep contentment and fulfillment, total fulfillment, fulfillment forever with never a moment of relapse… none of that exists for me, anywhere, not in this world and not in the next. I feel like I'm floating in a void, on and on and on from one to the next, and the next. And…."

Eve stopped talking and snuggled against me, tightly, pushing as if she was trying to find an opening into my flesh. Her words had emptied the heat from my belly also.

"Sometimes," I changed the subject back to her original question, "sometimes I look up at the night sky and wonder if the scientists are right and there are planets out there somewhere with intelligent creatures living on them, creatures like us or not, maybe little green men or maybe dinosaur-like monsters that think and can remember the past and meditate about the future and other abstract concepts."

"What if there are? What if there are thousands, or even millions of planets like ours, with billions of intelligent creatures on each one. Can you imagine a god who could care about each and every one of us? I can't in my rational moments. I can't even imagine how any god can love the billions of humans on this earth. How can an omnipotent, omniscient creature truly care about thousands or even millions or billions of us petty mortals? We have so many ugly habits and desires. We're so crippled by our natural polarity. We love and hate and create and destroy as if they're all part of the same process, all part of some giant Ferris wheel that's the essence of our lives. We treat each other miserably. How can any creature possibly love us unreservedly? How? We can't even love ourselves. We fight and squabble and maim and torture and kill, and so often in the name of some all-loving god. And then, like I said, there are the numbers." Eve paused in her diatribe, long enough to kiss me and press her cheek against mine. I'm sure her cheeks were wet with tears. "It's kind of unimaginable to really believe that a creature exists who can love billions of mortal creatures, love and care for and guide each and every one. My mind just won't fit over the numbers."

"You're making me sad, Eve," I mumbled. "I think we were talking about how beautiful the night sky is, with all the stars shining on us, turning the black dome velvety and soft, and the wispy clouds floating our way from the horizon, like bits of lace from a bride's veil. And the warm breeze. And the chirping of the tree frogs and an occasional cricket. And the way you cuddle against me. And...."

"You're right," Eve whispered in my ear, burning me with her heat. Her hand dropped softly onto my chest. Her fingers tiptoed along my flesh, over my belly, down to where my manhood stirred with pleasurable anticipation.

I rolled onto my side and let my hands imitate hers, on her flesh. Soon our bodies were once again straining under the guidance of fingers and sweaty palms. Eve moaned deeply. Her lower body surged upward, demanding, again, and again. I vaguely felt her hand caressing my erection. I returned the caresses. Her moaning became a symphonic background for my mounting pleasure. I rolled over. We fused into one. The soundless music reached a crescendo, rising inexorably heavenward.

Later, lethargically, we dressed and made ready to walk home. I felt that I had entered Eden, worn myself out in the process, and must now return to the dialectical world of human mortality and need.

14

And then Eve met the Dog Man. He lived a couple of miles southeast of the city limits in a ramshackle two-room shanty. The cabin's roof was a hodgepodge of varicolored, varitype shingles and irregular tin patches. One wall consisted of mixed stones and bricks piled helter-skelter on top of each other and kept in place with mortar, baling wire and pieces of tin ranging from a few inches to several feet in length and width. The other three walls consisted mostly of wood, with tarpaper, tin, or wooden patches applied here and there as needed. The result was unique, kind of like a child's toy house mended by the child and his friends with whatever materials they could scrounge from the town dump, or possibly like some of the poorer shanties in Mexico and other third-world countries.

Irregular wood poles and stumps, some sticking out of the earth like clumps of spiky hair after a restless night on the pillow, others attached semi-horizontally, more or less; concrete blocks, some piled loosely, others stuck together with globs of cement; several straggly saplings; a couple of thorny bushes; and sections of wire fence standing alone or interwoven with the other materials seemingly from some comic-horror flick—all formed an ambiguously trigonometric enclosure around the cabin. Inside the enclosure no plant survived on the rocky dirt. Outside the fence, weeds and underbrush struggled for supremacy as far as the edge of the clearing. Beyond that the dirt lane, barely wide enough for the Dog Man's bicycle contraption, continued to twist like a sidewinder for a couple hundred yards through primal woods, from what passed as the gate of the perimeter fence to the gravel road that led to town. The rotting, primeval woods surrounded cabin and weed garden, a dank, gloomy place where all living matter flourished on the carcasses of their own kind, the only potential escape to the heavens above hovering weakly in the occasional ray of sunshine caressing the middle of the winding lane.

The Dog Man lived in the cabin. His dogs, mongrels of uncertain temperaments, shapes and sizes, lived in the enclosure and in the cabin also except for the warmest days and nights of the year, at which time they were locked out of the latter.

The dogs raised an infernal racket day and night. Any movement, any noise—the least disturbance within several miles of their acute hearing set them off, although I don't think they needed anything except their own boredom to stimulate their vocal chords most of the time or, as one local wag used to insist, to wind up their barking mechanisms.

The entire menagerie invariably accompanied their master on his periodic rounds of Echo Creek. The master rode a bicycle that had probably been new several years before WWI and had possibly seen extended service in the South Pacific during the second world conflict, where it had contacted some unknown type of malarial fungus that had devoured its paint and the fluid in most of its joints, leaving it as creaky and spavined as Don Quixote's

Rocinante, not to mention as rusty and rheumatic as the cart the Dog Man towed behind the bicycle. This cart was one of those high-wheeled things that squealed and shrieked between Santa Fe, New Mexico and Independence, Missouri during the early nineteenth century, carrying trade goods in both directions over the old Santa Fe Trail. How the contraption made it all the way east to Echo Creek, though, is a real puzzler, but not more so than how it survived considerably more than a century of use and weather. The Dog Man claimed that it was a family heirloom, the only one, in fact, passed down through the generations of Dog Men until he inherited it from his father. If a person can credit his veracity, which is questionable, he brought it east with him when, after his parents died, he returned to the original family estate to live out the remainder of his life, by family estate meaning the two-acre clearing in which his cabin crouched during my youth. Of course there are no extant historical records with which he has ever been able to verify his claim.

He believed that the universe was circular in essence, as was evident in the eternal cycles of day and night, winter and summer, hot and cold, love and hate, life and death, body and spirit, the planetary spheres, and by all means the eternal expansion and contraction of the universe itself (which he still believed in in spite of all evidence and theory to the contrary). He believed that those people who best lived by the universal model became one with the divine principle and thus one with the divine spirit—they earned their place in the eternal paradise.

So the Dog Man completed the circle for his family by back-trailing from west of the Mississippi to Echo Creek. I never got around to asking him where his ancestors had come from before Echo Creek, and before that, and why he hadn't gone there. Most of my neighbors would gladly have paid his way.

And thus, in line with the same principles, it came to pass that several times a week for as long as I can recall the Dog Man made his rounds of the town, usually in the early afternoon. He rode perched high on the extended seat of his two-wheeled contraption, crooked back relatively straight and dirty hands gripping handlebars raised well above the norm by a long, thin pipe. He sported shoulder-length, thin oily black hair topped by an unwashed beaver hat ostensibly inherited from one of his mountain-man ancestors, a gray-flecked beard last trimmed the day his hat was trapped (about the same time the cart was roaming to and fro along the Santa Fe Trail, I always suspected), a fringed buckskin shirt of the same period as the hat, baggy, holey pants of indeterminate color and age, and high-topped sneakers dyed by the dirt and feces in his dog enclosure.

Behind him, tied to the bicycle contraption with ropes and chains, screeched his cart. And the dogs? A few of the smaller, yappier kind always rode in a wire basket draped over the handlebars. Others, yappies and more medium-sized mutts, rode in the cart. There were so many of them that I always wondered how the Dog Man had managed to stuff them all in without suffocating a half dozen or so. They bobbed up and down, fighting to get their noses above the sideboards so they could bark at anything moving nearby, like a colony of prairie dogs herded into a single small hole that had been sprayed with jalapenos run through a blender. The bigger dogs led, followed, and flanked cart and bicycle. They were tied to the contraption and cart with ropes that spurted in all 360 directions like spokes to some Cubist's rendering of a wheel. They added the staccato, thudding bass and the smooth-flowing tenor to the altos and trebles of their mates. What with the shrieking of bicycle and cart (the wheels of the latter never seeming to have been oiled or greased in my memory), the discordant barking, and the boisterous songs the Dog Man sang as he pedaled up and down the streets of Echo Creek—well, I think most citizens would have gladly traded the circus they had in their streets for a daily mock battle between twenty or so divisions of tanks and artillery. The noise level would have been more sufferable.

Of course, there was the accompanying chorus from the hundreds of dogs scattered around town, in homes and back yards, a chorus rising and falling like ocean waves as the menagerie passed through the streets.

Many citizens, the dog-some and the dog-less ones, complained about the noise to the authorities. But after having often thrown the Dog Man into jail cells, along with drunks, petty thieves, and a juvenile delinquent or two, and suffered the indignation and lawsuits that followed, and after having seen the havoc a well-trained company of dogs can cause in an otherwise peaceful, and controllable, dog pound—the city council, the mayor, and the chief of police agreed to ignore the citizen complaints and the street noise, hoping against hope that the lawyers had been satiated by their damned lawsuits in favor of pound and inmates and every citizen who caught a headache or the "insufferable aggravations," as the media called it, from the noisy pack of mongrels, or whose pets had suffered psychological trauma because one man's dogs were allowed to roam the city streets barking to their heart's content while they themselves were not. Our city politicos had no doubts that the generally silent, long-suffering majority would soon enough become tired of complaining and revert to their normal complacency. All our leaders had to do was shut up and wait, which was a heck of a lot easier than speaking or acting without actually having said or done anything, and loads safer politically.

So, they reverted to no comment or pled ignorance to public questions about the Dog Man and his pack of noise makers. And, as any intelligent person would expect, their problem disappeared except in the vocal chords of a few of our more prominent cranks and, of course, in the continued parade of the Dog Man, his mechanical contraptions, and his dog pack. Doubtlessly the majority of our citizens simply got tired of interrupting their daily activities to complain and then fill out the three or four hundred forms public complaints required before they became official and could thus be acted upon, not to mention the one hundred ninety-nine forms all citizens had to complete before a public servant could even listen to their complaints, or the hundred exactly they had to fill out before they could even get through the doors of the court house.

Eventually, as is generally the case in a democratic society such as ours, a group of concerned citizens formed under the leadership of one Paul Tall, a man who had unsuccessfully run for mayor of Echo Creek every election since he turned twenty-one, as an independent and with no financial or political backing except what his own wallet and ego provided. At the time he formed the Committee against Frivolous and Unnecessary Noise on Our Streets (notice the avoidance of in our yards or houses, clearly a ruse to allay the fears of pet owners), Mr. Tall was in his nineties.

The committee ran into a brick wall, or rather several of them. Early on, it was successful in pressuring the Town Council to approve an ordinance banning excessive noise in the city streets unless specifically licensed by the town marshal. Motorized vehicles, children, and the marching bands of the high school and college were exempted, as were football rallies and such.

The problem appeared resolved. But the Dog Man sued. He claimed the prohibition interfered with his religious beliefs. His daily romp through the streets of Echo Creek, he insisted, was the result of a directive from God. In order to obtain personal salvation he needed to make his daily round-trip pilgrimage, with a different, specific route each day of the week. In order to save mankind in general (including the multitude of sinners already condemned to the flames) he had to ride his two-wheeled contraption, pull his cart, and be accompanied by his dogs.

Our city fathers snickered at the childish simplicity of the lawsuit. They had no doubts but that it would be thrown out of court as frivolous. They didn't reckon with the power of the media, however. Papa Lizardus' media empire, as per usual, had seconded what it considered the majority of the town's citizens, thus portraying the Dog Man as a nut case, simple and unthreatening but a lunatic nevertheless, until one of their more thoughtful supervisors realized that the vast majority of Echo

Creek's citizens were pet owners, most of those dog owners. At first many of those citizens had been in the forefront of the anti-Dog Man movement, but they began to feel threatened by what they saw as creeping no-noise legislation, a law that just might move from the streets to their yards and eventually into their homes. Their dogs barked. They barked in their own yards, sometimes in the neighbors' yards. They barked in their homes, too often with the doors and windows open. They needed to bark, to blow off steam and express their dogness, something all dog owners know but try to keep from the rest of us. Any city laws threatening a dog's right to bark on its own property inhibited all dogs' rights to be dogs—think like dogs, act like dogs, feel like dogs. The good pet-owning citizens turned against their legally-elected authorities. Ballot rebellion was in the offing. Fear stalked city hall. Letters poured in to the media and the government. The Lizardus media empire made an about face. The Dog Man became their poster child.

Almost immediately he became a national celebrity as well. Within days pictures of him and his menagerie, along with an in-depth two-sentence analysis of his conflict with city hall, had appeared in every newspaper and on every newscast in the nation. Innumerable organizations rallied to his cause, the most well-known and thus the most powerful being the national Animal Rights Formation (ARF), the Committee on the Right to Personal Spiritual Expression (CORPSE), an international group with headquarters in both Washington and Tehran, and the ACLU.

At the same time, the lawyer representing the city in its on-going battle against the Dog Man resigned. He, Ura Shill, was a dog-owner and he too began to feel threatened. Almost as importantly, though, he learned of the imminent involvement of ARF and CORPSE on the Dog Man's side of the conflict. He didn't like to lose. He had dogs of his own, as his neighbors would attest to, and not necessarily with good humor. Moreover he didn't want to fight the two national organizations he most admired. So he did what was best for everyone concerned. He pled conflict of interest and quit.

The court approved the Dog Man's petition, as did the appellate and state supreme courts. Mr. Tall, his committee, and the city (represented by a total of only one Town Council member by that time; the others had gone into hiding) lost each step of the way. Eventually the town marshal was forced to issue a license to the Dog Man on grounds that the state had no right to interfere with a man's religion and that pets had certain inalienable rights which governments and individuals could not deny them. Under advice of ex-council Lawyer Shill, the city quickly rescinded the anti-noise law. Barking again became legal, and continuous, whether the Dog Man rode the streets or not. The majority opinion of the Supreme Court found that, in their own way and by reason of their unique and special relationship to humans, dogs have an inalienable right to citizenship, natural or naturalized, and to all of its benefits as expressed in the Constitution. Naturally there was no mention of responsibilities. Furthermore, the Court determined that barking is a form of expression, as natural for dogs as speech is for humans. Thus, to deny dogs the right to bark in any way or form they wished would be akin to denying humans the right to speak their minds.

Inasmuch as the Constitution guarantees our human citizens the inalienable right to freedom of speech, our dog citizens are ipso facto guaranteed the right to freedom of bark.

So the Dog Man and his menagerie continued their circular trips just as I continued my sporadic growth into and through childhood.

I think I was four or five, still immersed in childhood but trying to outrun it, when I first met the Dog Man. That day I had run away from home, not driven by an irrepressible call to adventure, as I would like to claim, but by several belt-strokes on my backside, belt-strokes which in turn were caused by my stubborn insistence on tormenting a younger sister. Wounded and furious, I shouted that I was leaving and wouldn't be back—forever.

"You'll be back when you get hungry," Dad laughed.

Angered even worse by his apparent lack of concern, I stormed from the house, muttering threats about joining up with some wild Indian tribe or terrorist organization, or a traveling circus, and a dozen other threats that flashed into my mind. For what seemed hours I wandered aimlessly up and down the town streets, ultimately winding up out in the country, lost.

And I met the Dog Man. He was headed to town with his menagerie. I was roaming the outskirts, frantically trying to find my way home. I had had enough of the running away bit and, besides, I was hungry and thirsty.

At first it seemed to me that I had walked smack-dab into a circus parade. An unwashed, bearded clown led on a bicycle with the front wheel a little larger than the rear one and a seat perched on what looked like the top two or three feet of a flag pole. Dogs of all shapes and sizes cavorted around him, barking and growling, playing or fighting as their tempers dictated at any given moment.

I froze in the middle of the road.

The Dog Man somehow halted the rapid advance of machines and beasts before they ran me down, although at the last moment there was some doubt as to whether I would be, first, deafened and, second, eaten alive by the horde before being squashed by the two contraptions.

"Do you stand in the middle of the road when a car is coming?" he asked me once the noise level subsided.

I think I shook my head no.

"So why didn't you get out of the way when you saw me and mine coming?"

I must have shrugged, idiotically perhaps.

"Can you talk?"

"I'm going to school this year," I volunteered, then immediately began to doubt my certainty and added, "or next year."

"Maybe you'll learn to come in out of the rain," he muttered as he dismounted and stood staring at the outskirts of the town behind me. "And maybe not. Kids don't seem to develop any commonsense in the schools nowadays. But what the hell, you can't teach commonsense if you don't have any yourself, or if it's a rare commodity in the culture you live in, can you?" His beard parted in what I took for a grin. I felt more comfortable in his presence. "What's your name, boy?"

His eyes clamped onto mine as he spoke. His pupils were round, shiny marbles of the purist ebony surrounded by white circles. His lashes and brows were as shaggy as his hair and beard, almost as black as his pupils. What I could see of his skin, on his nose and upper cheeks, around his eyes and on the backs of his hands, seemed grey in the sunlight, maybe from ground-in dirt, maybe not.

"Donald?" he mused to my mumbled answer. "Where do you live, Donald?"

I motioned behind me.

"That's a lot of help," he grumbled. "Do you mean you live in town?"

I nodded.

"Where in town?"

He was staring at what little could be seen of Echo Creek under its canopy of trees.

"We live on the edge of town," my mind began to function again, recovering from the shock of encountering such an alien spectacle.

"Well, boy," he groused, "there are four sides to this damned town, as there are to most towns that I've had any experience of. Which side of Echo Creek do you live on?"

I stared at him, trying to correlate his question to my limited knowledge.

"North, east, west or south, boy?" he pointed with each word, his voice rising as he spoke.

His frustration released me from my paralysis. My mind had experience facing frustration. Besides, I thought that maybe his finger had pointed toward my house when he said west.

"West."

He studied me more closely.

"Yeah," he said, "I think I've seen you by that old two-story building that appears ready to give up the ghost any day."

The next thing I knew I flew upward and landed on his shoulders. He grabbed my ankles. I grabbed his hair to keep from tilting backward. He clambered over the railing and into the cart, to the angry protest of every dog in there, and to mine, although mine was loaded with fear rather than anger because I thought he was going to feed me to his pack of mongrels. The little ones couldn't reach my feet and legs, but they made valiant efforts. The larger ones didn't seem to think I would make much of a feast. They ignored me. But a few of those in between sank a tooth or two in my shoes, and at least one must have nipped the Dog Man's hands because he began to curse and flail with his boots and an occasional fist. Every time he let go of one of my feet to punch some dog in the muzzle I tilted to one side or the other and squealed like a wild pig being ravaged by coyotes.

I began to realize that he wasn't planning on feeding me to his beasts, but at the same time I became terrified that they were going to make a meal of me in spite of his efforts. At one time or another during the melee, upwards of two animals were dangling from one of my feet, a tooth caught in the canvas or in a shoe string, writhing, growling, and twisting to free themselves, swinging wildly as the Dog Man whirled.

Eventually, however, he brought the entire pack under control and deposited me safely among them, which sent my heart to yammering again until I realized that I had become accepted as just another one of the dogs. So I rode the streets of Echo Creek in the Dog Man's cart. Most people ignored us. A few, though, gawked and pointed when they became aware that I wasn't really a dog, but a human kid, which eventually led to some of our younger admirers realizing who I was and spreading the news. By the time we traversed less than half the Dog Man's route, we had a following of two or three dozen kids of varied ages, sizes, and lung capacity, shouting and pointing. I felt like a circus freak or a kidnapped follower of the Pied Piper. There was no escape, no room to hunker down and hide from the taunting crowd behind the sides of the cart. Every square inch was taken up by four-legged critters and a lot of those inches by critter excrement that the idiot brutes didn't seem to mind tracking around. They soon began to accept me not only as one of them but as a friend to all, jumping all over me and licking my face and hands as an expression of friendship, more often than not right after they had taken a taste of the free excrement.

To me it seemed hours later, after a circuitous route through the side streets of Echo Creek, that the Dog Man deposited me by the curb in front of my home. I must have passed muster because, before taking his leave, he invited me to accompany him on his spiritual rounds the next day, or any other day I wished.

"You're also welcome to come visiting us any time you want," he added with a movement of his beard that I took for a smile. After a long-winded explanation of how to get to his home, he ended with, "My friends like you."

I accepted his invitation the very next week, when I decided to run away again. Why? I haven't the slightest idea, but doubtlessly it had to do with one of my periodic memory lapses or temper tantrums, both of which weren't always unintentional. Or should I rather say they weren't always deliberate?

Anyhow it was a nice day, I think. I don't know whether I slunk off noticed or unnoticed, or was given an amiable, scoffing sendoff by my mother and sisters. But somehow I stumbled on the Dog Man's driveway in one piece and with my flesh intact, in spite of the multitude of other people's dogs that challenged my right to the public streets, alleys, and roadways—and without getting lost more than a half dozen times; luckily most people knew where he lived and were willing to point me in the right direction, in spite of the suspicious looks they gave me.

The Dog Man was home. So was his pack of semi-feral animals. The latter greeted me with gusto, or hunger, or some such feeling when I turned into the lane. Our leaders, or should that be rulers, probably heard the greeting in the state capital, if they weren't talking, which would be a rarity. A few moments after the racket began the owner of the dingoes, or dingbats or whatever you want me to call them…the Dog Man appeared in the doorway of his hut, preceded by that friendly, toothless grin of his, a grin which could turn into an icy glare when crossed.

"Well, young Johnson, what brings you to this Eden I've created?" he shouted over the hullabaloo as he crossed the compound.

I explained, proudly, that I'd run away from home, but I don't think he heard me, or cared at all. He was too busy shouting, kicking and swatting, and the barking meter had soared too high. In any case, he eventually cleared a snarling path to the rickety gate, somehow forced it open without letting any of the wild animals loose, and snatched me into the enclosure and onto his shoulders before I lost a pound of flesh. His dogs liked me, he had said, but I disagreed and so did the dogs until they seemed to once again recognize me.

Torturously we made our way to the door of his cabin, and so began my understanding of the Dog Man as well as my friendship with him, I like to think. The interior of the cabin was as primitive as the exterior. The logs which formed the ceiling and walls had been caulked with wads of insulation, packing debris, old newspapers, tarpaper, and many other things you could find in a city dump, all glued or nailed in place, depending, I suppose, on what could be bought, scrounged or stolen at the time of constructing that specific part of the interior. Much of the debris, including what covered the floor, had been in turn covered with slats from orange crates, boards, some of which might have been purchased, a thin, wrinkled layer of tin in the corner that held a bedroll, and one huge, flat piece of metal that must have once covered a hole in some roadway, to keep vehicles from falling through, but which at that time functioned as the Dog Man's reading space, holding an ancient, mangled recliner, a rusted floor lamp run off a generator of some primitive make, a wooden box which served as magazine rack and bookshelf for the few books, magazines, and other items the owner had been able to pilfer, and a stool, as well as a vintage 1940s tv tray which the Dog Man had turned into a table for eating, writing, sewing, and anything else he might consider necessary.

I didn't visit long that first time. The Dog Man had his rounds to make and I had arrived just as he was preparing to depart.

So, after a rousing tour of Echo Creek, he and his pack of mongrels left me precisely where I had begun the day, at my home. Nobody there seemed to have been affected, negatively or otherwise, by my absence.

But back to the Dog Man, I heard the story of his life more than once or twice. He enjoyed talking about himself, which is not by a long shot the rarest characteristic of any human creature I've ever met.

He began life in an adobe cabin deep in the mountains of New Mexico. His sire several removed was the last standing in a long line of mountain men, his mother, again several removed, the only survivor of the Saguarito Apaches, a once populous group of nomads roaming our Southwest until decimated by the white man's largesse. The two lovers and eventual spouses met the first day of a blue moon many, many suns ago when Jake 'Grey Wolf' Smith, the sire of the Dog Man's great, great grandfather—one day when Jake appeared in Cactus Thorn's village on his Shetland stallion, his head high and his desire iron hard after a winter alone in his primitive mountain cabin. His annual catch, the pelts of two muskrats and an ancient otter with mange, rode in a ball on his pack pony, the stallion's mate.

Cactus Thorn was the only child of the then village chief, Big Bear (named for the size of his girth), although she was not heir apparent because of her gender, in spite of the chief's many attempts to promote her to the position since it entailed a hefty salary that the chief could have confiscated and used to buy another wife, one more amenable to taking orders than his other three, and one young and new enough to once again infuse his male tool with a proud vigor befitting a chief. Many hot and frigid suns had passed since he had had the wherewithal to pleasure his wives; of course he blamed them for having lost their luster as the years of their marriage passed.

Big Bear and Grey Wolf quickly became friends, so quickly in fact that suspicion ran rampant through the village about the nature of their relationship. For a few months Grey Wolf became known as Wrong Way Man, not to his face of course, which would have been fatal for the name-caller, but behind his back and only for a few months until, to cement their friendship and purchase the hand, and the rest, of Cactus Thorn, Grey Wolf gave Big Bear three horses (which along with several members of Big Bear's band, he had stolen from a neighboring tribe), a mountain lion skin (which he had won in an arm-wrestling contest), a fourth wife (who had come into his possession via a poker pot, poker being one of the games he taught the men of the village during the long winter months), and a virtually bald raccoon-skin cap (which Grey Wolf had taken from a long-dead raccoon, one that had died of old age after a long bout with mange).

The friendship between the two men, however, didn't last long. Big Bear soon tired of his new bride. It seems that, after the first few times, after the sheen of newness wore off, he couldn't get an erection with her no matter how hard she tried. He decided that she could better serve him at the cook fire. His other three wives were lousy cooks, so he had put them to other chores, like keeping his tepee clean as well as warm in the winter and cool in the summer, making sure his stock of arrows was continuously replenished and his bow was mended when necessary and his knife sharpened, and earning a living wage out on the back alleys of the village, in order to help with the family finances.

The problem he faced with this fourth wife was that she refused to work. She expected to be pampered—treated as a lady whose beauty and desirability were sufficient in and of themselves. She expected, nay, demanded, that Big Bear bring home not only the bacon but also the bread and all the other necessities that befitted a lady of her worth, not to mention a family the size of his.

Well, you can surely imagine Big Bear's reaction to his new lady's demands. He was no shrinking violet. Hmmm, or was that henpecked husband?

Anyhow, Big Bear had his image to protect. Elections were coming up. He needed to portray himself as the loyal husband till death. At the same time, though, nobody, neither the tribe's braves nor its squaws wanted a wimp for a chief. What they wanted was a loyal husband and father who was, at the same time, a man among men. Their chief had to be a man who could keep all his wives satisfied (but no other women—a fairly difficult task in both cases), could and would romp with his children (no matter how smelly and icky), could keep peace in his family and in the village (with an iron fist for those who sought vengeance and a carrot for those who exuded mercy from every pore), stood among the hawks as the epitome of warlike valor (belonged at the least to one militia or warrior society) and, at the same time, represented the tribal totem of justice and compassion.

Big Bear appointed one of the biggest braves of the village to give his new bride fifty lashes with a half inch, in diameter, willow switch. Then, before the lady could recover, he ordered the same man to take her back to her family. Her family consisted of a crippled old man, even older than Big Bear and considerably weaker, and his one wife, a fat squaw who couldn't have caught a possum playing dead.

And finally, when his wife was safely out of his tepee, Big Bear took a case of homemade brew and scurried off into the wilderness to do penance for his sins. But before he left the village he called a village meeting of all able-bodied voters and expressed his compassion for his ex-bride, told them in a long rambling speech how his decision weighed so heavily on his emotional state that he needed time alone in the wilderness, because of the tears he needed to shed and because of the need to beg God's compassion for a decision that had cost him so terribly much of his soul.

Well, to make a long story short, Big Bear lost his election. Before he could take vengeance on Grey Wolf, however, whom he blamed for his failure, the latter fled the village with Cactus Thorn and lost himself and his new companion in the wilderness, where eventually he settled down, took up farming, and raised a family, which included the Dog Man's great, great grandfather, or so the Dog Man said. It was not until many moons later when he and Cactus Thorn learned that her village had been wiped out by smallpox.

15

And so one Sunday afternoon Eve met the Dog Man. The two of us came across him as he was headed to town for his pilgrimage. We were walking the country road that passed his lane. He was exiting the lane. Several of his more vicious pets must have decided that Eve smelled like a good morsel of flesh, or maybe they were just hungry, or, more to the point, maybe they wanted to make a human sacrifice to their gods, it being Sunday and they being on a religious pilgrimage. Whatever the reason, a half dozen of the mongrels lunged. Eve squealed. I bellowed (fear? valor?). The Dog Man lunged with fists and boots. The dogs yelped and settled back on their haunches. Eve relaxed and gave us what seemed a forced smile. I breathed a sigh of relief at not having to rescue fair maiden. I think the Dog Man grinned proudly, or maybe scornfully, under that heavy beard of his.

"Don't worry, young lady. The dogs have devoured a couple of our fattest councilmen already this week; they're no longer hungry. Besides," he added, chuckling, "they don't really like human flesh. They prefer pigs and sheep and cattle and maybe an occasional pet cat or dog from my neighbors, town and country. They especially like the pets of the town leaders, or so I'm told."

He was referring to the dogs of a couple town council members. The dogs had both disappeared without a trace and rumors ran rampant that the Dog Man's animals had enticed the pets to follow them into the woods surrounding the Dog Man's cabin and there devoured the innocent creatures. Both incidents had been followed by full-blown investigations, including extensive searches of the Dog Man's cabin and surrounding woods. Nothing had been found, but that didn't stop the rumors of course. Nor did it stop the Dog Man's resultant lawsuit, which was eventually thrown out of court because he insulted the judge, calling him by his first name more than once, even after having been admonished several times to address the bench more formally.

After his explanation, and my introduction of the two, the Dog Man invited Eve and me to his cabin, for a bottle of pop and for him and Eve to get acquainted. I tried to beg off, having other plans for Eve, but she appeared fascinated by the man and his menagerie.

"Hey," I interjected facetiously, "you were setting forth on your daily prayer circle, weren't you? We don't want to interfere with divine plans of any kind. We don't want to get in trouble with your gods."

"In spite of all the hype I get…in spite of everything I tell people, including you, one of the major reasons I go on my jaunts through town is that the dogs need to run and bark off some excess energy, that and the fictional religious-prayer thing I invented in my desire to torment the good townspeople. But the dogs can run and bark at the town dogs tomorrow, and a man doesn't have to pray every day. No divinity, be He, She, It real or created, if you'll pardon a reverse pun, needs or even wants that much adoration. They doubtlessly get fed up with our continual crying for their attention as it is and probably feel a sense of relief whenever we skip a religious ritual, no matter what the reason. So, to placate our own souls rather than those of whatever gods are watching over us at the moment, we can return to my home and get acquainted."

He studied Eve for a few moments. She preened, as was her wont when some male, any male worthy of attention himself, showed her more than a passing notice. Or am I possibly chewing sour grapes here.

"I'd really love to see your cabin," Eve answered his invitation.

And so the Dog Man turned his circus parade around and we followed him home. The dogs didn't seem any more enthusiastic about the change in plans than I did, except that I kept my irritation to myself and they howled and growled theirs. "Are you two an item?" the Dog Man asked Eve once we had all settled ourselves in his hut, Eve on the ancient recliner; the owner on the wooden box that served as a magazine rack; and I on the floor.

"Sometimes," Eve shrugged, smirking in my direction. "Why?"

"Just curious," the Dog Man eyed her thoughtfully. "I think I've seen the two of you walking in the area more than once, holding hands like Romeo and Juliet. And Donjon, he seems to have matured a lot recently, become surer of himself," he grinned widely, "and strutting around proudly as if he thinks he's a man now, and not being as willing to take my advice as he used to be." He ended the last two phrases with a deep chuckle, meeting my eyes as he did so. "Not that most thinking creatures would consider that a bad thing."

His words sent a hot flood surging through my body. I could feel my face turning rosy red.

I started to speak but Eve did so before I could collect my thoughts.

"I've heard a lot about you," she looked directly at the Dog Man, ignoring me. "You're probably Echo Creek's most famous oddball."

"You really mean the most notorious, don't you?" The Dog Man actually preened as he spoke.

"Probably. I started to say infamous, but I decided to be polite," Eve laughed comfortably.

"I can easily imagine what all you've heard," the Dog Man laughed with her. "I'm the great rebel, Satan right here on earth. People scare their naughty children into behaving by mentioning my name. I break their silly laws with impunity because I have no ethical or moral values and their courts are too cowardly or corrupt to do anything about it. If a dog or cat, or some other pet, disappears, blame it on the Dog Man. If one of their pets loses control and attacks someone, man or boy, woman or girl, I'm to blame because I wander around town all the time with my dogs, getting their pets so worked up that they can never settle down. It's a wonder more people aren't attacked and even killed. It's a wonder babies aren't attacked in their cribs, women in their kitchens, men in their shops, whole families in their homes." The Dog Man had a huge grin plastered to his face. He was enjoying the conversation immensely.

"You like playing the role of the devil?" Eve asked in an innocent voice.

"Joke all you want, Eve, but any society, any cultural unit, has to have some common enemy in order to remain a cohesive unity. Churches have other churches of similar but different faiths. Religions have other religions as well as some character who serves as the representation of evil, evil as defined by the culture under consideration of course. Families have other families that are richer or poorer or not law-abiding, or immoral. Nations have…well, you get the picture. There's no need for me to continue lecturing on something so obvious."

"Do you have a name?" Eve changed the subject. "All I ever hear you called is the Dog Man. But I don't really want to call you that. It sounds so…, you know?"

"No, I don't know, but I can guess. You believe that it sounds demeaning."

Eve smiled and shrugged, "Only if it bothers you."

"Well, any man would prefer a more heroic, predatory-sounding nickname like Devil, Wolf, Mars, Samson or some such nonsense. But dogs are, or were, hunters, and besides, given my lifestyle, the name is appropriate. I live with dogs. I prefer living among dogs than among humans. They're much more honest about their needs and desires. They don't deal in hypocrisy by the minute. They don't expect me to carry on meaningless conversations when I'm with them, even though I don't feel like talking. I can be myself, completely. If I want to talk, I talk. They listen," his lips split in a huge grin that couldn't be covered by the unkempt beard, "although their personal hygiene as well as their comprehension level are both considerably limited, I have to admit, but that, given my own sanitary irregularities and incomprehensibly rambling nature, is probably a blessing in disguise. So, to be completely honest, no, I don't mind the nickname. Besides," he smirked, "why should I really care what a bunch of people for whom I have little respect call me?"

"Everybody cares at least a little bit what other people think about them, whether they pretend they don't or not. They're lying to themselves if they say they don't."

"Maybe. I suppose you could be right and I could by fooling myself. But I really don't think so. What I think is that way down deep you probably know better, but you've been trained—no, I should say conditioned, by an educational system more interested in turning out model citizens than thoughtful citizens, citizens who, if they do think at all, think within the box and not outside of it. Social life is kind of like those old coloring exercises where you have to stay inside the lines if you don't want to fail. You can't build even rational, logical extensions of what's already there, and color them. That's simply not the way it's done. You have to follow the rules of someone else's logic, take the same steps, and reach the same exact conclusions. If not, you'd better drop out of society and follow some other route to where you want to go, which will probably wind up leading you directly and quickly into some prison or asylum designed specifically for asocial creatures, which will thus destroy whatever plans or dreams you might have had long before they can be fulfilled."

"You're not only being terribly cynical but also a little pompous, and you're wandering way out there in left field somewhere, with a left-handed batter up to bat."

The Dog Man studied her for several moments. I was certain

that his eyes twinkled all the time. He liked nothing better than a good argument.

"Attack the speaker. It's generally more effective than dealing with the substance of what he said."

His eyes continued to twinkle but Eve didn't appear to notice.

"I'm sorry," she spoke contritely. "I didn't mean to say you're pompous, only that your reasoning seemed so. I agree that there's a lot wrong with our educational system. I really hate the waste, everybody in lock step even when they aren't learning anything anymore and really would rather be somewhere else, anywhere but where they are, studying something more applicable to their own likes than what they are studying, but they stay on because they want the good job and good life that they're sure will come with the degree they'll get if they stick around long enough, or they stay on because others who count do, or they keep plugging away because that's just the way it's done or has been done by the people who count. Education is supposed to help them learn to function in the gray areas of our world, to free them from being glued to one pole or the other, to black and white fringes of human feeling and thought. But it doesn't because most kids can't or don't want to cope with mental processes not linked to the clarity and ease of either/or, either this or that and nothing in between. Oh, the more intelligent ones believe they're learning to think, to reason, that is. But they aren't. They're learning to rationalize one party line or the other, while the others, the majority, quit thinking on their own way back in high school, or even junior high. One thing I have to admit, though, is that many of the more intelligent ones really know how to sound intelligent.

Like me," she added, a huge self-deprecatory smile lighting her eyes.

"Well," the Dog Man grinned happily, ignoring her final comment, "who's being a little pompous now, young lady? You're saying that young people by and large don't go to college to learn, and so don't learn?"

"No, that's not what I said," Eve disagreed, laughing. "I didn't mean just college. And most students learn some things in spite of themselves, because they want a diploma or degree in order to get a good job, so they have to study some. And a few really want to learn everything. But lots just want to get good grades in their major, in whatever subject matter it is they plan on doing after they graduate, and passing grades in everything else in order to graduate, but they'd really prefer not taking that other stuff. And, for most students, taking courses they aren't really interested in is a waste of money and time."

"If you really believe all of that, I can understand why you think our educational system wastes so much of our human resources," the Dog Man mused as if to himself. "If true, it's too bad. We put so much effort, so much time, money and human resources into educating our youth. With sufficient effort on the part of the kids themselves, and even more on the part of the educational system, we could easily have the most enlightened citizenry in our world, something direly needed, both here and abroad."

"That's the problem," Eve accused. "Most students, by the time they reach college, don't want to be enlightened if that means to go on studying liberal arts and sciences. Not the ones who aren't there for academic reasons anyway, and not the ones who know what they want to do in life. They want to study in their major, study what they'll be doing in the work world and to heck with all the boring general requirements. But they also want the prestige of a college degree, especially from a prestigious university, even if that means majoring in a subject they're not very interested in. Like most of us, they just go with the flow that they assume is going up the social hill. But," she smiled with what seemed to me to be self-derision at her imagery, "nothing flows uphill, does it? Except for maybe the excess of the moment, when liquid backs up a while before being forced to flow downhill again."

"What do you consider a moment?"

The Dog Man's irrelevant question was accompanied by a smirk that matched Eve's.

"I guess it's relative, isn't it?" Eve's smirk spread to her eyes, creasing her smooth forehead and causing a small dimple to appear on each cheek. I had never before noticed she had dimples. "Some moments are significant, others meaningless, like in your own life. A moment could be a long time in the history of the universe and in the history of humans, or even civilizations in general, or a thousand years might be of no significance whatsoever, so they seem short. But back to education, I've really felt sorry for all the kids that dropped out of school along the way. They always pretended they really didn't care, although you could usually tell that a lot of them were lying and too ashamed to admit it. They said things like they weren't learning anything they could use to get a good job, or use in a job after they got it. They weren't learning anything practical. Some of them even admitted that they weren't learning anything, period, except maybe in their shop or home-ec classes, or things like that."

The Dog Man started to interrupt but Eve ignored him and continued with her favorite diatribe. "But I think now that the system has betrayed them too. It didn't teach them how to do a job they could be happy doing. But the ones I never could feel sorry for are the ones that weren't learning anything but they kept going to classes anyway. I still see a lot of them in my classes here at ECU. That's where the prestige is, in taking college prep classes in high school and then going on to university," Eve's tone became sarcastic, "in preparing for a socially acceptable profession and at the very same time preparing to become a lady or gentleman out in the social world, studying the liberal arts and sciences so you can enjoy the good life in your leisure time and so you can impress the pretentious and so you can be a 'thoughtful' citizen. One who needs to be able to do something practical when they graduate?"

"Why in the world are you so bitter?" the Dog Man wondered out loud. "You've got everything a person could want—beauty, intelligence, personality, a country that tries its damndest to make your life easy. You don't just spout the normal party line. Rather you seem to think for yourself. But you seem so angry, or maybe cynical."

"I don't like waste," Eve didn't hesitate. "I don't like to see all those dropouts discarded and forgotten, especially not the ones who could have learned a trade if they'd been given the right opportunity or direction. And I don't like to see so much of our time and money being wasted on students that aren't really learning anything anymore. They're just doing enough to get by and graduate, doing that for sixteen years in some cases, when they would probably have been just as well off, financially, socially, even emotionally as well as intellectually, if they had spent ten years or so preparing for a specific career or vocation, with a few courses along the way that related the liberal arts and sciences to their major courses."

"And wind up unable to think beyond the elemental?"

"Most people can't do that anyway, even after going to high school and college. For a while after graduation they spout the few ideas they absorbed from their instructors and fellow students. Then, as time passes, they slowly absorb new ideas from colleagues, friends and television, or the internet, or they revert to the simple beliefs they had as teenagers, or that they picked up from family and friends, or a specific religious or political group. They don't read much of anything, and especially not of intellectual value, so they soon forget what little they learned in school, if they actually did learn anything. So they have all those years of education wasted, all those young lives that could have been filled with skills and knowledge that interested the kids and are needed by businesses and our country."

"You mean like the skilled trades?" I noted the mockery in the Dog Man's words. I wasn't certain, however, whom or what he was mocking, or even if it actually was scorn in his voice. His eyes seemed to deny what I thought his tone suggested. They gleamed with interest in Eve's words, or in Eve herself because of her words. I couldn't tell which. But there was no doubt that he found Eve fascinating.

"No, I don't mean just the skilled trades. There are lots of jobs in the marketplace that shouldn't require a liberal arts education—most of them actually."

"Why are you in college then? Why not get one of those jobs?"

"That's the problem, isn't it?" Eve frowned. "Or maybe I should say there are two problems. One, I've been just as indoctrinated as my peers have been. I don't want to be just a mechanic, technician, salesperson, or bookkeeper. I might have to start there, but I want to move up into management level positions. I want a good life, and that means enough money to live well. And for me that means climbing the corporate ladder to the top, or near it."

She quit talking and the Dog Man asked the obvious question, "You said there were two reasons."

Eve shrugged, "The other one is obvious. Only the exceptionally gifted or lucky get ahead in our society without a college education. It's kind of like a union card. You have one, you get to climb the ladder with the rest of the college graduates. You don't have one, you probably don't unless, like I said, you're either exceptional or very lucky."

"So, living the good life means climbing the corporate ladder to as near the top as possible. It means financial and social success. Or should I say that it is financial and social success?"

"Financial success, anyway," Even smiled. "The rest follows easily enough."

The Dog Man stared into space for several moments, letting the silence shroud the three of us. I could sense the gears working in his brain.

"Even happiness?" his question seemed almost like a plea.

"People living in huts and not having enough to eat most days, or the people who have miserable or demeaning jobs, or those who have no jobs or homes probably have a difficult time being happy, truly happy, much of the time. Oh, they'll have their high points here and there, I suppose. But life will be drudgery for them most of the time." Eve grimaced before continuing, as if what she was saying even sounded cynical to her ears. "If you're successful, though…if you have money, you don't have to live in a cramped house; you can drive one of your cars to work; you can hire someone else to do the dirty or boring things you don't like to do; you can spend more fun time with your husband and children, and friends. And you can make friends with the right people, and so can your children."

"And just who are the right people?"

I again detected a smirk in the Dog Man's voice.

A prolonged silence followed the question. Eve was no longer looking at her questioner, but rather her eyes were staring at one of the dogs asleep in a corner of the room.

"Friends are people you want to be with," her eyes focused on me. "They're from your childhood, or school, or college, or work. They're people you meet and like, and so you stay in touch with them."

"That's one thing you've said that I completely agree with," the Dog Man's voice was soft, almost tender, as if he didn't want to antagonize Eve. "Friends are people you meet that have something that attracts you to them, something in their personality, or in their mannerisms, something, but not necessarily money or social acceptance. However," he added abruptly, with another of his big grins, "I've got a problem with one of your basic assumptions. I don't see how you can blame our educational system for wasting its human resources." He held up his hand, palm outward, as Eve started to interrupt. "I'm not saying that I disagree about the waste. I mean, the whole concept of educating the masses in the liberal arts, or should I say gentlemanly arts, almost all of them through twelve years and the majority of those through four more years, is terribly wasteful, of our finances as well as our human resources. But I don't see that as an aberration. It's simply a natural outgrowth of democracy, which in turn is the logical result of an enlightened view of human social relationships. Moreover, I should also say that democracy is the only political structure I know of that even approaches being a 'humane' system of social relationships, and in that sense it is enlightened, the main reason being that it attempts to help as many of its citizens as it possibly can share in the good life, materially, politically, and intellectually. But in so doing, it becomes one of the most wasteful forms of government there is."

"What?" Eve interrupted angrily. "Why would you say such a thing?"

"Think a minute before you interrupt again," the Dog Man didn't or couldn't keep a note of irritation from creeping into his voice. "In most systems of government the majority of the citizens…the vast majority of the people are extremely poor and so, relatively speaking that is, use very little of the country's resources, social or natural, educational or financial or material, of native or foreign origin. Of course there are some other ramifications of that but I don't think they affect what I'm trying to get across here. But in a democracy there is a thriving middle class and they use a lot of resources, natural or otherwise, a lot, simply because of the numbers. And of course a great deal of what they consume is waste pure and simple, unnecessary to life, health and happiness."

He paused and stared into space as if trying to gather his thoughts before continuing.

"Now picture the natural world. Picture all the 'dust' blowing around out in space, lost, no specific destination or purpose, unless it's to give life to a larger object like a star or planet. Then picture all the stars, planets, asteroids, and comets wandering throughout space without destination or apparent purpose, unless it is to give rise to life. Picture all the plants and the animals existing on this planet without apparent purpose other than to eat and drink, expel wastes, propagate the species, and live as long as they can. And use the natural resources that keep them alive until they do die. The whole thing is pretty wasteful if you ask me. Megatons of dust just to form a few larger objects, out of which one in millions might give rise to life. And the living creatures themselves? What's their purpose? Just to live as long as they can? Or is it to eventually give rise to thinking creatures such as ourselves? Even if there is purpose in evolution and that is precisely the creation of us thinking creatures, how terribly wasteful that evolution has to go through so much meaninglessness just to create us." He grinned sardonically. "So we can be by far the most wasteful of all. Now that is truly ironic. And it's much, much more ironic if there is a god who created all of this so he could judge us worthy or not of a place in heaven.

"We humans are the most wasteful of all God's creations. We don't simply use the bare minimum to stay alive. We fatten the calf so we can eat it too, even when we're not hungry or are terribly overweight. Oh, not so much the poor people in the poor countries. They have to eat the calf before fattening. And they have to divide the meat with so many others that they themselves don't get fat either. But not so in a democracy with an advanced middle class! They eat their share and then much of what in all fairness should have gone to the poor people. So, to me, it only stands to reason that our educational system wastes so much of our resources. I would find it astonishing if it didn't because that is really what we are, the ultimate naturally profligate products of a naturally profligate universe. Too bad that our being thinking creatures hasn't led us to transcend the box (or lines) we exist in and somehow put a screeching halt to much, if not all, of our waste."

"I don't see most living creatures as wasteful," Eve interrupted.

The Dog Man shrugged, "Taken individually, I don't suppose they are. I mean, most carnivores kill when they're hungry and, if they don't eat all of their kill, the scavengers will. So I guess you can say that, in that sense, nature is not wasteful at all. But the individual body doesn't use everything it eats. Some is excreted as waste. And procreation? Look at the waste in sperm. And what's the purpose of the individual members of a species anyhow, other than to propagate the species, which has little or no purpose in existence as far as I can see? Individuals are born, and they die, and in between those two events they eat, sleep, urinate, defecate, fornicate and search for more food. And when they have some leisure time, they play or lie around. And what's the purpose of all this, I repeat, because I believe that, without purpose other than prolongation of the life of the individual or propagation of the species, the whole thing is a waste, a terrible waste."

"Just because you don't see a purpose is no reason there isn't one," I chimed in with my first comment since we had arrived at the Dog Man's cabin, sensing the pomposity in my words as I spoke them.

Eve and the Dog Man smiled at me in unison, as they would have at a child of their loins who had not yet reached the age of reason.

The conversation deteriorated into talk about mutual acquaintances until the Tynsdale brothers were mentioned.

"I don't know Reno," the Dog Man said, "although I've heard of him. But I do know Ron."

"They're my cousins," Eve told him.

"Oh?" my friend responded, an odd catch in his voice. I thought he started to say something more. He opened his mouth and an odd anger lit his eyes for a moment. But then he remained silent, glancing intently at me as if he expected me to add my two cents to the conversation.

I didn't say anything, of course, because at that time I didn't have any idea about Eve's real relationship to the two Tynsdale brothers.

"How do you know Ronald?" Eve finally shattered the silence.

"I exaggerated when I told you that I know him," the Dog Man responded slowly. "I know he's on the board of the Echo

Creek National Bank. I know that he's been one of the instigators in at least two of the legal actions against me and my dogs. And I've had several, uh, verbal clashes with the man, one of which turned into something of a pushing match before it was over. I don't much care for his attitude. He seems to think that I'm some kind of filth that should be shot and thrown on the city dump. On the other hand," his teeth showed through his beard and his eyes sparkled in one of his derisive grins, "I think he's a card-carrying member of the horde of usurious leeches that infest modern society."

I could see that his words hurt Eve. He too noticed the hurt and anger in her eyes.

"I'm sorry," he apologized. "I didn't realize how close you are to him. But you wouldn't want me to lie about my feelings, would you? Besides," he continued with a return of his toothy grin, "if you asked Tynsdale about me, I doubt he'd say anything positive. In fact, if he was aware that you had come to my luxurious abode," he waved his hand, his mocking grin showing even more teeth than before, "he might again attack me on the streets of Echo Creek. He has an uncontrollable temper, as he showed after our last legal confrontation, one that doesn't seem to abate until he turns it loose on what he considers its cause."

16

Eve and I headed for home a short while after the Dog Man made his comments. She was not in a very good mood. And neither was I. My plans for the afternoon had been destroyed by our meeting with the Dog Man. The pleasure Eve had received from her discussion had been destroyed by his comments about Ronald Tynsdale. After a few minutes walking together down the lane and then along the road, I gave up on attempting to restore my plans to our agenda. Although we had a little over an hour before Eve had to be home to get ready for work, I could see that she was in no mood for any lovey-dovey moves from me. So I gritted my teeth, promised myself that another chance would come along some other time, and pretended the world and all in it were hunky-dory.

"If he knew Ronald better he wouldn't have such a negative opinion of him," she growled when I asked her what she thought of the Dog Man. "Ronald is a successful banker. He gives to charity. He's active in at least three social clubs that I know of. He's a popular leader in his church. He has a family and a nice home. He's…what does your friend have but an old cabin and a bunch of mongrels?"

She was angry. I kept my face straight and my lungs from forcing a series of chuckles out of my throat, even though her temper tantrum tickled my funny bone. It wasn't easy.

"You're right. It doesn't look like he's got anything. But he must get money from somewhere. He doesn't work. But he supports himself and all those dogs. He's got a fridge out back, in a lean-to, that's always stocked with food. And the shelves in the lean-to are always jam-packed with dog food, and human food too. So he doesn't starve. And," I added, "the rumor mongers say that he's got lots of money in banks around the state. He must have some since he's had good lawyers every time the city or somebody has taken him to court. Besides, he's happy. What more can a guy ask?"

"Maybe he's on the government dole somehow," she snarled.

"I don't know," I mumbled.

She grunted but made no other comment. We walked on in silence until we reached the Carson house. When we approached the steps to the porch, she suddenly pecked me on the right cheek, bounced up the steps without a word, and slipped into the dark house. I stood quietly, alone, for a moment, unable to move, watching first her and then the shadowy doorway into which she had disappeared. Then, my thoughts as selfishly forlorn as the night air, I turned and crept off into the darkness broken only by an occasional gloomy puddle from a streetlight or a circus-lit home.

The following day Eve phoned. The next evening she and I had a date for dinner and a late movie. She reminded me of our plans. She also reminded me that her cousin Mr. Ronald Tynsdale drove to Echo Creek on business several times a month. When he did, he stayed over to spend the evening with her. And, to put the arsenic-laced icing on the cake, he would be in town the next day, which meant that he would expect to spend the evening with his cousin, which meant that the late movie Eve and I had planned would no longer be on the agenda and that Ronald would be joining us for dinner.

We had agreed to eat at Armando's Ristorante, the best and most expensive Italian restaurant in Echo Creek, although not by any means *the* most expensive of the city's dining establishments. Neither of us could afford the place, but we had decided to pool our pennies and splurge. Because the restaurant was almost exactly half way between my house and the Carsons' place, we were to meet in front of it at 7:30. Since the bus route avoided my street by a good mile, and since I had no car, I walked to the restaurant.

There was no sign of Eve when I arrived. I waited, not very patiently after the first few minutes. Eventually I stepped inside and, describing Eve, asked if the receptionist had seen her.

"Yes, that would be Miss Gardener, I believe. She and her uncle, Mr. Tynsdale, are waiting for your arrival," came the unexpected answer. My face must have shown my bewilderment because, after a fleeting glance up and down my person, the receptionist flipped on her heel and stalked off, not waiting to see if I was following in her wake. I was, but my mind was occupied with two questions: Why were Eve and her cousin in situ already even though I had arrived early? Was the reference to Ronald as Eve's uncle a slip of the tongue or had somebody told the hostess that that was their relationship? And a third question raised its ugly horns. If so, why?

The evening came a bust, for me at least. Eve remained distant, as if I was no more to her than an acquaintance who had rudely crashed a private liaison between her and her lover. Ron (as he insisted that I call him) exuded a cold charm, albeit one that resonated of excessive sincerity and goodwill. He was not a big man, standing about 5'9" or 10" and weighing in at maybe ten pounds or so less than 200. A sedentary life had already begun to soften a body that had probably once been trim if not athletic. Yet the threat of destruction smoldered in the air around him, a threat like the impassive force of a glacier moving, ever moving inexorably south and west, destroying anything that couldn't get out of the way in time. And worse, the threat of explosive violence lay hidden deep beneath that exterior arctic force, like the boiling magma of a volcano ready to explode. An involuntary tremor shook my body as Eve introduced us. In reaction an almost imperceptible smile flitted across Ron's face.

"So you're Donjon," he mused, standing to welcome me when Eve introduced us, his inexpressive eyes roaming over my rumpled sweater and too-tight pants on their way from my hair to my scuffed shoes, before I could hide the latter under the table. His tailored suit, blue with thin red pinstripes, almost hid a gut that had begun to form from the good life. His tie probably cost considerably more than every piece of clothing I had on.

Even my shirt blushed at the comparison it couldn't help but make.

"Eve talks a lot about you," Ron continued. "I can understand why. She has always been attracted to boys that seem to have suffered some irreparable damage because of something indecisive in their nature. You know, boys who are victims rather than perpetrators."

What the hell could I say to that? I grunted something unintelligible, words that I couldn't even understand myself. He turned back to Eve and continued a conversation they must have been having when I showed up. In a few minutes the waiter appeared. We ordered and almost immediately afterward my table companions continued their conversation, gossiping about mutual acquaintances in Midport, about her family, about his. Our food arrived. Ron and Eve continued talking to each other as we ate. I answered an occasional question directed my way, kind of like a scrap thrown to the dog sitting on the floor at its master's right.

Eventually we finished our meal. Eve excused herself to visit the restroom, leaving a chasm of silence at the table. In spite of my frantic efforts, I failed to come up with anything to say. Ron seemed amused at the silence, or at my easily apparent anxiety. He examined me as he sipped his coffee, like a biologist might examine a frog he's preparing to dissect.

"I followed your high school escapade closely, you know. You don't know how closely." He finally commented, almost seeming to be talking to himself. He was staring at me, but he didn't seem to see me, except maybe as a reflection of his own musings. "I've always wondered what going on a killing rampage would be like. I thought about it even as a little boy, long before I entered high school, often daydreaming about it when I was mad as hell at some person or group of people, visualizing who I would kill or mutilate and how, often killing the same people more than once and in lots of different ways." He quit talking for several minutes, although his stare remained in place. "Once I went so far as to pinpoint where I could get a rifle and some dynamite, and when and where I'd use them." He chuckled, a not very pleasant sound. His voice remained so low that I could barely make out the words. "I don't know what I would have done with the dynamite, however. I didn't know how to use it then, and I still don't. But that wasn't of any importance in my daydreams."

He shook himself, as if trying to break free of a trance, and focused his eyes on mine.

"But, like you and unlike your friends, I never carried through with my dreams of violence. I chose to fulfill other dreams—outward conformity and the success it can bring if you're bright enough and play your cards right. After all," he smiled at me, a knowing, sardonic grin, "what sane man wants to destroy himself before he's had a chance to prove what he's made of. I think, of the three of you, you made the wisest choice. Your friends sacrificed their whole adulthood, all their future of fun and games, and struggle and spoils, not to mention, possibly, their eternal souls, for a moment of infamy, because that's about as long as most people will remember them." He paused again. His eyes remained glued to my face but again didn't appear to see it. "I cannot sympathize with a man for sacrificing his very existence, his life, his real and imagined future, everything, to become a hero or martyr in the eyes of others. Maybe at the greatest extreme, at the level of the eternal, I can understand it, even drum up some sympathy for it. You know, if a person thinks that by martyring himself he'll live on forever at God's right hand, become one of the chosen of heaven—that kind of a desire and the resultant commitment I can understand. That is an ambition I can sympathize with. I can also sympathize with the other extreme, the desire to imitate the greatest rebel of all, Satan, the desire to commit the worst of sins and to forever be remembered for having risen far above the mediocre. What I'm saying is, I can understand the need to transcend this mundane world no matter what the cost. I understand your friends. I understand their need to become infamous if not famous. However, I don't sympathize with it at all, mainly because what they chose to do was really quite mediocre as far as rebellions go. The two of them should have chosen to destroy a town or something else of great value. Or they should have chosen as you and I did, to live on in this mediocrity and take what we want from it. We won't be remembered in history, but we'll enjoy what time we do have on earth, which will be considerably more than what your friends had."

"You don't believe in sacrificing your life to make the world a better place to live in?" I asked idiotically.

"I didn't say that," his voice held a note of disdain. "I said I didn't choose to destroy my own life for a moment of infamy, or fame either, as far as that goes. An eternity of either would be something else, if I thought it possible." He drummed his fingers on the table and smiled that cold smile. "It's not that I have any moral compunction against taking a human life. I could care less about other people, or about the moral and ethical values involved, except insofar as they affect my success or failure in any given situation. I only care about me and my life, and I choose not to sacrifice either just to find out what killing a human being would feel like, although I've often been very sorely tempted and, I have to admit, might actually have found out several times if someone else or circumstances hadn't stopped me. Lucky them and lucky me," he ended his discourse with a sneer.

"What about if you want to help change the world, if you think it's cruel or meaningless, and you want to make it better?"

"You're repeating yourself. Besides, that's not a profound insight at all, you know," he stared thoughtfully at his plate, but I knew he was really watching me. "It's a Darwinian world pure and simple. Only idealists and other fools think otherwise, or think that it can be changed. Men of real wisdom and men with the guts and ability rise to the top if, of course, they have sufficient luck on their side. Life is a play, a drama at times, at other times a comedy, just as Shakespeare said. The world is the stage on which the actors perform. The problem is, of course, that we all get only one performance with no chance at redemption. You're dumped on the stage at birth and you had better hit the floor running. If you don't, you'll be behind in the race even before you begin to walk. And it's next to impossible to catch up."

Eve returned at that point. Ron bounced up to pull her chair out for her.

"What were you two talking about behind my back," she smiled at her cousin as she slid into her seat beside him.

"Nothing, really," he answered lightly, "just filling in the empty space you left with your absence, Eve."

She turned to me and I was surprised at the flash of anger her eyes couldn't hide. "You tell me, Donjon. Ronald delights in keeping his little secrets."

"Ron, Eve. It's Ron, not Ronald," The flash of anger in Ron's eyes matched what I had spotted a moment earlier in Eve's. "You know I hate it when people try to turn me into a Ronald. You know it and you do it just to irritate me."

"Come on, Eve," I interrupted, wondering if I shouldn't just shut up and let the two of them continue their spat, see where it led. "We were talking about my two friends killing people at the high school. That's what everyone wants to talk about when they first meet me, you included."

"Did you decide why they did it?" Eve asked, curiosity replacing the anger in her eyes. She was fishing to find out what all we had said.

"No," Ron answered before I had a chance to. "But I'd bet a lot of anger was involved in the motive." He watched me closely as he spoke, an odd smile or smirk on his lips, an expression that didn't quite reach his eyes, seemingly daring me to contradict him and tell Eve what we were really talking about.

"Why do you say that?"

Ron shrugged, "Lots of reasons. Sometimes a person just dislikes someone, for no logical reason, not one he can articulate anyway. There's just something about them you can't stand. Every time you see them, or think of them, you want to smash their faces in. Then there are the people that stand in your way. They have something you want and the only way to get it is to kill them, or destroy them in some other way." He bared his teeth at me in what he must have meant as a smile of complicity. "Then there are the bullies, all those people who like to push others around just because they can and because they enjoy it. One of them bullies you around, you get mad. The anger and frustration boils inside you until you explode and kill them. It could be as simple as that," his eyes studied me coldly.

I wondered why he was talking 'kill' instead of simply 'attack' or some such less permanent word.

"Donjon's two buddies possibly got fed up with all the waste of time and effort in the school system and decided to get even."

"Why shoot school administrators and trustees?"

"They are the guilty ones. They make the rules, from afar, but they make them nevertheless. And, of course, like so many people who are in a position to legislate, they don't have to obey the rules they create. The teachers? They only enforce the rules," Ron pontificated. "Besides, student relationships with teachers are personal, and it requires a more vicious, more violent relationship to kill at the personal level, I believe. Or it requires a much greater anger."

I started to spout off, to tell him he didn't know what the hell he was talking about, that there was a lot more to the episode than he could ever imagine. But I had done that too often and it had never done me any good. Nobody believed my long-winded explanations of the attack on the school. Worse, I generally came off sounding like an idiot because I still wasn't completely certain why Cass and Adam had done what they did. Besides, Ron was right in his analysis, right in general human terms anyway, or so I thought.

"Let's talk about something else," I inserted instead.

The five words were meant to be a statement. They sounded more like a plea. And they were accepted as such. The conversation turned to student life in general. This time I was included in the conversation.

When we finally decided it was time to quit talking and head for home, Ron paid the bill and then offered me a ride. I was surprised. I had figured that Eve and I would have to pay our share. And I had figured he would take off with Eve and leave me stranded in front of the restaurant, a long, dark walk ahead of me. He further surprised me by taking Eve home first, and again when he pulled in at an all-night diner and offered to buy me a cup of coffee, saying that he wanted to talk to me about Eve.

The diner was full of sleepy drunks and half-awake ex-revelers, with a few workers getting their evening coffee fix before heading off to their nightly labors. We settled in a booth that had possibly been re-upholstered a few decades before. Ron ordered black coffee; I ordered an orange soda.

"You don't drink coffee?" my companion asked as the waitress trudged off to fill our order.

"No," I mumbled tiredly. "I can't stand the taste.

"So, you like orange soda."

"Not much," I answered even though he had not really asked me a question. "But I figured I should order something if I'm going to take up a seat."

"I see you're one of those who believe in fulfilling what he sees as his social obligations, no matter how foolish and costly," Ron commented with a straight face, but a sneer lurked somewhere deep in his eyes.

My shoulders shrugged of their own accord. What could I say? He was right. Since the loss of my two best friends in high school and my own last-minute escape from disaster, I had been plagued by what I thought ethically or morally correct. The trait too often kept me from transcending the mediocre, or from not ordering an orange soda I didn't really want. It was as if I had been bullied into keeping my head down for fear that someone might notice it and try to knock it off.

He said nothing else until our drinks arrived and the sagging waitress retreated, leaving a hastily scribbled check on the table.

"What precisely is your relationship with Eve?" he asked abruptly when we were alone again.

Startled by the abrupt question, I found myself unable to answer right away.

"What I mean is, what are your intentions toward her? Do you hope to marry her someday? Is she just a temporary friend? I mean, is she just a girl you hope to bed for awhile, until you tire of her and move on to another?"

"I don't…," I don't know what I started to say. I was too dumbfounded by the questions and the machinegun-style in which they were delivered. Maybe I started to tell him it was none of his business. I like to think so. But maybe I started to say that I didn't know or that I did not want to talk about it. To repeat, I don't know.

"Don't tell me it's none of my business," he growled irritably, his eyes poking daggers into mine. "Eve is like my own daughter. I want her to have a good life, to graduate from college and marry well. In fact, I have the ideal husband for her, a young man just a few years older than she is. He's from one of the oldest and wealthiest families in Echo Creek. I've already broached the subject with him and his parents. I've shown them pictures. I've told them that she's intelligent, ambitious, and tough as a whip. They're having a small party next Saturday. Eve's invited and has accepted. I'll be taking her."

That was it. He stopped and waited for my reaction, mockery not quite hidden in his eyes or in the sneer twisting his lips.

"You have nothing to offer Eve. I've had you and your family checked, thoroughly. It would be a compliment to say you're in the middle class. According to what I can gather, you yourself are not very ambitious, no more so than your father before you. You don't even know what you want to major in at ECU."

And that's when my temper finally flared, lending me the nerve to do what I had wanted to do all evening. I bounced to my feet and stood staring at him for an agonizing moment, my mind a fuming blank. I started to slug him. My fist clenched and my arm cocked in blind rage, but before I could complete my swing, my temper gave way to my natural tendency toward reason. I suddenly realized that if I punched Ron I would lose Eve and I would probably wind up in jail for attacking him and for destroying the property of the diner. Besides, I'm not really a violent person.

"You told me not to say my relationship with Eve is none of your business," I finally gritted when my mind had fully taken control of my reactions. "But that's exactly what it is, none of your business," I growled over my shoulder as I turned on my heel and stormed along the aisle toward the door.

Ron told Eve his side of the story before she and I got together again. She, of course, listened to what I had to say about the incident. But she didn't believe me and told me that she was disappointed that I couldn't control my childish temper. She didn't seem upset that Ron was trying to rip us apart at the seams and, at the same time, maneuver her into a relationship that he hoped would be permanent.

"He wants me to be happy," was her only comment about my complaint.

"Are you going to that party to meet the guy he wants you to marry?" I asked, with not a little jealousy.

"Of course," Eve took my hand as she talked, "I might meet the man of my dreams. Who knows?"

"I thought…," I started to remind her that the two of us had made a tentative date for the next Saturday.

"Don't be silly," Eve interrupted. "I'm going because Ronald wants me to. If this boy is like the rest of them he's tried to fix me up with, he'll be an arrogant pain in the 'you-know-what.'"

"So, why go?"

"I like Ron and he's been good to me. There isn't a lot I wouldn't do for him."

I pleaded my case for a few more minutes but I might as well have been pleading with an escalator to stand still while I stepped on.

But back to my clash with Ron, after leaving the diner, I moped toward home, furious with the man for interfering in my relationship with Eve, and especially for setting her up with another guy, and ashamed of myself for not having hit him square in the face. I was within several blocks of home when I had to cross the street. As I stepped off the curb I heard a motor rev to my left. Glancing in that direction, I noticed that a car had pulled away from the curb about a half block away, but the driver had not turned on his headlights.

The vehicle raced toward me, gathering speed as if it were trying to set an acceleration record on the Utah Salt Flats. For a split second I was mesmerized by the speed and sinister darkness of the car. I froze in place five or six feet from the trees lining the grass between the sidewalk and the street. There was nothing between me and the black beast bearing down on me. No cars were parked along there. No garbage cans had been set out for the morning pick-up, although my mind registered several on the far side of the street.

I watched the car come, increasing speed with each second that passed. I watched it swerve toward me and still increase its acceleration. I watched its headlights come on and blind me when night suddenly turned to daylight. And finally, luckily, my mind released my body from its paralysis. I dove for the safety of the curb and trees, bruising my knees on the asphalt of the street and the cement of the curb; and my hands, fingers and elbows on the roots of the tree behind which I was frantically trying to clamber for safety. Somehow I misjudged my speed and trajectory. My head smacked into the tree trunk. The rough bark took several chunks out of my skull. I felt myself slipping into a black void but my forward momentum kept me scrambling blindly, wildly, until I lay prone and barely conscious behind my chosen fortress.

I felt more than actually heard the car race past me a few inches from the curb. It didn't slow down until it reached the next side street, turning into it with screeching tires and unappeased wailing from its motor. When I finally blacked out completely, I don't know, but it must have been almost immediately after the car turned the corner.

I didn't see the vehicle clearly, but in the split second before its headlights turned on, I had no doubts that it was a black car and that the driver was Ronald Tynsdale. Did I just assume this because of the way he had treated me? I don't think so. Did I tell anyone about the incident or who I thought the driver was? No. Who would have believed me? Eve? I doubt it. And besides, I didn't want to take the chance of telling her and so possibly losing her because of the way she felt about the man.

17

And then I encountered Reno. Unlike with Ron, Eve didn't set up a meeting between us. He simply showed up at the service station where I worked, actually the very next Saturday night after my encounter with his brother. Reno arrived precisely as I was set to turn off the lights and lock the doors. At first I thought he was Ron, there to confront me for some infraction or other of his rules, or to continue his attempt to kill me. But I remembered that Ron should be at a party with Eve, introducing her to a potential husband and in-laws. Anyhow I was befuddled and not a little scared as a familiar face popped through the doors just as I was starting to flip the light switch.

My fright must have showed because Reno stopped just inside the door and held his hands at shoulder level, palms toward me and, smiling, introduced himself.

"You look exactly like your brother," I blurted, my relief overcoming my fear.

"Yes," he agreed, offering a friendly smile in, I'm sure now, an attempt to calm the panic that must have been shivering openly in my eyes, "but I'm not like him. I didn't come here to threaten you or in any other way try to make you give Eve up, which I have no doubts he has done already. In fact, I'm glad she found you. She's been a lot happier since the two of you started dating. And when she's happy, I'm happy too. She's like the little sister I never had, or the daughter I might never have," he added sadly, making me wonder if he might suffer from some sexual malady.

Next he invited me to go someplace for a cup of coffee with him, and talk, an invitation that reminded me of Ron's a week earlier and thus set me on edge in spite of his friendly demeanor.

We wound up in the same diner where Ron had told me to stay away from Eve. This time I ordered a hamburger, fries and Pepsi. I felt more comfortable with Reno than I had with his brother, and I was actually hungry, whether from the emotional rush his appearance had given me or from some more natural cause, I don't know.

"So," Reno said after the sagging waitress had taken our orders, "you've met the real Ronald Tynsdale."

"Yeah," I agreed hesitantly, uncertain about where the comment was taking us.

"Look, I don't know what Ron told you, or possibly did to you," he said, leaning forward and speaking softly but insistently, "He can be malicious. He's cruel, vindictive, and violent at times. He has a terrible temper when someone crosses him in any way he considers personal or important, or even sometimes over insignificant things. According to Eve he's been complaining lately that she has hooked up with what he calls some dud she needs to get rid of before it's too late. So I can only assume that, at the least, he threatened you if you didn't give Eve up."

"Too late for what?" I asked when he paused as if he was through talking. I was more interested in how the Tynsdale brothers affected my relationship with Eve than in anything else.

"Who knows?" Reno shrugged. "He possibly figures Eve is getting serious about you and you're not worthy of her. Or maybe he's afraid she might wind up pregnant and have to marry you."

"Yeah, he definitely said that part about Eve being too good for me," I grumbled. "What's with him anyway? He's not her dad or anything, so why's he think he can tell her who she can go out with and who she can't?" My nerve swelled as I talked, "And where's he get off telling me what I can or can't do?"

Reno smiled for the first time since he had appeared at the station, "He tries to control everybody associated with him. That's just the way he is, although with people who have any social status he's a lot more subtle about it."

"What if they ignore him, or tell him to mind his own business?" I asked, fishing for any information that might tell me about Ron's mental state, anything that might tell me if I was still in danger from that source.

"Well, he's my brother so I hate to say this, but he's a dangerous guy. When I cross him I watch my back until he's got his revenge. At times it's no more than a rumor he starts about me sleeping in my patrol car or parking that same vehicle too long near some woman's house, and not always a single woman's home, especially if he's also pissed off at a husband. The rumor eventually gets back to my boss and the husband too." He chuckled humorlessly at the picture his words conjured. "I've had to do a lot of fast talking from time to time. My career has taken a hit more than once." He paused as if wondering what to reveal and what not to. "Then there are the times he's tried to kill me."

I wanted to ask him why he didn't do something about his brother. Then the image of that black car bearing down on me made me tremble inside. I wondered what Reno's life had been like.

"I really doubt if he'd try to kill you," Reno went on, "although you never know what he's going to do, except in public. He's a true politician. He doesn't show the evil side of his nature in public, or to powerful people he wants on his side or thinks he might need in some way, only to those who cross him, socially, financially, or whatever, especially if he considers himself superior to them, which," he added with a shrug, "is most people."

"So, what you're saying is, I'd better give Eve up or he might find some way to hurt me.

"Might? That's not a word I'd use to describe Ron and his actions. He does something, or he doesn't do it. He's like a cross between a bulldog and a fox. He won't let go of whatever it is he wants done, ever, but you never know which beast is going to come after you, the fox that will figure out some way to annihilate or break you without you even knowing anything is happening, or the bulldog that will sink its teeth in you where it hurts most and never let go till you've breathed your last or have somehow broken free and run for the hills."

"You feel that way about your own brother?" I asked, not a little frightened by what he had said. At that time I had no idea of the physical attacks Reno had experienced.

"I feel that way about my own brother," he looked me straight in the eyes as he spoke.

"How could you live with him?"

For the first time a slight smile touched the corners of his mouth but not his eyes, "What choice does a child have? If he's lucky he gets a mom and dad that are good to him and he gets siblings he likes, ones that have a lot in common with him. If not, well, he can't just run away from home and find another dad or brother to his own liking. He can't just go out and select one that he gets along with most of the time, and one that won't try to kill him if he gets in the way at the wrong time. A boy can choose his friends, within certain limitations, but he can't choose his parents and siblings, and he can't avoid his family after he's got it, not until he grows up and becomes independent, and not even then unless he goes someplace else to live, which I don't plan on doing, so I guess I can't avoid Ron completely." He shrugged and his grimace grew into the tentative beginning of a gloomy smile. "I guess my major problem is that I believe we're all dealt a hand to play, at birth, and it's up to us to play it the best we can. Only the irresponsible try to avoid the task they're given at birth. I mean the hand they're given to play and the table they're given to belly up to."

"I don't know," unlike with his brother, I felt that he would accept a conversation. He didn't seem to be dictating ultimate truths but rather exploring ideas and tentative conclusions, maybe trying to give reason to some of the decisions he had made in his own life. "I mean, sure, we're born in a specific place and time, and into, you know, a specific family, like two parents and maybe some sisters and brothers." I felt like I was starting to stutter a little bit, trying to determine ahead of time where I was going, but I forged on, becoming surer of myself as he sat and listened without trying to interrupt. "But I don't think that means we have to stay where we're born. Sure, no one can escape the place or time he's born in, but it's a big world and there are lots of places a man can go, and some really big countries, so I don't see why you'd think it would be so irresponsible to leave your family and go somewhere else to live, in your own country or in some other country."

"I know," he smiled thoughtfully. "If there weren't any people interested in seeing what's over the mountain or on the other side of the ocean, or people wanting to find a better life some-where else, we'd all still be living in Africa, I guess. But I'm not like that." He smiled, ruefully, I think. "I'm a stay-at-home. My brother would be like that, I'm certain, if he didn't have such a good life at home." He remained quiet for a few moments. "I don't have any real reason to believe Ron would be a wanderer under different circumstances, but I do. Given his personality, if he couldn't be one of the top dogs where he is, I don't have any doubts he'd go find someplace where he could, or maybe be forced to because he used illegal or violent means to have his way, and got caught, and so failed to get what he wanted."

"You think he'll really try to kill me if I don't quit seeing Eve?" I asked the question uppermost in my mind, thinking now that I already knew the answer, but yet not convinced completely that Ron would have run over me if I hadn't dived out of the way. In spite of what Reno had said, I still wanted to believe that Ron had just tried to scare me, that if I hadn't jumped out of the way of his car he would have swerved at the last minute, missing me. But something deep inside me kept insisting that I was roaming in the nebulous land of wishful thinking.

"Watch your back," he frowned and shrugged, then changed the subject. "What do you think of Eve anyway?"

"I…well…," my mind seemed to have been startled into shock by the direction of the sudden change.

"That was a really dumb question and completely inappropriate," he interrupted my stuttering. "You wouldn't be seeing her all the time if you weren't attracted to her as a woman and didn't like her as a person. Isn't that true?"

"Yeah," I agreed, my emotions relaxed by the change of pace. "I like Eve but I don't know how much she likes me. I mean, we're not going steady or anything like that because every time we talk about it she says we need more time to get to know each other better. Then she blames me for the problem."

He smiled, too readily, I thought, as if my answer was precisely the one he had expected, maybe wanted.

"That's Eve," his smile turned into a brief chuckle. "A lot of her ideas about people and her own ambitions she's gotten from me and my brother, I think, although a lot more from him than from me. Her dad never had an idea in his life, let alone an original one. And as for her mother, she supports the norm in any situation. 'No' isn't in her vocabulary unless it has to do with someone trying to subvert the social norms established by the elite."

"I think Eve's awfully independent," I decided to be honest with him. "She's got this stubborn idea that she can order her life from beginning to end. It's like she knows the world is an irrational place and that humans are even more irrational than all the other animals. She admits that we're creatures of our emotions and desires. But she insists that we don't have to be and that she can live a completely rational life. She even talks about love as if it's something you choose rationally, and you choose it based on financial status, ability, and ambition."

Reno shook his head, "That comes from Ron. No doubt about that. His life proves the point too. But I don't see much happiness in him or in his family, except for their public face. Ron's too ambitious, too greedy, to ever be content with what he has. He'll always want more. In some ways I feel sorry for him. He's spent his whole life chasing something: a higher social status, more money, more power, more control. He doesn't appear capable of saying 'That's enough. I've got everything I need. It's time to relax and enjoy it all.'"

"Maybe Eve doesn't either," I said, wondering.

He shrugged, staring at me with a thousand-yard stare that seemed to see everything and nothing, "Who knows? As you said, she's one of the most independent people you'll ever meet. And she's all modern woman," he chuckled mirthlessly as he said that "Like a lot of independent people, especially the young, she doesn't always consider the consequences of her actions. It's almost as if she thinks she has the right to do whatever she wants and nobody, God included, had better interfere. Not that she's immoral or anything like that. Actually she's a good woman. She just demands all the freedoms men have, and damn the consequences, which I don't think she ever considers anyway because, like I said, she believes it's her absolute right to, uh, test the waters, so to speak." For the first time he seemed a little embarrassed, although I wasn't quite sure why. "What she really wants is just what most of us want, and like the rest of us she's not quite sure which of her dreams is the most important and whether the realization of some of them actually does exclude others. Sometimes she says her main goal is a happy life with a husband that loves her and beautiful children that do all the right things. Other times it's money and social status, or a career she can be happy with, which are her primary goals. What can I say? I don't figure she's much different from most kids. The uncertainty of the future scares her. So she maps it out with as much certainty as she can. Which is impossible, of course—mapping it out so there's nothing left to chance, that is. And it's especially impossible in a world where there's so much freedom of choice and action, with little social consequence."

He shrugged as if in embarrassment. "Anyhow if Eve has one characteristic that overrides the rest of them, it's that she doesn't like uncertainty in her life. She thinks if she doesn't have a plan for everything she's wasting her time. And she might be right," Reno continued thoughtfully. "Most of us just float through life, taking whatever comes our way and making the best of it, doing something because that's what our parents or our friends or society expects of us, or it's what we think we want. The lucky ones are the ones that find something they really want to do and go after it no matter what it takes, and still like doing it after years and years."

"That'll probably be Eve."

"Yeah, maybe, I hope so. But she's got one major weakness that bothers me. She's never faced a real tragedy. So far her life has been one success after another—parents with money, top student, top athlete, one of the most beautiful girls in school, all the best males chasing her. Life has been too easy for her. She thinks all she has to do is reach up and pick any apple she wants from the tree. She thinks all she has to do is make a plan and go for it, and it'll lead her one step closer to Eden. How's she going to react when life reaches out and bites her on the ass some day?" He paused and stared at me for a long time, making me uncomfortable. Finally he asked, "Why do you think she chose you to date? Out of all the star athletes and student scholars on campus, and wealthy guys, and really good-looking guys, why you?"

I couldn't answer that. He realized that his question had made me uncomfortable, and that to some extent it had been a little insulting, so he changed the subject to Eve's past, and then mine.

We continued talking for another half hour or so. Reno asked a lot of the same questions most people ask the first time I have much of a conversation with them, questions about my relationship with Cass and Adam and the reasons for their attack on Echo Creek High. In general, he seemed more interested in probing my character in the present than in the past, however. As usual I came off as indecisive and uncertain, I think, simply because that's what I was. Like my country, my mind, my interests, my inner being itself was split about almost everything, from my world view to my economic and political philosophy, and on down to how much control I should have over such things as my education, my career, and even my spiritual being. Some days I felt very decisive. In my mind I outlined what my major would be, how I would earn my living, and even what specific church I would join soon, none of these the same every time. Most days, however, I continued to float, reacting to the events and people around me. I had become a pendulum, swinging from right to left and back and back again from one extreme to another, never quite reconciling either with the other.

Eventually Reno drove me home, gave me a number to call in case I needed him, warned me one last time about his brother, and drove away into the night.

18

Once again my life appeared to return to normal. My affair with Eve continued with no apparent hitch. She refused to say much about the guy Ron had chosen for her intended, and I was too smitten to make much of an issue of her outing without me.

"He's only one of the several Ronald has tried to pair me off with, and he's not the most interesting or ambitious," she said when I first asked her about the evening. "He's not like you at all. He has big dreams, but he has no idea what he has to do to make them come true, except graduate so he can get a good job in which he doesn't have to do any physical labor; get married to a woman who will cook his meals, clean his house, and raise his kids; and go on vacations yearly to all the popular places." She shook her head in what I took for disgust before continuing. "He'd probably be a lot happier if he took a job in a factory or garage or something. In his spare time all he does is work on the car daddy bought him or drink beer with his buddies. I don't know why he's at ECU rather than at some technical college, or working and learning on the job." She paused thoughtfully "Oh, I guess I really do know. I just don't like to admit that I'm like all the others. It's what most of us do who want to get a decent job and live the good life, and maybe be somebody someday." She shook her head as if she were angry at something. "It's what the right people, from the right families, do. It's a game of follow-the-leaders, the leaders being those who have the money and/or power to do whatever they please."

After those words, she refused to discuss the guy any further, never giving me his name. I didn't tell her that Ron had tried to kill me, but I brought up some of the things Reno had said. Her reaction was irritation.

"I like Reno a lot but he shouldn't talk about his brother like that. People will think he's jealous.

Late one Sunday afternoon we walked out to the Dog Man's place. Eve said she hadn't seen him for some time and missed his wit. I hadn't seen him for a couple weeks either, so I was happy to traipse along with her wish. More to the point, of course, I was happy to keep her company anywhere, just in case something might happen between us.

My friend had just returned from a jaunt through Echo Creek. The two of us waited until he had unhitched his dog pack and turned them loose in their respective ambience, most of the little ones inside the hut and the rest in the enclosure surrounding it.

"Well, Eve, I have had three oddly humorous but not very pleasant encounters with your uncle—Thursday when I was meandering through Echo Creek, minding my own business; again on Friday in the late afternoon, during rush-hour traffic; and then again today," he drawled before we had any more than plopped down in our unassigned but expected seats, his eyes, almost hidden by the unkempt bush covering the lower half of his face, fixed on Eve. "Thursday I had stopped in Bronson Park to let the dogs relax awhile when he pulled up, jumped out of his car, and started ranting away like he was talking to a rather unruly subordinate. He seems to be under the impression that your friend here," he nodded at me, "and I are a corrupting influence on you, if in no other way by simply imposing our presence on you. He suggested, or should I say demanded, that we exit your life, the sooner the better."

"My uncle?" Eve asked, voice as well as expression conveying her bewilderment.

"Yes, Mr. Ronald Tynsdale, Esquire," the Dog Man's words dripped with sarcasm. "His very words were, 'You will stay away from Eve or I will make your life even more miserable than it is.' I swear that those were his very words, although spoken in a threatening rather than sarcastic tone."

"He's not my uncle. He's my cousin," Eve seemed both angry and upset, "although he likes for people to think he's my uncle. In that way, he thinks people are less offended by the advice he's always handing out, advice and half-camouflaged orders."

"Why do you put up with them?"

"He's good to me. He's interested in my welfare and my future. He wants me to be happy and successful. If I need something like money or clothes or an invitation to the right parties, anything, he makes sure I get it, from him or somebody else."

"Kind of a sugar daddy," the Dog Man commented.

"Yes, but there's no sex involved," Eve spoke with irritation. "He treats me like a daughter."

"Yes, well, your relationship with him is none of my business, and mine with you is none of his business. You might tell him that the next time you see him." The Dog Man grinned but not with humor, although you had to know him to realize that he actually was grinning, albeit sarcastically, rather than doing something else like frowning, pouting, sneering, or what not. His beard was so thick that you couldn't really tell why his mouth was hanging open. If you weren't looking closely, in fact, because of the jungle thickness of his eyebrows, you wouldn't notice the glint in his eyes that gave you the hint about what the mouth was doing.

Anyhow, he launched into the story of his second clash with Eve's cousin, on Friday. He was making a special pilgrimage through downtown Echo Creek. Only a few of the dogs were sounding off, mostly the yappy ones, the majority possibly intimidated by the heavier-than-what-they-were-used-to traffic of Echo Creek's central streets during rush hour. However, as far as the Dog Man was concerned, his real problem was not the traffic but rather that, during his most recent brush with the town's police and court system, although he was acquitted of the multitude of charges on which he was arraigned, and although he and his menagerie were given freedom of access to most of the streets of Echo Creek and, of course, to the country roads surrounding the city, the judge ordered him to avoid the downtown area at all times, day and night, under penalty of arrest and possible confinement. Like most judges and other rulers of our country, the Dog Man's judge felt that the freedom to impose one's attitudes, words, and actions on others was a Constitutional right for those in power, especially in judicial power, except when such would interfere with the personal world of any of those same people.

The Dog Man had not by any stretch of the imagination forgotten the judge's order. He ignored it. I asked him why.

"The old bastard died two weeks ago," he laughed, "so I decided to do what I damned well wanted to do. I got there about the time everybody was getting off work and trying to cross Main Street to get to the public lot where their cars were. And the traffic along Main was atrocious," again he sniggered, "as it always is at that time of day, especially on Friday. So you can imagine the frustration my cart and mangy animals caused, creeping along Main at a snail's pace, relatively speaking. I haven't had more fun in years. Drivers yelling and honking and cussing like the devil himself," he glowered, half mockingly, at Eve for a moment. "Even the buses had to stop and wait for me to get through so the traffic could clear out. I had a blast."

"The legal stipulation wasn't invalidated just because the judge that ordered it died," Eve enunciated each word, while a faint note of anger seeped out between each one.

The Dog Man's eyes glittered, "Sometimes a little rebellion is good for the soul."

"That's childish."

"Yes, in this case, I must admit. But I stand by my statement. We live in a democracy so I might add that sometimes a little rebellion is necessary, even if childish or even meaningless in the long run. We can't let authority become so sure of what it considers its own right to rule that it forgets, completely forgets, that the ruled have rights and that the rulers should only exist to make sure those rights are not infringed, that the rulers should not have any rights, or benefits, that the ruled don't have."

"My God," Eve exploded scornfully, "that's so foolish it's not even worth discussing. One way or another, leaders always have the power to be above the law to a greater or lesser extent, even in a democracy."

Again the Dog Man's eyes glittered, whether with humor or anger, I wasn't certain. All he said before launching back into his tale was, "The ideal generally is foolish when you think of consistently embedding it in reality rather than simply striving toward it, what with human nature as it is, but I shudder to think what this world would be like without a few noble goals, and especially a few noble souls to occasionally remind us of the rights of the masses, in one way or another, even if we and our institutions never come close to allowing, consistently allowing, those very rights."

Anyway the Dog Man was loafing along through downtown Echo Creek, at the height of rush-hour traffic, ignoring the crazed honking and shouting, and revving of motors that threatened mayhem, when suddenly a car started to pass him on the wrong side, scraping the curb as it did so, and blasting its horn like another maniac had been suddenly turned loose in the streets. Then, as abruptly as he had gunned his motor to pass, the driver of the black car swerved toward the dogs tied on the right side of the car/bicycle contraption, sending animals scurrying under the cart and almost upsetting the whole apparatus. The Dog Man slammed on the brakes. Luckily he didn't run over any of his pets. Nor did the attacker. A moment later the Dog Man, seeing that the driver wasn't going to smash into his cart or run over his dogs, continued slowly on his way. The driver paralleled him for almost a half block, then gunned his motor and sped up and into the driving lane because of the cars parked next to the curb.

No sooner had he passed safely beyond the entire menagerie, than the driver screeched to a halt. Realizing that he was too late to get stopped in time, the Dog Man braked frantically, lightly rear-ending the offending vehicle before coming to a halt. All of the lead dogs, to keep from being caught between the vehicles, clambered over the rear of the offending auto, winding up scrabbling on its hood and top, a couple of them with front legs scratching for purchase on the bumper and rear legs frenziedly trying to climb air itself, all of the mutts howling with fear and rage. Luckily, again, none were actually hurt, but that didn't lessen their indignation which, according to the Dog Man, they continued to express during the following confrontation.

"Between their barking and howling, and the horns and shouts and swearing of all those drivers trying to get around us, and the angry souls trying to cross the street, it was a real bedlam," he explained with about the widest grin I've ever seen on his face. "I mean, there I was, laughing my head off, with all the noise around us, and here came your uncle stalking back toward us like General Patton parking his tank and stalking toward Hitler's bunker, if he did such a thing." He grinned foolishly at Eve. "The crazy driver was your uncle."

The Dog Man said that, as soon as he saw the look on Ron's face, his laughter froze in his throat.

"Road rage," I thought. "The damn guy's gonna attack me, maybe shoot me if he's got a gun. So I jumped down off that bicycle like an impala trying to escape a cheetah's attack. My god, my damned old heart started hammering away like a steam engine gone berserk. Sweat popped out every pore on my body and my mouth and throat dried up so fast and furious I thought I'd choke on my tongue." He chuckled humorously before adding, "But you know me. I can put up a good front. I took an old karate or judo stance. Whatever. I squared the old shoulders and leaned forward like I was going to attack your uncle," he semi-grinned at Eve. "That made the bastard stop. Or maybe he stopped because he suddenly realized that the two of us weren't alone but surrounded by dozens of people, a lot more if you include the cars and drivers lined up for several blocks, some of whom might be witness to whatever happened. I don't know, but I like to think that I'm really the one who stopped him in his tracks. It makes me feel good.

"In any case, he stopped two feet from me, changed his murderous expression to one of irritation and concern, and whispered, 'You block my way like that again, I'll run over you and your whole mangy pack of animals.' And then he flipped around like some general or politician on parade and stomped back toward his car, or rather I think that was where he was headed. But I didn't keep watching him. I was too worried about all those other drivers slamming out of their cars, and the pedestrians all over the place, yelling at me."

At that point the Dog Man thought the confrontation with Eve's cousin was over and all he had to do was continue on his way, if he wasn't mobbed first by all the mad drivers honking and screaming curses at him. But, although Eve's cousin had disappeared into the crowd, he had left his car exactly where he had stopped it—smack dab in front of the bicycle contraption and animals, blocking the Dog Man's lane and thus his further progress. The lanes to the contraption's left held bumper to bumper traffic, unmoving. To the right, though, were the cars parked at the curb. The small truck behind the Dog Man's contrivance sat with its bumper touching the rear of the bicycle's cart, the dogs chained to the latter having scattered to right and left as far as their ropes and traffic allowed. The Dog Man could not back up, as could not the truck or any of the dozens of vehicles lined up behind him. He had no way to go except right, and that only through a narrow lane between two parked cars.

Reasonably, in spite of the hysterical voice in his gut screaming for him to run and hide, trying to ignore the frenzied honking seemingly rising from every corner of the planet, the Dog Man remained put. The vehicles in front of Eve's cousin's car began to slowly move forward as the stoplight in front of them changed to green. But Ron's car remained put, and Ron had returned to stand beside the bicycle, his angry stare threatening to decapitate and castrate the cause of the jam. The horns behind the Dog Man became even more rabid, the curses unruly in their promise of violence. The Dog Man's animals began to sound like a pack of wolves frightened to death by the mayhem around them. Their howls were full of terror and anguish and, some, of frenzied anger.

Keeping his eyes on the ground so as not to lock eyes with any of the drivers around him, most of them now standing beside or on top of their autos, and thus possibly initiate an attack on his person, and not looking directly at the angry man beside the car in front of the bike, the Dog Man finally scrambled down from his pedestal.

And that's when the attack happened, although not from Ron the uncle/cousin, but rather from an oversized woman who charged walrus-like toward the cause of the real traffic jam. The Dog Man actually did notice her approach but, seeing her size and the extreme effort it took for her to put one foot in front of the other, he ignored her, seeing no threat. He didn't know where she came from. He figured of course that she had been driving one of the cars caught up in the traffic jam, but which one he didn't know then or later, nor even if it was one of those nearby or one a block away.

What he did know was that she started swearing when she was still several paces away, cursing louder and raunchier than any one of the other nearby drivers.

And she didn't stop. Rather, she charged like an oversized but crazed rhino. She marched ever closer to the Dog Man, determination in each step, anger turning her face beet red, increasing her speed with each stride. Ten feet. Eight feet. Watching Eve's cousin for the least sign of danger, the Dog Man ignored her. Until she charged. Then it was too late, way too late to do anything except throw his arms up to protect his head from her swinging purse. Actually, too late for even that. The purse, swung overhand with well over two hundred pounds of furious female behind it, connected with his forehead, sending him sprawling into several of the dogs that were cowering under the edge of the cart.

"That damned purse must have weighed twenty pounds," the Dog Man commented ruefully. "I should have been watching more closely, but I was focused on Uncle Ron, expecting him to be the one who attacked me. My brain registered the woman's approach before she started her final charge, before she swung that damned purse into my face and then waddled in for the kill, but I wasn't quick enough to defend myself effectively." He shrugged his shoulders and shook his head as if disgusted with himself. "The thing is, I should have recognized that woman and realized she wasn't a person who would shrink from smashing me or my dogs, if given the chance. I don't know what she was doing in town at that hour. She lives on a farm about a mile south of here. Her husband is dead, I think, if she ever had one, which is pretty doubtful given her size and temper. Some young man farms the land around her house. I see him around the barn or riding a tractor in one of the fields sometimes, when me and the dogs ramble out that way. But anyhow," he realized he was rambling verbally and so returned to the story, "you might say she's got it in for me. She's got lots of cats, not as many cats as I've got dogs, but a lot. And they run wild, day and night, hunting anything they can handle. They're always slinking through the woods around my house. I don't mind, of course. That's what cats do and they keep the mice population in check. But a few times one or two of them have gotten into the enclosure here," he made a circling gesture, "trying to get some of the dog food I put out, I figure. Well, to make a long story short, the dogs have killed a good half dozen of her cats. I buried the dead monsters but somehow she found out about it and demanded that I pay indemnity for the dead things." He laughed. "Can you imagine? Her cats steal dog food from my dogs and they kill the thieves and she wants me to pay because my dogs protected my property and their food."

"I'd be upset if your animals killed one of my pets too," Eve cut in.

"Hey," the Dog Man laughed, "I'd be mad if one of her cats killed one of my dogs. But I wouldn't ask her to pay me for the dead animal, not if my dogs had raided her property. But that's not the whole story. She has several dogs also. They're mainly house dogs, I suspect, like some of the cats. She lets them out for an hour or so in the morning and late afternoon too. They chase anything that moves, me and my dogs included. Well, I finally got tired of her dogs chasing us and yowling and staying just out of harm's way every time we ambled out that way. So once, when her dogs came yapping and howling after us, I untied three of my biggest dogs and let them go after our tormentors." His eyes suddenly lost their sparkle and he paused before continuing. "My dogs killed two of hers and sent the rest kiting for home before I could stop them. I was sorry for that, but mad as hell about what came next. The damned woman sued me for a half million bucks. The luck of the draw is all that saved me. The judge we wound up with hated animals. I think he belonged to PAP. Most judges, given our screwed up judicial system, would have made me pay the money, maybe even more."

"What?" Eve interrupted. "You're being silly. And what's PAP?"

"People against Pets," the Dog Man sniggered. "You name it! This town's like any other; it's got a chapter of it."

The woman's attack was the spark for the inferno that followed. Car doors smashed open as more irate drivers and passengers tumbled from their vehicles. A short, thick-necked jockey of a man reached the bicycle's side just as the Amazon-plus clobbered her target the second time and retracted her arm for another swing. Her back-swing bashed the jockey with her anvil of a purse, sending him wobbling into the female of a couple who were also scurrying to help in the attack on the Dog Man. And that crash ignited the conflagration.

At first the Dog Man feared he would be the center of the violence. Everybody had been charging his way. But the vortex of the melee quickly moved away from the growling, howling dogs. Eve's cousin made the mistake of scurrying around the Dog Man's contraption to separate the Purse Woman from a fat man who seemed to know her and consider her the cause of some past wrong, only to be attacked by the man and wife team, who may have believed that he was the owner of the dogs and their mobile home. A small, lawyerly looking man in a gray suit and red tie was bumped by an elderly woman in a black pants suit and pink blouse. He retaliated by smacking her with his briefcase. A gray-haired man in tan slack pants and white tee shirt clobbered the lawyerly fellow, knocking him down and then trying to help the fallen woman to her feet. But a truck driver type in Levi's and flannel shirt knocked the old man flying as he charged toward the Dog Man, only to trip over the woman in black as she tried to stand. His chin hit the pavement, knocking him unconscious, but not before his legs kicked out and smacked into the face of the gray-suited man, who retaliated by punching another fellow rioter in the groin.

In any case the bleating of horns receded somewhat, but the pushing and shoving and swearing increased in tempo. Eventually finding himself on the fringes of the riot, apparently unnoticed by the combatants, the Dog Man began lifting his contraption and moving it little by little into the space to his right and slightly behind where he himself was parked. Soon he had the whole affair, dogs and all, in the narrow space between the two cars at the curb. He half pedaled and half lifted the whole mess over the curb and then rapidly pedaled to the corner, where he made a right turn to the far side of the courthouse and again turned right, this time onto a narrow, almost completely deserted street.

And so, in short order, he could no longer hear the community brawl behind him, although he did hear the sirens of the police as they stormed in to save the situation for another day. Not long after that he turned onto a city street that led into the countryside.

"The police came visiting the next day, in the morning, but there seemed to be a lot of disagreement about how the hullabaloo actually started, although most of the people who had been there agreed that me and my dogs were the real problem. You know," he chuckled, "some people blamed the person who attacked them, others some car that fled the scene, still others the city government for not widening the streets, and yet others the police for not having a patrolman directing traffic in the most congested part of town. Others were certain that I blocked traffic on purpose. Nobody seemed willing to accept even one iota of the blame."

"Did you accept any of the blame?"

"Of course not, Eve. I think of myself as honest, but not so honest that I wouldn't lie to stay out of jail, or court." His eyes glinted again. "I told the police that I was trying to turn onto a side street, to get out of the way of the traffic, when some character in a black sedan cut me off on purpose and then attacked me." He pushed his eyebrows and beard aside to show us a black eye. And then he pointed to several small bruises on his arms. "I showed the police these and a few others on my chest and back. "They seemed a little skeptical, but what could they really do? Everybody was lying and no one seemed to agree on how the melee started. And so your uncle couldn't convince the police that I was the real culprit."

"I doubt if he really tried," Eve seemed more disgusted than angry.

The Dog Man shrugged and said nothing.

"What about the judge's order?" Eve asked.

"Hell, judges are so arrogant they expect people to follow their orders no matter how wrong or inane, transcribed into writing or not. I expect old Judge Arsenic was one of those. He was a supercilious ass. Besides, all of them pass out orders like Santa supposedly passes out presents on Christmas Eve. The only one who probably ever saw those orders was the judge's clerk, and the judge himself, maybe, although he was probably too self-important to read them after he dictated them to his clerk. However, to continue my story."

He held his hand up to silence whatever it was that Eve started to say.

"But earlier today your uncle got his revenge," he glared at Eve and ignored her "cousin" murmur. "I was returning from a little jaunt by two of the town's most populous churches as they were freeing their flocks after the weekly sermon. Nobody paid me a damned bit of attention, I have to admit—no jeers, no curses, no catcalls or rocks thrown by the pious kids. Or their parents," he chuckled, his facial hair moving in the breeze. "I guess the story of Friday afternoon's riot must have made the rounds of the town. Nothing like violence and its aftermath to pacify the people. So, anyhow, I was returning after a kind of boring pilgrimage, about a hundred yards or so this side of the city limit sign, when I noticed a big black sedan barreling toward me. Well, you know just how narrow the road is that leads from town to my lane? And I have to drive in the middle so my pets on the right side aren't forced into the ditch.

"My God, I thought, that idiot will kill half my dogs, at least, and maybe me too. And the bastard didn't slow down. In fact, I swear that he speeded up as he got closer." He shrugged and sniggered. "There wasn't anything for me to do but take to the ditch. Which I did. Right into it bicycle wagon, dogs and all—and me." Fury suddenly flashed through his eyes, followed by curses and several rasping breaths before he got his emotions under control. "He ran over two of my pets, Grant and Abe. It took me an hour to untie the living dogs, tie them to the fence on the field side of the ditch, right the bicycle and cart, put the dead in the cart under an old tarp I carry, re-tie the dogs to the contraption, and then hunt down all the little mutts, who had spread all over the place, chasing anything that moved and lots of things that didn't. When I got home I buried Grant and Abe."

"Did you get a license plate or a good look at the car? Did you call the police?" Eve asked sympathetically.

"Yes and no. I couldn't see the plate. There was too much

dust. He was going so fast and kicking up so much dust that it was impossible to see much of anything, let alone a little license plate. After all, that's a dirt road we were on, as you well know, and it's really dry out, and the wind was following him, so there was even dust in front of him, as well as everywhere else. But I saw the car and driver all right, in spite of the dust. And I called the police."

"What did they say?"

"They sent an officer out to talk to me."

"What did he say?"

The Dog Man stared at Eve for a long time before he answered, "I don't think he believed me when I told him I saw the driver. I shouldn't have told him about the dust, but he asked if I saw the license plate and, well," he shrugged in irritation, "I would bet everything I have that he didn't believe I saw the driver. But he'll investigate. He seemed like an honest cop with a sense of integrity. I think he'll try. He'll talk to his superiors. They'll tell him to talk to your uncle. Your uncle will claim he's innocent. He'll have an alibi and he'll tell the cop about my part in the street melee the other day. The cop will go to his superiors for advice. And, since the man who killed my dogs is a respected member of the community, and since the officer will say my story isn't very credible, his superiors will tell him to drop the case. End of story."

"You can't blame the policeman," Eve commented.

"That's what I said," the Dog Man shrugged in irritation. "But I can sure blame the system."

"How? Why? You said yourself that you couldn't see a license plate because of the dust and that there was dust even in front of the car. So how can you expect anyone to believe that you got a good look at the man driving? Or woman?"

"I think I said all of that, even about not blaming the police-man. I'm also smart enough to know it's my word against your uncle's." The Dog Man's voice had turned sarcastic. "But I'd bet no one checks your uncle's car for damage to the front and left side."

"I wouldn't," Eve insisted, "because I don't think you like my cousin. You've got a grudge against him for some reason."

"Not really. I don't know the man. But the little contact I have had with him suggests to me that he's not a very honorable person."

"I think you'd change your mind if you got to know him."

"Maybe, but I'll pass on the getting-to-know-him part."

The conversation frittered into silence for several minutes. Eve sat glaring at the Dog Man. His eyes sparkled as he returned her stare. Me, I felt like a cat watching two dogs, one trying to intimidate the other with an unwavering glare and the second attempting conciliation with a slight wag of the tail and a laughing glint in his eyes. When the silence had begun to vibrate with Eve's anger and my fearful uncertainty, with an ironic smile on his lips, the Dog Man changed the topic, asking Eve about a test she had recently taken in a marketing class. Eve's anger melted as she explained the many hours of study and worry that led to an A.

19

Possibly ECU's most popular professor during my years there was Dr. I. Zacharia Quierda, Professor of Political Science, the latter actually being a serious attempt to fuse two academic opposites, inasmuch as politics and science are about as mutually inclusive as are expressionism and arithmetic, and not a tongue-in-cheek commentary on social studies, as some might think. Dr. I, as he was known among his students, was the youngest full professor ever to teach at the college. When I entered ECU he had just recently signed on to the faculty, maybe five or six years previously. According to rumors, his meteoric rise from instructor to full prof was a direct result of his prolific scholarly production. He turned out "studies" almost as fast as the local nail factory turned out boxes of nails and screws.

I believe Dr. I was 28 or 29, maybe a year or two younger. Eve told me once that the man had also earned his PhD at the very young age of 23, or so he had told her. In any case he was a dynamic lecturer, full of ideas and wit if not facts, breadth of perspective, or unbiased opinions. I took his Intro to Poli Sci course on Eve's recommendation, to fulfill one of my social science requirements. Mostly I was thankful for her suggestion, although ultimately I really wished I had taken anthropology or another psychology course instead. We spent most of our time on communism, socialism and liberalism as much maligned political species, on race relations or on how to overcome our prejudices in a sociopolitical system designed to further the same.

I have to admit I joined the class to learn about Marx and Engels, and Lenin and Trotsky, and the communist revolutions of the twentieth…. Oh well, it was an interesting class. And maybe I did learn a lot about my personal social prejudices, and those of my Indo-European compatriots, and nothing about those of my African-American, or Hispanic-American, compatriots. And maybe I'm just too hard-headed to change much, in any basic sense, although I don't find that such a characteristic distinguishes me from most of the people I've known: black, white or brown; rich, poor or in-between; believer or non-believer; Catholic, Protestant, Muslim, Hebrew, or atheist; ad probably finitum.

"You need to transcend your limited view of politics and human nature," Dr. I once told me at a party he hosted for his students old and new. "They're not separate, you know. Politics is inherent in everything, in the arts, in science and religion, in… it's everywhere. Every decision, every choice or desire is colored by your political views, actually determined by them. And your political views are colored by the way you see the world and human nature. The world is simply a kaleidoscope of the colors you paint it. They are so interwoven that they're like the human creature itself, a mind and a body inseparable. Just think of the mind as politics and the body as human nature. If you separate mind and body, neither one can function. The mind can no longer reason simply because it doesn't have anything corporeal to reason on. The body can't function because it has nothing to guide it. The exact same is true of politics and human nature."

I realized, as he spoke, that he was summarizing one of his course lectures...in fact more than one: his class intro and summary, and some of his discourses on Marx and the political movements Marxism set off. But, of course, I was no longer as interested as I had once thought I was in communism and its offshoots, or proponents, or in any kind of politics for that matter. Being a young, hot-blooded member of the American middle class, my primary interests were girls, girls, more girls, and how to make a buck or two in order to date a specific girl, Eve, to be honest. This I had realized after a few of Dr. I's class sessions. I couldn't find much exciting about politics or social problems, nothing nearly as much as I thought I would.

Anyhow, Dr. I liked to party with his students. His public reason, the one he himself broadcast anyway, was that, like politics, education was all pervasive, informally if not formally. And what we learned informally, even unconsciously, had a much greater impact on our lives than did our formal education, a much more profound and more lasting impact. So, being a dedicated teacher, he refused to limit his instruction to the classroom. Besides, he liked to forge close, personal relationships with those students he considered worth his time and effort. That appeared to be what really made his teaching worthwhile to him.

The rumors, on the other hand, insisted that the students chosen for his personal succor were primarily female, with the few chosen males thrown in as camouflage.

In any case, the sixth or seventh of Dr. I's parties that I attended was during my eighth week in his class, my second semester on campus. Eve and I went together. She had been personally invited. My invitation was more general inasmuch as all the students in Dr. I's classes at the time of any given party had an open invitation, something he announced at the beginning of each semester. The parties were always on Saturday. Those students and ex-students he deemed worth his while were invited by e-mail or phone. Eve was one of those. I was not.

Dr. I's house was concealed on a couple acres of wooded land at the far northwestern edge of what used to be the Barsell Farm, but was presently owned and farmed by a man named Zyco, who lived three miles to the east. Why he had rented two acres of land to Dr. I was a mystery. He owned several farms including the Barsell Farm and had destroyed all the buildings on each of them, except the house he rented to Dr. I. He had also turned all the wooded acreage on every one of his farms into tillable land, except for the two acres rented to Dr. I. He prided himself on being a grain farmer and on taking advantage of every acre of land he owned. "No waste," was his motto. "Profit" was his creed. "Money" was his religion.

One day, supposedly, one of his competitors asked him why he leased the land to Dr. I. His answer: "Everyone must do a good deed from time to time. How else does one earn a place in Heaven?"

"By the grace of God," his competitor answered earnestly.

"I'm afraid my God is too much like me," Mr. Zyco answered just as seriously. "He expects all of us to earn our way to his side through our good works. As far as He is concerned there are no freebies, none whatsoever, neither here nor there. Everybody has to earn his own way to Heaven, one way or another."

I never met Mr. Zyco so I can't really vouch for his beliefs, or his honesty.

But I can give some kind of account about what happened to me that one night at Dr. I's house.

Eve and I arrived about 8:00 pm. The house and its acreage stood at the edge of Echo Creek, the lane leading back to the house less than an eighth of a mile from the town limit sign. The house itself huddled near the rear of the trees and brush that made up the woods and was thus invisible from both road and town, although on the night of the party there were lanterns spaced along the lane and the trees surrounding the house were bathed in ornamental lights. We still couldn't see the house from the road, but the sky over it looked like someone had borrowed the sun for a light fixture.

When we entered the house we were met by the host himself. He nodded to me with a quizzical expression and then pulled Eve aside. I waited patiently, expecting him to return my date immediately. But the two of them, after a few moments of intense conversation, wandered together toward the back of the house. Neither one looked my way, nor spoke to me nor anyone else crammed into the living room. I was flabbergasted. At first. Then angry. I started to follow them. But after a few steps I hesitated. Some other feeling paralyzed me, possibly brought on by thoughts of the rumors about Dr. I and his relationships to his students. Maybe it was a sense of shame. Maybe a feeling of loss. Maybe both. Or maybe it was humiliation. I don't know. But after a few moments of standing in place, frozen by something sick and angry inside me, I headed for the door through which my date and professor had disappeared. The kitchen. It was the kitchen I found myself in, as I knew I would, with maybe twenty people standing around talking and laughing, seemingly totally unaware of my loss. They all had bottles of beer in their hands, or paper cups. Scattered around the floor were open ice chests heavy with bottles and cans of beer and soda. Every inch of counter space that didn't support a microwave, toaster, or other piece of kitchen equipment supported plastic cups and bottles of booze and mixers.

Nobody paid any attention to me as I entered the verbal melee. Eve and her kidnapper had disappeared somewhere else. I stopped, frozen, in the doorway, my eyes frantically searching the crowd, my mind dropping another notch toward emptiness and hurt.

I started to ask a couple standing nearby if they had seen Eve and Dr. I pass through the kitchen. But I couldn't. Eve had not been forced to go with the professor. She had walked off willingly, without saying a word to me, not saying don't go away because I'll be back shortly, or I've got to talk to Dr. I for a moment, or…anything. Nor had she prepared me in any way for the possibility that I might be deserted. I was devastated. And angry. Devastated and mad as hell!

I made my way through the kitchen, looking for my missing date. The back door was locked, as was the only other exit, a door leading to the left at the rear of the house, a door I had never entered in any of the previous parties I had attended. I tried the knob to each door.

"You can't go back there," a female voice spoke behind me and to the left. "Dr. I is having a private conversation with a student."

"Did he just go through here?" I tried to sound unconcerned, but what came out sounded plaintive and angry, even to my ear.

"Was that your woman he had in tow?" the male with the girl snorted sarcastically.

I glared at him, unable to answer.

"Don't sweat it," he sneered drunkenly. "He'll return her when he's through, either still as pure as when he borrowed her or at least not much the worse for wear, I expect."

"Don't be an ass, Dave," the girl elbowed him, giggling.

I turned and walked away, knowing full well that if the guy made another comment I might slug him, unable to keep my fury at Eve and Dr. I from exploding against an innocent drunk, my anger exacerbated by his sarcastic, snotty attitude. I hesitated in the doorway to the living room, thinking about returning and breaking the door to the bedrooms down. After a few moments, though, I threaded my way through the noisy crowd to the front door and left. Soon I was on the old road leading back into Echo Creek, my steps as heavy as my heart and soul, my mind frantically trying to find a positive explanation for Eve's desertion and my own cowardice, but coming up short in each scenario it invented.

I eventually reached home and crept into bed. Sleep avoided me until the sun was beginning to peek at my world from behind the horizon, hesitating in the pale grey dawn as if too self-conscious to show itself completely.

I didn't overcome my anger, or my sense of worthlessness, for days or maybe never.

Anyhow I withdrew from Dr. I's class.

Eve? I ran into her in the library the day after the party.

She glared at me and asked why I had deserted her.

"I had to bum a ride from one of the girls I know and her date. That was embarrassing. For a while I thought I'd have to walk back to town."

"I deserted you?" I sputtered angrily. "You go in the bedroom with Dr. I and lock the door. You don't tell me a damned thing; you just walk away with that bastard. And I didn't even know where you went until some drunk in the kitchen told me. And you expected me to wait until you two were through doing whatever the hell you were doing in the bedroom! You aren't that naïve, Eve. And neither am I."

"We were discussing my last paper, the one I just turned in on sex and women's rights."

"Yeah, and I'll believe that when Mars is repopulated with tiny green creatures who speak English. Nobody locks bedroom doors to discuss a damned paper."

"Are you calling me a liar," Eve swelled indignantly, her blue eyes sparking. For a moment I felt like apologizing. "We didn't do anything but talk about my paper. Dr. I wants me to rewrite it for publication. I told him I probably wouldn't have time until summer.

I almost laughed. Almost. But my suspicion had turned to an even deeper anguish as she talked. I couldn't wipe from my mind the drunken words of the student by the locked door. The vivid picture of his drunken sneer and the impact of his words still haunted my mind, forcing it into a jealousy that teetered on the verge of rage. I turned and walked away.

One plaintive word from Eve's mouth caught me before I got out of earshot: "Donjon...."

I kept walking, ignoring the new hurt invading the older one. Loss, a deep, cold, empty sense of loss and loneliness joined the hurt already embedded in my soul. I almost turned around and retraced my steps, but something, pride maybe, kept my spine rigid and my legs moving forward.

I didn't see Eve for several weeks after that day, not even walking around the campus or in the library. It was as if she suddenly changed her schedule in order to avoid me.

One day, though, Dr. I accosted me as I was headed off campus. I had just finished biology, my last class of the day, and was headed home to shower, eat, and study. As I approached the social sciences building he stepped out of the front door and came to a halt several feet in front of me. As I glared and started to go around him, he spoke, "We need to talk."

"What about?" I snarled. "I dropped your class."

"I know," he spoke softly, calmly, and a little patronizingly, I thought. "I wish you hadn't. You were a good student."

"Yeah, well, it's already done," I tried to control my voice but the underlying anger was impossible to hide. I moved to step around him and continue on my way.

"Please wait and hear me out," the softness of his voice seconded the plea.

I hesitated, wanting way down deep to ignore him and walk away. But an image of Eve stopped me. "Okay, so go ahead and talk," I tried to growl but my voice came out little more than a hoarse whisper.

"You're making a big mistake," he warned in the tone of voice he used in his lectures, albeit softer and insistent rather than thoughtful and loaded with energy. "Nothing happened between me and your girlfriend. I don't have affairs with my students."

"That's not what everybody says," I sneered in spite of my attempt to speak reasonably. "Rumors say you sleep with any student that's got a good body and a decent brain to go with it."

His face turned red, then white.

"You know better than to believe any of the rumors that circulate on a college campus, Johnson. Lord knows, there are enough of them." He paused, staring at me with his professorial look, the serious stare he used while trying to pour reason into the young minds in his classes. "You're an intelligent young man. And you've had your share of problems with gossip in the past, I expect." He paused, his eyes studying mine, before adding, "And maybe you still do, from what I hear. So you should know better than all of us how idiotic, false and damaging rumors can be."

I shrugged, no longer trusting myself to speak. My anger escalated at his reference to my past.

"I'm young. I'm single. I'm a normal male. So, yes, I've had a fling or two with students. After all, most college girls are adults both physically and legally. So there's no reason I can't date them if I want to and they're willing. I try not to date any of them while they're in my classes, of course, but that doesn't always work. Attraction to the opposite sex doesn't always conform to what is ethically correct."

"I'm not interested in your love life," I interrupted, wanting to turn and walk away but at the same time held in place by a perverse interest in what he had to say.

"Okay," he held up his hands, seemingly in an attempt to pacify my apparent anger, "to get to the point, Eve and I met at the party to discuss a paper she wrote. I think it's an excellent paper and, with a little more work, might be publishable."

"Why did you meet at the party?" I asked angrily. "Why not in your office? And why head for a bedroom and lock the door? And that was pretty damned rude and inconsiderate to take her away from me just when we walked in the door, without a damned word of explanation. It was like you and Eve both were telling me to go away, get lost. And, hell…," I sputtered to a halt, not having any idea what more to say.

"It was my mistake," he interrupted me. "I didn't consider the rumors and how it would look. But nothing happened. Absolutely nothing!" He smiled wistfully before adding, "I don't think Eve is the type of person you could pull something like that on anyway, no matter who tried it. Besides, she seems to be completely infatuated with you. Although I can't for the life of me understand why," he added with a smile meant to show that his words were meant as a joke.

I shrugged and again turned to walk away, this time pushing his arm away when he tried to stop me.

"Just talk to her," he called after me. "She's really hurt by this whole thing."

"And I'm not?" I muttered to myself.

The next Saturday I walked out to visit with the Dog Man. I needed a shot of his good humor, but I didn't find much of it.

"What's this I hear about you and Eve breaking up?" he asked as soon as I had waded safely through the outer ring of wildly friendly dogs and seated myself on the floor just inside the front door. "She says you two were at a party and you got upset because she left you to talk to one of her teachers about a paper she had written. She said...."

"Yeah, she said," I interrupted. "Do you mean she came out here to see you?"

He paused and glared at me before continuing, "She's really hurt, you know. You had no right to desert her like that."

"Hell," I snapped, unable to contain my anger. "You're not the first person to defend Eve and blame me for deserting her."

The Dog Man stared at me curiously.

"Why did you take off and leave her there anyway? Eve's not the type person that would go somewhere with one guy and then leave him to go make out with another. I have her figured as a pretty straight-forward woman, not a flirt or someone with loose morals. I don't think she's like so many of the girls I hear about nowadays. At least I don't have her pegged as a girl who has casual sex for the pleasure of it, either with a friend or with some stranger she's just picked up in a bar or at some party. I don't think she'd have sex with any guy unless she was willing to marry him, to make their relationship permanent. As far as girls nowadays go, she's pretty straight-laced, I think."

"Come on," I laughed cynically. "Most of the women I know would crawl in the sack with anyone, for whatever reason, if they wanted to, and moral values would have nothing to do with it. That's all old school stuff." I forced a grin at the triteness of my comment and continued ranting senselessly, "Morals don't have a damned thing to do with sex anymore, only with marriage, or commitment. If you promise to be true to someone, like in a marriage or if you're living together, or going steady, you should be true to your partner. That's true for men and women both. It's not just for women. That's what we have now. Equality. Men don't have any more rights than women. Why should they? We...."

"Okay. Okay." The tone emphasized the Dog Man's irritation with me. "So everybody's equal in this *Brave New World* we live in. Men and women only differ in their plumbing, and that's morally irrelevant, because plumbing only does what it's created for. People have to be loyal only to committed lovers, for legal and social reasons, not spiritual or moral ones, whether those lovers are of the same or the other sex, whether they're human or animal, or plants, for that matter. If they get married, sex partners are kind of like business partners. They sign a contract. If one of them breaches the contract, the other one can sue for dissolution of the business and separation of assets and income. If they're not married, well, then sex is just one more game, like tag or hockey or one of those crappy shoot-em-up games I see you playing on your I-pad or I-phone or whatever it is you have. Sex doesn't have to have anything to do with spiritual commitment or procreation and full-time commitment to raising a family in marriage. It's just a fun time, temporary, for a couple of partners to play with each other's genitals till one or the other or both have orgasms. No sweat." He glowered at me before continuing, seemingly daring me to interrupt. "That's one of the things that separate us from the animals, right, being capable of having sex for pure pleasure rather than pleasure and procreation, but in our case driven by pleasure rather than procreation? We're not only intellectually able, but also physically and morally and spiritually able, to separate the act from the potential end product of the act, the pleasure from the baby. Screw your partner, male or female, and throw the wasted seed and eggs out with the wash water. After all there's plenty more where the waste came from, and even when you're trying to get pregnant you waste a lot of the same anyway. So do the fishes and animals, the fishes especially, I believe. So why worry about it? Hell, nature's terribly wasteful anyway, and so are humans, so of what importance is one more wasteful practice, especially if there's a lot of pleasure attached to the wastefulness? Wasting seed is no worse than wasting food or water, I guess, maybe a lot less so in its consequences."

The Dog Man stopped talking and closed his eyes. For a moment I thought he was through. But then, eyes still closed, he began talking once more, or rather mumbling to himself.

"No wonder I'm happy living on the fringes of society, away from the hustle and bustle of social evolution, although I've always considered the word evolution to necessarily mean slow but steady, albeit too often hesitant, improvement, whereas what I see in society today I wouldn't consider improvement, just change. Change? Maybe retrogression would be a better word, retrogression in the spiritual realm as the material realm progresses. In other words, it is the inevitable journey to Sodom and Gomorra that necessarily accompanies the progress of civilization, that is, the evolution of civilizations from struggle to the easy life, from abstinence and sacrifice to indulgence and permissiveness. And ultimately comes the destruction, the rot from within long before the barbarians reach the gate."

Again he paused and sat silently for a long time, shoulders sagging, hands drooping in his lap, eyes closed.

"I guess, what I'm trying unsuccessfully to get at is that somebody has to have moral values and somebody has to be responsible for them. The church (or should I say the churches?) no longer has the spiritual authority, or sufficient loyal following, as far as that goes, to make much of an impact on individual morals, not to mention public ones. Television and other forms of modern news media have pretty much destroyed any high minded spiritual commitment we might have once had, by idealizing, whether intended or not, the immorality prevalent in the private lives of our cultural idols and other leaders, sometimes those of the church itself. Our government and its leaders definitely can't enforce moral codes unless they do so tyrannically. In that case, of course, they would come across as even greater hypocrites than they are. As for their leading by example, well, most of our political leaders would have to go through a thorough and intense soul cleansing before they could do so, and an about face in their life styles and personal practices. And I doubt that many people with money and power would do such, definitely not for the great unwashed masses." The Dog Man shook his head disgustedly, sadly. "From what I've seen of our government, and from what little I've read about the function of societies during peace time," again he chuckled, this time with a note of sarcasm clearly evident, "governments don't lead by example but rather by fiat or decree or some other such authoritarian method, or, if they're democratic rather than tyrannical, the leaders just get out in front of their subjects and try their damndest to stay there, no matter which way the flock is going, pretending to lead all the time, of course, and pretending to have solid moral and ethical values, so as to impress the masses and thus be allowed to stay up there in the front lines and so retain their modicum of power and cash in on the extra wealth thrown their way by those who would share in the power and acquire more easy wealth."

"Man," I laughed, "I thought Eve was the most cynical person I've ever met. And I always thought you were kind of a positive guy, seeing the bright side of things. But maybe I'll have to change my mind."

"You do that," he seemed to smile behind his beard. At least his lips moved and his eyes sparkled a tiny bit. "But as far as I'm concerned, and historians and other scholars be damned, highly developed civilizations bring about their own demise in one of two ways. They lose that spark, or that dynamic certainty, or whatever you want to call it—that absolute belief that they are right and the rest of the world is wrong. They lose that blind trust in themselves and their god, that oh so unshakeable conviction that God is on their side in all matters and that they, and only they, know God's mind. They begin to doubt that they are His chosen and thus are morally right no matter what path they choose, and no matter what or whom they destroy in the process. They accept more and more of the unbelievers into the, once, elite club of the chosen, simply because doubt grows among them that they are unique in any spiritual or biological sense. Along with that slow growth comes a sense of guilt toward all the people they have excluded from their elite club. To assuage that guilt they need to "save" those that they previously condemned. So in come the unwashed, the others, with all their unique needs and beliefs, all their different ideas—in family life, governmental rule, morals, ethics, in personal and social and spiritual relationships. All those varied differences that invariably bring discord with them.

"Or," he paused as if to gather his thoughts, "an old civilization loses its moral compass. Pleasure, comfort, the immediate gratification of any and all needs become the norm, rather than sacrifice for the future, the future of oneself and one's children, the future of one's extended family, one's neighbors, one's country, one's god. A vision of a future paradise for the chosen few, a new Garden of Eden, no matter how myopic and self-centered such a vision might be, no damned matter how personalized, or grasping and greedy, no matter what sacrifice demanded of the self and others—in my mind that is what builds great civilizations, not gratifying sexual desires any time and with any one you happen to want in a given moment, or gratifying any other material desires whenever and wherever they arise. Civilizations begin to die when self-gratification usurps duty and responsibility, no matter how misguided the latter are."

He paused and chuckled before continuing, "I think that's enough of a lecture for one day. I don't know why I got on my high-horse. I no longer even know what you said to set me off.

But whatever it was, if you don't want to be bored by my pedantic lectures, don't say it again."

"We were talking about Eve and somehow got off on morality and the fall of empires," I laughed at my own conceit. He was the one who got off the low path and onto the higher one. I just listened and tried to follow.

"Ah, yes, Eve. I can't believe you gave her up. She's got everything a man could want—beauty, intelligence, character, integrity, loyalty and, if I might throw in a characteristic which seems irrelevant on the surface, consistency." He paused and stared at me for several moments as if awaiting a reaction. I said nothing so he continued. "And you gave her up just because of jealousy? You know, it's your fate to live and search for happiness in this modern world of ours, a world of inconsistency and transitory gratifications. Oh, you could escape it to a certain extent, like I do. But you're too young to make such a choice, even if you wanted to. I can't see you happy living on the fringes of society. You're young and so still have that strong desire to experience life, with all its adventures and pleasures and heartaches." He almost cackled this time. "You've got too much curiosity about and desire to experiment with the opposite sex is what it boils down to, that and too much enthusiasm for the adventures of life, all aspects of life. No way could you withdraw like I have. And I could not have done so at your age either. I too yearned for adventure, for not only new adventures, but also for the anticipation of them and of the unknown future and all it held for me. I chased women, I got into trouble, I went to college, I worked at a job that I enjoyed, I got married, I had a family." I was certain I saw tears in his eyes but he had turned his face from me and was staring into space to my right, so I wasn't certain. "And then my world fell apart. Death came to visit my two children. I was driving the car when the accident happened. That's what it was, an accident pure and simple. Another driver ran a red light and hit my car in the back half, right where the back seats were. My two children were strapped in those seats. The rear half of the car was destroyed, as were the two angels of my life. My wife was not with us. For some reason she seemed to blame me. Oh, not at first. At first we grieved together. But slowly, over the next few months, she changed. She began drinking and running around, out till late hours, lying about where she had been and with whom. And I," the Dog Man's voice trembled. He stopped talking. I thought he wouldn't go on, but after a few deep breaths he started again, "Instead of trying to find help for her I walked out. That was many years ago. I haven't seen her since. And not a night goes by but what I dream of her, awake or sleeping. Not a day goes by but what I think of her at least once. That was a terrible mistake, my walking out, like you just walked out on Eve."

"What happened to her, your wife?" I asked curiously, made sad by his suffering and ignoring his comment about Eve.

"I don't know. She disappeared." There was a profound desolation in his voice. "I once returned to where we lived, in her home town, but she had simply disappeared. Her parents were dead. She had no siblings. Not a single one of her friends knew where she was or what had happened to her. As far as I'm concerned she might as well have disappeared into a black hole."

"You still miss her then," I asked tritely, unable to grasp the depth of the desolation in his voice and words.

"Miss her?" An angry emptiness, an echo as if seeping out of the very depths of infinite space, black, hurtful, despairing, as faint as a ghost of being wandering forever lost in the darkest night, howled somewhere behind his voice. "Miss her? Yes. All the time. Like part of me is missing all the time, every single moment of the day."

His voice broke. He turned and walked out of the cabin, through the dogs yapping outside, and disappeared into the woods. I waited for over an hour but he didn't return.

I left.

20

I started drinking more than usual, more often and more when I did drink, at times not even returning home but rather passing out wherever I happened to have my last drink and waking up the next morning. That's the only way I got much sleep, because when I didn't drink myself into a stupor I lay awake most of the night, any and all nights, thinking about Eve. I missed her terribly. Even during the day, at work, in class, with friends, I couldn't keep my mind from her. It simply fled from present reality, no matter what, into the recent past where Eve inhabited every single nook and cranny of my world and self, and every moment of my time.

Oddly enough, I generally made it to work and to class, and to the student gym. I guess I hadn't fallen completely over the cliff, although my self-pity often made me think that I had. Others thought so too. Dan Borrell confronted me one morning as I was listlessly walking toward the library, hung over and smelling of booze from the night before.

"Hey, man," he greeted me with those words and a light jab to the chest. "What's this about you ditching the woman of my dreams at Dr. I's big bash a couple of weeks ago? Are you sick or something, or is it just a rumor? I can't believe it." He threw his hands like a ham actor in some cheap play. "Bart told me. He said Eve told him at one of their study sessions. I called him a liar, of course. Nobody leaves Eve, nobody with any sense, anyway. So what've you got to say for yourself, Big Boy?" He grinned at his Mae West imitation. "Tell me it ain't so. Rumors are flying that you aren't quite right in the head, that you're drunk half the time, and that your breakup with Eve is the cause, which isn't hard to believe."

I thought about pushing him away and walking off. His frivolous mood grated on mine, irritating rather than soothing, although the latter is probably how he wanted to come across, to soothe whatever anger or frustration I might still feel about the breakup with Eve and thus get me to talk.

His attempt didn't work though. My anger was still too close to the flashpoint.

"I've got to do some quick research in the library and get my butt to class," I mumbled apologetically, stepping around him to continue walking, throwing over my shoulder as I walked away: "We're gonna have a quiz. I'll see you in the Union at noon." I wondered what kind of excuse I could come up with to miss that appointment.

"I'll be there, man. Don't stand me up. The rumor's out that you're avoiding all of us, all your friends, and that you're drinking way too much."

He said something else but I didn't hear what.

Noon came all too soon. All morning I had promised myself that I would avoid the Union. But finally I staggered out of the fog of booze and hurt and self-pity, far enough at least to realize that Dan was a decent guy and worried about my welfare. And he had become a good friend. So I headed for the Union.

Dan was waiting for me, holding down a table for two against the back wall. I had expected to find Bart and possibly some others with him, but Dan surprised me. He sat all alone. He hadn't even gone through the food line yet.

"Toss your backpack on the chair," he stood, pointed to where I would sit, and then stooped and moved his backpack from the floor to his chair. "Let's get food."

He took off instantly, without waiting for me to follow his commands. I tossed my backpack where he had pointed and followed.

When we were finally seated, backpacks on the floor and burgers and fries in front of us, he dug in, ignoring my questioning stare. After a moment my irritation got the better of me.

"Damn it, Dan," I swore. "What the hell's the matter with you? You wanted to talk. So talk!"

"I'm hungry," he spoke around a mouthful of hamburger. "Eat and we'll talk later."

So I ate, and waited as he devoured his second burger.

"Is it all true?" he asked when he had finished.

"Is what true?"

"Don't play innocent," he growled. "Did you really ditch Eve at Dr. I's party? Did you drop Dr. I's class? Have you refused to have anything to do with Eve since the breakup?" He suddenly grinned slyly. "And do you think there's any hope for me now that she's alone again?"

"Shithead," I laughed in spite of myself. "Yes, yes, no, and hell no. You gotta have looks and sophistication to attract Eve."

"Maybe, but I don't' think so. She liked me once, and Bart too.

Hell, she's dated lots of different types. And you're damn well no Casanova."

"I was kidding, Dan," I shook my head to show the absurd humor of my comment. I don't know what attracts her, or any other woman. Just when I think I've got it figured out, they do something that shoots my theories to hell. Or Eve does. Why she claimed that she planned on marrying some rich man and yet stayed with me, I don't have the slightest idea."

"Me either," Dan chuckled. "That is, why she stuck with you is way beyond me. I figure she must have been blind or sick in the head, or...."

"Go to hell," I laughed.

"Let's get serious," he stared at me as he chewed his last fry. "You don't really think Eve had something going with the old Professor Playboy, do you?"

"What would you think if you went on a date with a girl and she left you and locked herself in a bedroom with some other guy?"

"Yeah, I get your point. Anyone else but Eve, I'd say you got a big problem and you better stay away from her. Anyone other than Dr. I, I'd say you should take a poke at him. But the good professor? Well, I think there's something you don't know about him. Not many people do. And...I don't have any real proof of what I think. Just a few rumors, mostly limited to some of us in sports."

"What're you trying to say, Dan?"

"Well, I don't want this to get around. I'd feel like hell if it isn't true and the word got out that I was one of the guys that started the rumor."

"Okay, okay, okay," I forced a laugh in spite of my irritation. "You know I can keep a secret. I never told anybody about that time you got blind drunk and wound up in bed with that old hag. You know, the one old enough to be your great grandmother and ugly enough to pass for one of Macbeth's three witches."

"I know," he groaned. "And I'm damned glad you didn't. What a way to ruin a reputation."

"If you had one," I grinned.

"Yeah," he sarcastically imitated my grin. "Okay, rumors among the basketball and baseball teams say that the good Dr. I has had affairs with two former players, a forward and an outfielder. They say that it's Dr. I himself who started the rumors about his affairs with his female students. That and his parties are his cover. I guess he thinks the sun's too bright outside the closet."

Dan's words hit me hard. Feelings flashed through my body—doubt, denial, tentative acceptance, anger at myself, shame. I don't know what all, but for the first time since the night of Dr. I's party and my breakup with Eve, there seemed to be some relief sneaking in there somewhere.

"You're kidding me," I stuttered, trying my damndest to assimilate what he had said and what it meant for me and Eve. "Dr. I? I can't believe it. He's never given me any indication he's not straight. I've never heard anyone suggest such a thing."

"Yeah," Dan smiled weakly, as if trying to commiserate but not quite sure how to go about it. "Me neither. At first I didn't believe it either. I'm not certain I totally believe it now, but it's funny how so many of the guys on the team swear it's so. But," he shrugged, "you know how rumors are. One person says they've seen something, or heard something, and before you know it lots of them have heard or seen the same thing. Some of the guys that are talking though, you know, I really trust. I can't see them making things up or saying things they aren't real sure of."

That little session with Dan returned some of the cheap ego that I had lost the night of the party. I quit drinking so much and turned to women instead, exchanging one addiction for another. I couldn't seem to do anything in moderation in those days. And I had about as much self-control with my latest joy as I had had with the former one.

But before I became addicted to my latest craze I tried to connect with Eve again. The next Saturday I walked out to the Carsons' place, when I felt certain that Eve would be there. As luck would have it, though, who answered the door but Mrs. Carson, the last person in the world that I wanted to talk to. She wasn't what you would call friendly, of course.

"What do you want?" she asked as she opened the door. "I thought you and Eve had broken up."

"Yeah, well, we did," I stuttered. "But I really need to talk to her."

"She doesn't want to talk to you," the damned woman started to close the door in my face as she spoke.

I smacked it with the flat of my hand, effectively keeping it ajar a couple of feet, and then stuck a shoe in the opening.

"Come on," I felt a kind of whining plea in my voice and cursed myself for the weakness. "Just ask her. Let her decide if she wants to talk to me or not."

She glared at me as if she wanted to kick me or maybe spit in my face. Then a smirk slowly spread across her lips and her eyes took on a spark of light.

"Well," she hesitated before continuing, "she's not here right now. She went to an afternoon movie with a friend." Again that smirk, but it quickly spread into a mirthless grin. "A male friend, that is. I doubt if you know him, personally at least. But I'm sure you know who he is. His father is a lawyer, a wealthy corporation lawyer. Matthew Dwight is his name." Again she paused and studied my face, which I'm sure showed both my hurt and my anger. "Matthew's son," she emphasized the two nouns, "is Andrew Dwight. He's a nice boy, just what Eve needs to settle her down."

I almost turned away but, shoulders sagging, I tried to force the tremor out of my voice, before asking, "Do you know when she'll be home?"

"Now how would I know that?"

There is nothing I would have liked better at the moment than to wipe that sneer off of her face with the flat of my hand. But I held myself in check and asked, "Isn't she supposed to be home by ten?"

"That was when she was out with the likes of you, a good-for-nothing who couldn't be trusted with a nice girl like her. I trust Andrew. He's a little gentleman. He brought me a bouquet of flowers when he picked Eve up. He's thoughtful and nice. Now if you'll get your foot out of the doorway I'll get back to my television program."

"You think she likes this guy?"

A really dumb question? I knew it was but I just couldn't help myself. I was really upset that Eve was out with another guy, especially someone who could give her a heck of a lot more than I could. Suddenly I felt even more insecure than I had since the evening Eve and Dr. I had locked themselves in his bedroom, leaving me with that old lack of self-confidence that had often haunted me before, and even into my teenage years.

"Look," Mrs. Carson said in a tone that made it seem like she just might sympathize with me a little, "Eve is not for you. She's ambitious. She wants a rich husband. She wants a comfortable life with no money worries. She wants children who won't lack for anything. What can you give her? I know I keep asking that same question, but it's the most important one you should be asking yourself if, like you keep saying, you really care for the girl. If you love her, you want her to be happy, don't you?" She paused and the smirk appeared again. "Isn't that what love is all about? Wanting the person you love to be happy and rich and… well, have everything their little heart desires? Isn't that what you should want for Eve, if, as she says you've told her more than once, you really do love her?"

"How stupid is that?" I thought and almost said out loud. Yeah, sure I wanted Eve to be happy and have everything she desired, but with me, not with anybody else. But I wasn't about to admit to the old witch in front of me that my love was just one of those normal human emotions that have a large element of selfishness in them.

"Just tell her I stopped by to see her. Would you do that,

please? Tell her I'll be in the library tomorrow afternoon. I'd like to see her if she'll stop by there."

"No, I'm not going to tell Eve any such thing," the woman almost snarled. "She doesn't want to see you, ever. She told me that, actually more than once. We've talked about her little infatuation with you. She admitted that you had little to offer her and that she should have dumped you long ago. She said you were inconsiderate and jealous, and lazy, and didn't have any idea what you wanted to do with your life. She wants to make something of herself. You seem to be satisfied with mediocrity and just floating along like on some muddy creek somewhere. I agree with her. So go away and leave us alone."

"But I have some really important information for her. It should change how she feels about me."

I think she started to shout at me but her husband appeared behind her, his eyes glaring at me over her shoulder.

"You've taken up enough of our time," he growled.

I looked at him, then her again. They were both scowling at me. So I turned and left, shoulders heavy, gait dragging. I thought for a moment of waiting on the other side of the street, on the curb, in the dark, until Eve and her date showed up. But I immediately rejected that idea. Eve had avoided me since our last conversation. Mrs. Carson had left no doubt in my mind that she spoke for Eve, that most of what she had said were also Eve's thoughts.

I trudged on home.

The next day I headed for the business school building, where Eve had a couple of classes daily. It was a few minutes to three in the afternoon. I figured that Eve should be leaving her marketing class about that time. And I was correct.

When the bell rang I was standing outside the doorway to her classroom, leaning against the wall opposite the door. She ambled out talking to some guy I recognized but couldn't place in any specific context. She saw me all right. Her eyes darted my way and then slipped quickly away, back toward the guy. I pushed off the wall and started her way. She said something to the guy and then took off almost running. He stopped as if stunned, his eyes following. My actions were absolute clones of his. After a few moments he glanced around as if wondering what had just happened. His eyes met mine. He frowned and then headed in the direction Eve had taken.

I don't know how long I stood there paralyzed. But it was long enough to get bumped several times by students scurrying along the hallway, on their way to or from classes. After a while I lurched away, following the student movement on my side of the hallway, not knowing where I was going, or why.

I wound up outside the building, near some park benches, where I plopped my butt down and stared into space, my mind blank.

21

That night after work, an hour before midnight, my mind still feeling sorry for my body because of Eve's cold shoulder, I headed for the bars again, this time to a hole called Stinkey's.

Stinkey's was not a student bar. It stood belligerently on a side street almost a mile from the northern edge of campus, in an area dominated by companies catering to the skilled and unskilled trades and to businesses that service home repair and upkeep. After ten or eleven at night, the building was almost always bouncing on its toes to the wild rhythms of drunken music inside. You couldn't miss it if you happened to wander within a block radius, not because of neon lights or anything like that, because the bar's façade was actually dark, leaving the building itself with a forlorn, forsaken appearance, but rather because of the music and drunken, raucous laughter from inside the nondescript building. It seemed to escape through every pore.

As I entered, the smoke and stench of booze and frantic bodies punched me in the gut. I choked as I tried to breathe. But then, almost immediately, my body adapted. The music became a friend, a shoulder to cry on. The noise of laughter and shouting beckoned like a siren on the shore of a foggy sea. I felt at home as I headed for the bar to get a beer.

Three beers later I was dancing with a woman almost as tall

as I am, maybe twice my age, and probably outweighing me by a pound or two. I had sat down beside her at the bar, unwittingly. I was also so engrossed in my problem, so engrossed in feeling sorry for myself, that I didn't notice her; otherwise, being stone sober when I took one of three vacant barstools and ordered my first beer, I probably would have chosen one of the other two stools to sit in.

I didn't even know that a female was sitting beside me until the first graze of her knees as she swung around on her stool to stare at the dancers. My first beer had just disappeared down my gullet and the bartender was heading my way with another. At the light touch I glanced her way but she didn't return my look, just sat there staring toward the dance floor as if mesmerized by the wild rhythms on it. So I turned back to my despondent mood, noting vaguely that she looked somewhat like Groucho Marx from the side but seemed to have a decent figure, albeit a big one.

A moment later she grazed my thigh once more as she swung back to face the bar. Automatically I again glanced her direction. Nothing. Her gaze was lost in the bar-length mirror that faced us, or maybe it was lost among the dozens of bottles of booze that were stacked on the shelf below the mirror.

I returned to my self-pity.

She swung around again. Again her knee grazed my thigh and again she completely ignored my irritated glance in her direction. And again, a few moments later, she bumped me as she turned back to the bar.

"Do you like to dance?" I asked, not really caring whether she answered or not.

"I would love to," she answered.

"What?" I asked kind of stupidly. She hadn't answered my question.

"I said yes, I'll dance with you."

She was looking at me with this kind of false innocence, so what could I do. Say go to hell? Say that's not what I asked you? Say wait a minute; let's start this conversation over?

I took the coward's way out. I stood up and offered her my arm. And we headed out into the primitive melee.

I have to admit that she was a pretty good dancer, a lot better than I am. She wasn't at all inhibited by my clumsiness. But why should she have been? We never touched once we entered the combat zone. She immediately swung into some kind of war dance, maybe Sioux or Pawnee or some such thing. It definitely seemed like something out of one of the old John Wayne or Randolph Scott movies, or some movie about savages in Africa, or more probably a combination of the two—anyhow a movie with a scene in which the Indians (African savages?) are getting themselves psyched up to attack a wagon train, or maybe a white man's fort. She went whooping around in her space, body bouncing and twitching, legs kicking as If trying to knee any of the dancers that got in her way, arms shooting in all directions, face without a single damned expression, unless ecstasy is what you see on the faces of movie zombies.

But she definitely seemed to enjoy herself. When the music ended and I started to return to my beer, she grabbed my arm and held on for dear life, until the music began again, at which time she again stomped into her wild trance and frantic movements.

I just kind of shuffled in place as she stomped around me and every couple nearby. The only thing missing from her was the whooping. But the band furnished that well enough.

Once the band changed to a few slow dances, to give the dancers a well-needed rest before the tavern had several heart attacks to contend with, I guess, she headed back to the bar, me in tow, attached to her right arm by five sharp fingernails, uh, claws.

I chugged my beer and she immediately ordered me another. She rejected the bartender's offer to refill her drink, which I had learned was cranberry juice. Anyhow, I finished that next beer quickly, trying to return my mind to the sanity it had lost on the dance floor. My plan, hastily formed as she dragged me out of the horde of savages and wannabes, was to finish my beer quickly and get the "you-know-what" out of there. After the bartender slammed the next beer in front of me, I immediately formed another just as devious plan—finish that one even more quickly and get the "you-know-what" out of there. Neither plan worked. Before I finished the second beer there was another one in front of me. I could have gotten up and scuttled away, using any or no excuse, but I've always had a weakness for free beer. So, I thought what the hell, drink up on someone else's dime (I think the beer was actually selling for $5.50 that night) before the bank goes dry.

Ho, ho. That wasn't very bright of yours truly. Before I had finished that beer I felt myself being dragged into the war dance again. And then back to the bar where not only my unfinished beer but also another full one awaited me, complete with a wink from the bartender.

I was hooked. I'd had more than my limit in too short of a time. And the dancing had turned my body into a cauldron of sexual frenzy. Three beers later and my dancing buddy began to look like Sophia Loren, except for her face, which still had Groucho's nose added to Peter Lorre's lips and chin, the Hulk's ears, and Randolph Scott's hairline, if he had let his hair grow untended for a few months.

So, for another hour or two I drank beer at the bar with some really wild dancing, for both of us now, interspersed between every two or three beers. My partner began to look better and better to my psyche and my body began to yearn for a little social jitterbugging between the sheets.

I don't know when we finally left Stinky's. Nor can I recall much of anything until waking up the next morning…er, day; it was close to two in the afternoon when I groaned out of bed and glanced at the clock on the nightstand by my sleeping partner's head. I had missed a couple of classes.

Then I glanced at my sleeping partner, at her face that is, since the rest of her was hidden under the covers.

I shuddered and, suddenly wide awake, I dressed as fast as I could and beat a hasty, and stealthy, retreat out of the woman's apartment. I heard my latest heartthrob mumble some question as I opened the bedroom door, but I continued my flight, pretending I hadn't heard a thing. I passed through the living room, I'm sure, but I don't remember seeing it, I was in such a hurry.

I exiled myself from Stinkey's that day and I didn't return for some time. And I haven't seen that one-night stand again. I don't know what I'd do if I did, unless it would be to run like hell or douse myself in beer again.

And so began my second addiction, females and the games that go with them. I have to admit that I enjoyed this second addiction a lot better than the first one.

I started hanging out at the student bars. Women seemed to be plentiful and ready for whatever I proposed. The first one after Groucho was another one-night stand. I would have gone back for seconds, but she had a boyfriend. He had been out of town the night we met, visiting his parents in order to finagle some more spending money out of them, or so she said.

"Give me your phone number," she insisted as I got up to leave her apartment at 3:45 the morning after (or the morning still, since neither one of us had been asleep yet). "Tom'll be back the day after tomorrow, so I can't see you after tonight and tomorrow night, unless he leaves town again. I don't want you calling me and messing up our relationship, so I won't give you my phone number. We plan to get married as soon as we graduate next year, and I really want to marry him. His dad's got money and a good business, and he'll take over that business someday. That's why I don't want you messing our relationship up. But I'll call you when he takes off again. We can get together if you want." She grinned slyly at me, knowing damned well that I'd fall all over myself to get her in the sack again, if I hadn't found anything better.

She had told me about her boyfriend and future husband Tom after our second dance.

I had been sitting in a bar called Plato's, nursing a beer, looking over the merchandise, when our eyes met. She was at a table with two other girls, all of them dressed to attract the male population in the bar. One of her girlfriends was wearing a slinky black dress that showed more mountain on her chest than it did the valley in between the two peaks. She had a nice face too. Her hair was a little too blond for the roots that supported it, but she still had a nice do, and a sensual face that almost any guy wouldn't mind waking up to in the morning. The other friend was a little on the common side, not repulsive by any means, but a little too skinny and with a face that could easily get lost in a crowd, even a crowd of average citizens. She was dressed like someone's sister.

Betty, on the other hand, was about in the middle of the two in looks and dress. She was a brunette. Her hair was short, not even hiding her ears completely, nice little ears from which dangled loop earrings. She had a nice shape, one on the order of Marilyn Monroe rather than more recent movie stars for whom anorexia seems to be the latest fad. I was smitten.

I asked her to dance. She said yes. She was a good dancer—nice, sensual movements; always in rhythm with the music. But from the very beginning she started leading the parade. Try as I might I couldn't force her to follow me. Finally, after I had failed in my final attempt to force her to follow my lead, failed although I lifted her off her feet by pulling her into my chest and leaning backward, failed in spite of the fact that I was considerably stronger than she was, stronger but not agile enough to keep her from slipping back into the lead once I let her feet touch the floor again—finally she giggled and, with a smirk, asked, "Why do men always insist on leading when we dance?" She smiled at me, condescendingly, I thought. "All of you do it even when I'm a better dance than you are."

I was startled by the question, startled and at a loss for words. My face must have shown my bewilderment because she grinned happily, as if she had won some kind of battle, and continued, "I know what you're going to say, that it's the custom for men to lead women when they're dancing. It's the way it's done. And if a woman leads then the man loses some of his, what would you call it? Manliness? Manhood? Machismo?"

"Yeah," I mumbled, irritated. "It's the way it's done." I hesitated and then, suddenly, I thought the whole thing was too funny for words. I cackled. Or I guess it was a cackle, although that sound refers more to hens than to roosters. I moved a few dance steps on my own and we almost tripped each other. I cackled again, and let go of her and started dancing facing her but a couple steps away. Her feet were moving a little faster than mine, more in tune with the music, I have to admit. But I was suddenly in control of myself again and felt the music flowing through soul and body, something I hadn't felt while she was in control.

We danced that way for a while, to the slow rhythms of the dance. She smiled. I grinned. She moved her right foot. My left foot was only a heartbeat behind hers. I danced closer, took her right hand in my left, put my right hand on the small of her back. She smiled again and clasped my shoulder softly with her one free hand.

"Okay," she growled, "you lead, but please catch up with the rhythm."

"I'll tell you what," we locked eyes. "You squeeze my hand

when we need to go a little faster and my shoulder to make me slow down a tad. How's that?"

She smiled and we danced until the musical trio decided to take a break. She only squeezed my hand twice. But I think she was probably just being nice to me.

She wouldn't let me take her home that first night. One of her friends might tell her fiancé, she insisted. But we made a date to meet at another bar the next night, an off-campus bar where few students went. The bar had no dance floor, but it was quiet, dark, and a nice place to go with a date if you wanted a kind of hand-holding, steamy place to warm up, have some good conversation, and eat one of the best hamburgers in town at the same time.

And so we met.

"You know, I don't usually step out on my boyfriend," she claimed after we had ordered the house specialty: hamburger, fries, and onion rings, with a tiny salad to top it all off. "But I think you're something special. And I've seen you out with a girl I admire a lot."

"Who's that," I asked curiously.

"Her name's Eve. I don't know her last name, but she's got most of the guys I know and a lot of the male teachers wrapped around her little finger. She seems to be able to get anything she wants, even good grades, without much effort."

A look of admiration, mixed with a little jealousy, I believe, flitted across Betty's face as she mumbled the last sentence. Her words left me dumbfounded. I wondered if the only reason she was seeing me was because of my relationship, or rather ex-relationship, with Eve. But I soon shrugged that uncertainty off. I didn't really care what her reason was for wanting to go out with me. I wasn't planning on a long-term relationship, and neither was she. All I really wanted was a little sack time with her body, and I figured the reverse was all she wanted. Anything more than that didn't interest me, not after my loss of Eve, no matter who was to blame for our breakup. I don't know if it was a matter of my damaged ego or if, after Eve, no other woman seemed to attract me body and soul, but there it was. My body now wanted women instead of booze, any woman, while my soul remained back there in the past with Eve.

So I played along with Betty in hopes of getting a little sex without investing too much time and effort. But the longer we talked the more I liked her.

"Yeah, I dated Eve," I offered. "But no longer."

"The story is that she dumped you for Dr. I." Before I could react to her comment she giggled and added, "Really, there are two rumors. The other one is that you dumped her when you caught her making out with Dr. I."

"Shit!" I shook my head. "It's a good thing I'm a nobody or the student newspaper might publish an article about the whole thing. Of course they'd get a lot of it wrong. The news usually does."

Betty smiled, and then laughed uncontrollably. When she finally got control of herself, still grinning, she said, "That's not as farfetched as you might think, having it published in the student paper. Dr. I's an important figure on campus, among the students anyway. And lots of people know Eve. The only thing keeping the whole affair out of the paper is probably the faculty advisers. They wouldn't want to create a fuss that might get them too much notoriety, maybe get them fired, maybe get them sued, or at least get them relieved of their control over the newspaper. I've had a couple of them for classes. They're not the type to want any kind of reputation except as," again she grinned from ear to ear and her voice became imitatively pedantic, "professional scholars and teachers. They definitely wouldn't want to be associated with the seamy side of academia." The whisper of a giggle echoed in her voice as she finished.

"Not many professors would, although some of the things they say in class are pretty questionable and pretty one-sided," I agreed and added my own platitude. "They all seem to like an easygoing life, hiding up there in their ivory tower, with nothing but an occasional heated discussion to interfere." I hesitated before adding a little facetious sarcasm, "It must be nice up there. It's kind of like the news media, except they're in it for the money and the Profs are in it for status," I added.

"Are you jealous?" She smiled teasingly as she took a bite of onion ring.

I shrugged, "A little. I'd like life to be a little easier. Sitting around in an air-conditioned office and reading. Meeting occasionally with some student you can bully a little and give advice that isn't any skin off your nose. Lecturing to a class nine or twelve hours a week, to students most of whom are asleep with their eyes open. Answering a few questions at the end of class or in the hall afterwards. Strutting around like a big wheel in front of all those young innocents." I ate a few greasy fries with my fingers before licking them clean and then wiping them on my napkin. "What a life," I smiled, "if you can stand the boredom."

"Yeah," Betty ignored my forced chuckle, "at least it's one place where women can almost be equal to men."

"Almost?" I sputtered. "I don't see any difference between my male teachers and the female ones. Some are fun, some are interesting, some are boring, and some should probably be doing clerical or factory work somewhere. So anyway, what's your beef? I thought you were planning on going out into the business world and making tons of money after you graduate."

"I am, but I get tired of men getting so many more benefits than women."

I started to make some not-so-funny remark about male superiority, but she stopped me with a raised hand and a don't-you-dare look in her eyes; and, I have to admit, the thought of antagonizing her before I got what I was after did a lot to stop my trap also.

"If there's one thing that makes me madder than hell it's someone who thinks women being treated as inferiors is funny, so don't say what that gleam in your eye suggests you're going to. Or worse," she added, "don't say that women really are inferior."

"Well, crap," I sputtered, suddenly angry myself. "I don't think women are always treated that way, and I think a lot of women enjoy like hell leading men around by the nose and teasing them with feminine charms and using those charms to compete in the market place. Hell, look at a lot of the women on television and in the movies. They show lots of cleavage and leg as if that somehow makes them more attractive, and I stress attractive—as if being attractive to men makes them better reporters or actors… or helps them get and keep jobs they don't really have the intelligence or other abilities for." She started to speak and I held up my hand to silence her. "At least the female professors don't walk into class with skirts up to their butts and blouses open to show what they have upstairs."

"Damn you!" Betty hissed, starting to rise.

Suddenly my funny bone got the best of me again. I laughed, then chuckled and giggled uncontrollably.

She hesitated, an angry frown scrunching up her lips and eyes. Then a smile erased the frown. She joined my giggles and plopped back down in her seat.

"Sex is a really funny thing, isn't it?" she frowned. "It rules our lives whether we admit it or not. And it's so gross if you just sit back and think about it. Where it happens is about as nasty a place as any super-intelligent sane satirist could have chosen. I mean, right down there where we get rid of body wastes. The same damn place," for a moment I thought she would burst out laughing again. But she seemed to catch herself before she continued. "What kind of god would play a joke like that on her helpless creation unless she had a really wild sense of humor? And worse, men are always staring at women's butts, really fascinated by them. Gross!" Her eyes sparkled as she finished. "But what the hell, I'd really like to meet whoever decided to make us like we are. She must have one hell of a sense of humor. And," she held up her hand as I started to say something, "Why shouldn't women use their feminine charms to compete with men? Men are just as bad. They use everything they've got to lord it over women, like their strength and the old boy system, and...." She shrugged in a disgusted way and stopped talking.

I decided right then and there that I could really like Betty. It was too bad that all my body and soul wanted from her was a little close and hot time. If it got enough of that it might decide it wanted more. Who knows? But she had a boyfriend and had made it clear that she would damned well be true to him when he was around. I had to admit that in some ways I envied him, and figured he must be quite something to have got the girl in front of me.

"Yuck," she finally came out of her trance and shivered, with an odd grin on her lips and in her eyes. "Let's talk about something else. That kind of talk totally turns me off, even though I find it interesting. My mind does. My body just seems to wilt though, seems to lose all its sexual heat, when I talk like that with someone."

"So, what do you want to talk about? What I'm hoping to do to you later?"

"Talk about sex? I think that would be fun. I bet you don't think women should have all the sexual freedom that men have, do you?"

"Well, hell," I think my forehead frowned and my mouth grinned, "it's a heck of a lot more fun for men when they do."

"Yeah, I bet. But I mean way down deep, where you keep your morals."

"Of course not," I forced myself to turn serious, as she seemed to want, although my body really wanted me to be superficial and sensual. "Who the hell would keep some sense of morality in male/female relations if women were free to screw around as much as men?"

"Well, men could, you know. They're so damned shallow most of the time, only thinking about their own needs. Why don't they think about what we need sometimes?"

"You've got me," I admitted half seriously. "How often in a day do you think about what men need?"

"A heck of a lot," she answered, an honest, almost forlorn expression in her eyes, before continuing, "although I think it's more about what they want than what they need. I hate to admit it but I spend too much of my waking time worrying about what my boyfriend wants. Before I met Tom, I worried too often about what the guys would think of what I was wearing or what I was doing or how much I weighed…or if my breasts were too small and my butt too big, or my hair was too long. That's after I had, you know, gone through puberty and the boys were starting to stare at me and I liked it." She shook herself angrily, her voice becoming harsher. "And sometimes I hated myself for all that worrying and fretting. I'd tell myself it didn't make any difference what I wore or how much I weighed or…. I'd tell myself that I didn't give a damn whether I attracted the guys or not. But I knew I was lying because the next day I'd put on a sexy dress or tight jeans or something and stand there in front of the mirror trying to decide if I looked good enough to pass inspection from my girlfriends and attract the eyes of some guy I liked. Or guys," she ended with a giggle, followed by a deep frown.

"Well, hell," I shrugged helplessly, "guys aren't that much different. We try to attract the girls by dressing up too, or doing silly things or showing off our muscles or our agility or something. You know, showing how bright or strong or fast we are. I mean, that's what we all do. I don't see how that's a female problem. Guys want girls. Girls want guys. So they figure out how to get them. What's wrong with that? I'd say it's normal. And," I grinned and made a little slurping sound, "I for one like it."

"But don't you see?" she complained. "Girls like to show off their bodies. They know that's how they catch a guy. But most guys do things. That's how they catch a girl. Girls should do things to catch guys, and not things that show off their bodies. We shouldn't be things to look at and play with. We should quit worrying about what we look like and get out there to do things, like men. We shouldn't have to show off our breasts or butts or legs or anything just to attract men. Men should like us for what we do, not what we look like."

"Are you telling me girls aren't attracted to guys' bodies?"

"No, I'm not saying that. I guess girls are attracted to guys' bodies too, a guy's eyes, or how he walks, or his shoulders or smile. It's just not as important as what a guy can do. Guys try to get in the sack with any good-looking body that seems to be willing. Girls aren't like that. Not totally anyhow."

"Yeah, that's what I always figured. Men go after anything in a skirt that turns them on, unless they're hunting for a wife, I guess. They generally don't care much if a woman can dance or cook or bowl or fly to the moon, or would make a good mother. That's all just icing on the cake. They want someone that'll let them get in her pants. They'll worry about the rest of that stuff later, if they think about it at all. Number one interest is junior down there in their pants. After that, everything is just added attraction."

"That's pretty crass, I know," she added as she toyed with her drink. "I don't think I believe it totally."

I laughed, then began to muse as if talking to myself, "Neither do I, completely. But it's pretty damned close to the truth, I think. I suppose there's always the thought of kids and a home and all that somewhere hidden in a man's mind, especially as we get older. At least that's what some of my older friends tell me. But I still think the first order of business for a guy is a girl's body. That's the first thing that points him in her direction. That's the first thing he wants. Yours truly anyway," I added with a smirk. "The rest is secondary. And I think that's been true in most civilizations. If it hasn't been, then why so many female prostitutes and so few male ones, and the male ones that there are mostly sell to other males? Girls don't have to pay for sex, not many of them anyway," I smirked again.

She remained quiet for a while, still sliding her drink glass around in front of her, making rings and destroying them.

"Well, girls like sex just as much as you guys do." Her voice was insistent, almost angry. "And we should have the right to do it whenever we want, and with anybody we want to."

"I didn't say you don't," I shrugged and finished my beer without really tasting it. I laughed again, abruptly, without control of the emotion that caused it, and opted for the facetious route. "I've never been a girl so I don't know how much girls like sex. But they must like it or the baby population would take a hell of a plummet. They must like it or we wouldn't have the gross overpopulation we do on this old planet." I grinned and waved my empty beer bottle at her. "Now would we?"

"Don't be a simpleton!" She rolled her eyes with the rhythm of her rotating glass. "Of course we like sex. Most of us who are normal in that way, at least. That's so damn evident that even saying it sounds stupid. The question is if we like it enough to compete with males in the free sex market. I mean, do we women like sex enough to jump in bed with every man whose body or abilities turn us on, and to hell with any consequences or morality or anything else except our own pleasure? That's the question. Are we like guys in that sense? Or do we basically only sleep with guys we think we would marry, or have kids with, or at least have a long relationship with?"

I threw my hands in the air, shrugged expressively, and shook my head melodramatically, "I thought that had pretty much been decided by modern women, sex for pleasure and to hell with the babies."

"I don't like the way you say that."

"You don't like the way I say it, or you just don't like how it sounds out loud?"

"Neither one, really," she kind of smiled, sadly, I thought.

"Why did you pick me out to have a little fun with?" I dared to ask after a few moments of silence, not really expecting to get an honest answer.

"Your butt, of course," she grinned widely and stared at me. "You've got a really nice little butt."

"Damn," I grumbled with a return grin. "I thought you were attracted to my good looks and witty ways."

"That too," she laughed. "The other was what got me close enough to learn more about you."

We both stayed silent for a while, then she said, "I don't like it that we have to suffer any consequences and all you men have to do is get your orgasm planting the seed and then go on your merry way, with no problems for you if your seed catches an egg at the right time. You can just ignore the result or accept the consequences. You have a choice, unless the law steps in. But we women don't. You think that's fair?" She glared at me before continuing. "I guess we do have some choice, though, to abort or carry. But that puts all the responsibility on us, while you guys are free to go on your merry way."

I shrugged, not really bothered much by the reality of life. "Whoever said life's fair?" I smirked, feeling kind of guilty as I did but not able to stop myself. I thought it was kind of a dumb question. "But hell, isn't that what all these pills and things are supposed to do for you women, keep you from getting pregnant?"

"Don't be a smartass," Betty growled but immediately burst into laughter herself. "I guess I do sound kind of silly, like blaming God or something for what I am. But I still don't think it's fair. And don't give me any of your dumb comments." She glared at me for a moment and then suddenly giggled, "But she really is to blame, you know. She could have made us different."

"Yeah, well, okay," I decided to change the subject a little, avoid this idea of a female god responsible for us all and force my mind to think of an escape route from where we seemed to be going, "that's one of the things modern technology is all about, isn't it, making men and women a little more equal, a little more alike. Women can screw around all they want without getting pregnant if they're careful, and if they do get pregnant they can get an abortion. Or they can have the kid and still work because housework isn't the bear it used to be and they can put their kid in some kind of kid care or school. Sex as a moral thing for women has gone the way of the Model T and the old biplane, and washing clothes by hand. What the hell, there are even stay-at-home dads anymore, men who at one time would have been considered gigolos, and in some cultures still would today. And married women that stay at home are called stay-at-home moms. How's that for equality?"

"Stay-at-home moms are a lot more common than stay-at-home dads," her voice assumed an argumentative tone.

"Probably," I shrugged.

"It's kind of stupid when you really think about it," she mused. "Parents are so stuck on social status and money that they don't really think about how kids would rather have more time with them. And how it might be a lot better for the kid."

"Where did that come from?" I asked, startled.

It was her turn to shrug, "People shouldn't have kids unless they really want to spend a lot of their time with them. My parents worked long hours. I didn't get to spend much time with them, not as much time as I wanted to because of all the hours I had to spend in school and dance lessons, and piano, and ball practice and…and all the time mom and dad worked and then had club meetings or went out with their friends. I wish we'd spent more time together."

"Yeah," I was no longer in a giggly mood. "My problem was I wanted to get out and away more than my parents would let me. But I guess I had more of an adventurous spirit than a nesting one. So I broke away early."

"Are you trying to say that males are more like you and females more like me?"

"Not really," I answered seriously, irritated a little. "It's something to think about but I was just comparing my desires with yours." I hesitated for a moment, unsure of whether to go on or not. In general, when I got involved in any philosophical male/female discussions with the fairer sex, I wound up losing a potential sex partner for the night. Like so many people, the women I knew only wanted to hear their views about male and female relationships seconded. Angering them seemed to turn off the sex drive.

So I shut up and turned our talk toward the mundane, Betty's life, and how sad it was that she and I had no future. This latter was a little bit of a stretch because I didn't really care a lot if we kept seeing each other or not, except as occasional sex partners, even though I had begun to like her. That liking could lead to something more than the physical attraction I felt for her, but it wasn't the top item on my list of things to concentrate on. Not at that moment.

We finished our meal, headed to a student bar for drinks, and eventually wound up in bed together, at her apartment. It was an enjoyable night, not the best I've ever had, but decent. She was a good lover, passionate and willing. But there was something missing, as there was in all the liaisons I had during the first few weeks after I swore off booze—not completely, of course; I'm not that much of a purist.

Then the night, or our part of it together, was over, so damned quickly. I dragged home at three, knowing full well that the morning would be miserable, but also knowing that the time in bed had been worth the suffering to come.

In the next few months there was a string of Bettys, some really good, some rotten, some willing to do whatever I wanted, some willing only to use a hand or mouth, and a few not willing to do anything at all except wrestle with clothes on. The latter I got rid of as quickly as possible. I was out there chasing women for only one reason and if I didn't get that early on I didn't waste my time. There were enough girls who were ready, willing, and able. I didn't see any reason to keep dating the unwilling, or the teases. I was addicted to one thing and one thing only. And like any addict I went straight for that, no detours, no don'ts, no hesitations. And by and large, what I wanted was pretty easy to come by. All it required was a little pretending and a few lies. But even that was kind of enjoyable when it came with beer and dancing and led to my goal. I guess I had begun to really enjoy the chase. Or maybe I was practicing for a life role as Don Juan. I don't know. What I do know is that any sexual morals I possessed had flown the coop, at least temporarily, if I had possessed any. But then, that seemed to be the story of my relationship with the opposite sex, thus far at least. Eve and the widow were the only ones I had mourned for any length of time, and within a year or two the widow had become a faint memory, only resuscitated in an occasional dream. I wondered if Eve would go the same way. After all, women were women, and there was always another one to take the place of a previous one. The only problem was that I couldn't find a girl to take care of my emotional needs as well as the physical one.

22

Life went on that way, from one woman to another, from one moment of extreme pleasure to the next day's physical and moral hangover, and then another repeat of the cycle.

Then one day the Dog Man waylaid me on a street near my home, in the afternoon when I was returning from a class to get ready for work. He was riding his contraption but with only a few dogs along. A quick guess came up with an even dozen, out of a total of how many I didn't know, but I was certain that two times that number was closer to what had been with him the first time we met, a few more probably, and more than that out at his cabin.

"Where're all your dogs?" I asked him after shouting hello as he pulled up to the curb near me. "That cart looks almost empty." I wandered over and glanced in. As I had thought, there were only four little mutts in there. The rest of the barking mutts were tied around the cart. So my first estimate had been right on track.

He had been grinning at me as he pulled up. When I asked the question his gaze turned to the cart but didn't seem to see it. A sad, angry frown turned his face rigid.

"Somebody poisoned them. It happened at night. I woke up one morning and sixteen were dead. I was upset, really upset, more so because I thought it had been my mistake. I thought I had mixed some rat poison in their food by mistake. I keep some on the shelves near their dog food, as you know. And I sometimes use a scoop to put some poison in a bucket and take it out to spread around the clearing, outside the fence. If I don't use all of it I pour what's left back in the sack I took it out of." He winced. "I guess I was so upset that I didn't think. I just assumed, although I checked the dog food bags and didn't find any trace of poison. I didn't imagine that someone else might have poisoned them on purpose. But several nights later the same thing happened. Eleven were dead in the morning. The only ones alive were the ones that I'd kept inside the house for the night, and again there was no sign of poison in the dog food bags. But there were a couple little pieces of meat near the gate, just outside of the fence. Whoever did this must have dropped them. And the dogs couldn't get to those pieces." Again he stopped and stared off into the distance, shoulders drooping and anger turning his face rigid again. "I can't believe I was so stupid. I don't make mistakes like that. I'm too careful, too meticulous. I've been taking care of my dogs for too long to make a silly mistake like putting rat poison in their dog food."

"How do you know the meat was poisoned?" I asked innocently.

"I had it tested," he growled. "I had it tested and it did have rat poison in it, the same kind I keep on the shelves. And don't ask! Yeah, I went to the police. They were more interested in the fact that it was the same kind of rat poison that I had…they were more interested in that than in my claim that someone had poisoned the dogs. They said they'd look into it. But you could see they suspected me of poisoning my own dogs, by mistake or on purpose, especially when I told them about Eve's uncle trying to run me down. They thought I was lying."

"You can't blame them, you know," I commented, knowing full well that I should have been more sympathetic. He loved his dogs and I could see that he was suffering from the loss, and maybe even feeling guilty for not having realized what was going on and thus at least having protected the last bunch poisoned. But I'm kind of a bumbler in social relationships. "You haven't always been pleasant to them when they stop you for some complaint or other, like townspeople calling them about the noise your dogs make while you wander through town, or the fights your dogs sometimes get into with somebody's dog. You yourself have told me that you're sometimes too combative even though you know the police are only doing their duty."

He seemed to squirm a little, but his eyes remained cold and angry.

"Yeah, I know. I do get a little ouchy when they stop me, even when I know I did something wrong. But this is different. Some bastard killed my dogs and the police aren't doing anything to catch the killer."

"How do you know?" I think I sounded a little insistent.

"Don't you…," he started but stopped when he saw my hands outstretched, palms facing him. "Okay," he smiled sadly, "you win. They've been out a couple of times. And they've talked to the neighbors. I guess I can't expect much more than that. They're just dogs that died. And nobody saw who did it, or else they aren't talking. And there don't seem to be any clues."

He suddenly stopped talking and stared into space, anger and sadness mingling in his eyes. I waited, knowing that he had more to say but was too emotionally distraught at the moment to continue. A couple of times he started to say something but hesitated. His eyes became moist and a tear ran down his right cheek, into his beard. He ignored it.

After a while he whispered hoarsely, "I know who did it. I'm damned sure I know."

"How do you know?" I kept my voice low and emotionless.

"It doesn't take a genius. Who tried to run me over twice, in town and on the road out to my place? That miserable cousin of Eve's, that's who. He's just the type that would kill innocent beasts to get even with someone he hates."

"Why does he hate you?" I figured I needed to get him talking so maybe his misery would ease off a little.

"The same reason he hates you," the Dog Man laughed mirthlessly. "We're too close to Eve and he doesn't want her running around with anyone who doesn't have money or power or, best of all, both. From what Eve says, he must be a real control freak. And mean as all hell. From some of the stories she's told me about him, I figure he might be a sociopath, or at least have some of those tendencies. And he has a lot of political clout."

I wondered why Eve had told him things she hadn't told me. With me, she had always defended Ron the Hun, as I had begun calling him to myself.

"You know," the Dog Man changed the subject, "that you haven't been out to see me since you and Eve broke up. Why is that?"

I shrugged and gave a dumb snort that I meant to be a chuckle.

"Why?" he insisted.

"I've been busy with work and school," I lied.

"That's not what Eve told me. She said you started drinking heavy and then began chasing every skirt that acted willing."

"When the hell did you talk to Eve?" There was no hiding my anger. It was clear in the way my voice rose stridently as I asked the question. Or more honestly, almost shouted it.

"She still comes out to see me once or twice a week. So, I guess I can say she's loyal to her friends even if you aren't."

I had no answer to that, although it hurt to imagine Eve out at the Dog Man's place talking and laughing while I was getting stoned or, later, climbing into bed with some drunken girl. I had ignored my parents, and my sisters, as well as my friends since Eve jilted me. I suddenly wondered how Dan and Bart were doing.

"She misses you too, you know," the Dog Man stared at me accusingly. "The two of you would still be together if you hadn't ditched her out at that professor's house. That really upset her. Hurt her. You don't go on a date with a girl and just leave her in the lurch."

"Did she tell you what she did?"

"Yeah, she went with the professor to discuss a paper she had written for one of his classes."

"Yeah, all right," I answered sarcastically, not able to control the anger and hurt in my voice, an echo of the same thing boiling in my gut. "She went with him to his bedroom and locked the door. How's that for an innocent talk about a paper?"

"She said she didn't lock the door. It must have locked automatically. Or maybe the professor locked it without thinking. Besides, they weren't in his bedroom. That was his study."

"I was told it was his bedroom." I think my comment was a little surly because he stared of me for some time before saying anything, so I told him as precisely as I could recall what I had been told when I went looking for Eve that night.

"You know damn well not to trust what people say to you, especially strangers, not about anything much beyond simple directions of something like that anyway," he shook his head, but I couldn't tell if it was because of anger or disgust. "That girl might have been drunk, or jealous of Eve, or just some kind of prankster. Who knows?" He suddenly chuckled at his own words before adding, "But you should have known, at least known enough to be skeptical, like I've tried to teach you to be."

"I don't care if it was his bedroom or studio or office or rec room, or what." The childish anger and hurt, the same that I had felt during the incident and more than once since, surged into my gut again. "Eve just walked off with him. Just walked off, you know, without saying a word. I don't know how long they were gone but it seemed like hours. A girl doesn't just do that to a guy she's with, not one she's been going with for a long time. Does she?"

I think my angry words also sounded kind of accusatory, as if the Dog Man were somehow in collusion with Eve because he was trying to defend her.

"I can see how you would react that way," he stared up at the sky as if avoiding my eyes. "But Eve really didn't mean to hurt you.

She's not a flirt, or anything like that, not as much as she used to be, anyhow, if what she says and what I hear about her is correct. In that way she's changed. But she is pretty damned competitive, in everything. I think that's a characteristic that has developed as time passed and she felt the world changing around her. You damn well know how competitive she is, I believe. And she needed an A on that paper she wrote for Dr. I. If she didn't get it she would've wound up with a B in the course, she said. So she went in to talk the good professor into an A grade on the paper. You know how persuasive she can be."

I almost laughed. I wondered if he knew how ambiguous his words sounded to me, ambiguous or suggestive of what he was really trying to argue against. I think I knew Eve and her persuasive abilities a little better than he did. I also knew just how competitive she could be. But I also knew my feelings for her, so I shut up. He continued repeating that Eve and the good professor, as he called Dr. I, simply went into seclusion to discuss potential improvements to Eve's paper.

"Did she get an A?" I asked curiously.

"Yes, she did," he beamed like a proud papa, "An A+ to be precise. And she got an A in the course, as you would know if you hadn't had you little jealousy tantrum."

He almost lost me at that point. I felt my anger tromping on my bowels but, with an effort, I held it in.

"What the hell," I mused to myself. "I miss her, but I really don't know if I could ever be as close to her as I was. I don't think I could trust her like I did." I almost laughed out loud as that last sentence unfolded in my mind. The rumors I had heard about

Dr. I stormed through my brain. Was he homosexual? Really? Or was he bisexual? I must have laughed out loud at my childishness because the Dog Man interrupted my thoughts.

"I don't see that it's a laughing matter. Eve is hurt, deeply, even if you're not. Whether you get back together with her or not, you owe her an apology. She'll be out to my place Saturday afternoon. I'll expect you there."

Without another word or gesture, he mounted his bike contraption and took off. I was left with my mouth agape, you might say. My first thought was "Screw you." My second was a fleeting picture of Eve the first time we made love.

Mesmerized, I stood frozen for a long time after he had turned into another street and disappeared. Saturday afternoon began repeating itself in my mind, an echo from a mountain top all snowy and frigid on a sunless morning. Would the icy fog lift before Saturday afternoon? In spite of myself, I prayed that it would.

23

Saturday afternoon arrived, slowly, slowly but surely. I had to work that morning, but I got off at one. My mind and body had both been waiting impatiently for that moment. But my total being was still hesitant. I started for home, stopped halfway there and turned toward the Dog Man's place, walked a couple of blocks, retraced my steps for half a block, and then somehow made the necessary commitment to talk to Eve again, no matter what the consequences. I couldn't believe she would have anything to do with me, in spite of what the Dog Man had said. Moreover, my own anger and jealousy kept eating at my insides. Every several yards of advance brought greater anguish. When I reached the Dog Man's shack I was a nervous wreck. But I found the nerve to enter through the gate and then knock at the door. Eve opened it. The Dog Man was not in sight.

"Hi," was all she said, but I read a deep sadness, and some anger, in her eyes.

"Hi," I almost stuttered in response. "Where's Dog?"

"He took off," she stepped aside and motioned for me to enter. "He said we could use some time alone." She stopped talking as I hesitantly stepped over the threshold. "To maybe iron out some of our problems, he said."

I turned to look at her, startled but not overly surprised. I should have suspected that the Dog Man had some kind of trick up his sleeve. He wouldn't have made a very good referee if we got into a squabble. He didn't have the patience. But he was good at providing the right situation at the right time.

"Do you think we can?" I asked without moving, before adding, "Come to terms with our problems?"

"Problems?" she frowned. "I really think we have only one problem, you not trusting me."

I started to answer, not kindly, but turned instead and walked into the room to sit down. Eve pushed an old, sawed-in-two barrel in front of me and also took a seat. I had never seen that piece of furniture before, but then I hadn't been in the Dog Man's shack for quite a while.

"I was so mad when I came back to Dr. I's living room and you weren't there…I was so mad when I found out you had left that I took off after you. I almost ran all the way to town." I could see that she was still mad; she was shaking and her forced smile was rigid, frozen. "If I had caught you…," she shrugged and abruptly stopped talking.

At first I couldn't find my voice. It seemed to be hidden somewhere inside my chest, which had tightened so much that I suddenly knew what a dwarf star must feel like.

"Why do you think I took off?" When I did find my voice, I tried to control it but it shook like her shoulders and head were shaking. "You left me without a word. You went into a room with another man and locked the door. And somebody told me it was Dr. I's bedroom. And I waited and waited and you didn't come out. What the hell did you expect me to do? As far as I was concerned, the only other possibility was to break that damned door down and beat the crap out of the good professor." My voice had turned strident toward the end of my diatribe.

She was silent for some time, her eyes not meeting mine, before she said, softly, "We need to talk reasonably or we're not going to be able to resolve this…this…."

"Disagreement?" I offered.

"Yes."

"I can see you're still mad."

"Yes. I'm so mad I'm having a hard time talking."

"Me too," I added, my voice harsher than I had wanted. "My mad seems to be fading though, kind of. I guess seeing you changed my feelings a little. You know, made them a little softer. But I'm still having a rough time when I think of you locked in that room with Dr. I."

"You know Dr. I doesn't really like girls, don't you?"

Her eyes met mine for the first time since she had opened the door. I also noticed her for the first time. I mean, really saw her face and body. I guess I had been too self-conscious, maybe self-absorbed, up to that point. She had lost weight. Her jeans weren't as tight as they normally were and her breasts didn't take up as much of the slack in her blue blouse as they had before our abrupt separation. Her hair was still immaculate, combed into a pony tail, which was not like her at all except when she was playing tennis or something. But her eyes looked a little strained and her full lips were slightly shrunken.

I wondered if I had just not noticed those characteristics before or if she had suffered by our separation, as I had. My heart suddenly kicked me in the rump, a kick I probably deserved. At least I thought so at that moment.

I changed the subject of the conversation, but not the real meaning hidden in there somewhere.

"I've heard that. I've also heard that he's bisexual."

"He never made a pass at me, and I didn't want him to. I just wanted an A in his class and I know he likes for his students to show that they realize their inadequacies. One way to do that is to ask him to go over your papers or exams after he's already graded them." Eve smiled that subtle, suggestive way she has, as if she's sharing some deep secret. "That way he thinks your interest is in learning, not the grade."

"You could have done that in his office, on campus."

"Yes, I could have." She glared at me, unblinking. "But I guess I made a mistake. I thought you trusted me."

"I did," I answered, not at all sure I was telling the truth. I didn't really know the extent of what trust between a man and woman meant. Or maybe the problem was that I'm a male and so I'm not that trusting where sexual relations are concerned, because I know my own weaknesses and I know the weaknesses of some of the people I've had experiences with. Or maybe I'd just heard too much locker room talk, male talk that tends to exaggerate and even outright lie about the talker's escapades and the perfidy of the female of the species. Or maybe I had some kind of genetic distrust of the female that had developed through the evolution of us males, something that related to our minor and uncertain role in the creation of future generations. I don't know. At the time I was pretty well flustered about the meeting and intellectually as well as emotionally uncertain about what had happened and where my future with Eve might lead.

"You did?" Eve's tone left no doubt that her question was meant to be sarcastic.

"Look, Eve," I forced the anger and nervousness out of my voice. Or at least I tried to. "I did trust you. I didn't quit dating you, did I? I never complained about your study sessions with other guys. I didn't complain, much," I forced a chuckle on the word to accompany the word 'much,' "when you dated those guys your cousin set you up with, did I?"

"You didn't quit dating me?"

I could see the anger building as she blurted the question. Her eyes sparked and the words sounded like sand gritting in her teeth. "You...," her voice started to rise angrily.

"That's right," I interrupted. "I love you too much to let something like that interfere with our relationship, something as petty as your dating a guy just because your cousin insists on it, a guy you and I both know damn well you'll be bored with. And besides, like you always say, we're not engaged or anything, not even going steady."

"So, you've been going out with other girls too? And never told me about it?"

I thought for a minute she was going to attack me. The thought...the image made me chuckle, then giggle. Before I could control myself, I was laughing uncontrollably, or I probably should say cackling.

Eve jumped to her feet and swung a fist at me. Luckily I caught it in midair, or it probably would have caught me smack on the nose. I was still cackling. I couldn't stop and was fast becoming almost helpless from the uncontrollable laughter. Eve yanked her arm but, even more luckily, I had enough strength and control to hang on, barely. She yanked again. I couldn't hang on any longer. But something happened as she pulled free. Her eyes lost their anger. Her jaw relaxed. Her lips opened. And suddenly she was laughing with me.

Within seconds we were on the floor stripping each other and then I was in her and floating higher and higher into some paradise beyond the clouds until the universe exploded and I lost the last vestiges of rational consciousness.

Later, much later, I walked her home. We didn't talk much. I was thrilled to be with her again. I like to think that she felt the same way just being with me.

"If Dog hadn't made the effort to get us together," she asked me once, "would you have done it, eventually?"

"I don't know," I answered honestly. "I tried. I waited for you after class a couple of times. But you ignored me. I went to the Union several times when you used to be there. But I didn't see you. I saw you on campus a few times but, again, you acted like I wasn't there. You just walked on. And the library, I...."

"What did you expect? You could have stopped me and made me talk to you."

"And you could have stopped and acted like you wanted to talk to me."

I realized that I too was getting hot under the collar. With an effort I checked my anger. I knew that I didn't want to lose her. I looked at her, at the lips that had given me such pleasure, at the legs and breasts and arms that I loved so much to caress, at the shoulders I loved to put my arms around and squeeze softly, at the body that was so soft and warm when cuddling against mine. I couldn't think of another person that I had been so close to, physically and emotionally, and spiritually. Our eyes met and I believed that she was thinking many of the same things I was.

I rose to my feet and realized that she had done the same thing, simultaneously with my movements. In the next moment we were in each other's arms. Then we were moving toward the Dog Man's closet-sized bedroom. And soon she again took me to that physical paradise we had so often visited together, the one where soft, warm flesh carried me beyond reason or thought, into a heaven where only physical pleasure exists and even that seems like a dream, but what a dream.

24

So my love and I were back together. Not as smoothly or comfortably as before, but together nevertheless. We didn't meet on campus as often as we had before out breakup. Nor did I find myself heading for the Carsons' house during every spare moment I had. But our love life almost returned to the balm it had been for my ego and soul, balm with a little bit of some ingredient missing. Maybe the aloe. In my more rational moments I blamed myself for the jealousy that had made me ditch Eve at Dr. I's party. But that was only a temporary fix, very temporary, since I'm like so many human beings that have never felt total failure and have had a success here and another over there throughout his life.

Sorry, I should have said "his/her" life. I want to make sure the fairer sex takes its share of the negatives as well as positives in this game of life we are doomed to play.

I have to admit that nothing between me and Eve was as it had been before our problem—not the sex, which had been idyllic; not the moments of bliss afterward when we held each other and drifted off to sleep, her warm, soft, delightful body against mine; not the moments when I spotted her in the distance and waited expectantly until she spotted me and that wonderful smile spread from her lips to her eyes as she

approached closer and closer; and not the moments of antagonism that had been there so seldom before but now too often appeared from nowhere and crept deeper and deeper into
our conversations.

We met at the Dog Man's often now, much more than before.
He seemed to see into our souls at times, or at least into mine,
and a sad look surfaced in his eyes when Eve and I were together
and he looked directly at me. I don't think that same sadness
was ever directed at Eve. He became somewhat defensive of her
whenever I said anything that could in any way be construed as
negative. I believe that somewhere way down in his psyche he
believed that he was her father, in all ways but biologically, and
biology be damned in his feelings for her.

Our only meaningful disagreement was about Eve. The two
of us, Eve and I, had been wandering around the woods outside
his property on a Saturday afternoon. Neither of us had been
scheduled to work that day, so we met at the Dog Man's shortly
after noon and, after a long chat with him, walked hand in hand
out his gate and into the trees. I was feeling melancholy for some
reason, a feeling that had begun to haunt me more and more
after the breakup and get-together. Eve was in a chatting mood
and jabbered away about minor things as we walked. About
halfway through the woods we stopped in a grassy area, by an
old oak that must have fallen recently because it still had lots of
leaves covering its branches, leaves many of which were just beginning to get a tint of rusty color around the edges and hadn't
yet begun to take on the odor of decay. The grass around the
tree was tall. The earth was soft. The shade was delightfully cool

and the smell of the trees and grass still hinted of spring even though June was approaching.

We lay in each other's arms, the world around us slowly fading into a soft, warm euphoria. Around me, I guess I should say since, to be honest, I really don't know in any absolute sense how Eve felt. I only assume, since she kept coming back to me and since she lay there seemingly in the same romantic stupor I was in...I assume that she too was in a romantic daze. After all, her warm body cuddled softly against mine. Her eyes were closed. A slight smile curled her lips. Her breathing was regular. Her hand held mine. She was there with me, not somewhere else with someone else, I believed.

After awhile...a half hour, an hour—I don't know how long we lay there in our own world, but finally we woke as if we were one person and made love, slowly, rapturously, the pleasure building until we exploded, two wandering stars fulfilling our mutual destiny. Afterwards we again dozed. When we awoke we could see that the afternoon sun was turning into an evening sun. The air was cooling our skin. The brightness was fading.

"Oh, oh," Eve sat up quickly, leaving me still lying there watching her. "We've got to go. I have a date tonight."

"You what?" I clambered to my feet and stood there glaring at her. "A date? I thought maybe we'd go to a movie or something this evening. We...."

"I should have told you," she whispered huskily, "but I didn't want to spoil our afternoon together. Ron is throwing a party at the country club tonight. He invited me."

"And he plans on trying to set you up with the heir of one

of his rich friends," I tried to sound rational, but the anger in my voice easily gave the lie to my attempt.

"I'm sorry," Eve said, trying to take hold of my hand, which I jerked away spitefully. "I shouldn't have told you. I...."

"Shouldn't have told me?" I squeaked. "Shouldn't have told me? Like you didn't tell me that you were going off with Dr. I and what you were going to do with him? Like...," I couldn't go on any further. My voice quit. I almost wilted.

"But if you understood why...why I do it, we could talk about it."

"Hell, if we talked about it...if you had told me sometime why you do it, maybe I would understand," I gritted. "It seems to me that every time I get to thinking that you're mine and I'm yours, Ron sets you up with some rich asshole."

"Watch your tongue," Eve growled. "You know I don't like that kind of talk."

"Why?" I asked, my voice almost failing me. "Why? I thought we...."

"I told you a long time ago," Eve interrupted. "I told you I was looking for a man with money, or one who was ambitious enough to make lots of it. Besides, I owe Ron a lot. He's paying my tuition here at the college. And he pays most of my living expenses. So I figure I've got to give him something in return. And all he seems to want is for me to meet some guy who has money or will have it someday. He treats me like his daughter, you know, and I think I owe him for that. Besides, who knows," she shrugged and gave out with a little laugh that to me seemed forced, "maybe he will fix me up with the man of my dreams, eventually."

Those words cut me down to size. I had no answer. I felt kind of like a little male calf that had just been castrated.

"We'd better go," is all I could say. "You might be late for your party."

We started for the Dog Man's cabin. Eve took my hand. I started to yank it loose, but something kept me from doing so. I don't know what, any more than I know why I didn't tell Eve to take a hike, but rejecting her didn't even enter my mind. So we walked hand in hand through the shadowy woods, side by side, and silent. I knew that if I started talking my temper would get the best of me, and I would say something that might be the end of our togetherness, might shred Eve's feelings for me. On the other hand, I wandered if she truly had feelings for me, or if our being together was only because she hadn't yet found anyone she preferred being with—yet. I wondered if I was but a stepping stone on her way to that rich marriage she had mentioned more than once in our conversations. I wondered if I was no more than a trial marriage, a relationship with many of the benefits of marriage endorsed by religion and government, and culture, although culture or government not so much anymore of course. And religion? It shuts its eyes a lot.

At the cabin we parted ways. I wanted to walk her back to town, but she insisted that I stay at the Dog Man's and that she would walk home alone. So I obeyed. Irritated, wondering why she didn't want my company to town, but obedient nevertheless.

I waited, my mind dredging up all kinds of upsetting images. And I waited, wondering where the Dog Man was. I wanted to see him before I took off. Why? I don't know, except that I enjoyed his company and I figured he might ease my daytime nightmares of Eve partying at her "surrogate father's" house.

I must have been there a half hour or more, sitting on the barrel seat and staring into space, when I heard the dogs yapping closer and closer, until Dog and a bunch of them burst into the room. The Dog had a slight frown on his face, and his dogs, maybe sensing that their master wasn't in his normal blasé temper, were not as noisy as normal. Noisy, but not as noisy.

"I wondered why I didn't see you on the road with Eve. You should have walked her back to town. There are some nasty characters out in this neck of the woods."

"I wanted to. She said no."

"Well, hell, you should have anyway. You know that."

"Yeah, I know that," I growled sarcastically. "I also know Eve. And I thought you did to. That would have been a hell of a lot of fun, walking her to town when she didn't want me to. Like walking with a living icicle."

He chuckled, but the frown remained.

"That cousin of hers picked her up, about halfway to town. I was pedaling this way, not more than fifty yards from Eve when he stopped and got Eve, passed me, then made a u-turn, and almost sideswiped me when he passed by again." Dog threw out a couple of swear words before continuing. "On purpose for damn sure. I could see the look on his face. He was enjoying my attempt to miss him. I almost went into the ditch. One of these days I'm going to catch that bastard alone. Then we'll see what kind of a man he really is."

"What about Eve?" I asked, curious.

"I don't know. I was too busy trying to avoid that damned car. I barely caught a glimpse of the bastard's face, just enough to see that he was grinning. But you know Eve." A smile cracked his lips. "She's probably still giving him hell."

"Maybe," I disagreed.

"What do you mean by that?" the Dog Man exploded angrily. "Hell, Eve...."

"Yeah, I know," I interrupted. "Eve likes us and wouldn't put up with anyone trying to hurt one of us. But she's also under his control, so to speak. You know how much he does for her and how much she seems to worship him. She talks about it enough. I'm not sure where the line is, the line she wouldn't let him cross without a fight. I'm just not."

"Don't let his fixing her up with idiotic dates with rich kids get to you. They don't mean a thing to Eve."

"How do you know?" I spit the words out without thinking.

"Because I know Eve. And I know what she says about you. She talks about you all the time. She did even after you ditched her, before the two of you got back together again."

"Yeah, well," I growled, "according to her our relationship isn't going to go anywhere."

I told him what she so often said about marrying a guy who had money or the ability to make good money, so she and her kids would have a decent life.

"I doubt she means that," Dog grimaced thoughtfully. "She often says things like that to me too, how she wants a husband that can give her a nice home and smart kids, how her husband has to come from money or be a doctor or some other kind of professional who'll make her life and her kids' life easy, how she wants…, well, she pretends to be really ambitious, a kind of financial social climber, but I think it's all just part of her growing up, a façade she's created for herself out of her dream world. You know, that dream of the future we all create in one form or another when we're teenagers. She really just wants what we all want, a spouse and children she can love and a life that makes her happy to be in it. She just doesn't know it yet."

"Come on," I laughed, a kind of cross between a bulldog's growl and a hyena's cackle. "You make it sound like we're all the same. What about the ones who want some adventure? What about the ones who have wandering feet and can't wait to climb over the closest hill just to see what's on the other side? What about the ones who've given up on the dream about Helen of Troy or Paris and just want somebody, anybody who's willing to help make their life comfortable? What about…?"

"You've made your point," Dog interrupted with a chuckle. "But what you ignore is the great disparity out there. All you have to do is notice the physical differences and you should recognize that there must be great psychological differences to match them. Hell, some little ugly duckling or nut case isn't going to have the same level of dreams for the future as…," he grinned sardonically before continuing, "Eve does." His grin broke into a chuckle as he paused. "You sure as hell don't seem to have the same size dreams as she does."

I had to smile in spite of my irritation, "How do you know what kind of dreams I have. I've never talked about them."

"No," he continued grinning like the man who had just found a huge golden nugget, "you haven't. But I was a young man once, not a lot different from you, I suspect, so I have some inkling of your dreams. Like you want a woman for the night, and maybe a few beers before and after, and maybe a pretty rock solid promise for a few more dates in the future. You're not too interested in anything as permanent of marriage. Not yet. But then you think of losing Eve and something permanent doesn't sound so bad after all. Yet, when that thought pops into your mind, vaguely, so vaguely that it's not really a thought, more like a kind of feeling… when that feeling flows through your veins you find yourself withdrawing from you-don't-know-what. You don't even know that you're withdrawing, but you have this feeling that the world has you in its grasp and won't let go, that if you don't somehow backtrack you're doomed to lose your free will, that you'll never make another decision that is truly yours, without any outside influence whatsoever. Somehow, someway, through no action of your own, you've become enslaved by something beyond your ken. You've lost your free will."

"Good God," I exploded, refusing to admit that what he had said had hit me right in the core of my being. "Do you have any idea what you're talking about? I don't."

"Bull," the grin remained plastered to his face, actually growing bigger.

"I thought we were talking about Eve."

"I'm not sure whether we were talking about Eve or your feelings about Eve. And I'm not sure we can distinguish the two."

"Are you saying you think Eve is actually serious about me in spite of all her talk about a rich husband? Or are you saying that I haven't really committed myself permanently to Eve?"

Dog stared silently into space for a few minutes before answering.

"I don't know. Maybe both. Maybe Eve talks like she does because she knows how hesitant you are about committing to her permanently. Or maybe you can't commit yourself to something as permanent as marriage with her because you don't think you're what she really wants for a husband. Or maybe you're not in the least bit ready for that kind of commitment. I've wondered about those questions a lot over the past year, watching how close you two sometimes seem, yet how distant."

To tell the truth, I hadn't really considered why I had never asked Eve to become engaged. Nor had I ever discussed our getting married with her. Sure, we talked about marriage in general. But the talk never wound up in any kind of commitment between us, not even close. It was always a general discussion, about commitments or non-commitments, and all the potential consequences, never a discussion that involved the two of us personally. We also occasionally mentioned the fact that our relationship was a temporary one. But that usually came when I learned of one of Eve's "blind dates" set up by Ron. My jealously would surge to the fore and my tongue would do the rest, blaming Eve for not being faithful.

She would of course point out that we were not engaged or even going steady. Maybe I was naïve or stupid or something because it never dawned on me that she might actually want some kind of a permanent commitment, in spite of her comments about what kind of a man she wanted for her future. I decided that I would broach the subject the next time the two of us were alone.

"Eve is a really beautiful woman," Dog glared at me. "She's beautiful. She's smart. She's ambitious and she's a good person. I don't think a man could find anything better."

"What about love?" I asked, suddenly interested in getting his take on Eve and me. "Do you think she loves me?"

"She must have some feelings for you," Dog shook his head in disgust. "She stays with you in spite of all the crap you pull."

"All the crap I pull?" my voice must have risen an octave or so. "What the hell are you talking about? She goes off to these parties her cousin or uncle or whoever the hell he is plans. She knows damn well he has her set up with some rich snob. He tells her he does. And she sometimes even tells me the guy's name, and where he lives and who his parents are and…crap, Dog. Don't try to tell me she's some little innocent and I'm the one who pulls all the crap!"

By the time I finished my tirade I must have been shouting because Dog grinned from ear to ear and, with a wink, put his palms over his ears.

"Look," he became serious. "I had a girlfriend once—I mean, I was in love when I was young like you. It was that first love, you know—that fantastic innocent love that's like a dream." He hesitated and gazed at me for awhile before continuing. "No, I don't suppose you do know. Not intellectually. You're in the middle of youth and all its wild, uncontrollable feelings, so your mind can't define it consciously, not yet. It has no perspective, no second or third love to compare it to, and no aging distance to look back and say it was like this. Comparison and distance are the only way we humans have to create the proper tools for understanding and describing our feelings. Sadly, of course, by the time we reach distance and perspective, we no longer have the same feelings. Or, better said, those feelings have become different. They're no longer as intense as before, but more permanent, less susceptible to the winds of change, more profoundly embedded in the psyche and somewhat less so in the body, the material self."

"Wow!" I forced a laugh, which kind of sounded like I was drowning. "I didn't know you were a philosopher or I would have had you help me with my philosophy homework."

"Don't be a smartass," he smiled. "I can see what you feel for Eve. It's pretty evident in the way you treat her. I can see that she loves you. She was really down all the time the two of you were separated. She was out here a lot. Most of the time all she talked about was you and the fun times the two of you have had. She was always asking me if I thought the two of you would make a good couple, a permanent couple. She likes to say that she's looking for a rich husband, but she seems pretty stuck on you."

"Then why the hell is she always meeting other guys, for lunch or coffee in the cafeteria, for study sessions, at parties where Ron the Hun sets her up with a potential mate?"

"She's still young. She's checking out all the possibilities. That's what girls and boys do. It's kind of like choosing what profession you want to spend your life pursuing. There are a lot of them out there and so, unless you're one of the lucky ones who knows from the get-go what he wants to do the rest of his life, you check a lot of them out."

"So," I could hear the skepticism, and anger, in my voice, "Eve is not one of the lucky girls who from the beginning know which guy they want to spend the rest of their life with. That's the reason she checks out all the possibilities and, in the meantime, hangs on to me—because I'm the only one that, to this point in her life, she sees as a potential permanent mate."

"Something like that," the Dog Man shrugged.

25

That night I hit Stinkey's early. I was almost into my cups, sitting at a table near the rear wall, when Dan walked up and grabbed a seat.

"Hey," he grunted as he waved at the waitress and pretended to take a sip of beer, letting her know that he wanted one, "what the hell you doing here drinking all alone. I figured you'd have picked up some chick by now, and headed for bed," he smirked at me.

"Go to hell," I growled, grinning. "They probably need another joker like you, to keep the devil in stitches so he'll maybe leave his victims alone for a change."

"Funny, funny," Dan grinned. "I can see being back with Eve has already done you a world of good. You're no longer the grump you were when the two of you were at odds."

"What are you doing out alone on a Saturday night?" I changed the subject. "Lost your touch with the girls?"

"Nah, I've been at a party. But it was boring, boring, boring. So I took off to see what my little area of the world has to offer."

I looked around, making sure he saw what I was doing.

"You can say the same thing about this place. Boring. Not a lone female in sight."

"Who needs them," he laughed. "Maybe I'll become a priest.

Take a vow of chastity and spend the rest of my life just watching. See what people really are like. You know," he grinned, "see if they're really as sinful as I think they are."

"Wow," I mimicked his grin. "Aren't you the cynic tonight! What's the matter? Some girl stand you up?"

"I guess you could say that," he shrugged, keeping that shit-eating grin on his face. "I've been dating this chick. Her name's Sally. She's in my lit class. But we broke up last week. She wants a husband. Me," he did a little chair dance that could have passed for a lap dance if he had been a woman and there had been some-one sitting under him, "all I want is a little lovin' now and then. Marriage? Maybe someday, but only when the girl well goes dry or I get tired of swimming around in it."

I just shook my head. What could I say? I felt the same way most of the time, although not always when I was around Eve.

"Sally," he finished his beer and signaled for two more, one for me and one for him. "Now Sally, she's one sexy chick. And she's right up there with all the other modern females. You know, ready for a little roll in the hay if she likes you well enough, just for fun. But she seems to think that extended togetherness should ultimately lead to a ring and a ceremony and a happy-ever-after tale." He stopped talking and stared into space for several min-utes. "I'm just not ready, you know. There's too many ladies out there that I haven't tried yet." He grabbed the beers the waitress brought to our table, handed one to me, gave the girl the money she asked for, chugged half of his beer, and continued, this time without the grin, "I don't know, Donjon. I sometimes wonder if I'll ever find the woman I wanta spend my life with. Take Sally.

When I met her, I thought she might be the one. She's good to look at. She's smart. She dresses nice. She seems to like me. But damn it, something is missing. The sex vibe is there. I enjoy her company. But some little voice keeps saying, just wait ten years, and then what? Is she going to be the same girl or is she going to be a grumpy, sloppy housewife?"

He stopped talking and sat there staring at me, waiting for my reaction, I decided.

"Come on, Dan," I chided him. "What are you going to be like ten years from now? Are you going to be some professional with a good salary? Or are you going to wind up in a job with a mediocre salary? Are you going to be one of those guys that take their wife out to eat two or three times a week, and maybe to a play or movie or dance afterwards? Or are you going to come home after work, park your butt on the couch to watch a ballgame, and wait for your wife to get the meal ready? Or maybe you'll invite the guys over for some poker several nights a week. Who knows? I don't know what I'll be like ten years from now. And you don't either. We all change as we age, not always for the better. So how can you expect Sally to not change?"

"You've got a point," he shrugged. "Maybe I'm just not ready to tie the knot. And besides," he chuckled, "what I'm going to be like is not my problem. My problem is what the little old wifey is going to be like. She's the one I can put up with or not. I get to choose in her case, not in mine."

"A profound statement, that," I found myself grinning too. "Maybe you'll supplant Sartre or Dr. I in the intro to philosophy class someday."

"Hey, only one thing would be better."

"What's that?"

His grin spread and I knew he had been ready for that question.

"To be prime matter in an intro to a women's studies class, or even better, to be the professor's research aid."

"Or the professor who does most of the research himself."

"Um, yeah, agreed," he raised his bottle in a mock toast"

Silence reigned for several minutes before he commented.

"You didn't ask me whose party I was at."

I shrugged, not really interested. Dan, and his roommate Brad also, was always going to parties thrown by athlete friends. I had been to a few of them. Some of them were fun. Most weren't, because the girls there were interested in hooking up with an athlete.

Not really interested, but not wanting to irritate him, I asked the question.

"Ron the Con," his voice dripped sarcasm and his eyes searched my face for reaction. "Eve's boss. Or maybe I should say the guy that thinks he's her lord god or something like that."

"But he's really the devil in disguise," I could feel my temper seething in the words.

"Yeah, something like that," Dan agreed. "I had my rounds with him after Eve and I had a short fling. So did Brad, I think. And I know other guys who did too. He's a real bastard when it comes to guys chasing Eve."

"I wonder what the hell his problem is." I shook my head in disgust. "He surely doesn't want Eve for himself."

"I wouldn't put it past him, but just for a one night stand, or to get a little on the side. His wife's family is well connected. Eve's isn't. And he's an ambitious bastard. So I can't see him doing anything to screw his marriage up. But I guess his ego might tell him he can get a little on the sly and, if he's careful, no one will know."

"I don't think so," I disagreed. "From what Eve says, and Ron's brother, and you and Brad, I figure he's one of the few men I know who totally ignores the wild urges of that little monster down below. Or maybe his monster doesn't have any desires. I don't know him well enough to say yes or no. I…"

"He's too damn coldblooded to have uncontrollable desires. Hell," Dan almost giggled, "he probably plans out his weekly, or monthly," he sniggered again, "trips to the bedroom with his wife, down to how many times he's going to squeeze each boob, and with which hand, and the number of fingers he'll use each time, and how many and what kind of kisses he'll exchange with her, and how many minutes and seconds coitus will take up, and…," Dan burst into laughter at his own jokes, almost knocking his beer bottle off the table.

I couldn't help laughing with him in spite of the coarse image he evoked.

"I shouldn't tell you this," he finally calmed down enough to talk again. "I shouldn't but I've liked you since we met. You seem like a good guy and so I think you should know what you're in for if you stay with Eve, and not only from Ron the Con. She's a flirt. She always has been and she always will be, I expect. She can't help herself."

"Come on," I couldn't help but agree, although his words pushed my temper up a few notches. "I don't think I've ever known a girl who wasn't, if the moment and the guy were right. I figure you can probably say much the same about guys."

"Yeah, you're right,' he agreed with a frown. "But Eve isn't alone to make her own decisions. She's got Ron. He's always pushing her toward some guy whose parents have money and power. I don't know. It's like he's some medieval lord who's trying to get the best bargain for his daughter. You know, marry her off to some other lord with a big castle and lots of land and peasants so he has a powerful ally. And he's dangerous, man. Guys have chased Eve until they clash with Ron. Then they back off, fast. They don't say anything but the rumors make the rounds, that Ron threatened them or had one of his boys knock them around. Things like that."

He paused and stared at me.

"I like you, Donjon, and I don't want you to get hurt. But the rumors are that Ron is after you. They say he's going to get you out of Eve's life, one way or another."

"Whoa," I spluttered. "He's got a lot to lose if he comes after me."

Dan started moving his beer bottle around his side of the table, forming and destroying watery rings.

"Maybe. Maybe not. He's gotten rid of all her boyfriends to date. You're the only one he hasn't been able to squash easily."

I studied his face for awhile. He seemed worried.

"Did something happen at this party?"

He hesitated and I thought he wasn't going to answer, but he finally looked up at me and said, "Yeah. I shouldn't tell you this; I don't want to get Brad in trouble with you. But he was at the party and was flirting pretty heavy with Eve. I think he'd been drinking a lot before he got there, but I don't know for sure because I hadn't seen him all day. I left for the party early and he came a lot later, all spiffed up like he'd been to the dorm to shower and shave and all. And he started flirting with Eve, as soon as he walked in the door. And the strange thing is, Ron the Con didn't seem to care. He even seemed to egg the two on." Dan hesitated and smiled ruefully before continuing. "Knowing him, I figure he thinks it'll be easier to get rid of Brad if Eve starts running around with him, easier than it has been to get rid of you. And he's hoping Eve'll dump you for Brad."

"Did they leave the party together?" I asked, knowing full well that my anger showed on my face, but unable to control myself.

"I don't know," Dan shrugged. "Like I said, I left early. The two of them were still dancing. Knowing Eve, though, she'll do what she wants to do. She's as headstrong as Ron the Con." He chuckled, but without any humor in the sound. "Brad, he's like the rest of us. He'll jump if Eve gives him an okay sign."

"She wouldn't do that," my words were more hopeful than confident.

26

I had a couple more beers with Dan, then left. I needed to go somewhere alone to do my brooding, and to get my temper under control. The former was easy, the latter impossible. I wasn't angry with Brad, however. Hell, I was also young and hormone-driven. I didn't have to think much about the situation to realize that in his place I would have done the same thing. Eve was one sexy woman and fun to be around. I figured that any male would come running, slavering all the way, if she beckoned. But Eve? In spite of her insistence that we weren't engaged or even going steady, and in spite of all the chances I had, I didn't step out on her or spend any evening hugging and dancing with another woman, except for the time we had been separated. Yet she went to all these parties that Ron the Con threw, went and, as far as I knew, flirted and played around with the date he chose for her on that specific night, or with some other male of her choosing. What she did with them after the party was anybody's guess. I tried to think the best, the best for me, that is.

I figured that I should break up with her. We didn't seem to be getting anywhere with our dating. No plans for the future. We, actually, seldom talked of a future as a couple anymore. Yet there was something that cemented us together, although maybe I should say there was something I couldn't break free of, something like a monstrous magnet that kept pulling me back to her side and simply wouldn't let me get far from her, in my emotions especially because she was seldom out of my thoughts for more than a few seconds at a time, even when I was busy, and even during those moments I could sense her existence at the periphery my senses.

But, of course, I slowly talked myself out of my anger and kept on seeing Eve. Why, I don't know, but I think she was my drug of choice and I had become inescapably addicted to her.

That didn't keep me from grousing the next time we were together, though. Which didn't get me anywhere, except for another semi-sleepless night. And it didn't stop my continuing to date her, something any addict or ex-addict should understand.

The day was the next Wednesday. The time was late evening, maybe around nine or so. The weather was next door to perfect for spring—cool, windless, and with our world blanketed by a black cloudless sky covered with bright pinpoints of stars, some twinkling as if laughing at me, most staring without blinking. Eve and I were walking toward the Carsons' after a movie. I brought up her evening with Bart.

"I heard you danced all evening with him, and maybe let him see you home."

I felt Eve tense.

"Who told you that?"

Her voice was irritated, almost angry.

I forced a chuckle at the question, "My source wants to remain anonymous."

"So do most liars. And it upsets me that you believe such nonsense. He was the only boy my age, except for the boy Ron set me up with. And he was a complete dud. He didn't know how to dance and he didn't want to do anything except sit and hold hands. That got old pretty quickly. So, yeah, I danced with Bart a few times. And, yeah, I let him drive me home. It was better than going with that dud and letting him try to slobber all over me."

We were walking hand in hand and, if her hand was any indication, she was heating up. I decided to shut down the conversation before we got into a real argument, because I could feel my own temper also warming up. Jealous? Yeah, you might say that. I was ticked and I wanted to know what she and Bart had done either on the way to the Carsons' or after they got there. But I knew that probing her for the answer just might get me into a situation that I didn't yet want. So I changed the subject to her classes and her job.

When we reached the Carsons' all I got was a quick peck on the lips and a mumbled "Call me tomorrow" before she turned and disappeared into the dark house.

Me? After a few silent curses I turned and made my way home, where I slipped into another dark house, sneaked up the stairs, stripped, and fell into a cold bed.

Nothing much happened for a couple of weeks. Eve and I got together several times. I kept my mouth shut and reaped the benefits. Was it worth it in the long run? I don't know. Would we have been better off if I had spoken my mind immediately? I don't know that either. I've learned over the years that keeping some secret knowledge bottled up inside me is generally good for a relationship but not necessarily for my emotional health, which can also affect my relationships. But one thing I have also learned is that truth is not all it's cracked up to be. Sometimes it is even more dangerous, personally, than a lie.

In any case, one evening Ron the Con (or should I say Hun) accosted me as I was walking home from work. I was on a kind of deserted block. To the right of the sidewalk stood a high wooden fence extending the whole block. I couldn't see anything on the other side of the fence except a tall crane glaring down at me. The sidewalk and the street were deserted. I hadn't seen either a pedestrian or a car since I entered the block and I was about half-way through it. Nor were there any cars parked along the curb, on either side of the road. On the far side of the street stood a line of small businesses, all closed for the day and no sign of life within. The sun had set but it was not quite dark yet, just a mute world stuck in that period of day in the Midwest when silence reigns in the atmosphere and the world has been deserted by daylight and darkness both, leaving a gloomy Neverland that, you often feel, might or might not change, ever.

So you can imagine how a car suddenly zooming around the corner in front of me and accelerating in my direction, on the wrong side of the street, caused me to look for a hole in the fence, frantically. I found none and, by the time I had turned to run toward a huge tree I had just passed, the big black car had screeched to a halt beside me, bumping the curb but not quite bouncing over it. I think my heart almost jumped over the fence and left me behind to fend for myself.

Ron surged out of the car, leaving the motor running, and strutted around the front bumper to face me.

"We need to talk," he commanded. "Get in."

"No, I don't think so," I said, easing farther away from the curb and ready to make a dash for that tree at the first physical threat. "The last time I saw you, you tried to run me down. I sure as hell don't trust you."

He glared at me before answering, "I didn't really try to hit you. If I had, you'd be dead. I was just trying to scare you."

"That's bull shit and you know it," I almost shouted. My heart was beginning to thump even harder in my chest, and I almost took off running for that big tree. I think he realized my fright because his next words gave me an out.

"I'll meet you at that diner where you and I talked and later you talked to Reno. That should make you feel safe. There seem to always be customers in there, and, if not, the owner and at least one waitress are always there."

I sensed the sneer in his voice, but at the moment I could have cared less. The relief of meeting him somewhere where there were people, witnesses, slowed my thumping to a more acceptable rhythm, although the fact that he knew I had talked to Reno there made me wonder, nervously.

"As soon as you can get there," he almost chortled, before jumping back in the car, gunning the motor and driving away. At the next cross street he turned around and sped back past me, on his way to Mike's.

I hesitated, not completely certain I wanted to meet the man, even someplace where there were witnesses. I didn't trust him, not one teeny little iota. I didn't like the idea that it would really be late if we talked for even a half hour. Simply walking back there would take about twenty minutes. Getting served another five or ten. And it was after midnight already. There would be little traffic, if any, between the diner and my home at that time of night. Yet there would be witnesses in the diner, people who saw us together. I decided that he wasn't dumb enough to do anything after being seen in public with me. And he knew damn well that his own brother and the Dog Man, and Eve also, would be witnesses to my stories about him trying to kill me.

I decided I was safe for the night, in spite of the fear in the pit of my stomach, and the anger that kept trying to push it aside.

Ron was waiting when I walked into Mike's Diner, in a rear booth. Mike himself was waiting table and doing the cooking as well. There were four other customers, one couple in a booth near the front door and two lone men also in the front of the store, sitting on stools at the counter, two stools apart. So there was no one nearby to hear our conversation. Ron ordered coffee only. I ordered a coke and hamburger. I had planned on raiding the fridge at home but figured I could afford a sandwich. However, Ron must have been feeling generous. He said he would pay. I didn't argue with him; he had invited me to the talkfest. And he supposedly had plenty of money.

Ron didn't say a word until Mike brought our orders and left. I wondered if he was trying to intimidate me, but I kept quiet, not having anything to say anyway.

"You know what this conversation is going to be about," he commented as soon as Mike left.

"My relationship with Eve," I shrugged.

"I plan on convincing you to quit seeing her," he stared at me for several minutes without saying another word.

I said nothing, just stared back. What was there to say? I knew what he wanted. And he did scare me. But I have a stubborn streak. And besides, I figured what Eve did was none of his business. What I did was less so. I would keep dating Eve until one or the other of us decided to end the relationship. And I didn't figure that person would be me. Not that I had definite plans for a long term relationship like marriage. Oh, there were times when I considered asking her to marry me. But every time, after several hours or even days of thinking about it, I generally rejected the idea, either consciously or unconsciously. I was still a student. I was a student with only a part-time job. I couldn't even afford living on my own, let alone afford to support a wife. And Eve had made her feelings quite clear about men without money or potential. Moreover, although we often talked about the future, and about marriage and having a family and such, she always made it abundantly clear that she didn't consider me as prime marriage material, mostly because I was poor, didn't seem to know what I wanted out of my education, and didn't seem to have much ambition for the future. Besides, she always laughed at the end of our conversations and added that I wasn't the marrying kind, not yet. So I had no doubts that she would reject a marriage proposal coming from me, no matter how much I might protest that I really wanted to marry her.

"You know," Ron continued when I didn't reply, "there are lots of people in this country but for my purposes here there are only two types: those who want to rise about the masses and those who are happy just blending in and being a nobody."

He just stared at me with those cold eyes. I had to wonder if his heart was as cold as his eyes. From what I'd heard and seen, it probably was.

"You, I have no doubts," he finally continued, "are in the last category. According to Eve, you don't seem to know what you want to major in. You seem to be happy working in that greasy garage, washing cars and changing their oil and putting air in tires when asked, and changing tires and batteries. It doesn't take a great deal of drive to clean up other people's messes. You keep hanging around Eve in spite of her ambitions, and her drive, holding her back from making the proper decisions about her future. You know she'll never marry you." He shook his head as if disgusted. "She's got more taste than that. She wants a man who is going up in the world, or is up there already."

I almost asked him what he meant by "going up," but I kept my mouth shut. I was still a little intimidated by him. And, besides, a lot of what he was saying was true. I didn't have the slightest idea what I wanted to do with my life, and that included whether or not I wanted to marry Eve. And I really didn't have a lot of ambition to become rich. What I wanted was to be happy, I guess. I didn't know if money would make me happy or not; I'd never had much, nor had my parents and they seemed happy enough to me, happier than I pictured Ron being, what with all the rumors I'd heard about him running his family with an iron fist and his wife being a kind of wishy-washy type who did as she was told and had never been known to cross him. And his daughter, supposedly, was a clone of her mother.

I wondered if this was why he was so attracted to Eve, her independence and her refusal to knuckle under to anything she didn't approve of. Or was it that he saw her as a challenge, a woman to eventually force into submission.

"I figure she can make up her own mind about who to date and when," I finally commented after he had quit talking and was again sitting there staring at me. "She's a big girl, you know, an adult in the eyes of the law. She sure as ever doesn't need some relative telling her what she can and can't do. I don't know where you get off trying to tell her who to go out with. She's not your daughter."

He just smiled although, as usual when he talked to me, his lips were pulled back in more of a sneer or snarl than a friendly grin.

"Why do you try to control her life?" I finally asked when he didn't say anything.

He shrugged as if that was one of the most stupid questions he had ever heard, "Because she's like most young people these days, or any days as far as that goes. She needs someone to guide her in the proper direction. Otherwise, like so many kids, she'll meander for several years and screw up her life, and maybe the life of some man, before she gets on the track she should be on, if she ever does get back on the straight and narrow, which is sure as hell not a given. Look at you, you and those two high school friends of yours. They must not have had the proper guidance at home, or in school. If they had, they might not have died before they grew up. Two dead kids. Killed more or less by their own hands. What a waste. And you. I have to admit that you made it to college after high school. But hell, you're still frittering away your life." I was becoming pissed and started to interrupt, but he held up his hand like some teacher commanding silence and me, well, I had been well trained over the past thirteen plus years. I shut my mouth down before it could get me in trouble.

"Just look at you. You command about as much respect as any nonentity, grease and all. You're definitely not in control of your own destiny. You don't know what you want to major in. You could be experimenting with some basic business courses, or science courses, but Eve says you haven't taken anything along those lines except a required science course, and that was in geology, something about as financially worthless as the literature and history electives you've taken." He suddenly changed direction, startling me. "What do you plan on majoring in?"

How could I answer such a question? I shrugged and mumbled, "I don't know. I'm thinking about English."

"That figures," he sneered. "What do you plan on doing with it? Teach?"

I shrugged again. What the hell. He was right to a certain extent. I didn't know what the hell I wanted to do with my life. On the one hand there was all the pressure to go to college and get a good education, pressure from teachers, friends, family, and the whole culture to be exact. Somehow, if seemed that if you didn't have a college education you just weren't worth anything. I guess I was like most of the other kids I knew. I followed along, blindly, without much dissension.

Yet I knew some older guys who had graduated from college, and some girls too. They didn't seem to be any smarter than a lot of the people I knew who had quit after high school. They didn't read any more, and what they did read wasn't any different from what the other group read. The same was true of art and movies and television programs. And games. As a group they did have better jobs usually, and better homes, and better clothes. But that wasn't always true, not by a long shot. And I couldn't see that they were any happier.

I sometimes wondered if I was wasting my time, if I would be better off just working, since I really enjoyed my job even though I didn't make a lot of money or receive a lot of respect. At the moment I thought, fleetingly, that Ron might be right. Maybe I was wasting my time, and worse, wasting Eve's.

When I didn't react to what I considered a rhetorical question, he continued, "Like I said, I don't want Eve to ruin her life with someone who'll never amount to much, if anything. And no, I'm not her parent. But she's part of my family. And she is like a daughter to me. She's attractive. She's bright. She's a go-getter. And most of all, she has ambition of her own. And I don't want any of those assets frittered away until she too becomes a loser. Understand?" he glared at me, the sneer still on his lips.

"Besides," he continued, the glare gone but the sneer still in place, "I'm kind of old fashioned. I think one of the surest ways the head of an extended family, a clan if you will, can move the whole group upward and keep the young from wasting so much of their potential, not to mention their time, is to use those same young people to forge bonds that not only lift one clan socially and financially, but also make the other clan stronger and more capable of also moving upward. I think our ancestors, and even some modern cultures, were smarter than we are. They didn't accept all this romantic claptrap about the young searching for and, hopefully, finding their soul mate, their personal human Eden. That's the way it should be. Use what the young have to get the whole clan ahead in this world. Quit wasting our young and what they have to contribute to their families by letting them roam around looking for the person of their dreams until they've wasted the best years of their life. After all, sexual attraction isn't love. Not by a long sight. Love comes from spending time together, from suffering together and struggling together to get ahead and working together to have children and raise them right and to make a better name in society. It…." He shook his head and frowned. "But I don't know why I'm telling you all this. I doubt if you have the slightest idea what I'm talking about. If you do, you're doubtlessly too young and close-minded to understand."

I just shook my head, disgusted but also impressed. I didn't know many people with independent ideas of their own. Most of them simply believed what everyone else believed, with maybe, occasionally, some variation which was generally not of their own creation. But accept what he was saying? Not by a long shot. It would destroy a basic freedom, or independence, that I for one don't want to do without.

"So," I tried for a thoughtful tone, "you're telling me that you want Eve, through marriage, to connect your clan, as you call it, to another a little higher on the social rung, hopefully both financially and politically."

"You can actually understand ideas that aren't simply part of the normal tripe, can't you?" For a moment he seemed impressed and the sneer disappeared, but only for a moment. Within seconds the sneer had returned. "But the important question is, can you buy into them or are they too different for you?"

"Buy into them? Hell, no. I believe in independence, no matter what the cost in time, money, and effort. Besides, I don't like the idea of anyone being prostituted to the social status of their family, or of themselves." I forced a harsh laugh, "Especially me or someone I want."

He shook his head with disgust. "That's pretty damned naïve. And selfish. But what else could I expect from you."

"And what you want isn't selfish? Come on!"

He shook his head disgustedly, that sneer still plastered on his thin lips.

"No. I don't see it that way. In some ways individual freedom is one of the most selfish aspects of our government and culture. The young go their own way, often with little or no guidance from the time they're in school. Little or no guidance about the kind of spouse they should search for, or the kind of career that would mesh with their personality, inclinations, and intelligence. Or they get the wrong kind of guidance. Especially if they're good at sports, and can play at the college level but not the pros. I wonder how many kids wind up in college just to play sports, or because a friend of theirs is going to college, or because their parents insist that they go, or...kids who aren't interested in learning or in any specific career that has to do with college-level learning. Kids who have never read an entire book in their life, and who probably won't, even during their college years." Ron paused and glared at me. "I wonder what percentage go to college and don't have the slightest idea what they want to major in and, after a couple of years, kind of stumble into a major they aren't really interested in and won't use or be able to use after they graduate."

When he paused for breath I commented, "I guess that's part of growing up, making wrong decisions and going down wrong paths until you find the right one."

"The problem is, a lot of people never find the right one."

I shrugged. I was getting a little bored with our one-way conversation. And irritated because I felt that he was talking about me.

"I figure most of them could with the right guidance. And I plan on guiding Eve down the right path. Right now she needs help breaking free of you. And that I'll give her."

I almost sniggered. This was where all his wind had really been headed for.

"What if she doesn't want help? What if she likes the path she's on?"

"It's a dead end and, one way or another, I'll help her change to a path that's going somewhere."

"One that benefits you, I expect," I imitated his sneer.

"One that benefits both of us, and our family."

As he spoke he rose and walked away. At least he stopped at the cash register in the front of the diner and paid our bill. But he left me with a long, dark walk home, although I don't think I would have accepted a ride with him if he had offered. He still scared me.

<h1 style="text-align:center">27</h1>

The next afternoon I walked out to the Dog Man's place. He was not at home so I used his floor to take nap. I had just awakened and stood up when the Dog turned into his lane from the road, his hounds broadcasting his approach to the four winds.

"Hey, hey. Company," he shouted as he burst through the door. "I just talked to your nemesis. He stopped me about half-way between town and here, pulling squarely in front of me and so not giving me much choice but to stop and chat." He grinned. "The guy's so damned full of himself that I sometimes wonder why he doesn't weigh several tons."

"What did he want?" I felt my temper rising and made an effort to squash it.

"What do you think, Donjon? He sure as hell didn't stop to enjoy my pleasant personality or infinite wisdom."

"Probably to make some kind of threat. That seems to be all he knows how to do."

"You win the cigar," the Dog Man shouted.

I could almost see his grin through his wild beard.

"He wanted to let me know that he, not you or me, is responsible for Eve and her future. Although that's not how he put it. I think 'control' comes closer to what he was saying, although I doubt that he would admit it. I can't believe that character. He should have lived back in the Middle Ages."

"Or been born in the Middle East," I interrupted.

"Yeah, there's that. But he threatened me...and, of course, you. He was ranting so much that what he was saying wasn't easy to follow."

He paused, again shaking his head, this time with anger flashing in his eyes.

"So you're not sure what he was trying to say."

"Oh, yeah. There was no doubt about that. It's just that his reasoning was all over the board. And mad. I thought he was going to start frothing at the mouth any minute. I was startled because he's usually calm and rational, even though what he says is so damned irrational from our modern perspective." He paused and, shaking his head, grinned. "But the essence of what he was saying was pretty damned clear. Either I stop you from chasing Eve or he'll make sure both of us are sorry for all the trouble we've caused...and will cause, I think. That wasn't at all clear. I sometimes thought he was angrier about your having, what he called, chased after Eve and kept her from finding some more acceptable guy to date and sometimes I thought he was madder about your still keeping after her and so keeping her from finding an 'appropriate' mate this last year or so of college. But I expect that it was probably both, past and future."

"What a nut case!" I exploded.

"Agreed," Dog stared at me for several seconds before continuing, "but a dangerous nut case. I'm not sure what to advise you."

"It doesn't make a damn bit of difference," it was my turn to shrug. "I'll date Eve as long as I want to. Or as long as she'll have me."

"That's the right answer," Dog mused. "But it's not the safe one. I think the guy's a real psycho. But then, psycho isn't the correct word here either. He knows what he's doing. He's almost always pretty rational, actually cold and calculating. He just seems to have this control fixation when it comes to Eve, as if somehow she's his prized possession, one with tremendous sentimental and financial value, and you're trying to steal it from him. He really does see her as a possession, it seems to me. I sometimes wonder if she isn't the woman he'd really like to have for his spouse but can't because of the age disparity and their genetic relationship."

I forced a laugh, "He thinks he's some feudal lord and she's one of his 'people,' one who keeps ignoring his commands. But he's so attracted to her that he can't bring himself to punish her for her recalcitrance. He thinks that, someday, if he links her up with some dumb wimp, she'll wind up in his bed."

Dog chuckled, "You've given it some thought, I see, and come up with an answer that suits your personality, something that you wouldn't mind doing yourself with some good-looking chick."

I answered his grin with one of my own. I was tired of Ron the Con and his attempts at manipulating Eve and me.

"Yeah. But not just with one chick. With a dozen or so. You know, a harem all my own."

"Uh-huh," Dog rolled his eyes sarcastically, "as if you could handle that many of these modern girls. Hell, you can't even control Eve."

"Come on, Dog," I complained in fun. "Do you know any guy you think could control Eve? I mean any guy, without using force. Hell, I don't even understand what she wants half the time. There's no way I could lead her in any direction she didn't want to go, without a whip and stool anyhow. You know, like lion tamers use. And then she'd just wait until I got careless and then pounce. And that'd be the end of me."

Dog laughed and joined the fun, "You're right about that. She might not know the exact direction she wants to go in, but she sure as hell won't go where you or I or any man tries to get her to go, unless that's the precise direction she wanted to go in in the first place, or the direction she has just decided that's best for her. She's got a mind of her own and she reacts negatively to force. So your best bet is to use the carrot, not the stick. Or better yet," his eyes sparkled, "use sweets because I don't think an old carrot would tempt her in the least. In fact, I'm not even sure sweets would. Maybe money, a lot of it. We're all susceptible to money. Or love. A lot of the time that works even better than money."

"Love?" my pessimistic self blurted the question before my reasonable self could stop it. "What's that exactly? Some people love money, or what it can buy. Some prefer power, or both. Some want fame, or maybe I should say adulation. Then…."

"That's enough," Dog interrupted. "You're becoming worse than I am at my most cynical. But they all really want other people to admire them, even worship them."

"Okay, okay," I laughed halfheartedly. "You win. Down deep Eve wants love. But it has to be in the same package as money, lots of money."

"I think you've got Eve all wrong," Dog shook his head in disgust. "She's really looking for love. She just pays lip-service to all those people around her, that couple she rents her pad from; this guy Ron the Con, as you call him; maybe her parents, for all I know; and probably all those teachers who've advised her to go into business or some other money-making occupation, because they think they know what her personality wants, the teachers she talks about sometimes and seems to admire."

At my blank look, he laughed and added, "She does seem to have paid attention to some of those people who have shown an interest in her, and who listened to her occasionally, rather than always worrying about their own image or whether she really does like them or not."

I think I probably blushed at that one.

He must have noticed because he added more softly, "You've got to admit that you always seem worried about how she perceives you or whether she really is being faithful."

With an effort I pulled myself together, "Is it that easy to see?"

"Yeah, it's that easy, and I expect Eve thinks so too. But I don't think you should worry. She likes you or she wouldn't always be hanging around you. She'd be off tempting other guys to chase her."

"Well, hell, she does enough of that."

"I think you're wrong," Doug growled, staring me in the eyes. "At this point in her life you're the only man for her. That's pretty damned evident even if she's not aware of it. She comes out here quite a bit, and all she ever wants to talk about is you. She seems to think that I know more about your whereabouts and character than she does. I get the feeling that she associates me with you like you associate her with Cousin Ron, that I control you in some way." He laughed like he had just cracked a hilarious joke. "But you and I know damn well that you listen and then do what you want to, just like she does. You're both damned independent, which is actually the problem here. Can two truly independent people live together for years without major clashes? Or does it take one with more independence and one with less? Answer me that," he grinned and stopped talking, apparently happy to have added a little philosophy to the conversation.

"I always thought marriage was a partnership, two people living together equally."

"Do your parents treat each other as equals?" He stared at me, demanding an honest answer with his eyes.

The question caught me off guard. I had never thought about it before. My parents had always been there in the house, two people ruling my life sometimes and at other times letting up on the reins. They were like some of my friends' parents, unlike those of others. They weren't drinkers. They weren't nasty. They could be fairly strict around the house, but they didn't seem to bother themselves, or me, about what I did when I was out on my own, not any more, although there had been a lot of questions and comments and rules when I was younger. Now that I thought of it, anyhow, those rules had slowly relaxed over the years. But were they equal? They seemed to be. When push came to shove, Mom ruled the house, the day to day things. But Dad made the major decisions, I thought. And he seemed to win most disagreements.

"I don't know," I answered Dog as truthfully as I could. "I don't think so." I explained what I had been thinking. "But you know, I think that's their personalities. They're not the same person, you know."

"Let's don't spout truisms," Dog growled. "I've never met any two people who were exactly alike, physically or mentally."

"Damn it!" I growled back. "I know that. But what I'm trying to do here is figure out what the word 'equal' means when we're talking about two different people sharing the same space and duties and responsibilities. People in our country don't all do the same thing and make all decisions alike. Crap, what kind of a crazy country would that be? And don't tell me I'm still spouting truisms. I know I am. But I'm trying to work my way truthfully to your question about my parents."

He clapped me on the shoulder and gave a please grunt, "You're doing fine."

"Well, Dad does certain things and Mom does certain things. It seems to me that they both act according to their likes and abilities, and let the other one do the same. A division of labor, I guess. Both doing what fits their personalities and abilities." I paused for a moment. Dog waited patiently, his eyes seeming to sparkle. "But what Dad does is more like what our bosses and political leaders do. And what Mom does is more like the duties and responsibilities of a worker, blue and white collar. But then Dad does some of the white collar things." I hesitated, realizing that I was meandering and a little mixed up. "But then he does most of the fix-it work too. And Mom does most of the house work and laundry and cooking, what us kids aren't assigned to do, and makes most of the decisions about us kids and our lives, even contradicting Dad at times."

"Different but equal?" Dog did a little jig to show that he approved of my long-winded explanation. "That sounds like equality to me, but I expect some of our fellow citizens would disagree."

"So," I finally interrupted after he had stopped his dance and silence had set in for several minutes, "is that good enough for me and Eve, do you think?"

"Hell, Donjon, who knows? That kind of a relationship would be great, if it fits your two personalities. But Eve is really strong-willed, not really happy unless she can have her way in most situations. And you, you're easygoing, most of the time, but you refuse to allow anyone to run over you. That's pretty evident in things both you and Eve say. And that's the problem we all face when we decide to hook up with someone in marriage, which at one time was meant as a life-time relationship, although I'm not sure that's true anymore. And maybe that's for the best, because long-term relationships can turn sour and get mean as hell, even violent. Hell, that's true of the relationships of citizens in nations, like ours. We humans can only live together for so long in peaceful togetherness before we start squabbling. And unless we purge our psyches of the urge to violence they hold, or unless we can separate equably and peaceably and go our individual ways, our squabbling will get nastier and nastier until it becomes all-out warfare. And maybe even separation won't soothe the hatred that has built up over years of disagreement." He paused, grinned, and did an exaggerated eye-roll. "And that is my kernel of wisdom for the day."

His movement to the general and philosophical took the personal immediacy out of our discussion of me and Eve. I felt kind of let down, mostly, but in some ways felt guilty because I realized that Eve had her right to freedom, to build relationships and experiment with them, just as I did. My only problem was that I didn't want to experiment with new female relationships anymore. I was happy with Eve, and only Eve. But I still wasn't sure about commitment. I guess I just wanted our relationship, mine and Eve's, to continue as it was. My commitment to a future with her was uncertain, which was maybe the problem she had in remaining true to me and only me.

But I still couldn't keep from feeling that she was being untrue to me. Was that my ego having its way? Was it my feelings for her? Was it my culture, one in which men have little control over the dating process, relatively speaking—men chase, women choose, I believe, unless force is involved? Or was it more basic? Was it my being a male, which, by the nature of the flesh, I think, gives me less certainty about the whole male/female relationship than it must women? I'm talking about the connection of the birth of a child all the way back to the procreative moment that created that child, and the knowledge that women have considerably more certainty, and thus peace of mind, and thus control, than their male counterparts do.

But then, again, maybe I simply have problems facing a reality that I can't control. Another all-too-human characteristic?

So, after some more conversation with the Dog Man, kind of desultory compared to the above, I left, definitely unsatisfied in my gut. I had to accept that a big part of the problem was of my making, my hesitancy about making a definite commitment. But then Eve had made it abundantly clear from the beginning that, for a permanent commitment, she was looking for a man with money or, at the least, lots of potential. My reaction was that I didn't fulfill that requirement.

28

I didn't see Eve for almost two weeks. She had looked for me, she later said, both in the library and out at Dog's. She had never tried to contact me at home. Why? She never explained, just changed the subject when I asked. So I stopped asking, assuming that she either didn't want to meet my parents and siblings because that would put us another step along on a path to a togetherness future or she really hadn't been that interested in finding me.

Anyway, I had been working extra hours at the service station and spending my few spare hours studying either at home or in the library. Then final week jumped in and I was busy studying for and taking exams. I assumed that she was too.

The weekend after finals, though, on Saturday evening I walked out to the Carsons' house. I knew Eve would be working full time that summer, but I also knew she would be off evenings and some weekends, and my schedule had me off a couple of days during the week and every other weekend.

Mrs. Carson answered the door and, as usual, made me feel right at home.

"You again," she greeted me with her pasty frown. "I guess you want to see Eve."

"Yes, Ma'am," I wasn't very quick on the trigger with sarcasm or I might have used 'madam' instead. And she was definitely not the madam type. So maybe I should have used sister, but, as I say, I'm not very quick with the humor and, anyway, she wouldn't have understood that either. I had never heard her laugh and Eve said that she hadn't either, not once in the time she had boarded with the woman and her husband.

Mrs. Carson stood there glaring at me for what seemed like several minutes, not saying a word. I was struggling to not fidget when she finally commented, "I can't understand why you keep chasing the poor girl. With the other young men after her, and the dates she goes on, you should take the hint."

"What hint?" I blurted, my temper starting to rise, although whether at Eve or the woman standing sentry before me, I don't know.

"Well, if you don't know, it's not my place to clue you in. That's up to Eve."

With those words, she turned and disappeared, letting the door close behind her. So there I stood, the closed door maybe six inches from my nose, no light on in the vestibule on the other side of that door, although I could make out a dim flickering light somewhere in the distance. I figured it was the television in the living room.

But what I didn't know was whether Mrs. Carson had gone to get Eve or had simply returned to her program, whatever that was. I didn't move for some time, paralyzed by uncertainty. Then I swore angrily to myself, closed the screen door, and sat down in the porch swing.

I must have been there for ten or fifteen minutes, waiting

uncertainly, and was just about to get up and stomp off, when the porch light came on and then Eve appeared a few seconds later.

"Hi," she greeted me without stopping. As she tromped down the stairs she said, "Let's take a walk."

After a startled moment of indecision, I bounced up and almost ran to catch her.

"Hey, why the hurry?" I asked, a little on the angry side, as I caught her. "You're acting...."

"Just don't talk for a while, okay?" she grunted, grabbing my hand in hers. "I've been fighting with the Carsons."

I started to ask why, but thought better of it and began walking silently beside her. Walking? She definitely wasn't just strolling along. She was tromping or stomping along, and her hand was doing a little squeezing on mine, and not gentle love squeezing. So, like a good boy, I shut down completely and followed along. I had never seen her this angry before, and most definitely not at the Carsons, whom she only very occasionally criticized or spoke disparagingly of. I wondered if this meant that she would be moving out, but I didn't pose the question.

We had gone maybe a half mile when her hand relaxed in mine. A few minutes later she slowed to a stroll. Maybe twenty minutes later we were passing a small, grassy city park. It was deserted. We had almost passed it when she seemed to make a decision and, with a slight tug, led me to a bench near the far end.

There we sat silently as more time passed, watching an occasional car pass on the street and hearing occasional shouting from the distant houses.

Finally she spoke, "I can't believe the Carsons can be such snobs. They've been after me for the past two weeks to stop seeing you."

I shrugged, "This isn't the first time, is it? They don't like me, especially Mrs. Carson. I've known that for a long time. So have you. And you've said more than once that they bitch a lot about me."

"I know. But that was always just a comment now and then, derogatory or referring to your friends in high school, or your family. But this time, it's been every day, all the time. I'm getting sick and tired of it. I don't like people telling me what to do or talking bad about my friends."

"Well," I thought for a few moments, "I can't think of anything I've done recently that would set them off."

"It's nothing you did. Ronald visited me twice the weekend before last. He took me out to dinner. But he came over in the afternoon, when I was still at the library, and talked to the Carsons until I got home and ready to go out. I figure that's what did it because Mrs. Carson started in on me right away."

"So Ron's to blame?"

"Maybe, I guess. He definitely doesn't like you. And he tries to talk me out of seeing you all the time. When he can't, he just changes the subject or makes some kind of derogatory comment when your name comes up and suggests that there are lots of nice, rich guys that would like to date me. And then he's always saying that you're a loser. And now the Carsons! They keep bringing your name up, out of the blue, and saying all kinds of nasty things. And telling me I can do better and that you're not worth my time and that you're...."

She stopped in mid-sentence and squeezed my hand.

"Well, I've known since we met that the Carsons don't like me. Mrs. Carson has made that pretty clear. She thinks my family is trashy. And that definitely includes me, maybe because of what my friends did in high school. I figure that's part of it anyway. And I agree with you. She's snobbish as hell. She thinks she's one of the elite, I guess." I think I was grumbling by the time I finished. "It'd be nice if you lived somewhere else."

"I know," Eve took my hand and squeezed it. "But I can't find any other place as cheap and clean. And they don't have too many rules that keep me from doing what I want to. And Ronald pays part of my rent as long as I stay there."

We were quiet for several minutes. I wondered why Ron paid part of her rent but decided not to ask.

Then I said, "Ron seems to think you'll come around to his way of thinking. And he thinks he'll scare me away from you."

"I know. He thinks he can control me like he does his wife and daughter. But he's got another think coming. This isn't the Middle Ages. And I'm not some peon. Nobody's going to marry me off to a man I don't want to marry. And nobody's going to tell me who I can date and who I can't. Not even Ronald." She quit talking for awhile. Then, "Ronald has always been good to me. I like him, although he can be way too assertive, wanting… no, demanding that people around him do what he wants them to do. But I'm not a simpering idiot like his wife. I do things my way, thank you."

"An emancipated female," I laughed, although she didn't have to tell me that she was untamed. I'd had plenty of experience with her free spirit. And to tell the truth, I liked it. But at the same time, I wondered if we moderns weren't going too far with our insistence on freedom, often at the expense of responsibility and the feelings of others. "But who's going to mind the store if all you women decide to be footloose and fancy free like men."

"What do you mean?" Even asked, irritation not very carefully hidden in her tone. "Do you mean we should stay home and keep house and do what we're told?"

I forced a laugh, knowing I was irritating her, but forging ahead anyhow.

"Not really, although that's part of it, I suppose. But staying home? You know as well as I do that technology has made housekeeping a hell of a lot less difficult and time-consuming than it was, hell, less than a century ago. And kids are a lot less time-consuming because there's school and pre-school and.... You also know that a lot of women work outside the home and a lot of men work around the house. But that's not really what I meant. Work is work—two people living together can damn well decide on their own who does what. If they're satisfied, then it's nobody else's business, I don't think."

"But like most men you still think the house and kids are the main responsibility of the woman and the man's duty is to bring home the bacon."

"I didn't say that."

"Maybe not, but you've hinted it enough."

"Well, I'd sure want my wife to oversee the house and all that goes with it. If it was left to me," I chuckled and I think that irritated her more, "the place would become a pig sty. That's what my mom says anyway."

Eve had been holding my hand in hers but, after a few moments of absolute silence between us, with only the angry beep of a horn in the distance breaking that silence, she let go and scooted away a few inches.

"So, if we were married, it would be up to me to do all the housework and the cooking and cleaning up after the kids and...."

"Come on, Eve. I didn't say that. I said 'oversee,' which means be the boss. That's a lot different than doing the work yourself. That's what my mom does. Of course, she does plenty of work herself, but she also hands out the chores in the house, to us kids and," I chuckled at some memories of her giving Dad hell for his not having done some chore she told him to do, "to Dad too."

"What does you dad do, nothing unless he's told to?" Eve's tone of voice had turned sarcastic, as if she expected only one answer.

"He keeps the yard and garden up, and keeps the car and lawnmower running. And he keeps everything working in the house. You know, like the electricity and heat and paint on the walls."

"And your mom does the cooking and washing and housework and takes care of the kids and...."

I shrugged, but I doubt that she saw it in the dark, "Like I told you, us kids have to do certain things around the house, like clean our rooms and help with the cooking. And the girls help with cleaning the rest of the house and I mow the yard a lot of the time, and other things."

Eve took my hand again. She seemed mollified. For a moment.

"But you still think the house and children are the woman's responsibility."

I mulled over her words before answering.

"Yeah, I do. The woman's the one who carries the kids in her womb and, from what I read, has the nesting instinct, whatever that means. But I don't know how we got off on this married responsibility stuff. We were talking about men and women and women being as free any more to do whatever they want, as free as men think they are. I don't agree with that completely, you know. There's the pregnant thing and who carries the baby and all. You know, the basic biological difference between men and women. When they screw around and mess up, it's not the man who is going to have a baby, for someone to take care of over the next twenty years or more. It's the woman. So I guess I have to say that real responsibility for sex and what might happen is hers. The man can always run like hell the other way."

I would have continued but Eve interrupted me, angrily, "So it's the woman's fault, you're saying?"

"I don't think I said that, but being at fault and accepting the responsibility for it are two different things."

"There's always abortion," she stated as if we had not had that discussion before and as if she were a judge handing out a sentence to a man just pronounced guilty by a jury of his peers.

"Yeah, we both know where we stand on that one. But we're talking about responsibility here, personal responsibility in general, not after the fact, and not after a crime or anything like that." I think I was sounding a little pretentious, but I couldn't stop myself. "Somebody has got to be responsible before the act. Somebody has to be morally responsible for the sexual relationship between man and woman. And it sure as hell isn't going to be men. Men aren't built to be responsible." I paused, trying to collect my thoughts but found that impossible. So I continued weakly, "If no one's responsible, then I guess sex just becomes a game of pleasure, like basketball or tennis. Or maybe more like eating an ice cream cone."

"That's silly," she laughed, taking my hand again.

"Yeah, probably," I agreed. "But it's still a lot of fun."

"Ummm," she agreed, snuggling closer to me. "A lot more fun than eating an ice cream cone or playing a game of tennis. But, you know, you keep talking about how women control men and sex and all. I don't agree. Look at some of the countries around the world and the difference in the rights of men and women in them. Look at a lot of religions around the world. Look at marriage. It's a manmade institution created to keep women from changing partners when they're not treated right. I'm glad I was born in the age of technology, when women aren't forced to stay at home and take care of the children and home."

She glared at me.

I decided to quit the discussion while I was ahead.

We soon decided, without discussion or comment, to play the male/female game and to hell with the consequences, I guess. Or more than likely we both simply forgot about (ignored?) the possibility of consequences and lived for the pleasure of the moment.

It was a pleasant evening. Warm with a full moon on the horizon. Silent except for a cricket somewhere and a distant car every ten or fifteen minutes. Nobody around. The children who often populated the park and neighboring area were nowhere in sight, probably home eating the evening meal or watching television; they definitely weren't on the streets. The rows of windows on the other side of the street shed very little light to disturb our sense of peace and safety.

By mutual consent we made our way to a large clump of bushes near the back of the park, and to the grassy, hidden space in the middle, a place we had used before. It was a satisfyingly wonderful evening.

Later I walked Eve back to the Carsons' and took off into the darkness on my own.

29

Events moved rapidly after that evening. I don't know whether Mrs. Carson told Ron about Eve and me going out together a lot again and the fact set him off, or if Ron visiting the Dog Man's was the culminating factor. But I saw Eve a couple days later in the college library and she told me that she and Ron had had a long and bitter argument about me. He had mentioned having gone out to the Dog Man's and getting into a heated argument and a near fight with the man. The supposed upshot of the argument between Eve and Ron was that Ron had told her in no uncertain terms that she was to stop seeing me. And she had told him that she would make such decisions without help from anyone, including him.

She had stormed off, leaving him angrily but ineffectually shouting after her.

Later that same day I saw the Dog Man in town, riding the streets with his barking dogs. He told me that Ron had driven out to see him, the only time Ron had ever been out there. When I asked him about the argument Eve had mentioned, he laughed and said that he and his dogs had chased Ron off his property.

"And mad?" Dog burst into happy laughter. "The wet hen doesn't tell half the story. He was frothing at the mouth, and when I told him to get lost and quit bothering people who didn't much care for his bullying ways, or his interfering in matters that were none of his business, I thought he was going to attack me right then and there. I think the only thing that stopped him was that I had let a couple of the Rottweilers in the house when I let him in. They didn't much like the way he was carrying on and they let him know it, snarling like a couple of guard dogs at a dangerous intruder. Twice I had to order them to sit down and be quiet. I finally told him to get out or I'd set them on him. I pointed at him and the dogs started his way. He backed out of the house making all kinds of silly threats, but he sure as hell didn't stop. And as soon as he was through the gate, he jumped in his car and took off, cussing me through his open window."

He was grinning by the time he had finished his tale. So was I, but then the memory of some of the things that Ron the Con had done hit me like a sledge hammer. I made Dog promise to be extra careful.

"He loses control when he's mad," I insisted. "That's what Eve tells me, and so does his brother, Reno. And you know yourself that he's tried to run you down."

Dog just kept on grinning. He was pleased about his run-in with Ron.

"Don't worry about me," he winked. "I've lived a good life. And I'm pretty good at taking care of myself."

If only we'd known.

A week later he was dead. A pickup truck hit him while he was returning from town to home. The driver of the pickup swore that he was traveling at the speed limit and completely in control, but that the Dog Man's dogs had for some unknown reason stamped from the side of the road right into the path of the truck, giving the driver no time to react except to automatically and wildly swing the truck wheel to the right—the wrong way in fact, according to the police, since it swung the truck right into the Dog Man on his bike rather than into the dogs surrounding him.

Four dogs were killed anyway and six injured as well. What happened to the rest of them I don't know for sure. By the time I got my nerve up to go out to his place, the dogs were all gone and the place was boarded up, with a for sale sign at the head of the driveway. Eve didn't know either, but she had heard that the Dog's neighbors had contacted the police and an animal rights group to have the dogs moved somewhere else. They barked all the time and there was no one to feed them. She had also heard that the bank in town foreclosed on the property because the Dog was several months in arrears on his mortgage payments.

I'll miss the Dog Man. He was a good friend and a funny guy. A good man. He lives on in my memory, beside my high school buddies, Adam and Cass.

I also had no doubts that Ron had somehow engineered the Dog Man's death. So I set out to prove it, somehow.

The first thing I did was to scour the newspapers to get the name of the pickup driver and any information I could glean about the accident. That wasn't much of course. Real facts are usually pretty sparse in the press. All I could find was the summary of the accident as related by the driver, and a few additional facts added by the police. They accepted the driver's account of the accident and didn't charge him with anything. According to them, he hadn't been drinking but was rather on his way home from work and wasn't speeding or driving recklessly. They also maintained that his tire and skid marks suggested that everything had gone as he said. But, according to the papers, nothing at the wreck site indicated where exactly the bike and dogs had been hit, toward the middle of the road or along the side. I knew there was no need for me to go out to the wreck site; I wouldn't have any idea what to look for.

I also didn't have the slightest idea how to go about checking up on the driver and his story. So I called Ron's brother, Reno. He was a police officer. I figured he might be able to dig out information that I couldn't. When I told him about Dog and his relationship to me and Eve, about his encounters with Ron and what had happened to him, Reno became interested, although he had already known much of what I told him. We made plans to meet the next evening at Mike's.

I didn't get off work until six but, after hurrying home to shower and eat, I made it to Mike's at seven thirty. Reno was waiting for me, devouring a hamburger and fries. I ordered a Pepsi and sat down across from him in his booth.

When he had finished his meal, he pushed his plate aside and, coffee cup in hand, said, "Let's have it."

I told him everything I knew and what I thought and why.

"The police assigned to the case didn't mention that Ron had visited the man before the accident. Did you tell them?"

"Are you kidding me?" I asked, more indignantly than I should have since nothing had been his fault and I wanted his help. "I went to the station and asked to talk with anyone involved in the case. The officer at the desk asked me what case. I told him that it involved the accident and he said that's precisely what it was, an accident. There was no case."

"I can understand that, from what I've read in the papers and seen on television. And from what my colleagues have told me." With those words, he gazed at me searchingly before asking, "You didn't know I'm now a policeman here in Echo Creek, did you?"

Startled, I shook my head, "Since when?"

"I was offered a job several years ago, but I didn't take it until about six months ago."

"Does Ron know?"

"Of course. Ron's got an in with every department in this town, and most of the little towns within twenty miles. In fact, the way my colleagues and others talk, I suspect that Ron's influence got me the job here. He probably figures that, us being brothers, he can count on my backing if he gets in a real mess."

"Can he?"

"No more than anyone else, and probably less than many. I've seen and experienced too much of his violence and lying ways." Reno frowned before continuing with our previous conversation. "Knowing Ron, I think it sounds fishy that he visited this Dog Man guy shortly before the accident. But the police probably only know his good side, and he knows so many of the top people in town, so they reject out of hand any meaningful connection with the dead man or his killer. Ron can be very impressive when he wants to be and he seldom does anything in public that would shed a bad light on him. The question is whether he knows the driver of the pickup and how well. I'll check around to see if that driver has any kind of record and if there's anything to connect him to Ron. It there is, I'll check in with the officers who covered the accident, to find out what they have, if anything, other than what the news has carried."

After that, the conversation turned to Eve and my relationship with her. We soon left, parting outside as Reno got in his car and took off. I headed to the college library. There were still a few hours I could study before it closed.

A couple days later, early evening, I was on the sidewalk headed home from work when a patrol car pulled up next to the curb. At first I thought I was in trouble for some unknown reason. But I recognized Reno when he rolled down the window and called me over to the car. I climbed in and we talked. He had learned that the pickup's driver was named Pete Dirkel, a fact I already knew. Dirkel had been in minor trouble with the police several times, twice having served time in jail, once for six months, once for two years.

"He's a bully type," Reno said. "He picks on people, fat guys, old men, women, usually in bars, and works them over, usually with his fists, but the two times he wound up in jail he used a club. The first time, he was lucky. The bouncer and some other guy stopped him before he could do much damage, so the judge went easy on him. The second time? Well, the victim spent several months in the hospital. The judge sentenced Dirkel to two to five and ordered him to pay for the victim's medical expenses. Dirkel got out on good behavior after a year, but he never paid the medical expenses." Reno paused and shook his head scornfully. "I can't believe the court never followed through on the order for Dirkel to pay up. But they didn't and the victim refused to press charges. Some of my colleagues think somebody got to the victim and scared the crap out of him. If not, why the hell wouldn't he press charges? And it couldn't have been Dirkel because he was in prison. So...."

"Ron?" I asked.

"I don't know. But rumor has it that some of the people Dirkel beat up had had problems with Ron. Nothing I can substantiate, and the rumors are pretty vague, but they're still out there."

It didn't seep through my thick skull that I too had had troubles with Ron, that trouble being my relationship with Eve. I could only think about the Dog Man's death and how it might not have been an accident. But I didn't have the slightest idea how to go about finding out if my suspicions were true. I did find out that Dirkel lived in a tiny ramshackle house on a bramble-infested lot in Echo Creek, a couple of blocks east of where the Dog's country road entered town. And he had his own plumbing business, a one-man business. So he could have been heading home from a contracted plumbing job when he hit the Dog Man.

But I had no way to find out where that plumbing job was, short of checking with the police, assuming that they had that information. And checking with them was not an option, so I decided to wait until Reno got back to me and ask him to check it out.

In the meantime Dan and Bart had asked me to meet them for a few beers Friday evening, at Stinkey's. I had accepted the invitation since Eve would be working.

I got there a little late. They had said eight. I arrived a little before eight-thirty. Their greeting was boisterous, suggesting that they had already downed a few.

"Lover boy finally made it," Dan shouted.

"I'd suggest he buy a watch," Bart grinned, "but I don't think he can tell time yet. Too young and innocent."

"You're both full of crap," I laughed and told the passing waitress what I wanted.

"Look at that," Dan shook his head in mock distress. "He didn't even order us a beer."

"You didn't really expect a tightwad like Donjon to pay for a round, did you?" Dan took a long swig of his beer. "Hell, I hear he won't go out with a female unless they go Dutch."

"I can see this is going to be a rough night, what with two drunks to take care of," I grinned, paying the girl who had just brought my beer. "When did you two get here anyway?"

"Was it yesterday or the day before?" Dan turned to Bart. "Or maybe it's only been an hour or so. Damn, time flies when you're having fun."

I shook my head, thinking he was joshing, but he nodded toward the back of the room, where two girls had just come out of the hallway leading to the restroom.

"We picked them up just after we got here. They're both in one of my classes and may be worth our time and effort. So watch what you say."

I started to ask where the girls were sitting, but then noticed the two drink glasses between my friends. I had noticed that they were sitting at a table for six but had figured that it was the only one available. Looking around now though, I realized that there were several smaller tables empty. I also realized for the first time that there were two chairs between Dan and Bart.

"Oh-oh," I blurted. "I don't want to cramp your style, so maybe I should sit somewhere else."

"Nah," Bart's voice had become almost a whisper, as he stood to greet the approaching girls. "Just stick around and see how real Casanovas work their prey."

Yeah, I thought sarcastically. Boys chase. Girls decide.

The rest of the evening at that table was pretty boring. My friends introduced me to the two girls, but the names went in one ear and out the other. I thought from the beginning that the girls were playing Dan and Bart. They spent more time talking to each other than to their would-be pick-ups, except when their glasses were empty or when Dan or Bart insisted on carrying a conversation with them. I had downed three beers and was seriously considering heading for home and bed when, suddenly, without warning, the two girls stood up, said they had to leave, and took off.

My two friends stood up stuttering, trying to talk the girls into staying or let the two guys walk them home. It didn't work. The girls turned their backs and walked away, hurriedly it seemed to me. For a moment I thought Bart was going to chase them. He took a couple of hurried steps, then stopped, disbelief written all over his stance. Dan just stood there, swearing under his breath, I think. I forced myself not to laugh at the spectacle, but I couldn't suppress a grin.

"Grin, you bastard," Dan growled, before himself bursting into embarrassed laughter. "What a wasted evening."

"The damned bitches played us," Bart sputtered as he returned to his seat and chugged the rest of his beer. "I'll sure as hell remember that."

"For all the good it'll do you," I was still grinning at their discomfiture, although inside I felt sorry for them. I'd suffered the same consequences more than once and knew damn well how angry they were.

"Oh, I'll get even," chagrin was still plastered all over Dan's face. "I've helped both of them get ready for quizzes and exams ever since the class started, and I know they're planning on taking a couple of the classes I'm taking next year. I helped them figure out what was going to be on a quiz or test and helped them better understand what the prof might expect in answer. And Barb, I proofread her last class paper for her. We've got another one due in a week and you can be damned sure I won't give her any help."

"Being a little nasty, aren't you?" I gave him a lopsided grin.

"Screw you," he grinned back. "We bought them drinks all night. And what thanks did we get?" he laughed and I realized that he was coming to terms with the let-down. "We bought those two drinks all night and they sure as hell didn't offer to buy a round. Then they get up and take off, without even a thank you. What would you do? Tell them we'll buy the drinks any time we meet in a bar again?"

"Nope," I answered. "I figure I'd do exactly what you did. Nothing but bitch and moan."

At that both Dan and Bart grinned, sheepishly. By silent but mutual agreement we changed the subject.

"Have you figured out yet if your weird friend's death was really an accident?" Bart asked after the two of them had ordered more beer.

"With proof? No," I answered, sliding my beer bottle around the table in front of me and watching the lines of moisture it made. "But the guy who ran over him is meaner than hell, I hear, and has been in jail for beating people up. I've also heard that he knows Ron."

"That's damned suggestive," Dan blurted. "Ron's sure as hell not above something like that, especially if someone else does the dirty work."

"Yeah," Bart agreed. "There are plenty of stories about mean things he's done, but no one talks about them in public. And I don't think anyone has ever accused him of anything, not in public anyway."

"No one talks about them to anyone except close friends," Dan added. "Ron's not the type of guy you want to cross."

"Well," I groused, "I'd sure as hell accuse him, if I had some good proof."

"Proof of what?" Dan scoffed.

I shrugged, thinking.

"I guess the first thing I have to do is make sure he knows the pickup driver, Dirkel." I threw my hands in the air, feeling despair at not knowing what to do. "After that, I don't know. Maybe find out if Ron has given the guy any money recently."

Bart had taken an interested pose, his face lighting up with a smile, "Hell, let's spy on the guy. See if Ron contacts him. You know where he lives, right?"

"Yeah," I answered and started to tell them where, but Dan interrupted.

"Why not watch Ron, see if he contacts this Dirkel?"

"Not me," Bart burst out. "That guy's too dangerous for my blood. He had a friend of mine worked over, bad, put him in the hospital for a month."

"Why?" I asked, figuring I knew the answer.

"For the same thing you're doing, chasing Eve. Eve was willing, my friend said. But Ron told him twice to keep away from her. Jim, my friend, laughed in the man's face. The next thing any of us knew, some guy caught him after dark, walking home from another friend's house and taking a shortcut down a dark alley. Jim never saw the guy. He knew someone had followed him into the alley but, when he turned to see who it was, the guy hit him with a club. All Jim saw was a big shadow swinging something at him. Two broken and three cracked ribs, a broken chin, and bruises over most of his body. Luckily he never felt most of it. The first swing had put out his lights. He almost lost an eye too, it was bruised so bad."

"So maybe we should forget the whole thing," Dan piped in.

"Not me," I disagreed, although what Bart had said sent shivers through my body. "I owe the Dog Man to find out if his death was more than an accident."

"What I said doesn't scare you?" Bart interrupted when I started to say more.

"It scares the crap out of me," I admitted. "But Dog has been a good friend."

"I didn't know him, and neither did Dan. But you've been a good friend, so I'm in."

After a brief moment of silence, Dan agreed with Bart, then asked, "So, how do we go about this?"

It took us another hour and a couple more beers to come up with a simple plan we could all agree on. I was going to continue dating Eve, knowing full well that it would irritate Ron and maybe set him off. I was going to find out when Dirkel was off work. And we were going to share spying on him during those hours, as much as we could, given my class and work hours and their class and practice hours.

The next day I phoned Reno; he was working alternating days and nights—one week days, one nights. He promised to find out Dirkel's work hours and get back to me.

In the meantime, however, I started checking Dirkel out. I began hanging out in the bar he frequented, decked out in my work clothes (grease-spotted jeans and tee shirt, scuffed and dirty boots) to try to fit in. At first no one would talk to me about anything except the weather and sports. But I soon learned which ones had already enough booze to dissolve their inhibitions. On my fourth evening I hit pay-dirt. He was an older guy, still working age but approaching sixty. I had seen him there every night, and by the time I had been there almost an hour, nursing my single beer, he would be starting to slump on his stool.

So this night, after he had finished two beers and was starting on his third, and that during the time I had been there, I moved to the stool next to him, trying to quell my nervousness by dint of psychological effort alone.

"Trying" is the key word here.

"Hey," I said after I'd been beside him while he finished the third beer and ordered another. "Where the hell are all the women that are usually here?"

He squinted at me before asking, "How the hell would I know. I'm married and too old for skirt-chasing anyway."

That startled me all right. Before I could stop myself, I stuttered, "Married and you're here alone? Why?"

I guess I hit the proper nerve because he spurted a drunken laugh and said, "What do you think? To get enough nerve to go home and face the old woman. I can't handle her bitching without a few beers under my belt"

Those words brought on another fit of drunken laughter.

"I'll tell you, young fellow. Make sure you know what a woman's really like before you get hitched. Make damn sure she likes to have a few beers now and then, and that she likes a roll in the hay more often than that. If you don't, you're in for a hell of a life."

"Why don't you leave her?" I blurted, again before thinking.

"That's not really any of your business. But I'll tell you anyway because I'm in a good mood tonight. My boss gave me a good raise today and my wife's sister is visiting so she'll be in a decent mood when I get home." He stared at me for several minutes without saying a word. But he kept waving his empty bottle a few inches over the counter.

I took the hint and ordered another for him and one for me, although my bottle was still half full.

After that we jabbered on for awhile, about life and women and marriage. He was bitter as all hell about all three, and about his wife especially. If I could believe his story, he had started hanging out at the bar after work because, if he went home before she was ready for bed, all she did was criticize him, their life, and the fact that they had no children. He never did tell me why he didn't get a divorce, though.

"Hell," he sputtered after an especially nasty comment about her, "the fact we have no children is her fault. She's barren as a damn desert. We had her checked out twice when we were younger. But somehow over the years she's decided that she's innocent as a dove and I'm the sterile one. Go figure. Women!"

While we had been talking, Dirkel had come in and downed a couple beers. As my drinking partner wound down, Dirkel left with two other guys.

"Who is that big guy, the one wearing the bib overalls?" I asked as Dirkel and his two companions approached the door, bumping into anyone who didn't get out of the way quickly enough.

"His name's Dirkel, Pete Dirkel," my companion muttered. "You don't want to have anything to do with him. The bastard thinks nothing of walking up behind anyone he doesn't like and clobbering them with his fist or anything else available. Mean as hell and not a decent bone in his body."

That was my cue. I pretended that a friend of mine had had a run in with Dirkel and Dirkel had beaten him badly.

My drinking partner (I'd learned that his name was Jim) opened up.

"Yeah, I was in here one night hiding from the old woman," he winked at me and chuckled. "Dirkel and his two friends were sitting at that table over there," he nodded toward one of the tables in the middle of the room. "Some guy, a young guy, maybe a student or something...he walked by and tripped on an empty beer can Dirkle had thrown on the floor. He bumped the table. Didn't spill anything or even touch one of the guys sitting there. But Dirkel, he jumped out of that chair and began beating the crap out of that kid. By the time the bouncers got there, the kid was on the floor and Dirkel was kicking him. The paramedics came for the kid and the police showed up. But by that time Dirkel and his buddies were long gone."

"Did the police arrest Dirkel?"

"Are you kidding me? No one told the police anything, not even the bouncers. No one knew the guy that did it. Not in this place."

"You didn't say anything?"

"You're crazy. I'm not about to get on Dirkel's bad side. Besides, what good would it do? The courts wouldn't do anything to him. Maybe fine him or chew him out. Then he'd go after the squealer. That's happened more than once." He paused, glancing around as if he was afraid someone was listening to our conversation. "Rumor has it that he's killed before, and that that was no accident when he killed that guy the other day."

"Why would people say something like that?" I asked, my curiosity roaring like a riptide.

"There was some dude in here last week talking to him. I'd never seen the guy in here before but several people called him Ron. And some of my buddies said they heard him and Dirkle talking about somebody called Dog something or other, saying he needed to be put in his place. Then Dirkle and this guy Ron went outside. One of my buddies was lying in his car, drunk as a skunk and afraid he'd get sick, but still awake. He had all the windows rolled down. He said Dirkel asked for $5,000 to do the job, but he didn't say what job. The other guy said he'd get the money when the job was done, and then he told Dirkel how this Dog guy rode his bike around town and out to his place most days. He seemed to know what time the guy often headed for home and he told Dirkel where the guy lived."

"Did anyone tell the police?"

Jim shook his head and glared at me with an irritated look on his face, "You don't listen too good. Or you've got a lousy memory for such a young fellow. I said I don't plan or getting on Dirkel's bad side. He wasn't the most likeable person in the world. Always causing problems around town with those damned dogs. Getting in dog fights and disturbing peaceful neighborhoods."

"So you think Dirkel killed him on purpose?"

"Yeah. Maybe he had it in for the guy. Maybe that Dog Man's dogs had attacked his dogs; he's got several hounds of his own. I hear he's a fox hunter."

"Do you think he'd kill for money? Like maybe this Ron fellow really did pay him $5,000 to kill the man."

Jim shrugged, "Hell, I wouldn't put anything past Dirkel. It might've really been an accident. It might not have been."

"What about this Ron guy?"

"I don't know him myself, or anything about him. But I've heard a couple of times since the accident that he's another guy you don't wanna cross."

With those words Jim changed the subject to sports. Every time I tried to change it back to Ron or Dirkel, he ignored me. I finally excused myself and left.

30

Reno never did come through with Dirkel's working hours. When I ran into him one day downtown and asked about them, he told me he had decided not to give me the information. When I asked why, he said, "Two reasons. One, he has his own business so his hours are when he has a contract to work on someone's house or business building. Two, I don't think I have the right to give you what information I was able to find out. The info might get you in trouble. I know you want to use it to put a watch on the man and that could get you hurt, maybe even killed. I don't want that kind of guilt on my conscience. Besides, you're not a police office, so it would actually be illegal."

Before we parted he reiterated that I didn't have any legal authority to spy on Dirkel and should stay away from him.

When I told Bart and Dan what he had said, they agreed and backed out of our plan to try to catch Dirkel and Ron together.

"It's a stupid plan anyway," Dan added. "We could get in a barrel of trouble with the police if Dirkel spotted us and told them what we were doing. Or Dirkel and his friends could come after us. And what good would it do if we did see them together? That wouldn't prove anything."

I couldn't change their minds, even when I told them what Jim had said.

"Who would take the word of a couple of drunks against some-one with Ron's pull?" Bart asked before continuing in an irritated tone. "And I'll bet you couldn't get Jim and his drunken friend to talk to the police anyway. You said Jim clammed up when you started asking too many questions, probably afraid you might say something and it would get back to one of those two bastards."

So I was on my own and I didn't know what to do. I didn't know Dirkel's working hours, if he had any consistent hours, which I doubted since he worked by contract, if Reno was right. From what I could gather, he didn't frequent any bars consistently but rather appeared inconsistently in several. And I didn't have much time what with classes and homework, my job, and being with Eve whenever we were both free. For more than a week I tried to come up with a plan of action, but I had no experience in police work, so I couldn't come up with anything. I had given up and was thinking about going back to Reno, when Dirkel brought the action to me.

Or rather, to us.

Dan, Bart, and I were leaving Stinky's one night when Dirkel and his two friends accosted us, right outside the doorway.

"Well, well," Dirkel almost chortled and crowed to his friends, "Look who comes struttin' outta the bar, pushin' people out of the way like he owns the damn sidewalk. What do you think?"

"I think we should kick the shit out of them," one of his two shadows growled.

I felt the door open behind us and glanced nervously behind me. Bart had disappeared but Dan was still standing there, a sick but angry look on his face.

"We're just minding our own business," I said and tried to move forward.

But Dirkel stepped in my way and put his hand against my chest, stopping me in my tracks.

"You're not goin' anywhere until I say so," he sneered, his voice as happy as a lark's, or better said, a buzzard's when it spots a road kill unattended. "We've got some business to hash over, like you botherin' old friends of mine."

"I don't know what you're talking about," I sputtered, my mind flying all over the street and back into the bar, trying to come up with a quick, safe retreat.

"You callin' me and Jim a liar?"

Again a happy note had entered his voice. I realized that it didn't make a bit of difference what I said. He was a bully, in this case a bully with a mission, and he had found his mark. So I stepped back and waited, anxious, wondering when he would throw the first punch. But he didn't want any interference, I guess, because he and his two friends began maneuvering me and Dan toward the alley a few yards away, the alley that ran behind Stinky's. I tried to hold them back. I could see that Dan did too. But it didn't do any good. Each time we took a nervous step backward, they just moved in again, close, their body odor and flesh forcing us to move back each time. We had just reached the mouth of the alley when Bart and three big guys came out of the shadows and stopped behind Dirkel and his pals, each of the big guys placing himself behind one of our three antagonists and Bart joining me and Dan in front of the three.

My heart suddenly slowed its fearful rampage. I recognized the three guys. They were football players at the college, linemen, and one of them was also on the wrestling team. I didn't know them well, but I had joined them for a drink now and then, in Bart's company. They kind of dwarfed our foes.

And suddenly Dirkel and his pals were the ones trying to escape, trying to back away from the alley. But the three linemen pushed them forward, and Bart, Dan and I gave way, willingly, but remaining close.

"Okay," Dirkel suddenly shouted as he found himself pushed further and further into the darkness. "Get out of the way. We're leaving."

"Are you now?" the wrestler laughed. "A moment ago you didn't look like you wanted to leave. Why's that?"

"None of your damned business," Dirkel growled, maybe thinking that the wrestler's words suggested a weakness.

But they didn't. Quick as a wink the big guy stepped in and punched Dirkel in the gut. As Dirkel grunted and bent over, gasping for breath, the guy moved behind him and kicked him in the back of the knee. Dirkel fell sideways, cracking his head on the wall of Stinky's on his way to the ground. For a moment there was no sound. Then, between gasps and groans, Dirkel began protesting and begging for help. His two friends, however, weren't in a mood to help him. They had their hands in the air and were trying their damndest to get out of the alley, but were held in place by the two football linemen.

"Now," the wrestler growled as he picked Dirkel up and slammed him against the wall he had earlier smacked with his head. The big guy hit him in the gut again, holding him upright as his body tried to force its way into a ninety degree bend. "Now, I don't like bullies. Especially when they pick on friends of mine. Do you understand?"

When Dirkel didn't answer, still gasping raggedly for breath, the wrestler smacked him on the side of the head.

"Do you understand?"

"Yeah."

"Say yes, sir."

The big guy drew his arm back for another swing. Dirkel must have seen it because he quickly sputtered, "Yes, sir."

With that the wrestler hit his victim in the gut again and, as if he were tossing a cardboard box, threw him back into the alley.

Then, turning toward his friends, he motioned with both arms. The linemen grabbed Dirkel's two friends and threw them into the street down which, as soon as they stopped spinning, they took off, no apparent concern for Dirkel in their flight.

Needless to say, Dan and I bought several rounds of beer. Bart and his three friends must have gotten tired of my expressing my thanks, because they finally told me to shut up about it.

I was pretty stoned before the night was over, so much so that one of the linemen, the only one who seemingly had a car, drove me home. I was thankful for that also. I still haven't paid him and his friends in full, I don't think, but Bart had gotten his share plus a lot of theirs.

A couple of days later I was at work. It was late evening, maybe nine o'clock and I had just finished changing the oil in a customer's old Ford Escort, when the guy I worked with came in the garage part of the station and said, "There's some guy out by the pumps. Says he wants to talk to you."

I glanced out through the row of windows in the overhead door. My heart skipped a few beats because it was Ron's car and I could just make out Ron himself sitting behind the wheel.

"Know the guy?" asked Jack, my co-worker.

"Yeah," I growled.

"You don't look too happy to see him. Want me to tell him you're busy?"

"Nah," I knew that wouldn't work because Ron would just make a nuisance of himself until I took the time to talk, or listen. He wasn't one to be put off. "I'll go talk to him. Wait till I get some of this grease off my hands.

When my hands were relatively clean I strode outside, trying to make my walk more of a strut than slink, but I don't think I did a very good job of it. Neither did Jack; he gave me a worried look as I exited the door. As I made my way toward the gas pumps, I glanced over my shoulder to make sure he wasn't following me. I didn't want any witnesses to the humiliation I knew was waiting for me.

"Finally decided you could spare a few minutes from your important job?" Ron greeted me, still sitting in his car, with the window open, sneering at me, making no effort to pretend that he was going to buy some gas or ask for any other kind of service, or play the nice guy.

It took an effort to clamp down on my own temper. I wanted to tell him to go to hell and then turn around and walk off, but I didn't. I figured he would tell Eve, changing the story to improve his side of it, and she would be upset.

So I kept quiet and waited.

Ron let the silence hang between us for several minutes, maybe thinking it would intimidate me.

Finally he asked, sarcasm heavy in his voice, "You plan on buying a service station when you graduate?"

I couldn't hold back any longer, "Don't be an ass! What business is it of yours whether I do or don't?"

"I'm making it my business, and you know why, so don't get smart."

"Don't get smart?" I sputtered. "Don't get smart? What the hell are you talking about, don't get smart? You're no relative of mine. And you sure as hell aren't a friend. And you're no parent of Eve's, no guardian, no nothing. So get on with what you want to say and get the hell out of here."

"You know," he hesitated. It was easy to see that he was on the verge of storming out of his car and attacking me, "if there's one thing I hate, it's some worthless kid, some know-nothing worthless piece of trash getting smart with me." He glanced around and then toward the door of the station, where Jack was standing, just inside the closed door, watching us. "And another worthless piece of trash standing there like he's on guard duty or something. I could dispose of both of you without breaking a sweat."

"That's a laugh, and you won't try," for some reason I felt my bravado rising. "We both know you only work in the dark and on the sly."

"Don't be too sure of yourself," he sneered. "You and that friend of yours with all the dogs might wind up seeing each other in hell sooner than you think."

In spite of the chill, and then the anger, that swept through me, I laughed and returned his sneer, "Are you telling me you had Dog killed, and you'll do the same to me if I don't do what you want?"

He stared at me and then answered, "You said it. I didn't. But you never know." When I didn't react he continued, "I came here to be nice and give you one final warning. Stay away from Eve. I don't care what excuse you use, but stay the hell away from her. Otherwise," he shrugged, stopped talking, and just stared at me before continuing. "Otherwise you're going to have an accident, a nasty accident."

Since he seemed to be in a talking mood, I decided to probe further, "Why?" I hesitated. "Why do you think you're Eve's boss, her controller, like maybe she's really just a robot and you own her? What the hell! This isn't medieval Europe. We don't live in the Mideast or Africa or someplace like that. And Eve's not really anything to you. She's not your daughter, or your wife, or your mistress or slave or anything. She doesn't even work for you. So why do you even want to control her? Why?"

By the time I had finished talking, I really wanted an answer. I was not simply telling him that he had no right, legal, moral or otherwise, to impose his will on Eve and our relationship. I wanted to know why he thought he had a right to control Eve and her life. I guess I was still pretty naïve. He probably didn't really know why himself. But doubtlessly he thought he did.

"I don't see that it's any of your business. But Eve's like a daughter to me. She has been since she was a little girl. And you're not only worthless and headed nowhere, but you've also got a past that stamps you as a coward and potential killer, or a criminal at least. I don't want Eve ending up with someone like you. I want her with someone I can trust, someone who has a decent future."

"Someone you can control?" I stated although in the form of a question. "Someone you can control and through him control Eve?"

"I'm not going to tell you again," he gritted, a mask of fury on his face. "Drop her. I don't care how you do it, but do it. And keep my name out of it." With an effort he controlled the anger. "She won't believe you anyway if you tell her what I've said here. I'll convince her otherwise. But you do as I say or, like I said, you'll be joining that friend of yours before long." Again the sneer replaced the fury on his face, "Or maybe I should say, those three friends of yours." He laughed, a forced sound that came out an evil cackle, "And nobody's going to believe you if you tell them what I've said here." He stared at me, then added, a sneer on his lips but not in his eyes, "But maybe that's an overstatement. Those two idiot ballplayers you run around with might believe you. Let's just say, nobody in any position of authority or with a rational mind will."

With those words, he turned on the engine and, glaring at me one last time, drove off.

The next night, Saturday night, I had a date with Eve. She had borrowed her dad's car for the weekend, so we had transportation other than the bus or shank's mare. After a movie and a hamburger and fries at a drive-in, she drove us out to an isolated area near where Dog had lived, parking in a wooded curve through which Echo Creek wound its way after having turned south out of town. It was a peaceful, beautiful spot at night, especially when the moon was up, with the creek darkly visible several yards in front of where we were parked, its moving waters occasionally sparkling through the trees surrounding us. The place was frequented by young lovers, but that night only one other car sat among the dark trees, a car maybe fifty feet from where we sat and invisible except for the bumper and one taillight, both visible because a sliver of moonlight was glancing off them.

I was horny and in the mood, so I started my moves as soon as she turned off the motor. But it wasn't to be my night.

"Let's talk," Eve said in that no nonsense tone she could adopt when she was upset.

"Talk?" I think I kind of squeaked the word. "Talk about what?"

"You know what," she proclaimed.

Of course I knew. Ron had talked to her. I tried to control my anger. The bastard had ruined my evening.

"Not really," I groused. "But I can guess that it has something to do with that damned Ron."

"I would rather you didn't speak that way about him. He likes to look out for me, no matter how much I tell him I'm a big girl and can look out for myself. And I like him, even though he makes me mad at times. He's good to me. And I feel safe knowing he's around to help me if I need help."

"Come on, Eve," I complained. "He doesn't look out for you. He's a selfish bastard only interested in what he can get out of people."

"You don't know him," I could tell that my words had irritated her further. "He's always got my best interests in mind. He can't help it if I'm no longer the nice little girl I used to be. He just doesn't want me to get hurt."

"Doesn't want you to get hurt?" I spluttered. "You think that's why he had Dog killed? Because he didn't want you to get hurt?"

"The police said Dog's death was an accident. So quit trying to blame Ron."

Eve's voice raised an octave or two with the last two sentences. I realized my plans for the rest of the evening were shot. But I still tried to salvage our feelings for each other by shutting up and trying to put my arm around her.

"Don't touch me!" her voice was still higher than normal. "I want to talk."

"God," I exclaimed and moved back to my side of the car.

We sat for a long time in silence. I wanted to say something, but couldn't. I didn't know what to say to ease her anger. I didn't know why she was angry but assumed that Ron had told her something about me.

Finally she broke the silence, "I've never seen him so mad."

Her voice had dropped to almost a whisper. She sniffled and I could tell she was crying, but I didn't know what to do since she had told me to leave her alone.

"What do you mean?" I finally asked when she remained silent. "Did he hurt you?"

"No, of course not," she mumbled through her sobs. "But I thought he might. And he said some nasty things about me and some of the things I've done and the guys I've dated."

"And me in particular."

"Yes. He called you a loser who would do anything to get out of a jam, even sell out your best friends, or your wife if you had one. I couldn't change his mind, and the more I defended you the madder he got. Once I actually did think he was going to hit me."

"That bastard!" I spit out without thinking.

"Don't call him that," suddenly Eve was no longer crying. "He just wants what's best for me."

"Wants what's best for you? Wants what best for you?" I was beside myself. "He wants what's best for Ron. He could care less about anybody else. He's…," I stopped myself, with an effort. "Has he ever made a pass at you, or anything like that?"

"Don't be silly," Eve began crying softly again. "He doesn't care about me that way. He's got a wife and daughter."

I suddenly laughed, in spite of trying to control my emotions. I wondered how ridiculous what we were saying might sound to an outsider, someone who didn't know any of us. And I wondered why she couldn't see Ron for what he really was.

"God, Eve," I shrugged in the dark, "married men have been known to have affairs, you know. Don't be so naïve. You know better."

My words must have sobered her up because the muffled sobs stopped and she sat there staring at me in the semi-darkness of the moonlight. I couldn't see her eyes or make out the expression on her face, so I didn't know if she was suddenly angry, simply serious, or what. I shut up and waited, hoping.

"I know. I'm not that stupid. But Ron isn't that way. He's dedicated to his wife and family."

"You've never heard any rumors about him, huh?"

"Oh, don't be silly. In a small town there're always rumors, especially about anyone who amounts to anything. And Ron's one of the town leaders, and even powerful in large towns like Echo Creek. So, yes, I've heard plenty of rumors about him. People are always trying to cut him down, saying he hurt this person or that person, or ruined someone else."

She quit talking.

I suffered the silence for awhile, then asked, "No affairs, or pushing women around, or anything like that?"

This time Eve's voice came out muffled and thoughtful.

"Gossips always like to accuse young, successful guys of sleeping around and being a little rough sometimes. Kind of like having vicarious sex, I guess. So, yes, there are rumors about Ron. But a person's being silly to believe rumors. They're usually made up by jealous people."

"So, he didn't threaten you?"

"No, not really."

"Not really?" I couldn't help repeating her words, although in a serious tone. "Not really, but he still scared you?"

For a moment I thought she wouldn't answer. Then her voice came trickling out in a whisper, "Yes, but it was only the way he was moving. He couldn't seem to stand still. He kept taking a step in my direction, and backing up. And doing it over and over, all the while talking trashy about you, and threatening you. It was like you were some kind of demon haunting him."

"Or he's the demon and I'm his next victim."

"Don't be silly. He was just mad. He gets that way when he's mad. He was just worse this time, worse than I've ever seen him." Eve paused for a long time, until I thought she was through talking and I started to say she needed to be careful of Ron, then she again whispered, "Like I said, more than once I thought he was going to hit me. But he didn't. Later I decided it was just my imagination, because he ended our talk by apologizing for his anger."

"And blaming us, especially me, for making him mad."

"Well, yes. He was honest about that."

"Yeah, I'll bet. Every time I talk to that guy, he tries to make me feel like I'm to blame for anything bad in your life, and thus in his. Dog felt the same way. And see what happened to him."

Big mistake, Donjon. I realized as soon as the words were out of my mouth that I had made Eve mad.

"He didn't kill Dog," Eve almost yelled the words, a far cry from her earlier whispers. "Quit suggesting that he did! It's not fair and I don't like it."

"Okay, okay," I tried to mollify her, although I really wanted to argue the point. "But you be careful. I really think he's got a screw loose when it comes to me and you dating."

Those words basically ended our evening together. The conversation languished. I tried to dig deeper into the rumors she had heard about Ron, but she refused to answer, or to continue the direction our conversation had taken before. So we talked half-heartedly about school and our work and then called it a night. Even our goodnight kiss was a little on the cool side. She let me out at my house and then drove off. My depression gave me a fitful night, with only a few hours of real sleep. Mostly I dozed and woke and fretted in my subconscious mind.

What with later events, I don't think I'll ever forget that night, or be able to forgive myself for the tepid nature of our final hours together.

31

A little over a week later, I was on my way home after work, walking the darkened streets of Echo Creek, about half way between the downtown area where I worked and home, my mind dreaming of Eve and bedtime, when I decided to go for a midnight swim in a gravel pit at a bend in Echo Creek itself. I was young and so potential danger seemed to disappear into the heavens when nothing happened for a few days. I had decided that Ron had given up for the time being on separating me and Eve and was accepting the inevitable. I hadn't seen him or his hitman, Dirkel, since the night at the service station.

My home was on the edge of town, with the creek about a hundred yards behind it and the pit another one hundred yards to the right. I skirted to the left of home, through a vacant lot and soon reached the creek. The sky was cloudy, no stars or moon showing, and I had been passing under trees since reaching the creek bank, so without street lights my vision faded to only a few yards. I was familiar with the path I was following, though, and the path was well worn. I made decent time.

Once, when I was only about twenty yards from the pit, I heard movement behind me, a brushing of leaves or grass. I stopped dead still, my heart jumping around in my chest. But nothing happened. No more noise.

I decided that some small animal had made the noise, so I continued on my way. I didn't hear anything else and my heart slowly returned to its peaceful beat. When I reached the edge of the pit the clouds had cleared from around the moon, leaving it free to bathe the middle of the pit in a beautiful glow. Quickly I stripped and dived in, swimming out to the middle to lie on my back and gaze up at the night sky. The moon was still smiling at me, and a couple dozen or so stars twinkled around it and to the east. I stared at the moon, returning its smile. I don't know how long I floated there on my back, but eventually I tired and swam back to shore, ready to dry off and head for bed. But that was not to be.

When I clambered onto the shore, a voice, low, threatening, close, asked, "Enjoy yourself?"

I didn't recognized the voice and my heart did its flip and then began its hammer stroke again.

"Damn!" I almost shouted. "You scared the crap out of me."

"I'm gonna do more than that before I'm done."

"Who are you?" I demanded, struggling ineffectively to keep the tremor out of my voice.

I knew though. Something in me said "Dirkel."

"You can call me Mr. Dirkel."

I finally made out his dark form. I was standing on a sliver of land that jutted out into the gravel pit. He was standing on the land side of the tiny peninsula, between me and my clothes, and between me and flight.

"You're a slippery bastard," he continued. "And a trouble-maker. I saw you with that drunk, Jim, a couple weeks ago. I talked to him later and he told me what he told you. I don't think he'll talk to you anymore. You or anyone else," he forced a chuckle, cold and threatening.

I tried edging toward my cloths, but he moved sideways, placing himself directly in my path.

"You're not goin' anywhere." Again he laughed. "But hell, I guess you are goin' somewhere. You're gonna join Jim in hell."

He pulled something out of a pocket. It sure looked like a pistol.

"Why?" I asked, more to play for time than anything else although my heart was jumping around like mad and my lungs had quit functioning well enough to suck in sufficient oxygen for my body's needs. I realized that my only chance was to turn and dive into the dark depths of the pit. "What have you got against me?"

"I ain't got nothin' against you. Or least I didn't until you talked to Jim. But Ron wants you outta the way. He don't like you chasin' the girl he's tryin' to raise to do his biddin'.'"

"That bastard!" I couldn't stop the words from forcing their way out of my lungs and off my tongue.

"Yeah, he's a bastard at times. But he pays damn well for getting' rid of people he don't want around, like that Dog guy."

"He paid you to kill Dog."

"Christ, you're dumb as a rock. That's what I said. And he says he's gonna give me a lot more to get rid of you. So…."

Suddenly another voice came from behind Dirkel. The guy was wearing such dark clothes and standing so close to a huge tree trunk that it was almost impossible to make him out.

"I suggest you drop that pistol and take two steps backward, Dirkel."

The voice I knew. It was Reno.

But I was in the line of fire, almost straight behind Dirkel from Reno's position. If Reno missed…?

I threw myself backward into the dark water, my legs so weak they almost dropped me on the bank itself, but I made it. And the water dropped off, straight down, within a foot of the shore line. I stroked deeper and deeper, and out toward the middle, until I had to breathe or suck in water.

When I broke the surface I was twenty of so feet from shore. I sucked in several mouthfuls of air and started to dive again, uncertain about who the form standing on shore belonged to, Reno or Dirkel.

But just before my head dropped beneath the surface, I heard a voice yell, "Donjon, it's okay"

I re-surfaced quickly.

"Is that you, Reno."

"Yeah, it's me."

"Dirkel?"

"He's down, dead I think."

I dog-paddled to shore and the standing form was in fact Reno. My relief was so overpowering that it took several tries to force my legs to hold the rest of my body upright, but I finally made it, to see that Reno was talking on his cellphone to some Lieutenant Walker. I glanced at Dirkel, who was spraddled on his belly beside a large boulder, unmoving. I couldn't see his face in the dark or tell if he was breathing. So I waited for Reno to get off the phone.

When he did, he turned to me and said, "An ambulance and several of my colleagues will be here shortly. In the meantime get dressed and we'll talk."

"What about him?" I pointed in the dark.

"I believe he's dead, and you might have been too if you hadn't jumped in the water." He paused before continuing, as if he really didn't want to continue, "and me too maybe, because I didn't know whether to pull the trigger or not with you in the line of fire. It's lucky for both of us that Dirkel hesitated for some reason, just like I did, but a fraction longer. Maybe he didn't want to kill a police officer. Maybe he was afraid of dying. I don't know. All I do know is that we were both lucky and Dirkel wasn't."

He stopped talking, as if he was an engine that had run out of gas. But he started again when I had finished dressing. His voice had changed, become sad, hesitant.

"I've got some bad news for you, Donjon. Do you think you can handle it? Or would you rather wait until you're over the shock of this set-to here?"

"What now?" I asked myself. I wondered if Dad had had a heart attack. He had been having some heart problems and the doctor and Mom were worried about him. He was scheduled for some kind of procedure in a week. I didn't think of Eve as being the object of bad news.

"Ron is dead," Reno said. "So is Eve."

I sat down on the boulder by Dirkel's body, unable to stand.

All I could say was, "Eve? How?"

"Ron killed her. Shot her. He also shot that couple she lives with, both of them. Why? We haven't sorted that out yet. But the shooting was called in by neighbors."

Reno's voice seemed to fail him. He sat down, appeared to almost fall down, on the ground near me. For several minutes he remained silent. When he finally continued his voice was no more than a whisper, almost indistinguishable from the night sounds around us.

"I was the first officer on the scene. I didn't know what was happening or who was inside. Only that there had been a shooting. Then, as I walked up to the door…almost sneaked, I guess. I had my gun out…you know, because of the shootings reported… I had just stepped up on the porch when the door swung open and this dark form rushed out." Reno's voice faltered again. "It rushed out. I don't think it saw me at first. Then it did and it stopped dead in its tracks and raised its arm. I saw the gun in the hand and shot… from the hip almost. Just like that. Bang. And it was over. The guy stopped dead in his tracks and wilted. Just slumped over and fell on his face. Not more than a foot from me. God, I felt an immense sense of relief." Again Reno stopped talking and, this time, rubbed at his eyes as if wiping tears away. "I really felt relieved," he repeated in a tone that seemed guilty, self-accusing. "I did until I turned the guy over to see if he was dead or not. God, Donjon," his voice rose almost to a wailing shout. "It was Ron. I killed my own brother."

Again Reno stopped talking. For what seemed an eternity he just sat there on the ground, unmoving, so quiet I wasn't sure that he was still breathing. Then he began talking, fast, the words almost running together.

"Ron killed Eve. And he would have killed me. But I don't know if he recognized me or not in those few seconds when he opened the door and charged out. I don't even know if he realized that anyone was out there, in his way, until he was moving… trying to run, I think. I know I didn't recognize him. The house was dark and so was the porch. I couldn't do anything else but shoot. But I don't know how the hell I'm going to live with having killed my own brother, even if he did kill Eve. I just don't know."

"How did you get here?" I asked, more just for something to say than for any other reason.

"I realized that, if Ron was willing to kill Eve and face off with the police, he might have set something up for you. He wasn't one to not get his revenge on people he considered enemies. So after I checked the house and the other guys began arriving, I came looking for you. The guy you work with said you had left a few minutes before I arrived, walking. So I followed the streets I thought you would take. When I was approaching your house I saw a guy slinking along toward the creek behind your house. I remembered that you and your friends liked to swim back here at the pit. Long story short, I followed the guy and, well, we both lucked out."

"God," I shook my head disgustedly, "I don't know why I felt so safe. I should have known that Ron or Dirkel would be after me, just waiting to get me alone. I didn't think. I…I just wanted to swim and clear all the crap from my head. And I needed to do something to take my mind off of Eve, and our last time together. I just wasn't thinking," I repeated, my mind trying to absorb what he had said about Eve and Ron. "Why did he kill Eve, do you know? The other night, the last time I saw her...," I couldn't go on for awhile, my body almost shaking with anguish. "The other night she said he had been to see her and scared her with his attitude and threats and all. She said he seemed fixated on me, as if I was some kind of devil threatening her and him. I tried to warn her to be careful, but she got mad and told me to quit saying bad things about him. She said he just wanted what was best for her."

By the time I finished, the tears were streaming down my cheeks. I tried to wipe them away, but I couldn't, and I couldn't suppress the occasional sob that wracked my body.

"I think you'd better not talk anymore," Reno said, his voice soft and sympathetic. "You'll need to tell the officers who are coming about what Eve said, and about your run-ins with Ron and Dirkel. So just listen for now. I know you might not want to hear this, but now is as good a time as any. You might as well hear it all, from me, not the news media, so you can start the healing process."

He hesitated for a few moments, as if he was searching for the correct words or trying to force himself to talk.

"I think Ron tried to rape Eve. Or at least he got rough with her and she defended herself. Anyhow, the people Eve lived with were both shot in the chest, twice each, no other wounds on them. But Ron had some deep scratches on his face and neck. And Eve's fingernails were bloody and had bits of skin and blood under them. Her face was bruised like she'd been hit with a fist several times. She was shot in the face five times, at close range, like the shooter was maybe mad as hell or trying at the last moment to fend off her attack, which I think is probably a little farfetched, knowing Eve. Her blouse was also torn, most of the buttons ripped off, and her bra was about half off, like it had been torn almost straight downward." He paused again, sucking in a huge lungful of air. "I loved Eve. You know, like a sister. I watched her grow up and helped her with some of her personal problems. So I think we'd better leave all of this for another time, when we both have enough distance to talk without getting all upset. Okay?"

"Yeah," was all I could say.

But it was enough for our purposes. We remained silent until the other cops arrived, me sitting on my boulder and Reno standing silently nearby. Soon after the cops came, the ambulance guys arrived; they were walking and carrying a stretcher because they couldn't drive back to the pit, no streets or lanes wide enough for a vehicle. I found out later that they had parked in front of my house, waking my family and all the neighbors.

I was never really ready, emotionally, to talk to Reno about Eve's death, but we did talk after the funeral, about our feelings for Eve and the good times we had had with her. Her parents refused to have anything to do with me. Reno said they blamed me almost as much as Ron for what had happened to her. Their refusal to talk was okay by me. I had never met them and would not have known what to say.

Besides, I think they were right in what they said. I still feel guilty about how Eve died. I should have quit seeing her until she could free herself from Ron's control. Or I should have confronted Ron and made sure, somehow, that he couldn't harm her. For a long time after I lost her I felt worse than I had after I lost my two high school friends. I felt guilty and suffered a deep sense of emptiness in my gut. I still do.

The guilt and emptiness have softened some with time, but I don't think they'll ever go away completely. And on empty nights, when I can't sleep, memories of Eve haunt me, sometimes for hours. Nor will the rumor that seeped out of the woodwork several weeks after Eve's death go away: that she was pregnant when she died. I've asked everyone who will talk to me if the rumor is true. Nobody seems to be certain one way or the other, not even Reno. He checked with the coroner for me, for us rather. The coroner said he hadn't checked that far because Eve's parents had demanded the body and he had had no reason to refuse their demand, since the cause of death was so obvious.